A LOVER'S KISS

Maria Greene

D1447490

Zebra Books
Kensington Publishing Corp.

http://www.zebrabooks.com

ZEBRA BOOKS are published by

Kensington Publishing Corp.
850 Third Avenue
New York, NY 10022

First Printing: September, 2000
10 9 8 7 6 5 4 3 2 1

Printed in the United States of America

Chapter 1

Sussex, 1749

He was too late.

If only he'd worked harder at winning Marguerite's love, he might have been the one to stand by the altar waiting for her now. Nick Thurston sweated as he watched the woman he had loved walk the length of the flagstone floor of the chapel toward Charles Boynton, Lord Ransford, his best friend. So much had stood in the way of Charles and Marguerite's love—fear, vile rumors, and a villain named Montagu Renny, but they had overcome their difficulties.

Nick and Charles had competed for Marguerite's love while they tried to free her of the threat Renny presented. It was right that Charles had won her in the end, but that didn't make the pain easier to bear.

Marguerite wore a creamy brocade dress with a profusion of lace at the elbows and around the neckline. Her hair had been piled high, powdered white, and studded with pearls. Glittering diamonds circled her throat. Such a vision of loveliness.

Her sparkling smile made Nick's chest clench, and he fought to control the sadness spreading through him and creating a burning sensation behind his eyes. He could not remember when last he'd experienced his world in ruins. Perhaps at his father's funeral. He hated the feeling of hopelessness.

This was a joyful event—for Charles and Marguerite. He ought to be happy for them, take delight in their bliss, and he was; but he also tasted the ashes of his loss. Why hadn't he fought for her harder? What weakness in him had made him give up so easily?

He'd told Charles he wouldn't attend the ceremony, but he hadn't been able to stay away. He had to see them at their happiest moment. He pressed back into the shadowy corner of the chapel and looked with envy at Charles's joyful smile. *Damn it, I shouldn't have come here. Why torture myself?*

Charles looked like a king in gold-embroidered cream satin, a coat of excellent fit, and a waistcoat of gold brocade. The king of hearts who had won the greatest gamble of all—for love, Nick thought.

Charles was a deuced fortunate fellow, but had also shown a rare persistence as Marguerite kept rejecting his suit. Charles had helped to solve a mystery from the past that tarnished her reputation, winning her heart in the process.

She placed her hand in Charles's, and Nick felt the surge of emotion between them—a powerful fusing of hearts. The current of their love filled the old stone chapel at Mortimer's Meadow, and traveled farther—the entire length and width of Sussex. Pure golden joy, damn it.

Nick swallowed hard and swiped at the unfamiliar wetness in his eyes. He *was* happy for them, plague take it! They belonged together. He had known that from the start. Perhaps that was why he hadn't tried hard enough to win Marguerite's love.

No, he had to discard that thought—to be honest with himself for once. Truth to tell, he'd been afraid; he hadn't dared to go the distance to win her, especially as she had insisted that he had no chance of making his courtship of her a success.

He could not accept rejection, and he knew that would have been her final response. He would have stood to lose too much. Under no circumstances would he put himself in that vulnerable position, not after what he'd lost in the past.

The sweet scent of late roses filled his head, imprinting the memory of Marguerite's wedding day on his mind. He would always remember her in connection with roses. In five seconds, she would be the Marchioness of Ransford, and she would forever be out of his reach. Charles would carry her away to the wedding breakfast, and when they were alone later, sweep her into his arms and make her wholly his—love her until their hearts soared free.

Nick squeezed his eyes shut and cursed himself for submitting himself to this mental torture. The drone of voices penetrated his hazy mind, a surge of movement and the rustling of silk as the vows were said.

The guests mingled in the aisles. Suffocated by the air of excitement, Nick stumbled out of the chapel and strode down the brick path without looking left or right. Someone shouted his name, but he walked faster.

Away . . . away from the pain and the memories.

From now on, he would concentrate on the one part of his life that brought true contentment, the orphanage. One hundred children depended on him, and their smiles made up for the failure of his life as Nicholas Thurston, idle aristocrat.

Not that he ever called himself an aristocrat, but he had been legally adopted by a baronet, one of the few truly decent people he'd ever known.

Sir James Leverton had been a good man, a rock of kindness and tolerance, and Nick missed his father more than he could put into words. Sir James had left an aching emptiness behind as his coffin had been lowered into the ground three years ago.

From him, Nick—as the oldest son—had inherited the responsibility of the Leverton family, if not the title. It was a yoke Nick carried with uneasiness. A feeling of inadequacy mingled with his grief. He could not see a way to heal the rotten core of his family, not as long as Ethan kept ruining the foundation he'd tried to build. But Ethan, the official head of the family, had one goal in life, an early death from gambling and drinking.

I've turned my back on the wedding chapel, and now I'll have to turn my back on the past. Forget my hopeless love for Marguerite and move on. He grabbed the reins of his stallion from a stableboy and threw himself into the saddle. As soon as darkness fell, he would go to work.

Night came with a blustery wind that carried the scent of wet soil and decaying leaves. Late September brought a frosty nip to the air, a hint of the winter to come. Nick did not pursue his work in the cold months as fewer travelers took to the roads and the weather grew more treacherous. But the winter was months away still.

He pulled on a black shirt, black velvet coat, and black cravat that he tied into a careless knot. The only bright spots on his person were the white gloves, the Midnight Bandit's emblem. Always spotless as he held out his hand to catch the travelers' purses and jewelry flung at him in outrage.

Nick put on the black leather mask that concealed his entire face except his eyes and mouth. He made sure his long hair was tied back and covered with a powdered wig. Sweeping his black cloak over his shoulders, he waited in the cottage deep in the woods north of Cuckfield.

The hovel and the land belonged to Noah Bishop, an old groom who had served the Leverton family for thirty years. Noah had been Nick's loyal servant and friend, a man of many talents.

Nick needed an accomplice in his work, and he had two. Noah was tending to Pegasus, the great black stallion with two white stockings on his front legs—the secret horse, notorious on the roads.

The other accomplice was Raphael Howard, another highwayman who had joined Nick one evening in the road as they had chosen to hold up the same coach. Nick knew little about

Rafe, who had suffered from a loss of memory ever since returning from the war. A strange friendship had sprung up between them during the last year.

Nick planned to help Rafe discover more about his earlier life, but Rafe had claimed he wasn't ready to face his past. He always appeared at ten o'clock if he planned to join the mission. More often than not he did, speaking little, never smiling.

Nick glanced at the clock on the wall as it struck ten. A fire burned in Noah's grate, lending a cheerful note to the otherwise bleak cottage with its rough furniture and moth-eaten textiles.

The door opened and Rafe came in, dressed in black and treading soundlessly, as always.

Nick chuckled. "On time as usual." He looked at the masked face of his friend, sensing Rafe's cool wakefulness. A wave of subdued suffering always entered with Rafe, and he carried his powerfully muscled body with a stiffness that spoke of pain. Not that Rafe ever mentioned where he'd received the injury that gave him problems. Nick did not want to pry. If Rafe had the desire to speak about it, he would.

"I'm ready," Rafe said in his deep slow voice. "I've heard that the Duke of Atwood is celebrating his son's coming of age with a ball this evening. Ladies hung with jewelry. Fine pickings as the guests leave, and they're bound to be inebriated."

Nick grinned and smoothed each finger of his white gloves. "Atwood? Well, well, rather daring to rob the guests of the chief magistrate in the area."

Ladies hung with jewelry. He knew their sort, the kind of persons who looked down their noses at the less fortunate, called starvation and misfortune a just reward for sins of the past. As if poverty were something a child would choose at birth. Blast and damn, Nick swore silently, his old anger nagging at him like a thorn embedded in the flesh. "Rather ironic to rob Atwood's guests."

Rafe did not smile. He only tilted his head to one side as if considering the odds of stealing from the people who most wanted to see the Midnight Bandit hang. " 'Tis a challenge we cannot ignore."

Nick pressed the three-cornered hat low over his eyes. "You're right. I'm ready; let's go."

Pegasus pranced, evidently sensing the tension that tightened Nick's muscles as the sounds of a coach moving along the road reached his ears. Wind whipped leaves off the trees, snapping twigs and forcing the branches into a mad dance.

Nick exchanged glances with Rafe in the gloom. His eyes had adjusted to the darkness and he could read the taut lines of his accomplice's shoulders. There was always the chance that the robbery would go wrong. A well-aimed pistol shot. Death. Or capture and a public hanging from the nearest gibbet.

"The ball must be over; the guests are coming," Rafe said under his breath. "Let's watch for outriders before we attack."

The coach rumbled past, only weakly illuminated by two lanterns on each side of the coachmen's box seat. "No outriders," Nick said. "Foolish travelers."

"They probably don't have very far to drive," Rafe said and turned his mount onto the path that wound through the woods along the road.

Nick followed. Within minutes they had passed the carriage and cut through the thicket and onto the road. Nick pulled one of his loaded pistols from the saddlebag, removed the rag in the barrel, and aimed it at the coachman. Closely followed by Rafe, Nick rode to meet the carriage.

The team pulling the vehicle tried to rear as Pegasus appeared out of the darkness. They shied and neighed in terror.

"Stand and deliver!" Nick shouted as Rafe rode up to the coach and jumped onto the box. He held a pistol to the coachman's head as Nick slid from the saddle and stuck his pistol through the open window of the coach.

"Hand over your valuables without a fight. No one will get hurt if you obey." He flattened himself to the wall just in case someone were aiming a weapon at him from inside. He cautiously opened the door. "Step out!"

Two passengers, a tall thin man and a plump older woman, staggered outside. The gentleman wore velvet and silver lace, a powdered bagwig, a diamond pin in his cravat, and silver buckles on his shoes. His face twisted in an angry expression, and he swung his walking stick high in Nick's direction.

Nick had expected as much and ducked. The man swore and lurched back as Nick twisted the stick from his hand.

The lady gave Nick a haughty look, but her whole body was trembling. Nick eyed the strand of diamonds around her neck. Without a word, he held out his hand, and she fumbled with the clasp of her necklace.

"You're the Midnight Bandit," the man said in outrage.

"And I presume you're a very rich man who has lined your pockets at the expense of the cottagers on your estate."

"That is a lie!" the man cried.

Nick deftly slipped the diamond necklace into his pocket. "I'll take the rings and the shoe buckles as well," he said, pointing his pistol at the man's chest. "Don't dawdle!"

"You shall hang for this," the stranger said in a tight voice. "My best friend is the Duke of Atwood—"

"If you're his friend, you can easily afford to donate your baubles to a worthy cause."

"I can't live without my diamonds," the lady wailed, teetering as if on the verge of fainting. Nick caught her hand in his and bowed gallantly, never taking his eyes off her escort. "My lady, it distresses me to hurt you this way, but savor the thought that your diamonds will feed the hungry in due course."

"I do not give to charities," the man said stiffly. "The poor are pathetic. I don't care if they stay poor forever. They are lazy and ignorant, and they multiply like mice." He threw the buckles at Nick, who caught them in one hand as anger surged red and hot through him. He knew it was no use arguing with the nobleman. His opinion was one shared by many of the upper classes.

"Well, you will give now whether you like it or not, sir."

"You shall pay for this, sirrah! I shall get my valuables back—with interest."

"Greed will be the downfall of mankind," Nick said and recited the poem that was, besides the white gloves, the hallmark of the Midnight Bandit.

> *"Traveler alone, travelers of riches*
> *despair ye not*
> *as the Midnight Bandit will stop the witches*
> *of greed*
> *from boiling your hearts in their pot."*

"An outrage!" the man sputtered.

"Now your purse, sir. Then you may leave."

Nick bowed to the lady, who whimpered and fluttered her plump hand in front of her face. He recited another poem, one he'd taken from the popular poet B.C. Rose's third volume.

> *"I met you at dawn*
> *worshiped you in joy*
> *in awe before thy splendor.*
> *In golden valley and rounded mound*
> *Love I found."*

"Now, listen here, you scoundrel. Don't sully my wife's tender ears with filthy rubbish," the thin aristocrat whined. He dropped his leather purse on the ground, gripped his lady's arm, and dragged her into the coach.

The lady stared round-eyed at Nick and clapped her hand to her bosom. Nick smiled as he could almost see the blush on her face. He flourished a graceful bow. That damned poetry touched the ladies every time. It had been a stroke of genius to recite romantic verse to the female victims. They did not mind parting with their jewelry after that.

Nick scooped up the purse. He ran to his horse and jumped into the saddle. Rafe flung himself straight from the box onto the back of his mount and slapped the rump of the wheeler horse. Within seconds, the coach lurched forward.

Nick and Rafe silently melted into the darkness of the woods. Nick knew their first prey would raise hue and cry within the hour. "We'd better move to the south side of Atwood's estate and find another coach there. The militia won't believe that we would dare to stray anywhere near the chief magistrate's residence after the first attack."

"You're right," Rafe said tersely. "We'll have time to plunder many plump pockets before Captain Emerson gets wind of our strategy."

Nick laughed. "Emerson thinks we've moved north to the London roads. This new strategy will keep him unbalanced for months to come. He won't give up, though, and I respect the damned fellow for it. Besides, he's my friend."

"He's a splinter under my fingernail," Rafe shouted as they galloped across a meadow.

"'Tis his stubborn Scottish blood. Never gives up before he catches the villains he's been sent out to catch. I heard he nabbed a group of seasoned smugglers red-handed last week. They've always been wily, but he's been showing more patience, lying low and waiting for them to reveal themselves."

"As long as he does not catch us red-handed, I don't care what he does," Rafe replied and kicked his heels into his horse. The gelding flew over the dry grass. With ease, Pegasus stretched his powerful limbs to keep up with the other horse. Nick enjoyed the speed. It was a great pleasure to call this stallion a friend, he thought, as he held onto his hat in the gusting wind.

They successfully robbed another coach, stuffing the saddlebags with a ruby tiara and more diamonds. One more, Nick decided, as they rode along the winding paths through the woods on the east side of the enormous Atwood estate. This was close to the main road to London, and it offered many hiding places for those who knew every nook and cranny of the forest. Nick did, and he chose a secluded path to await the next guests foolish enough to leave the Atwood mansion without armed guards to protect them.

Pegasus trampled the ground nervously. The earthy scent of torn moss reached Nick's nostrils and the air held a faint promise of rain.

Rafe whispered. "By thunder, there's the coach we've been waiting for."

The squeal of unoiled wheels could be heard from the road. This carriage was moving at a spanking clip, and Nick debated whether to wait for another, more leisurely conveyance.

"Come on!" Rafe snapped, making the decision for him. "No guards in sight."

Rafe and Nick barred the road as the carriage horses slowed their pace in a sharp curve.

"Whoa," the coachman shouted and pulled desperately at the reins. The horses pawed the air; the coach lurched dangerously, tilting over on two wheels, then bounced back with the sound of jarring steel and groaning wood.

"Let's be quick about it," Nick said.

As usual, Rafe rode up alongside the coach and aimed his pistol at the coachman. Urging Pegasus forward, Nick advanced cautiously and, bending down, wrenched the door open, shoving the barrel of his weapon inside.

"Stand and deliver!" he shouted.

Nothing. Not a sound came from inside—at first. Then the world shattered as a pistol barked. The explosion knocked Nick's hat off as the bullet passed close to his head. He ducked instinctively as the acrid stench of powder filled his nose.

Pegasus pawed the ground and pranced. Nick fought to control the frightened horse. No one appeared in the door opening, only the fluted black barrel of a blunderbuss.

This traveler came prepared for nasty surprises on the road, Nick thought and urged Pegasus around the back of the carriage.

He whistled once, a signal to Rafe that they should retreat before one of them lost his life.

But Rafe did not react. The traveler stepped out as the moon emerged from the clouds. The silver moonlight outlined a fur-trimmed cloak, a wide-brimmed feminine hat with plumes. A woman holding a blunderbuss. Was it the spent weapon, or did she have another that was loaded? Nick could not say, but it made him cautious.

She stepped farther into the road, looking for him, and Nick watched from the deep shadow cast by the coach. She took one wobbly step, her plumes whipping back and forth as she searched the lane.

She could not see him; but by the tense set of her shoulders, he sensed that she was frightened. He rode around to the opposite side of the coach and realized that it was streaked with mud all the way up to the windows.

Not one of Atwood's guests. She had traveled a long way, but had she journeyed alone? He peered through the dirty window. The moon gave enough cold illumination to show that the coach was empty.

Soundlessly, Nick slid out of the saddle. Pegasus remained motionless, waiting, as he had waited many times before. Rafe snagged the reins as Nick sneaked back to his observation spot. The woman had her back turned toward him.

Nick pounced, gripping a handful of velvet cloak and feminine curves. The wide panniers under her gown made her an unwieldy prisoner. The weapon exploded aimlessly, nearly making him deaf.

He held her as she spat, hissed, and kicked. He twisted the weapon out of her hand and tossed it aside.

She twisted away and whirled at him, cloak flapping, hands flying. She punched him hard in the chest and on the jaw.

Nick grimaced and caught her hands. "An ill-tempered handful, aren't you?" He held her so close he could see the angry glitter in her eyes. Her breath came in ragged gasps. She was short and slim, her head barely reaching his shoulder. The moon bathed her face with silver.

"Unhand me, scoundrel!" She kicked his boot, and winced with pain.

He kept her fists trapped in his. "I'm not a scoundrel," he said. "I'm the Midnight Bandit, the darling of the ladies. I will not tweak a hair on your head as long as you hand over your valuables.''

"I have no intention of obeying your command," she said haughtily.

"Stubborn as well, I hear," he said, amused. "I shall help you. I am rather experienced in undoing difficult bodice lacings and unclasping reluctant jewelry."

"I don't care what skills you possess. Let me go."

He couldn't rob her. He'd known that the moment he'd discovered that she was alone and unprotected. Yet . . . as she trembled with fear against him, he could not release her. Her eyes were dark pools of terror and he wondered what other features the shadows of the night concealed. Brown hair? Blue eyes? He would never find out. "Why in such a hurry, and why alone?"

"I am not alone! My coachman—"

"Much protection he is," Nick said with a laugh. He placed his gloved hand against her throat, feeling her racing pulse. One of her hands remained against his chest, her body tense and alert. A wildcat in his arms, graceful but frightened. She would take the first opportunity to flee, just as soon as he lowered his other arm.

With startling swiftness she gripped the edge of his mask and tore it off. His powdered wig fell to the ground as the cords dragged across his skull. Stupefied, he stared at her, and she studied him as if memorizing every characteristic of his face. She glanced at his white gloves. "You are the infamous Midnight Bandit. I've heard of you."

She, unlike all his other targets, had seen his face.

"I shall give them a description of you," she cried angrily. "You will soon hang."

"We shall see about that," he snapped.

The silence shattered with the sounds of galloping horses. The riders were bearing down from the north, the militiamen's jackets faintly scarlet in the weak moonlight. Redcoats. The blast of the blunderbuss had attracted them. But why all the horses? Most members of the militia were foot soldiers. A private army? No time to figure out the answer. They had to move, and move fast.

"Blast it," Nick swore under his breath.

Rafe shouted and leaped onto his horse. He brought Pegasus around and Nick ran toward the stallion, his arm firmly latched around the women's waist.

"Let go of me!" she demanded.

"Drop her," Rafe said, but Nick did not listen. He could not take the chance of her describing his face to the authorities. With difficulty, he managed to swing himself into the saddle while hampered by her struggling body. He hauled her up into his arms.

Rafe disappeared into the woods, but the lawmen were already level with Pegasus's tail. The woman screamed as Nick pushed her flat across the horse's back. He leaned down over her, pinning her, and setting his spurs to Pegasus's side. The stallion took a giant leap over the ditch and tore through the undergrowth.

Saplings slapped Nick's face and twigs grappled with his cloak. He leaned farther forward, almost smothering himself on the women's velvet cloak. She waved her fists and kicked out, only to be whipped by the dense vegetation. Fabric ripped, and she moaned in pain. Nick swore under his breath and held on to her tightly.

Pegasus pressed through the thicket, hurling himself and his burden free of the suffocating trap. A path wound through the forest, and the horse instinctively followed it. The militiamen were close behind, but still hampered by the foliage.

Nick urged the horse off the path and in among the trees. It would be the only way to shake off the soldiers. The stallion ambled over moss and rock-covered ground, more than once losing his footing.

The woman muttered and moaned. A curse flowed over her lips, then a shriek that almost pierced Nick's eardrums. "Shut up," he demanded, "or I will throw you off. You'll break your neck."

Evidently she feared the possibility of such an injury and quieted down.

The tracks in the woods were as familiar as the lines in the palms of his hands. He headed Pegasus around a huge boulder and over a fallen tree. The women's head jostled his jawbone, and he groaned with pain. His arms were aching with the struggle of keeping her from falling off.

Pegasus jumped over a shallow stream and soon reached a smooth path. Nick let the horse have his head until they reached the hidden turnoff to the cottage where Noah waited. Nick reined in and threw a glance over his shoulder. He did not see any militiamen, but he could hear them in the distance. It was unlikely, however, that they would see the overgrown path leading into the heart of the forest.

Drawing a sigh of relief, Nick turned his mount onto the path. His arms trembled with fatigue, and his blood still raced even though the danger had been averted—for the moment. The woman lay limp in his arms.

Pegasus slowly wound between the trees and entered the clearing where the cottage squatted among the weeds. There was no sign of Rafe and his horse, but Nick had no doubt he'd found another haven for the time being. He never worried about Rafe.

Holding on to one of her arms, Nick eased the woman to the ground. She moaned and crumpled into a boneless heap. Nick slid out of the saddle and kneeled beside her in the dry brittle grass. She had fainted, and he carefully lifted her into his arms.

The door opened a crack, and Noah stuck his nose outside. "That you, Mr. Nick?"

"Yes, open the door wide, Noah. We have a guest." He carried the woman into the dimly lit cottage and placed her on the cot where he sometimes slept after his raids on the roads of Sussex. He laid her down, noticing her grimy hands that had been scraped raw by the thicket.

Her long curling lashes were sable black, as was her hair that had escaped from the arrangement at the back of her head.

The plumed hat had disappeared during their wild flight from the militia.

Midnight black and as shiny and supple as cat's fur, her hair rippled and curled over the tattered pillowcase and framed a pale face of wide cheekbones and pointed chin. He noted her sensuous lower lip, but what worried him was the tired downward curve of her mouth and the bruiselike smudges under her eyes. She looked as if she hadn't slept for a week.

"Damnation," Nick swore under his breath and peeled off his gloves, cloak, and coat.

" Got more than ye bargained for this time?" Noah asked with a worried glint in his brown eyes.

"You're right on that score. She could use some nourishment. Seems that she's spent a long time on the road."

"Cooked some soup for ye, knowin' ye would be 'ungry as ye came back. There's a loaf o' bread as well."

Nick retied his hair, which had come loose and was hanging over his eyes. He sat on the edge of the cot and chafed the woman's hands, so thin and frail in his own larger ones. He knew already that she was small, but the thinness of her bones had been concealed under the voluminous panniers and her bosom was modestly crossed with a white muslin handkerchief. Her throat, unadorned by jewelry, looked slender and vulnerable, and he had a sudden urge to touch her, to trace the graceful line of her jaw, to clutch her chin until she awakened and looked into his eyes.

She gave the impression of careful grooming despite her disarray, and under it all, a core of sensual femininity that he somehow longed to touch, to cup in his hands—not that he could hold her essence in his hands, but he could not deny the sudden longing.

She stirred, writhing slowly and tossing her head back and forth. With a groan, she opened her eyes. They were deep dark blue and curiously slanted upward at the corners, giving her a slightly fey air. They focused, seeing him, and slowly darkened to a dangerous glitter as she recognized him.

"You have ruined everything," she said hoarsely. She coughed to clear her throat. "May your head rot on a pike!"

"A rather severe curse on a hapless fellow, don't you think? I have not hurt you."

She flung one slim arm over her eyes, and he noticed the angry scratches the forest had given her as a memory of their mad flight. "Why did you abduct me?" she asked in a tired voice. "You could just as well have left me to go on with my journey."

"So that you could describe to the law a clear picture of my face. No thank you, miss ..."

"You can demand my name, but I'd rather cut out my tongue than give it to you," she said coolly, and looked at him with those deep inscrutable eyes. God, something inside him stirred every time she fixed those incredible eyes on him. He'd never seen such dark disillusioned eyes on a woman, or such bone-deep sorrow, and it bothered him. Two profound pools of pain stared back at him.

God's bones, he thought, and swallowed hard to remove the sudden catch in his throat. He inhaled deeply before he dared to speak again.

"I don't care if you call yourself Eve of Eden as long as you don't call yourself Adam, for I am he."

Her lips curled in a cynical smile. "Are you easily beguiled, as Adam was?"

"I might have been beguiled once, but there's a limit to my stupidity. At least I'm proud to admit that a woman beguiled me, not a snake." He tried to help her to sit up, but she pushed his hands away.

"Don't touch me," she said.

"Very well, Eve of Eden, suit yourself." He rose and stretched his tired frame. His arms still felt slightly numb from carrying her, and his neck was stiff. He joined Noah by the fire and accepted a bowl of barley-and-onion soup. As he spooned the simple fare into his mouth, he watched his prisoner from the corner of his eye.

She struggled to get her legs over the side of the cot, and

he noticed the blood that had caked along her ankle. He set down the bowl on the hearth and strode across the small room.

"You're wounded," he said and dropped to his knee to examine her foot. He expected her to kick out, but she meekly let him investigate the injury. Too tired to protest, he thought. "It needs bandaging." He turned to Noah. "Please bring a bowl of hot water and some clean rags."

He glanced at her face framed by the curtain of black silky hair and saw that she was on the verge of falling back into a faint. Her entire frame drooped, and a tremulous sigh fluttered on her lips. He touched her check—pale as a sheet, and skin as cold as marble.

He eased his arm around her slim waist and laid her back down. Fairy creature conjured from mist, he mused. He had the sensation that if she exhaled hard once, her breath would never return and she would just dissolve into a wraith of fog.

"I'm so very—so—" she whispered, and her voice left on a hiss of air.

"You're exhausted," he said, and spread a moth-eaten blanket over her. He took the steaming bowl and rags from Noah, who stood nearby, scratching his head and muttering. "See to the horses until I'm done here," Nick said under his breath. The old man obeyed.

He'd better make her more comfortable, relieve some of the pressure of her clothing, Nick thought. Lifting the corner of the blanket, he gently extracted the wounded ankle. She struggled to pull away, but he applied firm pressure on her leg. She fell back against the pillow, her eyes dazed.

He carefully folded the blanket to the side and untied the overskirt at the waist. The wrinkled velvet came free as he inserted an arm under her waist and elevated her insubstantial body. He rubbed the fine cloth between his fingers. A lady of standing, if her fine gown were any indication, but who was she?

She moaned, her head tilting to one side as if her neck lacked solidity. He quickly released the panniers and the petticoats, freeing her slender legs. He gasped at her beauty, the perfect roundness of her thighs and her calves, the fine ankles. Through the silk shift hitched high on her thighs, he could see the dark triangle of her femininity and the indentation of her small waist. He found himself staring—breathless—at the temptation of her nakedness barely concealed under the ivory silk.

He clenched his hands into fists as a wave of desire flooded him and tightened his groin. He'd waited and waited for Marguerite, hoping that she would slake his thirst in the end. It had not happened, and now he stood here like a moron, awash in such a torrent of lust that he thought he was going to explode. Just because of slender female forms knit together in such a way to drive a man insane. Rounded perfection. Her loveliness stunned him, and he cursed himself for his weakness.

He almost could not make himself unlace the tight bodice. His rampant lust somehow violated the injured woman, and he'd never dream of violating a defenseless lady. The bodice came apart in his hands, loosening the embroidered stomacher attached to one side. He supported her upper body with his arm as he peeled off the garment. Underneath, the shift was edged with a froth of lace that directed his gaze to her firm thrusting breasts, somehow taunting him with the clearly discernible nipples under the fabric. Forbidden fruit.

"You are ridiculous, Nick," he told himself. He groaned and tilted his face toward the ceiling. Rubbing his neck with both hands, he took deep breaths and forced his attention elsewhere.

He thought about the warts on his grandmother's chin, an exercise that cooled his ardor somewhat. In addition, the memory of her black nose hairs and steely disciplinarian eyes made him see sense.

This tempting bundle of sweet curves, mounds, and delicious valleys would probably one day have nose hairs and warts. He let out a long breath of relief. He could think clearly again, but after a quick look at the sinuous body, he wasn't so sure she would turn into a wart-faced autocrat like his grandmother.

He slid one hand over her thigh and swelling hips, tested the narrow waist, and skimmed over one taut breast. Her nipple tightened in response, a nub that taunted him under the soft fabric. She moaned and moved her hips erotically, blast her soul.

His heart hammered dangerously as he slid one hand under her and caressed one sinfully rounded buttock through the slippery silk. Her hips rotated in response, and he quickly covered her with the blanket, all except the injured ankle. Damn the erotic creature! She had the most perfectly rounded forms he'd ever beheld, and he yearned to crush her against the mattress and bury himself in her feminine softness.

His groin throbbed with arousal. He hung his head and forced himself to focus on the task at hand.

He pulled her torn stocking off and bathed the wound, then bound it tightly to stop it from bleeding. An angry bruise had formed around the injury, and he realized she must be in some pain. Not a word of complaint came from her, but he noted the pinched look of her lips as he knotted the bandage. She was no longer in a faint.

He traced the frail lines of her foot, the graceful arch, the slender ankle, and her cold pink toes. The intimacy caused more than desire. Something overturned in his chest, like a crushing weight. For a moment, he thought he would start to cry, but the burning behind his eyes subsided at last. He had no idea whence the emotion came.

Her head shifted on the pillow. How embarrassing to cry in front of woman, especially a woman who was staring straight through him with her mysterious eyes, as if reading his every secret. The Midnight Bandit never cried openly, and he wouldn't start now.

Chapter 2

Serena awakened much later. Early morning sunlight slanted through grimy windows. She turned her head and winced. Every part of her body ached, especially her ankle. She remembered the thrill, the soft caress of the stranger as he traced a finger along the arch of her foot.

A strangely intimate gesture, and the way he'd looked, as if his world had crashed around him, had touched her heart. It was as if she could still feel the pressure of his warm hand on her foot . . .

He had sucked in his bottom lip as if a spear tip had pierced his chest. For a second she'd thought that tears glittered in his eyes, but as quickly the illusion had been gone.

She struggled to sit up. Her muscles felt as if they had been pounded with a mallet, and her ankle throbbed ominously. A lesser pain would have put her in a foul mood; this was worse. Now her head was filled with the red-tinted haze of wrath.

"Why am I still here?" she shouted, and glanced around the cottage. She pounded the pillow. "I did not ask to have my journey interrupted by thieves and robbers."

The bandit was stretched out on the floor beside the cot, an old blanket wrapped around him and another one folded under his head. There was no one else in the room. He turned slowly at the sound of her exclamation and pushed the blanket from his face.

"For such a slender body, you have a large voice," he grumbled, and yawned. Dark whiskers shaded his jaw and cheeks, and Serena realized she'd never seen an unshaven man before—or one carelessly dressed in rumpled clothing. Where she came from, the gentlemen were always impeccably groomed and neatly shaved.

Come to think of it, this was the first time she'd seen the inside of a peasant's cottage. The pronounced state of dilapidation distressed her, and she wondered if her father's—no, Sir Luther's—peasants lived in such squalor at High Crescent. It was a distinct possibility.

"I demand that you take me to my carriage," she said, and gave him what she hoped was an imperious stare. "I refuse to be a pawn in your games any longer."

"Miss Eve, I decide the next move, and you will have to accept my decisions whether you like it or not," he said with a lazy grin. He pillowed his head on his hands as if he would stay prostrate for the rest of the day.

Lazy so and so! A criminal, a common criminal.

The heat of her rage pounded through her, as it had so many times before in her life. She'd learned to control her explosive temper, but this man almost goaded her too far.

"I did not ask to be abducted and locked into a tumbledown cottage with a highwayman," she retorted, and flung aside the blanket. "Besides, I don't have time to linger here."

"As far as I know, the door is unlocked. We don't get thieves in these parts very often. No need to lock the doors."

"I'm surprised," she said at her haughtiest. "I daresay thieves would not mind stealing from other thieves." She glanced down at herself and gasped. The gown was gone and so were her panniers and petticoats. The only thing concealing her from nakedness was her silk shift and one white stocking with its blue garter. The other one lay crumpled on the floor.

She tried to cover her state of undress with her hands, but they could only shield a small part of her body from his wicked gaze. A mysterious heat covered her entire body.

"Not as pale as you were last night," he drawled as the warmth rose in her face.

"*Where* are my clothes?"

"I thought the restriction of your tight bodice would hamper your breathing. One thing led to another once I had unlaced you. But have no fear, Eve of Eden, I did not ogle your pearly skin or take advantage of your weakness."

"I'm delighted to hear it," she said scathingly. She pulled the blanket back up around her. It felt stiff and rough against her skin and smelled suspiciously of horse hide. She, who bathed every day, had never worn a horse blanket next to her skin. She was about to complain bitterly, but restrained herself. If she incensed his ire, he would never let her leave this dreadful place. And he might do other unspeakable things to her person.

"Can you please tell me what happened to my coachman? I do worry about him after what occurred last night."

He grinned. She glanced at him twice. The scoundrel had a heart-stopping smile, and she noted the broad shoulders and the whorl of black hair in the opening of his shirt. A lean face and hair as startlingly dark as her own, waving away from a high forehead and clinging to his neck. Had he but worn a gold earring and a striped jersey, he could have been a perfect pirate. His keen blue eyes were deeply set and framed with long black lashes. She noted his thin arrogant nose, a wide sinfully sensual mouth, and a pugnacious chin.

"Probably in London by now," he said, his voice velvety as if he were well aware of her scrutiny. "I'm certain he would not linger to find out if a lead bullet had been molded especially for him."

"Your flippant remark annoys me," she said and clenched her fists around the edges of the blanket. She would gladly drive them into his jaw if they could gain her freedom. She doubted that they could. His fists would swallow hers. She had noted their iron strength last night. "I would like to go on to London, if you don't mind."

"I suppose that could be arranged somehow, but your ankle has a decidedly purple tinge this morning and looks very painful."

"All your fault! If you hadn't dragged me through the woods like a sack of flour, I would not have injured myself. I don't usually dash off without thinking about it first."

"It appears to me, Miss Eve, that you did just that. Your coach was hurtling down the road in the dark; you had no one to protect you, no luggage, not even a chaperone to lend respectability to the journey. The mystery intrigues me no end."

"And will continue to do so as I have no intention of answering your questions." She stood, gritting her teeth at the pain shooting up her leg. For a moment, dizziness overcame her, but she struggled against it—just as she struggled against the deep black pit of grief that beckoned.

Due to the harrowing events and her current predicament, the sharp edges of her grief had lessened somewhat, but she feared it would soon return in full force. Already that dark ghost of anguish was billowing in her stomach, predictably expanding throughout her body. She would not cry. She would not. There weren't any tears left. She bit the inside of her mouth hard to stop her sorrow from traveling up her throat and choking her.

She bent and scooped up her rumpled garments, noticing the mud and grass stains on the hem. The panniers attached to her petticoat had been torn, and the padding protruded like the innards of a pillow. She pressed the garments to her. They were all she had now. Embarrassed at her disarray, she asked, "Where can I wash and dress?"

He nodded in the direction of a corner where an ewer and a cracked basin stood on a stand. She eyed the utensils dubiously. "I would like my dressing case. It was in the coach." It hadn't been, but the lie gave a hint of respectability.

"I'm afraid you'll have to make do with a bone comb and

leather thong to hold back your hair. Your case is most likely in London by now."

She took a deep steadying breath and closed her eyes for a moment. She would not complain, even if reality were worse than her darkest dreams.

At least she was alive, which was one small consolation. If Luther caught up with her, she would die.

Memories of a vicious fight, memories of blood and death overwhelmed her, and she fought an urge to throw up. Bile rose in her throat, and the dizziness returned. If she collapsed now, she might never dare to move again. The horrors of the past would overcome her, crush her until nothing was left of her.

"Are you in pain?" he asked, close to her ear. "You look very pale."

She had not heard him move. He was standing next to her, the warmth of his hand penetrating the blanket slung over her shoulders. "I'm fine," she snapped. "Splendid, in fact. Give me that bone comb—as long as it is not filled with lice."

She held out her hand, but instead of the comb arriving upon her clipped demand, his hand enclosed hers. He laughed. The scoundrel dared to laugh while her father was waiting for his burial somewhere—never to open his slate gray eyes, never to smile at her again, never to shout at her or scorn her again. She was sure his body had been hastily hidden, but he was waiting nevertheless.

"I do not see any humor in the situation," she said stiffly and snatched her hand away from his. She walked toward the basin, her legs protesting with every step. "I do not appreciate being abducted by a highwayman."

"You invited me," he said and set to work on the fire in the hearth.

"That is utter nonsense." The room soon filled with a thin haze of wood smoke that smelled of autumn, moldy leaves, and seasoned logs. She glanced at him before discarding her blanket. He rose with one fluid movement, and his gaze caught hers as if riveted by an arrow. The air hummed, intensified, until she averted her gaze. Her heart raced alarmingly. "You're staring at me."

"You stared at me first," he replied in an unfamiliar husky voice.

"I wanted to make sure you weren't ogling my ablutions," she said, clutching the blanket more firmly around her.

"I've already seen what I am going to see without removing all of your garments, and I would not consider doing such a foolhardy thing. Not when your eyes fill with murder every time you look at me."

She whirled away from his disturbing gaze, facing the cracked and spotted wall. Murder ... Why did he use that word? Another wave of terror swept through her.

"I've never killed anything," she said woodenly.

"You tried to shoot my head off last night."

"Self-defense."

Silence fell as she struggled with the dark memories. She heard the sounds of horses outside and glanced quickly out the window. It was the old man who had been in the cottage earlier. He sat atop one horse and led two more by their reins.

"Your wish to go to London is about to be granted if you get dressed," the highwayman said.

With a whimper of relief, she dropped the blanket and scrambled to tie the panniers around her waist and pull the skirt and bodice on. They were ripped in places and mud clung to the hem of the dark green velvet gown. She pulled the yellow lacings tightly over her bosom and arranged the fine spill of lace around her neckline. Not that the lace had remained delicate and snowy; it was spotted and ripped. She could have cried at the ruin of her finery, but only gritted her teeth.

He strolled across the floor and handed her a comb. She eyed it dubiously.

" 'Tis mine; I am not infested with lice."

He touched her hand in a strangely intimate way, like an echo of a touch she'd known before. Strange. It left a waft of softness in her heart, but it was gone as she blinked her eyes. She tried to untangle the snarls in her hair. Her scalp was tender like every other part of her body, and she flinched as the comb snagged in the tangles.

"I'm afraid I'm not a lady's maid, but I could offer my service." He grabbed a handful of her hair, but she slid away from him, leaving him empty-handed.

"Don't," she said, and coiled the thick tresses into a simple chignon that she fastened with the comb. She glanced at her reflection in a mottled mirror, but saw only her eyes. They looked different, as if weighed down by the burden of her dark memories. How would she go on without breaking?

She felt into the pocket sewn into the side seam of her skirt and was relieved to find the key tied to a piece of satin ribbon. She had taken the box and key from her father's desk before throwing herself into her flight. "I take it you brought my cash box with you. A highwayman would not leave a coach without some spoils, would he?"

"Under regular circumstances, no; but as you recall, we were forced to escape from the militia. All I got for my efforts was to have my hat shot from my head, and sore arms from carrying you."

"I wish my aim had been better," she said as she lifted her torn cloak from the floor. " 'Twas too dark to see clearly, but I'll have you know I'm an excellent shot."

He laughed as he arranged his rumpled cravat and pulled on waistcoat and coat. These were not black, she saw, but various shades of blue with fine wool embroidery along the facings. A criminal dressed as a gentleman.

"*Who* are you?" she asked as she tied the cords of her dusty cloak at her throat.

"Adam—the first man foolish enough to fall victim to female guile."

"No—truly."

"Call me Nick. I'm Old Nick, the devil himself."

"I dislike your flippancy, and I know you're concealing your true identity," she said, and picked her way daintily through the debris on the floor. She found her tattered slippers beside the cot and, with a sigh of disgust, put them on.

"So are you," he said matter-of-factly, and bent to retrieve a black pot from a trivet by the fire. He poured warm milk into a tin mug and handed it to her. "This is not much, but better than nothing."

She accepted it since her stomach growled in a very unlady-like fashion. She also accepted a slice of bread and sat down on the edge of the cot to eat.

Noah entered and pulled off his worn three-cornered hat. He wore a leather jerkin, gaiters, and coarse knee breeches. "The horses are ready."

Nick nodded and finished the rest of his milk. "The carriage?"

"Waitin' and ready on the road. Th' 'ead groom did not want to believe me when I tole 'im ye needed the travelin' chaise, but I said ye'd journeyed a'ead wiw 'nother party an' needed the coach to bring Miss Delicia back 'ome."

Nick grinned. " 'Tis indeed fortunate that my sister is away from home today. She asks far too many uncomfortable questions."

He turned to Serena, who had followed the conversation with great interest. "I will convey you to the capital. Your belongings will be returned to you as soon as we catch up with the coachman. Where was your carriage headed?"

"To the Pig and Goose posting inn on Pall Mall." Serena lowered her gaze, not wanting him to read the lie in her eyes.

She sensed his suspicion across the room. "Strange. I've never heard of that inn before, and I know London as intimately as my own pocket."

She would not tell him about her only hope of shelter in London, a milliner in Haymarket, a relative of her old nurse. Most likely, the coachman had gone there to await her arrival, or he might still be in this area, talking to the local magistrate.

She shuddered at the thought. If the magistrate discovered that— She swallowed hard. If Luther found out— Her mind skittered away from that terrifying possibility. She gulped and set down the mug.

"I don't like milk with skin on top," she said peevishly to

avert the highwayman's attention. She *had* liked the milk and the bread, more than she cared to admit.

He looked at her, his eyes filled with contempt. "I daresay this hovel is unworthy of a true lady. I am sorry you had to sully your noble feet on this floor."

Knowing it would incense him further, she put up her nose. "Yes. Can we go now? The grime and the squalor is getting on my nerves."

"You are a spoiled, heartless woman, Miss Eve," Nick said, and flung a cloak over his shoulders. He brushed the dust off his three-cornered hat of black beaver.

Old Noah gave her a dark look, and she silently apologized to him. She knew about poverty, even though she'd always had the best of everything. She might never have seen the insides of a hovel, but her heart had ached when she'd seen the suffering of the poor in the neighboring town.

Her father had been a heartless landlord, a cold, ruthless person whom she'd detested, but also loved. He'd had the power to control her until now. Two weeks ago she'd come of age and had seen her freedom from his tyranny on the horizon, but then it had happened—

She hugged herself to contain a violent shiver.

"Let's go," Nick said. "If we want to reach London before dark, we'll have to leave now."

Nick assisted her into the sidesaddle of a gray mare, and twenty minutes later they were out of the woods and traveling along the London road in an old chaise with creaking leather and stiff springs. The conveyance was a far cry from her own well-sprung carriage, and the upholstery had seen better days.

So far, Nick hadn't said a word during the trip. She could see by the angry line of his mouth that he wished he were rid of her.

"I am surprised that you would consider escorting me all the way to London, Mr. Nick." She added a stiff "Mister" to his name to put more distance between herself and him. "After all, in your line of work, heartlessness and cruelty are important traits."

"Be that as it may, I want to make sure you arrive safely. A *lady* would not be so foolhardy as to travel on the roads alone; but since you've chosen to do so, I'm honor bound to protect you."

"*Honor,* sir? A jest, surely. I doubt you know the meaning of the word. You ought to hang." She pulled her tattered cloak more tightly around her and stared him squarely in the eye. His color heightened, and his eyes glittered dangerously. Even though he didn't move a finger, his powerful anger seemed to envelope her, crush her until she could not breathe.

She jerked the window down and leaned out to inhale the crisp autumn air. She pulled her head back in and glared at him. A show of arrogance would conceal her fear. It had been successful in the past. His anger reminded her of the violence she had learned to hate.

"Mr. Nick, I expect you to halt at the first respectable inn in London and let me off. Our roads will part there."

A startling coldness had crept into his sharp blue eyes, and a pallor had replaced the flush of anger. "I think not. I don't trust you. You've seen my face. I might as well escort you to Henry Fielding, the chief magistrate at Westminster, so that you can denounce me. I believe he works zealously to capture the highwaymen that infest the heaths and roads to London."

"You are one of them, a criminal who preys on innocent travelers, so you deserve the worst punishment."

"You would gladly denounce me, wouldn't you?" he asked in a harsh voice. When she didn't reply, he spat, "That does it!" She wondered what he meant by those words.

It became clear as the coach rumbled past a series of inns in the derelict Southwark area without stopping. It was clear the coachman had no orders to stop. The conveyance continued across the Thames on Black Friars Bridge. She recognized it from a painting she'd seen, but this was her first visit to London.

"I demand that you let me off at the nearest inn!" she said, and delivered a glare that usually reduced her servants to cringing obsequiousness. He did not even blink.

"So that you can rush off to the closest magistrate's court?"

His voice held an icy soft quality that made her flinch. "No, my dear. I shall not hang due to some spoiled damsel's demand. I shall take you where I see fit, and not to the fictitious Pig and Goose inn, or any other London hostelry."

"What about my carriage?" she wailed.

He crossed his arms over his chest decisively. "If your coachman is honest, he will safeguard it for you; but if he's dishonest, he will approach a fence in Field Lane to sell it and the horses. Either way, you are destitute. If I let you go, you would not be able to find your servant."

"That is not true," she said, then could have bitten her tongue as she realized her error.

"Ah! So you know where he is then? Just give me the address."

She shook her head mutely.

"Then I shall make sure to keep you safe until I see fit to let you go. I cannot trust that you'll keep my secret identity a secret for very long."

"If you let me go, I shan't say a word to anyone," she said as the implication of his words sank into her. "I promise. I do not want to be your prisoner as I have just left another such circum—" She abruptly dropped the rest of her statement. Damn her slippery tongue! She was too tired to think clearly. What if he found out the truth? She desperately needed a chance to prove Luther's guilt before he found her and silenced her for good.

God, what was she to do? Had it been only three days since she'd fled from Somerset and her well-ordered life there? A lifetime had passed since then. She felt old.

"Well, well, you have a secret to keep. Why am I not surprised?" His mouth lifted up at the corners in a derisive smile. "I did deduce that you were escaping from something, and now you've confirmed it." He shrugged carelessly. "But since you won't confide in me, I'll be patient. We have ample time to discover the truth."

"I won't tell you anything," she said icily. "You can keep

me a prisoner until the day I die, but I will not reveal a single detail of my life.''

"So haughty, so cold. A spoiled aristocrat to her fingertips who expects the world to bow and scrape at every turn.''

"Is that why you rob aristocrats? Because you hate them so much?'' She let her gaze wander over him and noted the flush of discomfort rising in his lean cheeks. "I'd say you aspire to become one, Nick, but fail on the finer points of conduct. Your rough edges cannot be concealed by any degree of refinement.''

Anger blazed in his eyes, another wave of barely restrained violence that left her weak with fear. Oh, God, had she gone too far? She struggled to breathe deeply, feeling the familiar catch in her throat, and the rising panic.

"I . . . I didn't mean—'' She floundered, wet her lips, and said, "That was a cruel observation.'' She could not say, *I'm sorry.*

"Verbal cruelty is an art the ladies have refined through the ages. I daresay I'll survive the blow. 'Tis not the first time my lack of refinement has been commented upon.''

Silence fell and Serena looked out the window at the passing pedestrians. The clang and thunder of the metropolis assaulted her ears. Laughter and shouts mingled with the sounds of iron-shod horses and creaking wheels. Flower sellers holding baskets offered their wares at the street corners, and a muffin vendor bore a covered tray past a row of sedan chairs and their burly carriers.

She saw pale and emaciated children dressed in gray tatters, street sweepers, and buxom maids wearing white aprons and huge mobcaps under the hoods of their homespun cloaks. Footmen dashed along in powdered wigs and livery. A painted and bewigged gentleman walked arm in arm with another gentleman, and Serena noted the jewel-hued brocade of their coats and their fine silk cloaks.

She had never seen so many people assembled in one place, all classes mingling. The largest town she'd ever visited was Bath, and it did not come close to gathering this size of crowd. The smells of the capital both enticed and repelled her. The scent of newly baked bread made her stomach clench, and the elusive fragrance of flowers made her think of summer. Horse dung and other noisome odors more often than not overpowered the finer scents, but a brisk breeze soon cleared the air of the foulest aromas.

"Where are we going?" she asked as the streets grew narrower, the houses more squalid. The carriage bumped over uneven cobbles and jostled her until a headache started behind her eyes.

"To a place I call my own," he said, not looking left or right in the gathering darkness. Evidently he'd seen all the sights before.

"I'm famished." She swallowed to ease the empty ache in her stomach, but failed. Despair at her predicament came over her. She had nothing, not even a clean change of clothes. She was wholly at the mercy of a criminal. Wasn't this what her old nurse had warned her about? But she'd had no other choice but to flee.

Chapter 3

The house Mr. Nick called his own was tall and narrow, next door to another tall and narrow structure of whitewashed wattle with latticed windows. Mr. Nick's house was cross-timbered, paltry windows its eyes to the world, but it sported a sturdy oak door. Most of the buildings, cheek by jowl along the narrow street, had been constructed in a similar manner, a seedy air clinging to the area.

At one end of the street sagged a gin shop, and beside it a rough stand for selling meat pies. At the other end, a coffee house stood beside a reeking smithy. A sedan chair bobbed past the coach window, the carriers red-faced and grim.

Noxious fumes rose from the cobblestones, Serena noted as she stepped down from the carriage. If she had a choice, she did not want to step onto the street at all, but her gaoler's sardonic smile forced her to walk through the slime.

He pounded on the door, and it opened a crack. A suspicious bloodshot eye peered at them. " 'Tis me," the highwayman said.

The door opened reluctantly, and Serena met an old dwarf, as bent as a bow, neck sinewy, gray hair bound at the nape of his neck, and face leathery. His sullen expression did not change. "I know 'tis you, Mr. Nick. Me eyes still work, ye know."

Mr. Nick the man had called the criminal. It had to be his real name then, Serena thought, unsure of herself. But didn't he have a last name?

"I'm bringing you a guest, Lonny."

"I don't live 'ere, guv. Ye take care o' yer own guests."

"Still as rude as ever. I don't know why I put up with you," Nick said and pushed past the tiny man into the hallway.

Lonny shrugged. " 'Cause ye din't 'ave a choice. Ye do what yer bleedin' 'eart tells ya to do." He made a motion as if spitting on the floor. "Fool!"

Serena cursed the moment she'd met the highwayman and now this disgusting fellow. A deep revulsion for the place—she could see furniture covered with dust—came over her.

"I don't want to stay here," she said, and turned as if to make a mad dash. Noah, who had driven the coach, stood right behind her. She collided with his chest. Tears of anger blinded her. "Damn your eyes," she swore as he propelled her around and pushed her into the hallway. It smelled of dust and disuse.

"Where are your servants?" she asked Mr. Nick in her iciest voice. "By the state of this hallway, I'd say they have a lazy attitude."

The highwayman gave her a look full of scorn. "There's only Lonny. And don't expect him to bow and scrape and obey your every command. He's no one's slave."

"I ain't a chambermaid, an' I don't plan to become one for th' likes o' 'er," Lonny said with a dark look in her direction.

"How long do I have to stay here?" she asked, not really expecting an answer. She loathed the little man, but held out her hands toward him entreatingly. "Please help me to get away. This man has taken me prisoner against my will."

Lonny and Nick exchanged glances, and Serena felt her stomach clench with worry.

"All I do is collect me wages an' make sure vagrants and thieves keep away from this 'ouse. Don't expect 'elp from me.'' Lonny grimaced and ambled off toward the back where stairs evidently led down to the kitchen.

"Don't worry, miss," Noah said close to her ear. "Mr. Nick's an honorable man. 'E won't 'urt ye."

"Honorable man?" Serena cried as Mr. Nick pulled her up the dusty stairs. "He's a *criminal*." She tried to twist free of his grip. "Let me go!" she shouted as she realized he was about to pull her into a bedchamber off the second landing on the stairs. She struggled against his greater strength, but his grip could as well have been iron manacles chaining her to a wall.

Only her laborious breathing filled the room. He was quiet, his gaze never leaving her face. Her spirits—already low— sank even further. The chamber had the dismal air of neglect, every surface covered with a thick layer of dust, the bed hangings limp and giving out a decidedly musty scent.

"I refuse to stay in this house a minute longer," she said, cursing her trembling voice.

"Unfortunately, your wishes carry little weight with me. At least I'm not leaving you by the roadside to fend for yourself. Within hours you'd be the victim of robbers and other unsavory characters."

"A much better fate than this. At least I would be free. Besides, I'm already the victim of a robber."

He slammed the door shut and dust whirled off the floor in gray eddies. "If I could trust you to keep silent about your adventure in my company, I might set you free, but . . . Truly, I would like to get rid of a termagant like you."

"I won't say a word to anyone," she hastened to point out.

"Your tune was different in the coach, Miss Eve. You must understand that I cannot trust you. As long as I suspect that you'll denounce me at your earliest convenience, I'll keep you here."

"You can't do that! I am a victim. I have done nothing to deserve this kind of treatment."

"You should have thought of that before you ripped off my mask. You've seen my face, and I can't take the risk of letting you go. Not until my work is over—or you have changed your attitude.''

The scoundrel smiled, damn him, that wonderful soul-stirring smile that had startled her before.

He continued. *"That* would be a miracle, of course, and I don't believe in miracles.''

"I'm a trustworthy person,'' she said coldly, but heard how unconvincing she sounded.

He barked a laugh. "And I am King Henry VIII.''

Filled with loathing, she gave him a dark glance. "Two robbers alike, you and he.'' If she had a chance, she *would* report him to the authorities for what he'd done to her. Her ankle still ached. Close to tears, she averted her face and stared at the dismal room. At least she was safe from Luther. He would not be able to find her here and kill her. The thought brightened her spirits somewhat.

She raised her chin a fraction. "Very well. I'm tired of arguing with you. Bring me a cup of tea.''

He leaned back against the door. "I am not your servant; nor are there any others except Lonny, and you've already heard his opinion on servitude. If you want a cup of tea, make one. You might as well make a whole pot for us all.''

His eyes twinkled nastily. Anger pounded through her in waves. Not only was he holding her a prisoner, he was humiliating her. "I have no intention of serving you, or any of the shady characters with whom you surround yourself,'' she said, drawing herself up to her full height, her back straight and unyielding.

He shrugged. "If you want to eat, you'll have to cook. I can always go to the coffeehouse on the corner. They serve excellent stews and roast meats and white bread to those who can pay.''

"I have nothing to pay with or I would send for some food.''

"Then you are at my mercy,'' he said. He pushed away from the door and came to stand over her. She flinched as his gaze bored into hers. She swallowed in fear as he dragged the pad of his thumb around her chin.

"Don't touch me.''

"I have difficulty staying away since your skin is as soft as that of a peach and your plump lips are as inviting as ripe strawberries."

If he hadn't spoken in a slightly chiding voice, she might have believed him—due to the intensity of his eyes; but she didn't.

If only he had been ugly and horrifying, not this handsome, virile man with a smile that made her knees weak, it would have been easier to loathe him. Now she could only think of his stirringly blue eyes and masculine form so close to her. No one with such broad shoulders and powerful physique had ever before pressed against her or looked so deeply into her eyes ... so deeply that she lost her thoughts for a moment, lost her memory of the horrors of the past, lost her anger.

She held her breath, then tore her gaze away. "You speak nonsense, sirrah."

He gripped her jaw none too gently and forced her to look at him. Anger flared in his eyes. "Don't belittle my every effort of gallantry. Are you so conceited that you cannot receive a small amount of flattery from a humble person like me?"

She wrenched his hand away from her face. "Humble? Hardly. Listen to me. I'm an heiress. Since you evidently need money, I'd be willing to pay for my freedom."

"No amount of your money would be enough to dare risk losing my life. My hide is precious to me."

"Please move away from me," she said, glaring and knowing he would not listen to her demands. He was so infuriating she could scream. "I dislike your person so close to mine."

He kept crowding her, touching her in small ways, rearranging a curl on her forehead, tucking another behind her ear, rubbing his finger along her jaw, and staring in a strange dreamy way at her throat. She feared she was disheveled and dirty, and she disliked the thought.

"I know I look a fright," she said hoarsely. He said nothing. She coughed to break the mounting tension. "I never go out without looking my very best," she added. "I take pride in my appearance."

"I'm sure you do," he whispered, his breath wafting intimately over her face. "My guess is that you dress at the height of fashion if you're an heiress. Unfortunately, I don't keep gowns and petticoats on hand for fine guests like you. You'll have to make do with what you're wearing. Or not wearing . . ."

His eyes had darkened, fired with something she could not clearly read. A pulse beat at his temple and his hands moved slowly around her head and into her hair, shaking the comb free.

"How dare you!" she cried as her hair tumbled down. She took a step back, away from him, and he followed. "Go away."

He closed her in an embrace, her breasts pressing hard against his chest. His heartbeat slammed against her intimately as if nothing separated them, not a single layer of clothing.

Somehow her own started pounding as if answering his urgent message. Heat filled her abdomen, and moistness gathered in her secret place that had started to tingle with longing. She felt faint and weak-kneed; and if he hadn't held her so tightly, she would have sat down on the old bed, dust and all. His lips were so close she could see the bold inviting curves close to her own, his expression projecting a hunger, a hunger that had nothing to do with food.

Her thoughts spun, a riot of confusion. His mind seemed to have flown out the window if his dazed look were any indication.

Nick dragged air slowly through his nostrils, wondering if he would shatter if he moved even an inch. The perfume of her skin intoxicated him, *the female smell of her;* the wild curls of her sable hair made his thoughts congeal into a searing heat of lust that centered in his groin. He'd never been overcome with such raw longing from just inhaling the scent of a woman who wasn't much more than an alluring wisp of smoke that curved and curled tantalizingly in his vision. He had to force his hands down lest they maul her breasts or grope through the layers of her clothing at the juncture of her thighs. *Brute,* he thought, disgusted with himself. *Animal.*

He took an unsteady step back, his body rigid, suffering the torture of his ravaging lust. "Don't be afraid," he muttered. "I won't hurt you."

A flush washed her cheeks, and he could not take his eyes off her luscious bottom lip, moist and inviting. He dragged his hand over his face trying to gather his thoughts. Her eyes were dark, unreadable in the gloom. Mysterious, like time itself, pulling him in.

He could drown and he would barely notice as he sank into their soft hypnotic depths.

The night had almost fallen, and there wasn't a single light in the room. "We'll see about making a fire in the grate. There is plenty of wood downstairs, and candles." He was about to take back his words and demand that she make her own fire, but somehow the command had left him. He only wanted to make a fire for her and look more closely at her magical face, ever-changing expressions lit by the leaping flames.

He had to break the spell.

"Let's set to work, or you'll sleep in a cold and damp room tonight."

She sighed, her shoulders slumping. " 'Twill be the death of me. I abhor damp bed linens."

"Well, that's all I can offer at this time. Better than sleeping in the woods somewhere, or in the carriage." He did not understand it, but he wanted to wrap her and himself in bed linen, damp or not, bury himself in her searing heat, rut like a bull, and never surface again.

No woman had incensed his passions in that manner. The strange thing was that he didn't even like her. She did nothing but complain. She took delight in taunting him and showed no inclination to beg further for her freedom. She had even said she would go to the authorities. That's why he couldn't let her go. She would go straight to the law, her pointed chin stuck into the air. Damned infuriating.

He didn't even know her name. *You have lost your mind,*

he told himself as his loins throbbed. He turned on his heel and strode out of the room. He would make sure she was comfortable in her prison; then he would stay away from her—until such time that he could not decently keep her a prisoner any longer.

When Nick left the room, Serena rushed to one of the windows and slammed a piece of firewood against the glass. Her hand wrapped in a towel, she picked the jagged shards from the frame and tossed them on the floor.

"Help!" she cried, leaning outside. The roar of London filled her ears, but no one heard her scream—or perhaps no one wanted to hear her. Hawkers and servants continued along the street without looking left or right. She kept shouting for help, but the windows opposite did not fly open to reveal concerned neighbors and the door remained closed. Two drunks' rowdy singing defeated her voice. They wove from one side of the street to the other, stumbling over the cobbles.

"I'm kept prisoner here," she yelled, but the drunks only laughed at her and waved a bottle. Deeply disappointed, she watched them turn a corner.

Nick arrived before she had a chance to convince anyone else of her plight. He hauled her inside, and she shivered in the cold breeze coming through the broken window.

His grip on her shoulders tightened painfully. "Bloody hell, what are you doing?"

"Someone might help me," she said tonelessly, filling with despair at her failure to raise public sympathy for her predicament.

"If anyone sees you, they'll think you are my 'moll,' my paid companion. When you yell through the window, the neighbors will think you're inebriated and want to make a show of yourself. This is not a very respectable area, so don't expect help from strangers."

Distraught, she wrenched away from him and sank down on the edge of the mattress. *Paid companion.* She shuddered in revulsion. "I am ruined," she said, as much to herself as to him.

The room was already growing uncomfortably chilly. He sighed. "Ecod, it might not be as bad as that. After all, no one knows your identity. Your reputation is safe as long as you stay here."

He was right. As long as Luther didn't know her whereabouts, she was safe. She threw a quick glance at her gaoler.

Nick looked handsome in a white shirt with frills at the wrists, his hair hanging loose upon his shoulders. He made a disturbingly intimate picture, and she despised herself for feeling any kind of attraction for the villain.

"I'll bring Noah up here with some boards to close off the window. I wouldn't want you to die with inflammation of the lungs."

She could not speak as anger and humiliation filled her throat with bile. There was no way out of here, not until Nick decided she could go. Only one bright hope remained, her imprisonment would give her time to plan for her future—for when she did find a way to escape.

"Don't try anything while I go back downstairs. You might as well set about making a fire while I'm gone."

Nick could not believe his eyes as he watched "Eve" trying to light the fire in the cold room. He'd carried up a pile of wood and returned downstairs for kindling, food, and soap and water.

She was crouching on the floor by the fireplace, the logs piled willy-nilly onto the grate, not a stick of kindling to be found anywhere, except right below the tinderbox in her hands. She was working hard to strike a spark against the bark shavings, but showed no result for her efforts.

"Give it to me," he ordered. He kneeled beside her and tore the tinderbox from her inept hands. " 'Tis evident you've never made a fire in your life."

She gave him a defensive look. "There has never been a need to—"

"I see. Someone has always waited on you hand and foot," he said with a cold smile. "Born never to do a decent day's work. Born to demand, born to order others around. Born to expect fires made and hot food served."

"I resent your slurs on my character," she said darkly. "I might have been born to order servants around, but I don't mistreat them; nor am I a complete dimwit."

He barked a laugh. "Yes, just as you wouldn't mistreat your thoroughbred mare. They are no more than animals to you, are they?"

Two red stains of anger glowed in her cheeks. "That is unfair, *Mister*. You don't know anything about me, so don't apply hasty conclusions."

The heat of her anger stirred his, but he only pinched his lips together. Not another explosion of tempers. He was too tired. With a sigh, he retrieved the logs and made a pile of kindling in the grate. Striking flint against steel to ignite a spark, he watched the bit of rag tinder flare up. He lit the kindling and, as it took, fed thinly split logs to the fire. The room slowly warmed, and she rubbed her hands in front of the blaze.

Her face had a closed, stubborn look, and Nick suspected his own face bore the same expression. He rose abruptly as her alluring scent slowly crept into his senses and weakened him.

"There's a bowl of stew and some bread. Unfortunately, there aren't any finer dishes for your tender palate and you'll have to make do like everyone else."

"I dislike your sarcasm," she said and flew to her feet. "If I have to be your prisoner against my will, you might as well treat me with respect. I don't deserve your taunts."

He threw a glance at her over his shoulder as he walked to the door. "I daresay our definition of respect is quite different." He left the room. Noah was already attaching a heavy bar to the door frame.

"I don't like this," the old man said morosely. "Ain't right to keep the lass locked in. Som'un is bound to search for 'er, and when they find 'er, ye'll be 'ard put to explain yer treatment o' 'er."

"There's no other way to protect myself. Before I let her go, I'll have to be convinced she won't denounce me to the authorities." He felt a strange uncertainty inside, but added, "She needs to learn some humility. Only then will she become reasonable."

Noah muttered something under his breath, but Nick did not stop to listen. Where Miss Eve was concerned, he would not show any indulgence.

Chapter 4

"Another night of bacchanalia, brother?" Nick asked the next morning as he stepped into Ethan's bedchamber in the Leverton mansion on Berkley Square. The word *brother* was bound to annoy Ethan who disliked being in any way associated with a person who had drawn his first breath in Hell's Kitchen. Not that they were real brothers; Ethan was his stepbrother, a kinship he longed to sever for good.

Sir Ethan Leverton looked as if he suffered from an incurable illness, his narrow face pasty pale and puffy, his eyes streaked with red as they focused on Nick. Already old and world-weary, Nick thought. Ethan was three years his junior, twenty-five, but had the dissipated look of a much older man who had spent his life in brothels and gaming hells. If Ethan kept up his life of debauchery, he would not live long past thirty.

"Don't shout at me," Ethan said with a feeble wave of his hand. He pressed his pale fingers to his temples. "My head is bursting."

"I'm speaking in a normal tone of voice, but with your brain pickled by—how many bottles of port . . . five, six?—you would consider a whisper a shout." Nick walked across the handsome Persian carpet to the man sitting on the edge of his bed wearing only breeches and a shirt evidently soiled with his own vomit. Nick almost gagged on the stench in the room.

"You have soiled your father's carved bed, Ethan. He was very proud of that cherry wood headboard. Said the bed had once given rest to Charles I on one of his travels."

"Faugh! Father was always taken in by such stories," Ethan said with a derisive snort. He braced his elbows on his knees and leaned forward, moaning.

"Better that than creating your own infamous legend. Your exploits in the underworld will go down in history as a bad example to mankind. I'm ashamed of you, Ethan."

Nick flung back the heavy curtains and opened one of the windows. He looked outside at the quiet square, seeing only a servant walking a fat dog, and a milkmaid with a yoke spanning her shoulders.

He stepped back and almost stumbled on the clutter of garments strewn on the floor. He lifted a costly embroidered waistcoat, noticing the missing silver buttons—stolen most likely—and the torn gold thread. He flung the article at his stepbrother.

"If you keep running through the Leverton fortune gambling and ordering new coats every day, you'll be a pauper before the year is out."

" 'Tis none of your business," Ethan spat, turning his head with obvious difficulty. He gave Nick an angry glare that also held a hint of hatred. The wave of animosity saddened Nick, but also angered him. Ethan had no right to ruin the Leverton name.

"It doesn't matter to me what *you* do with your life, Ethan; but if you try to break the trust and run through Delicia's portion as well, you shall answer to me. I know that legally you inherited everything from Sir James, including the protection of your sister. You'll have to live up to that responsibility and avoid muddying the Leverton name. Not only you, but Delicia will suffer from your debauchery."

"Damn you, Nick, you preach just like Father—as if you

have such a lily-white reputation, which you don't. You've done your share of carousing over the years."

"Be that as it may, I have never lived—nor acted—like a pig. Nor have I sprinkled money around like water." Nick crossed his arms over his chest and walked around the room glancing at Ethan's possessions, a series of dirty crystal glasses, an empty wine carafe, soiled and wrinkled cravats, stick pins, torn lace cuffs, high-heeled shoes with loose silver buckles, boots, handkerchiefs, and stockings. A watch with a cracked glass, wigs, hair brushes, and hair powder lying like drifts of snow on the carpet.

The stately bedchamber where Ethan had been born looked more like a trollop's boudoir than the private room of a baronet. The mint green silk panels on the walls had stains that Nick could not remember, and the serene painted landscapes in their gilt frames hung crooked, as if a brawl had taken place. One of the bed hangings had a long rip, and the fringe on the canopy had been torn off in places.

Ethan's manservant entered, and Nick rounded on him. "Clear out this mess, Shepley! How can you let Sir Ethan's belongings fall to such a state?"

Ethan glowered at Nick. "Don't berate my servants, Nick. I can do that myself when necessary. You don't have any say in this house."

"By the state of it, yours shall be the first house in Berkley Square to transform into a pigsty. Sir James would turn in his grave if he knew."

"Father is dead. He can no longer pour his litanies of displeasure over me." Ethan threw up his arms. "Thank Heaven for that!"

Nick suppressed an urge to slam a fist against his stepbrother's whiskered jaw or twist back that stringy blond hair until it tore loose. But violence would not lead to a solution. Nick had learned that years ago, but Ethan always tried his temper sorely.

"You'll never know how much Father loved you. He loved you more than life itself," Nick said acidly and leaned against one of the carved bedposts. The green silk hangings had some suspicious stains on them, some new, some old.

Nick slowly and deliberately grabbed Ethan's grimy cravat and squeezed it tight around his stepbrother's throat. "If he hadn't spoiled you rotten, you might have turned into a decent person. I will personally see to it that you won't desecrate Father's memory further. If I hear any more rumors of your careless gambling and drunken escapades, I will—"

"*What,* dear . . . Nick, will . . . you . . . do then?" Ethan chided as the cravat slowly cut off his air intake.

"I don't know," Nick said, so softly that only Ethan could hear him. "But I promise you won't forget the lesson." He let go his grip abruptly, and Ethan fell back against the bed.

Ethan sputtered, clearly unable to find air to speak his reply. His face turned red, then puce with anger, and Nick pushed away from the vicinity of his stepbrother.

"You smell like the sewer, Ethan. No wonder only whores find you—or rather your well-filled purse—attractive."

Ethan rubbed his thin neck and gave Nick a glare, his pale gray eyes blazing with hatred. "There isn't much left of that purse, if you must know. Father gave you The Hollows. The estate should rightfully be mine."

"So that you could gamble that away, too?" Nick laughed incredulously. "My mind boggles at your stupidity. How could the brilliant and kind Sir James have fathered an ignorant— lazy—pig like you?"

Ethan's eyes ignited with fury. "You have no right to lecture me. Father was out of his mind to adopt you."

Nick did not continue the discussion until Shepley had left the room. "As you well know, Ethan, the Leverton blood runs through my veins just as it does through yours. The only difference between you and me is that I was born on the wrong side of the blanket." He leaned over his stepbrother. "Anyhow, I have always been grateful for what Sir James did for me, and

I loved him like a father. I respected him. That's more than can be said about you.''

"Saint Nick," Ethan chided. "Your halo is slightly tarnished from all that boasting."

Nick straightened his back abruptly and changed the subject. "Why did you want to see me? Your note sounded like a matter of life or death."

Ethan clutched his head and rose from the tumbled sheets with difficulty. He brushed back his long thin hair and stretched himself to his full height. Slender but wiry, he stood almost six feet, shorter than Nick by two inches. He staggered to the window to lean over the windowsill. Nick could hear his deep labored breaths.

He finally faced Nick, his features drooping with worry. "I'm in debt, Nick, so deeply that it'll take a miracle to pay off what I owe."

Stunned, Nick remained standing in one spot. A wave of rage swept through him slowly, and he thought, *This time, I will surely kill him.* He could not say anything. His tongue failed to follow his command.

"Ecod, I was sure I was going to recoup at the tables last night. Had stupendous luck this last week at Watier's, but I've lost everything—to Lord Erskine."

Nick groaned. "You lost everything to that card shark?"

"You'll have to help me out of this. Erskine has given me a month to pay my debts, or lose this house, lose the Berkshire estate, everything. I gave him a draft on the bank, and that covers about half of the debt. If I don't pay the rest, he's bound to demand satisfaction in the field."

"That was mighty generous of him."

Nick strode across the room and gripped his stepbrother's bony shoulders. "Why didn't you put a pistol to your head already?" he snarled. "You want the family to live with the humiliation of your profligacy? And how will Delicia hold up her head now? She'll die of mortification."

Ethan's thin mouth lifted at the corners. "I'm sure you'll contrive to soothe her ruffled feathers."

He shook Ethan. "Blast it! Why do I always have to pick up the pieces after you?"

"You always contrive something, Nick. You'll have to save the family honor that means so much to you, won't you?" A note of triumph slid into Ethan's voice. "As you said, we can't let the family name be dragged through the mud. I'm sure you'll come up with the rest of the money somehow."

Nick let go abruptly, and Ethan stumbled back, hitting his shoulder against the window frame. His expression darkened with wrath.

"This is the one time I will not pay your debts for you. I'm sick and tired of acting as your guardian, Ethan. This time, you've gone too far. The family name be damned! At least the world will know that I did not lose Leverton Court, this town house, and everything in it."

"You're only blowing smoke. In the end, you'll come up with the funds as you so revere the memory of *my* father."

Loathing welled up in Nick, a dark red wave that threatened to engulf him completely. "Even if Sir James wasn't my real father, I respected him immensely. But I don't care to ruin myself to save you from ruin. This time, you're completely on your own."

Nick turned abruptly toward the door.

"You'll regret this, Nick," Ethan shouted after him.

"No, *you* will regret that you were ever born."

The serenity of night was slashed to ribbons as the shouting started, disembodied outraged voices. one male, one female. She recognized the nasal tones of her father, peevish, vicious in his condemnation. Father. Spewing out his hatred, his frantic displeasure at what Fate had given him. Mother's voice had lost its melodious tone; it shrilled with accusations of infidelity and cruelty. "Damn you, woman . . . Damn you all to the fires of hell! . . . So much better in town . . . bosom of kindness . . . not the cold witch of my nightmares.

Nightmares. The beasts of darkness. Mother, mother, *she*

whispered. Mother with the eyes of burning coals, suspicion,
pain, loathing. Father ... mother, beasts of unrest. Fingers
long and vengeful, talons curled. Forever clawing the life out
of each other.

Serena gasped and jerked upright in bed. Where was she?
Cold sweat coursed the length of her spine and rolled down
the sides of her face. She raised her trembling hand to wipe
her forehead, but she had barely any strength in her arm as the
icy terror of her dream still froze her limbs. She squeezed her
eyes shut and breathed deeply.

Only after ten deep breaths did she dare to open her eyes
and take a cautious glance around the simple room with its
whitewashed walls and uneven plank floor seen in the cold
light of morning. Rough-hewn pieces of furniture, a settle and
a table, and a woven rug were the only pieces of furniture
except for this bed with its lumpy mattress and mold-scented
blankets.

The memories returned, and with them coldness. The sweat
froze on her skin and she started trembling. Prisoner, reduced
to nothing—without even a name or belongings.

"I'm an heiress," she said to herself and rubbed her arms
to get warm. "I have a clothespress full of gowns for all
occasions, finely tooled kid shoes, hats and plumes, jewelry
cases, and carriages. Everything a lady would wish for." Saying
the words aloud helped her dispel the disturbing memories of
her dream, but she could not quite shake off the horrors of the
past.

They had fought. Andrew and Helen Hilliard had fought
with a frenzy that had finally taken its toll on her mother. No,
lung fever had; but in the end, her father's hatred had ground
down any resistance Helen might have sustained. A bitter
shadow, skin and bone, Helen Hilliard had died with an obscen-
ity on her lips.

Serena could still not decide whom she'd loved more, if
either of them. She had hated them for their corrosive quarrels,
but in her heart she still loved them, longed for their approval.
They had been her parents. She had loved them always, but

had been torn from one to the other, like a joint of bone snatched from the jaws of one mad dog to another.

I'm tired. So tired of it all, she thought in a daze. She dragged a hand over her eyes. It was over. They would never shout again as they were both dead now. Father had been dead only three days—or was it longer?—and Mother five years. Mayhap they were fighting on the Other Side. Serena shuddered at the thought and cried silently. She choked back a wave of grief as tears blazed a wet trail down her cheeks. She hugged herself and rocked back and forth until the hollow ache slowly subsided in her middle.

She shook her head to clear it of the disturbing memories. The grate held only charcoal and ashes. She would make a fire, but first she would dress to keep the cold and damp from her bones.

The blankets had given her scant protection against the cold, but they were infinitely better than nothing. She held up the rags that had once been a sumptuous gown of the finest velvet. Tatters now, but they would have to do.

She grimaced as she poured the icy water from the ewer into the washbowl. Without soap, she would not get very far in her ablutions, but the chilly touch would burn away the last shreds of fog in her mind. Her injured leg ached, but she could see that the bruise was changing color and the wound had healed to a rough scab. She scrubbed away the grime on her hands and feet. Without a mirror, she could not do much with her hair, only comb out the tangles.

Her ablutions did not make her feel much better, and as she came fully awake, her stomach ached with the knot of anguish wedged within. The burden of her secret weighed her down until she suspected it would be easier to die than carry it around for the rest of her life. Added to that, the burden of her imprisonment, the uncertainty, made life unbearable.

If she breathed too deeply, she might crack apart and all her memories spill out like a river of bile. Fear threaded through her, but she refused to think about the future. She would have to learn to manage the present until she grew strong enough to go on.

Feeling utterly brittle, she slowly slipped on each garment, adding what dignity she could to herself. Not that the tatters lent her much of that quality, but to stroke the soft velvet gave her a small measure of confidence.

When she was ready, she set to work making a fire, remembering every step that her gaoler had taught her. Kindling first, then split logs before she could pile on the big logs that would fill the room with warmth. At home, the fires never went out and candles had always been lit for her.

Her fingers were icy cold and she fumbled with the tinderbox. Clumsy, useless, she thought, not used to lifting anything heavier than an embroidery needle or a paintbrush. She had artistic skills, but she was sure that Nick would scoff if she ever mentioned those. He would not call artistry a useful skill, merely something with which to idle away the time. Well, she would prove him wrong—when the time came to escape.

There had to be a way to break out, but she didn't have the strength to worry about that for the moment.

Serena heard Nick when he slammed into the house. The very walls trembled as he threw the front door shut behind him. Serena flinched, and her heartbeat accelerated with fear. Tense, she listened for more sounds, but she could not hear his heavy steps on the stairs. Evidently he would not visit her right away. She drew a sigh of relief and clamped her hands to her cramping stomach. It ached from the lack of food, and from tension.

The fire fizzed and popped as the flames consumed the kindling greedily and licked around the logs. A sense of accomplishment came over her as she warmed her hands over the blaze. "You will be able to take care of yourself," she whispered to reassure herself. "You will have to, from now on. No one will ask for you, or care if you live or die."

Tears burned in her eyes as the truth of those words sank into her awareness. No one cared. Well, Luther did, but he would rather see her dead than alive. Then he could add her inheritance, funds she'd acquired from her mother's side of the family, to his name. Greed was what propelled Luther in this life.

The bolt on the outside slid roughly against the door and Serena glanced toward her only barrier against her enemy. She licked her dry lips and tried to swallow the clump of fear in her throat.

The gloom of the hallway poured forth her gaoler, dressed like an aristocrat in a dark green full-skirted riding coat embroidered with whorls of black wool, a paler green waistcoat that sported a long row of buttons buttoned all the way up under the snowy cravat edged with lace. His black breeches showed off muscular legs, and the power of his stride told her that he was not a man with whom to trifle.

His sun-bronzed face wore the dark aspect of imminent thunder, the expressive eyebrows pulled into a scowl and his nostrils pinched as if he'd inhaled foul odors.

He towered over her by the fireplace, his eyes stormy dark and seeing far too deeply into the corners of her soul. She rose from her crouching position slowly, forcing herself to meet his hard stare unflinchingly.

"What has put you in such a sour mood?" she asked boldly. "Did one of your other prisoners break out or wasn't the breakfast to your liking this morning?"

His mouth curved in a cool smile. "I see that your sharp tongue did not soften with a night's rest."

"The situation does not exactly induce a softening of one's tongue."

"Well, mayhap a well-filled stomach will change your disposition." He held out his arm toward her as if they were at a formal ball. "Let's go downstairs to the kitchen and find out what Lonny has left for us—if anything."

She refused any physical contact with him. "If he is the cook, I doubt the food will inspire in me a more positive frame of mind."

Mr. Nick gave a mirthless laugh. "I doubt anything will. Anyway, you'll do your own cooking in this house, Your Ladyship." His voice took on a hint of mockery. "You shall soon learn the difference between a cauldron and a frying pan."

"All I know is that I will soon boil your head in a pot and serve it on a platter to any stray dog that comes by."

His incredulity washed over her like a palpable wave. "S'faith, I'm shocked at such unfriendliness! So young, but so bloodthirsty. I suspect you did not receive such an unladylike upbringing from your mother."

"My mother had a heart of steel, and the temper of a vicious dog. She did not care to bring me up one way or the other. My old nurse saw to it that I learned the ways of a lady."

She could almost hear his unspoken critique, but he did not voice it as he led her into the dim kitchen below stairs. She'd noticed the cramped parlors on each side of the front entrance and realized the house must have belonged to a modest tradesman or an official. Even if it once had held a humble elegance, it now sported peeling paint and damp spots in the corners.

The kitchen in the basement had small windows high in the wall. They were grimy and let in a meager light. Her attention turned to an enormous stone hearth at one end of the room. There were two three-legged stools in front of it, a large wooden table on the flagged floor, a tall settle with drawers under the seat, and a cupboard. An oven had been built into the wall of the hearth, and iron spits and a copper kettle stood in front of the grate.

The scullery beyond had a lead sink that held a bucket of water and a stack of stoneware basins. The room smelled of previously cooked meals—of onions and roasted meat.

Lonny, the surly dwarf, stood by the table, his chin almost resting on the top. He wiped his hands on a grimy apron. "I see that I'm not needed 'ere," he said. "Won't do slave work for any of you." He glared at Serena. "But it's my kitchen. If ye ruin somethin', I shall flay ye alive."

He gave Serena another dagger-sharp glance and waddled out of the room. "What a rude man," she said, disgusted with the whole business.

"He's a misogynist. You're intruding on his territory."

"Against my own wishes, I might add," she said stiffly.

A dark loaf of bread, a head of cabbage, carrots, a bowl of eggs, a slab of salted pork, and a string of sausages rested on the table. Mr. Nick gestured toward the food.

" 'There. You should be able to make a hearty meal out of this."

"Bacon and eggs," she said faintly. "I usually eat a piece of toasted bread and drink a cup of coffee in the morning."

"Unfortunately, my hospitality does not stretch to white bread, unless you bake some. There's a sack of flour in the pantry. Help yourself."

Serena exhaled slowly, this new obstacle seemingly unsurmountable. She wiped the palms of her hands on her skirt and stared at the food on the table. She had been in the kitchen of High Crescent, her father's estate, but she had no idea how the servants cooked the family meals. The staff had consisted of the cook and her minions—a scullery maid, and a boot boy who did a little of everything besides polishing her father's boots and shoes. Not that he would any longer. She suspected the servants had left High Crescent in droves after her father's demise. They disliked Luther.

Serena wondered what would happen to the ones who stayed. Had she been a coward to run away? They had needed her to protect them from Luther's vile temper.

"I take it you know how to fry bacon and brown the sausages?' '' Mr. Nick asked, his eyes glittering with something that stirred her anger.

"Of course I do!" she spat. "But I'm only going to eat a slice of bread and drink some water. That's all my stomach can take so early in the morning."

"I would soon fade into nothing if I lived on that meager diet," Mr. Nick said. He sat down on a chair by the table, his legs sprawled out in front of him.

"If you want something other than bread to eat, you'll have to cook it yourself," she said pertly and looked around the room for a knife to cut the loaf. She couldn't see any sharp implements, and she certainly was not going to ask him for the location of the cutlery.

She aimed her steps toward the pantry and brushed against his leg as she passed him in the narrow space between the chair and the table. His warm hand closed around her clenched fist, and she stared at him with suspicion.

A wave of some powerful emotion rushed between them and filled Serena's stomach with a strange breathless feeling that had nothing to do with her hunger for food. She glanced defiantly into his keen blue eyes, knowing she should pull away, but she could not. An invisible silken thread held her to him, or was it the steel beneath his veneer of tranquility?

"Why do you always have to stop my progress?" she asked irritably. "Unhand me and let me work in peace."

"The knife is in the drawer under the table," he drawled, his voice insinuating that she did not know the first thing about the design of a kitchen.

"I knew that," she sputtered. "I still want to investigate what else this gloomy household has to offer. Mayhap an escape route through the pantry window."

"I must dash your hopes, alas. The pantry has no window."

She longed to punch him to remove the triumphant smirk from his face. She tore herself from his grip and opened the creaking door to the larder. A stack of plates and dusty bowls stood side by side of a basket of apples and the promised sack of flour.

She lifted an apple, its skin fragrant and cold, from the bowl and bit into it. Juice dribbled down her chin, and she wiped it off with the back of her hand. Her stomach cramped painfully as she swallowed. She hadn't tasted anything that good in days.

"Ravenous, are you?" he chided.

She said nothing, only concentrated on devouring her apple before he got the idea to take it away from her. She eyed the sausages and bacon suspiciously, and wondered how the cook at home had managed to arrange thin crisp slices of the pork every morning. She could almost conjure up the scent of fried bacon, and she found she could eat the whole slab herself if left alone. He didn't seem to have any plans to leave, however.

"Mr. Nick, why don't you carry up more wood to my prison, and I will arrange breakfast for us both while you're busy?"

"So that you can try to bribe the guard and escape through the kitchen door?"

She hadn't thought of that. She darted a glance at the fan-shaped window at the top and noticed a sturdy man sitting on the steps outside. "Another turnkey?"

"Someone who will assure your safety," he said.

Safety . . . She jumped in surprise at his words. Why would he think she needed a safe haven? Did he know something about her secret? Had he figured out where she came from? Had he somehow ferreted out why she had fled? "Safety?" she said aloud and plucked aimlessly at the frayed end of her bodice lacings.

"As far as I know, 'tis the gentlemanly thing to do—to offer sanctuary to a lady."

"Sanctuary? In the den of a notorious highwayman? Surely you are jesting."

"I'm not. A woman alone would be prey to every ruffian in London. I would not want you to be robbed and beaten, or worse. Your life is only worth a farthing in these parts—if that is the amount you carry in your purse."

"You make London sound like a very dangerous place. Surely, it can't be that bad. And why do you care what happens to me? I'm but a pawn in your lawless game."

She fingered the bacon thoughtfully, then eyed the frying pan on one of the iron stands. A thick layer of grease had congealed on the bottom of the pan.

"I know everything about London. I was born in a thieves' rookery. As you so eloquently pointed out, I am a villain. I was born a villain, so I know of whom I speak, but I don't care to see you abused."

She turned toward him slowly. For a moment she'd forgotten

that he was a highwayman; he had dressed and acted like a gentleman. But now she only noticed the cold anger in his eyes, an anger that held many bad memories, perhaps even worse ones than her own.

Chapter 5

She found a knife in the drawer and pulled it out. For one wild moment, she had an urge to attack him to gain her freedom; but even as she raised her gaze to his, she found that he'd read her thoughts. She quickly lowered her eyes to the task at hand. Slice the bread, cut the meat. That could not be too difficult.

She sawed at the slab of pork, finding it extraordinarily tough. "This is a very blunt knife."

He leaned his elbow on the edge of the table and propped his chin on his hand. His eyes twinkled with amusement. "You could always try the opposite edge. I believe you would find it much sharper."

She blushed and contemplated the knife. A slice off his hide would be most satisfactory ... She could have sworn both edges looked equally blunt, but she found that his suggestion made a difference in effectiveness. She managed to saw off a crude slice. The greasy meat kept slipping from her grip, and she feared she would top one of her fingers if she wasn't careful.

Still crushed with mortification, she carried the bacon to the frying pan and placed it atop the grease. She eyed the embers of the fire dubiously and realized that they would not heat anything in their current condition.

"I refuse to be part of this!" she said, straightening her back and raising her chin. "You can't force me to act as your cook or kitchen maid."

He shrugged, his gaze lingering on the bacon in the pan. "If you want to eat, you'll have to cook."

"I refuse." She stepped toward the table. "As I said before, I'll be content with a slice of bread." She pulled the loaf eagerly toward her and hefted the knife, now slippery with grease. As she started sawing through the bread, his hand closed around hers, stopping her work. Anger flooded her being instantly and she tried to pull away, but his grip brooked no rebellion.

"I like a more substantial breakfast," he said and got up. Standing behind her, he hemmed her in with his arms so that she could not leave the table.

"You can't order me to cook your breakfast, highwayman," she said in as contemptuous a tone as she could muster.

"No . . . but I know ways of persuasion." He forced her fingers to open and the knife fell from her hand to the table.

With his other hand he parted her hair at the nape of her neck and, while holding her, started kissing her there, quick hard kisses that caused her senses to turn over in confusion.

She fought, frightened now that she'd discovered that the nape of her neck was a tender, erotic—treacherous—spot. The mad dance of his lips made waves of hot sensation rush through her body.

"Stop it!" she cried when she could find her voice.

He groaned in her ear.

Her blood sang, and she was terrified of the powerful effect of his touch on her composure. He turned her around to face him, and she gasped for breath, a molten sensation coursing through her limbs. What was happening to her? Her head spun; his eyes burned with a hunger she'd never known before.

He clutched her shoulders painfully and crushed her against his hard chest and muscular thighs. His mouth assaulted hers; and when she struggled to ease her breathing, he invaded her more, his tongue raiding her mouth, a silken robbery that made her head spin. He was pushing her back against the table, his chest crushing hers in a most disturbing intimate manner, his hands buried in her hair.

She gripped his shoulders and pushed . . . pushed him back with all her might. He let go his iron grip in slow stages. His tongue made a wet trail along her throat, dipping into the hollow between her collarbones and farther down until stopped by the edge of her bodice.

"How could you!" she cried, tossing her head from one side to the other to get away from his onslaught.

"Cook!" he ordered, "or I'll find other ways to slake my hunger." He breathed hard against her neck, and when he raised his gaze to hers, she gasped at the fire at the depth of his soul. It burned her with its heat, making her blood rush wildly through her veins.

"I won't cook," she croaked defiantly. "I refuse."

He stared at her for a long moment, then slowly pulled away from her.

"You will."

His words hovered in the air, Damocles' sword hanging by a hair above her.

Finality. She sensed he would not change his mind. Unless she cooked, she would starve to death—or perish in the fire of his passion and be ruined beyond redemption.

Her body rigid with tension, she only stared at him as he sat back down. Her blood still raged through her, waves of heat and humiliation. She wished she would turn to stone and remain in that spot forever—as long as she did not have to obey his orders. She could turn the knife on herself, but that would only bring victory to Luther, the man she detested most in this world, along with this highwayman who assaulted her senses without respect or refinement.

She read in his indomitable eyes that he was more stubborn than she, and she let her gaze drop to the table. Hunger gnawed at her insides.

Filled with self-loathing for giving in, she lifted the knife and started sawing off another slice of bacon. Tears trembled on her eyelashes, but she would not wipe them off while he was watching. She could tell herself she was giving in to her hunger, not his demands. She dared not think beyond the most immediate task at hand; mulling over her situation would only make her panic.

She tackled the problem of the dying fire, placing bark shavings on the faint glow, praying they would catch. The hearth was so large she could actually walk into it, with a brick ledge to one side where she could sit and pots on the other.

"Blow on the embers gently or use the bellows," he advised, and she knotted her hands into fists of frustration.

"You might as well make the fire as sit over there ordering me around," she scolded, but not too loud lest he bother her again. She blew on the embers, seeing the glow quickening to tiny flames.

The minutes dragged on into eternity until she had managed to create a hearty fire—on which to put the frying pan? She didn't know, but logic said that cinders and ashes might fly onto the meat if she put the pan right on top of the fire. Besides, it might fall over. She eyed the pan uneasily. She might burn herself . . .

Why had she never been taught these simple things? Because no one had ever expected her to lift a hand in the kitchen.

"The trivet," came his infuriating voice behind her. "Use the trivet and put it up close to the fire."

She bit the inside of her mouth to prevent herself from shouting at him. He must mean the black wrought-iron stand with three legs that stood next to the spit. She saw how it could work standing by the fire, frying pan on top.

She shot a dark look at her tormentor and fetched a towel slung over the back of a chair. She folded it and wrapped it around the trivet so that she could put it at the perimeter of the fire. Pan on top. Breakfast would be done before a cat could lick his whiskers, she thought, her dark mood brightening at the thought of food.

She watched until the grease started sizzling. With a smile, she returned to the table to slice the loaf. The kitchen soon filled with the delicious aroma of frying bacon. So very easy.

He was still watching her, his eyes unreadable. A wave of dark hair had fallen over his forehead, giving him a rakish air. She wondered what went through his mind. A silent judgment of her incompetence, most likely.

Nick was dazed, still tasting the honey of her mouth, still remembering her soft curves pressed against him. He had never met a more impractical or inept woman, but somehow the character trait added to her charm. It was difficult not to interfere when the bacon started smelling burnt or when the grease welled out of the pan like a dense cloud. But it was as difficult to keep his hands off her body. The mere view of her slender neck under that silky flow of black hair drugged his blood. God, he could still smell the sweetness of her skin. Bemused, he watched her mouth, now a tight line of concentration as she sliced the bread.

"The bacon," he reminded her at last as he feared the lot would catch fire.

She gasped in surprise, gripped the towel, and pulled the frying pan from the trivet. She set it on the brick seat and grimaced. "The meat is ruined," she wailed. "Burnt black."

"Make some more," he said, shrugging.

She threw a quick glance at him, evidently to see if he was angry with her for ruining the food. Why would she care what he thought? he wondered.

She made a show of hiding the pan behind her voluminous skirts. "Since you work at night, shouldn't you be asleep during the day, Mr. Nick?"

"I sleep when I'm tired, and just call me Nick."

"I could wake you when the food is ready."

"Just throw the bacon in the swill pail and start over." He leaned over the table and took a slice of bread. "I'll eat this before I faint with hunger." He went into the pantry for a crock of butter and a tankard of ale, and when he returned, she'd disposed of the ruined bacon and was slicing some more. The color in her cheeks was high, and her eyes burned with resentment.

"I think you're laughing at my expense," she said, her soft lips trembling. "You take pleasure in tormenting me."

"That is not true. If you did not busy yourself with chores, you would get very bored locked in your room all day."

Her eyes were like wounds of pain when she glanced at him again. "Will you ever let me go?"

"When you realize that denouncing me would be worse than death."

She slammed the knife down on the table. "What are your plans for me? Are you going to skin me slowly? Pull out my nails before you boil me in oil or cut my throat?"

He did not reply. He wished he could let her go, but that would jeopardize his whole mission. He wished she would give him a solid reason to trust her.

"You won't have time to torture me," she taunted. "I will escape, and by the time you realize that I've denounced you, your wrists will be clapped in irons."

He shrugged. "I suppose I'll have to be very careful so that you don't escape. The more you taunt me, the longer you'll remain a prisoner in this house." He took a bite of bread, chewed, and stared her down—which wasn't very difficult. She was clearly used to surrendering to stronger wills than her own.

"Tell me something about yourself," he said when he'd finished chewing. "Are you from Sussex?"

He noted her hesitation. She set her lips into a rebellious line. "If you are," he continued, "I've never met you before, and I've had connections in Sussex for many years."

" 'Tis unlikely that a highwayman would mingle with the gentry," she said haughtily. "So there was no reason for us to meet."

He chuckled. "An astute observation. Nevertheless, I doubt that you hail from Sussex."

She carried the bacon to the fire as tenderly as if it were a newborn babe. Struggling with the handle of the frying pan, she managed to put her new "experiment" back by the fire. She remained standing with her back toward him.

"Since I don't know your name, it won't hurt to divulge your address."

"Somerset," she said, and ran to the table for the knife. Wielding it clumsily, she successfully turned the bacon without burning herself.

"Hmm, you're a long way from home. Won't your family miss you? Send out someone to look for you?"

She shook her head mutely, her neck a slender pale stem that seemed to carry too heavy a burden. The weight of misery. He sensed her sorrow more than knowing for a fact that she grieved.

He pondered the lovely picture of her; her tattered dress could not conceal her lovely form, a hothouse flower that had been tended with care in the past. Now as out of place as a rose in a desert.

"I can take care of myself. I learned that a long time ago," she said in muffled tones.

His heart constricted as he realized that she was crying. She would not want him to know that. He decided to pretend that he didn't notice. "In London you would be vulnerable, and I'm tired of repeating that."

"I don't think *hatred* is any different in London than it is elsewhere. I am not afraid of dealing with disillusioned people."

He sprawled in his chair and laughed. "Disillusioned? You are very naive, Milady Mysterious. People in this city do not have time to be disillusioned; they kill to survive."

She pulled away the frying pan with the folded towel and said, "They are angry at the injustice, so they inflict pain on others to feel they're worth more. I know. I've lived with hatred all my life—not directed at me specifically, but corroding others."

Her words punched him in the stomach, and he found himself without a glib reply. He inhaled sharply through his nostrils as thoughts raced like rats in his head. Memories of the degradation of his childhood. Memories that irrevocably triggered his anger.

"Survival is the only law here," he said at last. "I doubt *you* had to suffer such ultimatums every day you were alive to see another sunrise." He glanced at the black-edged bacon she pulled from the pan with the tip of the knife and put on a pewter plate. "As I've noticed, you've lived a very sheltered life."

"Be that as it may, I have seen enough misery to know that evil lives everywhere, in palace as in hovel. I was no safer at home than here." She shot him a glance that was bruised with disenchantment.

His breath snagged in his throat, and he felt the weight of her misery through those eyes. So young, yet so old. "Dare I ask what happened to you? What happened to force you into the night behind racing horses with only a coachman to protect you?"

She slammed the plate in front of him and shoved the bread across the table. "Here. Eat your breakfast."

He eyed the curling bacon slices with the burned edges and was on the verge of rejecting them. Then he thought better of it and reached for the knife in her hand. She seemed reluctant to release her convulsive grip around it.

"May I? I like to cut my meat into smaller pieces before devouring it. And what about the eggs? I'd like mine fried— on both sides."

"Don't force me," she said, her voice savage. "You have no right to order me around."

"Your sour demeanor inspires the rude side of me," he said with a grimace. "If you use some female charm, you might cause me to wait hand and foot on you."

"I do not waste my finer qualities on criminals," she spat, and swung around. She grabbed an egg. It slipped from her hand and crashed against the flagstone floor. Embarrassment heating her cheeks, she cursed under her breath, "Damn."

"A very unladylike expression," he taunted and cut the bacon into small pieces. Then he chewed the charred bits and chased them down with some ale. "Think of all the work the hen had to do to produce that egg."

"You're chiding me, and I find it highly annoying."

"You're annoyed because you're not used to waiting on others. It must gall you no end—hurt your royal pride."

"You know nothing about me."

"I know you're fleeing from something. I also know your flight was not well-planned. A lady of your standing would not travel without a mountain of trunks. You did not bring your belongings—"

"You know nothing about my belongings! My trunks might have traveled in a second coach with my maid, who also carried my jewelry case."

"Somehow I don't believe you." He pointed at her hand. "You have egg hanging from your finger."

She swiped at the offending slime with the towel, and he softened at her distraught expression. "Actually, your secret is safe with me. As I am keen to keep my own, I would not blurt out your secret to the world."

"It doesn't matter if you speak of it or not. Nothing will change the truth, and *that* part you don't know." She took another egg and contemplated it as tears rolled slowly down her cheeks. She did not emit a single sob, or sigh. Her silent grief unnerved him.

He stood abruptly. "Let me show you how to fry an egg," he said, hearing with surprise that his voice trembled. Without waiting for her answer, he took the frying pan and the egg from her and went to the fire. He placed the pan on the trivet and waited until the grease started bubbling. He cracked the egg on the edge and watched it spread in a circle in the pan. "There. Not difficult once you understand how to open the shell."

She stood beside him, dejected, and stared unseeing into the fire. He rose from his bent position, found the towel in her hand, and dabbed at her wet cheeks. "This egg is for you," he said gruffly.

"Are you going to place it hot and sizzling on my bare arm?" she asked in an almost inaudible voice.

He laughed incredulously. "No! I would never do anything that cruel."

"That's what my father did to my mother. She got a perfectly oval puckered scar from that. Always had to wear long sleeves, but she suffers no more. She is dead, and soon I will be, too."

Nick froze, feeling the chill of her words. He read the terror—the revulsion—in her eyes. Evidently she thought she would suffer equal indignities at his hand. He had never raised his hand to a woman, but he knew there were many abusive men who did not hesitate to take out their anger on hapless wives.

"You will not die while you're under my roof," he said, and knew he would protect her to his last breath. He could not stand abuse, nor injustice.

Chapter 6

He would kill Serena when he found her, nosy bitch that she was.

Sir Luther Hilliard clenched his hands until they ached. Frustration poured thorough him, a bubbling liquid that was hard to contain as the dirty traveling chaise barreled along the Sussex roads in the dark. God, he couldn't wait to fit his hands around her slender throat and squeeze that bright life out of her eyes. She'd always been a thorn, looking at him with dislike every time he came to High Crescent. Even as a child she'd shown her disdain. He'd had enough of her cool, condemning eyes.

She would go the same way as her father—just within days.

With a fervor he'd never felt before, Sir Luther planned his strategy as his coach got ever closer to London. She could not hide from him forever.

In her dream, Serena said good-bye to everyone, even hugged the stableboy. His mouth twisted in a grimace. "Don't go," e said. Everyone echoed his sentiment, but finality had taken deep hold in her mind. She had to leave. There was no looking back at the horrors, the blood congealing on the floor. The rage. The faces contorted in savageness.

The terror washed over her in icy torrents. Stiff as a pillar of salt, she could not tear her gaze away. Her hand was frozen around the edge of the velvet curtain, and she thought incongruously that such softness under her fingers could not exist at the same time as the hard fury of death. A drawn-out scream echoed in her ears, and her eyes flew open.

She lay rigid with fear, seeing the gray ghost of her nightmare playing out the familiar scene of her father's death even though her eyes were open. Below, on the street, she could hear the watchman call out the hour, "Three o'clock and all is quiet."

A lie, she thought, a barefaced lie. Quietude is but a pretense. Violence is right beside you, ready to erupt, she thought. Don't look for it; just pretend it isn't there.

She sat up and punched the pillow into a backrest. The headboard creaked as she leaned against it. Pulling up her knees to her chin, she stared into the night outside the only window in the room, a faint gray square against the surrounding blackness. Noah had boarded up the window she'd broken.

London pulsed with faint sounds of life. The night was old. She heard the remote sounds of voices and laughter, the *clip-clop* of a horse, the distant creak of a carriage. The clanging of a bell somewhere.

She felt weak and drained. Hopeless. This was the second night in her prison, and she could not find a spark of resolve not a flare of defiance that might push her through the long days ahead or the even longer evenings. She could not remember a single night of uninterrupted sleep since that awful evening when her whole world had crashed around her.

The bolt on the outside of the door slid back, the rasp of wood against wood a loud sound in the stillness. She tensed dragging the cover up to her chin.

She saw his dark silhouette, recognizing the broad shoulder and his narrow hips. The tall form of her tormentor.

"I heard you scream," he said, stepping inside and closing

the door behind him. "Is something the matter? Is something frightening you?"

"Did I scream?" she asked, the "sounds" of her nightmare washing over her yet again. She hadn't known she'd issued those screams. "It must have been a bad dream, but I can barely remember any of it."

He went to the window. "Do you suffer from nightmares?"

"Everyone does. Don't you, sometimes?" she asked, her terror slowly draining from her body.

"I have nightmares," he confessed. He got down on his haunches and set to work on the fire. Soon a small blaze filled the chilly room with an orange glow.

"If I lived a dangerous life like yours, I would, too," she replied as she watched his measured movements. He placed every stick perfectly, each one feeding the fire until his whole body was reflected in a golden blaze. He wore only breeches, boots, and a shirt. "After all, a criminal can't sleep with an innocent conscience."

"Is that what keeps you from your rest?" he asked in a cool voice. "Conscience?"

"No . . . only a disturbing memory that will not stop chewing on my mind. It is as clear as the day it happened, every color, every scent. Even the sounds keep echoing in my head, over and over."

He threw a glance at her, and she felt the probing heat of his gaze. "They can't be pleasant if your horrified scream is any indication."

"Nightmares are never pleasant," she said, her voice trembling.

"You're right." He kept looking at her, wondering, sensing her pain. She did not respond, only pulled her arms more tightly around her knees. Her eyes were huge and guarded, her hair a wild tangle of curls that gave her a vulnerable air. He found himself longing to put his arms around her and hold her until the tension left her body.

He reluctantly averted his eyes and gazed into the fire. "I feel that our lives touch somewhere—like two dark roads leading nowhere, surprisingly meeting at some windswept and barren corner.''

She didn't respond, but he sensed her unspoken sympathy. He also sensed her struggle to keep up her guard toward him, and that she failed.

He continued. ''I was born not far from here, in a rookery in Spitalfields, a warren of thieves and rats. A murder for a silk handkerchief was not uncommon. I stole my fair share and sold them to an old crone in Russell Street. She did brisk business in stolen goods—had enough gold stashed away to live to a comfortable old age. We were a group of boys, most of us no more than five years old. Snatching handkerchiefs and cut purses without the victims noticing anything were our trade.''

''Did you enjoy the thrill?'' she asked. ''Taunting death. Stealing is a hanging matter—even for a child.''

He shrugged and put another log on the fire. ''I had no choice. I tried to save my pennies. I knew of no better world, but I longed to leave the filth and the degradation. The hopelessness, the gin shops that feed the men of London with a liquid frenzy that more often than not end in violence and murder. The reek, the filth, and the all-pervading stench of gin. It's all still there, only a few streets away from here,'' he said as if speaking to himself. ''But I'm no longer part of it.''

''I suppose you really rose in the world to become a highwayman,'' she teased.

He grinned at her taunt. ''A very famous highwayman at that!'' He rose and stretched his stiff back. ''I was fortunate more fortunate than most. Someone lifted me from the rat-infested rookery and put me in a castle. At least I saw my new father's house that way. One can't but be in awe of a king who saves you from poverty and degradation.''

''You speak in riddles.''

''Let me explain. My real father was a handsome traveling actor who swept my mother off her feet. She was a real lady you know. She made the biggest mistake of her life when she threw in her lot with his. She soon learned that he found hi inspiration in gin and brutish behavior, but she was too proud to crawl back to her family. Father drank himself to death when his theatrical star fell into oblivion, and Mother and I ended up in a room, a vermin-infested hole in a warren of such holes. She was bitter and started burying her failures in the gin bottle. Then my uncle came, my mother's brother, the only person who has truly cared about me. He saved me, but my mother refused to be saved. My uncle, whom I called *Father,* died three years ago, and I've lost the finest friend a man could wish for."

"You speak of him with great reverence."

"He was a truly good person. I'd never met a 'saint' before."

"Bosh and nonsense! Saints do not exist. Most people look to what they can gain personally with every action. Most are willing to go to any length for greed."

He strolled over to the bed and looked at her. "You sound very bitter."

"That's the side of humanity I've always seen. A constant battle of wills, of greed."

"Come now, you must have made friends with some kindly person along the way."

"Yes, there was my nurse," she said. "Nurse Hopkins was as close as you can get to a saint. She is the person I trust most, and she gave me love. She literally brought me up single-handedly, but she had to leave when I was grown even though she was too old to fend for herself and nearly blind." She sighed and plucked at the coverlet. "I do worry about her. Who will slip food and money to her now that I am gone?"

He contemplated her downbent head as something squeezed his heart. She had a deep measure of compassion even though she made the most of hiding it. "Probably one of the other servants. They stick together, you know."

"Like thieves, then?"

"My best friend in the rookery was a thief. He's now my steward and honest to a fault. Desperation—hunger—force people to become criminals. Not all choose voluntarily to rob travelers and break into houses. To learn an honest trade costs money, and thieves are seldom born with a groat to their name.''

She stared at him, searching deep blue eyes that tugged at his heart. He didn't know why. He did not admire her acid tongue and haughty manner, but he sensed her despair, her aching loneliness. She needed his compassion. *He* needed her alluring body, which he wanted with an ache that surprised him.

''I did not know that highwaymen had enough property to employ a steward,'' she said.

He chuckled. ''You're very astute. However, being a high-wayman is a profitable business.''

She wrinkled her nose. ''I don't see much evidence of wealth in this house, only poverty.'' She gathered the blanket closer around her as if to separate herself further from him. He sat on the edge of the mattress. ''In this area, fine things get stolen if you're not here to guard them every day. Besides, I don't stay here much. This area holds mostly bad memories for me.''

''I can understand that,'' she said softly. Her eyes darkened, questioned, as she looked at him.

She pushed against the pillows, the cover slipping from her shoulders to reveal creamy hints of skin among ebony curls. She hurriedly tucked the cover back around her body.

He imagined her delicious curves under a clinging silk shift, and he instantly grew hot. Desire plunged through his stomach and tightened his loins. He'd never asked for this, and the overpowering sensation annoyed him. Animal lust, something he'd never felt for Marguerite Lennox, now Lady Ransford. He had admired and revered her.

All he felt for this woman was an urge to break down her barrier, conquer her, force her to reveal her secrets, make love to her until she was soft smiling compliance in his arms. His desire was laced with anger; yet something in her pulled at his heart incessantly.

He slowly reached out and brushed the pad of his thumb over her luscious lips. Velvety, and the most vulnerable part of her face. Her skin stretched tautly over her cheekbones and her jaw, giving her an air of tension and suffering. And her eyes, the eyes that could make him speechless, now made him lose coherent thought. Inscrutable deep pools of eternity, as if she saw far beyond the limits of this world. Lady of mystery.

She didn't pull away, only sighed deeply and stared at him until the images tumbled together in confusion. He leaned forward, touching his lips to hers, lightly, the brush of a feather. He craved her warmth, her scent, her taste.

Did she feel the pull of their attraction as acutely as he did? He plowed his fingers under her hair and cupped her tense neck. So slender, so beautiful. So mysterious, so unattainable.

Serena couldn't pull away even though she sensed the danger, the tug of his powerful magnetism. Male allure, so alien, yet so familiar as if she'd known it all her life even though she had never been close to a man before. Every inch of her responded to his attraction. She longed to abandon herself with him, mingle her soul with his. Her cold control was slowly slipping, her heart softening, like an eggshell cracking. *God, so help me.*

A bell clanged somewhere, slow and somber, warmly comforting. She shook her head in wonder as she realized it was clanging within her, not outside. His hand felt hot on her neck, his sensual mouth hovering just above hers, breath caressing her, his darkened eyes, desperate and searching in the night gloom.

She sensed his frustration. She feared surrendering to his dark desire. If he kissed her, she would fight him. Yet, as soon as his mouth sought hers, she felt only a tingling that traveled through her body like a series of tiny bells that set off an explosion of yearning in her blood.

She did not protest when he gathered her into his powerful arms and clutched her close. The blanket puddled at her waist, leaving her open to his touch. His chest was hard as granite against her softer breasts. They flattened against him as against a wall; and in a daze, she heard him groan as if in pain.

"Oh, my God."

He wound his hands through her hair, and she savored the onslaught of his plundering mouth that compelled her to respond. She touched his tongue boldly with her own, her heart racing madly at the rough-soft feel of him.

He read her invitation, and crushed her harder to him, delving more intimately into her mouth as if drinking the essence of her. She felt as if her very life had drained and flowed into him. Too powerful, too urgent. Fear swam through the thick syrup of her desire and surfaced in her mind.

She pushed against him. He lifted his face away from hers abruptly. She breathed harshly, struggling to find her voice.

"You can't take advantage of my body because I'm your prisoner," she said when she could find her voice. "I won't fall for your seductive smiles."

"Methinks you have already softened."

"You're taking advantage of my weakness."

"I have never forced a woman, and I don't intend to start now," he said hoarsely. Seconds sank slowly into minutes before his tension relaxed. He pushed the cover back up over her shoulders, his forearm brushing the hard tip of her breast. She gasped as a jolt of pleasure shot through her. His barest touch made her breathless and confused, and she wondered why she'd let him touch her and kiss her. Her mind might be repulsed by him, but her body wasn't. How long would her resistance hold up?

She wiggled down until her head was propped against the pillows and the blanket pulled to her chin. She was going to protest as he brushed back her hair and caressed her head as if she were a child. No one had done that since Nurse Hopkins' days in the nursery. Her hand had been gnarled and dry, not warm and soothing like the highwayman's. Serena liked his hands. They were strong yet gentle, direct somehow. He didn't move through the world crablike, like some people she knew.

He crashed into others' lives, plucking what riches he could. There was something vital, wildly attractive in his character, despite the fact that he was a criminal.

Her eyelids grew heavy with sleep, and with his every caress, they grew heavier. She was slowly gliding into a place of peace, of blessed emptiness where the specters receded and thoughts became unimportant. With a sigh, she concentrated on his rhythmic stroking and let herself fade into nothing . . .

Nick watched her tense face change as sleep overcame her. Without the mask she wore to protect her vulnerability, she looked young and defenseless. And sad. Her soft mouth drooped. He could not leave her like this, lonely and prey to nightmares. Mayhap he was the cause of those. Certainly she must experience fear and panic even though she would not willingly let the world see any signs of her emotions except for a tensing of her jaw and the hunted look of her eyes.

He slid down beside her, slowly pulling part of the cover over himself. The room was pleasantly warm, but he wanted to share *her* warmth; he wanted to feel her curves pressed against his body. He pulled her head onto his shoulder and tucked it against the hollow right under his ear. Her hair flowed silkily against his neck, making him hold his breath as another wave of desire rolled through him. It surprised him that he'd revealed so much of his past to her without even knowing her name. Sometimes it was easier to open up to a stranger than it was to confide in a friend. Charles was the only one who knew the horrors of his past.

For once Nick could forget the pressures of his secret life and only *feel*. Her presence had the power to stop all his thoughts, as if she would not allow him to be aware of anything but herself. For once he could relax, sink into the mattress and slide into the warm cocoon of sleep. The last thing he noticed was her slender thigh thrown over his, and her breast thrusting against his ribs.

Serena dreamed of a muscled chest rubbing against her silk shift and persuasive hands that touched her in places no man had touched before, gliding over the flat plain of her stomach, cupping her breasts and holding them to a greedy mouth that sucked her nipples into hard pebbles.

A hand moved over her buttocks, slid along her inner thigh, and rubbed the mound at the top of her legs until the silk grew wet and she moaned. She dissolved in pleasure, gasped ... writhed in wanton abandonment ... Her breath was captive in her throat, and she coughed, waking.

Regret flowed through her as she realized the rich, warm feeling had seeped away. She turned to her side, finding the hardness of an obstacle. Memory flooded back, and she realized he was still there, breathing deeply in his sleep. He had not touched her, only held her securely in the crook of his arm. The feel of his solidity pumped the desire back into her blood and it turned into a warm liquid pool in her belly, pulsing like a heartbeat.

Cursing herself, she pressed her face against his throat and inhaled the musky male fragrance of his skin. His arms tightened around her, but he did not wake up. Her body throbbed, and she pressed herself against him, longing for so much more than his innocent embrace. God, he felt so good.

She had lost all sense—as much was clear, she thought. She lay awake for the longest time, contemplating what had happened since she left Luther behind at High Crescent. Even though she had ended up a prisoner, her fate momentarily in the hands of this man—Nick—she had no desire to leave his arms. For once she felt safe. *Safe.*

But she could not rely on him—a highwayman! It would be imbecile to expect him to protect her. She would have to get away sooner or later, leave him behind. There was no doubt in her mind that she would find a way to escape. Until then, all she had to do was survive and outwit her gaoler. She would have to forget his attraction and only think of herself and her future. It wasn't easy when his muscular chest rose under her arm and his hip rubbed against her female parts with every breath.

Chapter 7

Nick had dressed as was expected of a gentleman, in a fine embroidered waistcoat, a dove gray coat with a long row of gilded buttons, and gold braiding along the facings and the wide cuffs. The morning after he'd spent the night in his prisoner's bed, he'd been invited to an "evening" at the home of Lotus Blossom, a popular courtesan living on a side street off Piccadilly whose real name was Gladys Sutton.

In earlier days, he'd been an eager customer at her house whose bedroom walls depicted provocative Oriental scenes of lovemaking between gods and goddesses in lurid reds and golds. The rest of the tall town house had been decorated in demure pastels and expensive art. Furniture, frail and elegant, in the style that Queen Anne had introduced, was accented with marquetry and placed on luxurious Persian carpets. Chrysanthemums and boughs of autumn leaves in Chinese urns, porcelain figurines, and carved wooden boxes gave further proof of Lotus's discriminating taste.

A haven, a warmly welcoming house that only nurtured the needs of gentlemen—if they had deep purses to pay for it all. Lotus Blossom offered discreet if passionate lovemaking, girls of refinement for every man's enjoyment, excellent meals and wine, and high-stakes card games.

Her blond hair elaborately curled, pomaded, and powdered into rolls above her ears and clustered in the back, Lotus raised a glass of wine to him in a silent salute. A velvet star-shaped patch at the corner of her lips tilted alluringly as she smiled at him. Voluptuous breasts barely concealed under a golden bodice, rounded arms, sparkling blue eyes, sultry smiles beckoned Nick, but he only raised his glass toward his old mistress and drank a quiet toast.

Nick had found much pleasure in the arms of Lotus in the past, but the ardor had subsided, leaving friendship in its wake. Even as he sipped a glass of claret, he kept remembering the soft curves of his prisoner's body, the juncture of her thighs intimately pressed against his hipbone. God, he wanted to kick himself for letting the memories of her cloud his vision and his thoughts. Ever since he'd taken off her clothes in Noah's cottage, he'd been in a frenzy to bed her. He yearned to capture the elusiveness of her being, find her pliant legs locked around his waist, her breasts filling his mouth . . . his manhood buried deeply, deeply inside her feminine heat . . .

The front door opened and admitted a group of inebriated gentlemen. With a grimace of displeasure, Nick watched Ethan enter the house dressed in a full-skirted silver blue brocade coat that must have cost at least one hundred pounds. Ethan, annoying his stepbrother, waved his hand languidly as if to show off the profusion of Mechlin lace at his wrists. He acted as if nothing had happened, as if he weren't on the brink of total ruin.

There was something steely, a flash of icy hatred in his eyes, as he strolled across the polished floor to Nick's side. Nick did not blink or retreat from the wave of animosity pushing against him.

"Good evening, stepbrother," Ethan drawled, his rouged lips parting in a cold smile. "Didn't expect to meet you here, but since you are in London, I suppose I will have to run into you at various gatherings."

Nick did not return the smile. "Very disturbing, isn't it?" He viewed the powdered cheeks of his brother, but the powder could not conceal the hectic color of his skin, a sign of deep inebriation. "I can tell that this is not your first stop for the evening, and probably not your last. But rest assured, we shall not meet again tonight—not if I have a choice."

Ethan took on a friendlier expression. "Be that as it may, I am glad I ran into you, Nick. Have you had time to think about what we discussed yesterday morning?"

"Your disclosures gave me nightmares, but I have not changed my mind. I never will."

Ethan snarled, dislike flashing in his eyes. "You'll *have to* give me the money—or at least part of it—or the whole family will be ruined."

Nick sighed profoundly. "*I* won't be ruined. Nothing that you'll ever do to ruin yourself will touch me. I won't allow you to drag me down with you."

"Delicia will be destroyed by the scandal of my insolvency," Ethan said peevishly. "You know that Father would not have wanted that."

"The rumors will certainly tarnish her name, but I will try to protect her. She's staying at The Hollows—where you won't be able to reach her since I've forbidden you to set foot on my property. I won't protect you any longer, Ethan. And Delicia must discover the depth of your debauchery, and when she does, her love and admiration for you will be destroyed."

"I'm sure you take the opportunity to speak ill of me at every turn," Ethan said, his voice trembling with fury.

"You brought this onto yourself. I shall take care of Delicia and make sure she won't suffer more than necessary from your idiotic conduct. Fortunately, she does not know many people in London; the gossip might not touch her. But if she comes up to Berkley Square, she will understand your complete disregard for the Leverton name. She will hear of your exploits."

Ethan's high color deepened, and he gripped a glass of wine from a nearby table. "You think you're safe at The Hollows?" He gave a derogative snort. "The king of a few acres. Those should rightfully have belonged to me—not you. 'Tis no more than right that you assist me in my time of need.''

"I'm tired of discussing this matter," Nick said and set down his glass with finality. "You won't get a groat from me, or from The Hollows, and Delicia shall discover your rotten core."

Nick stiffened, not at Ethan's lengthy cursing, but at seeing the figure of Captain Trevor Emerson, the friend who also was a deadly foe should he find out the identity of the Midnight Bandit. Emerson, out of his red uniform and wearing an elegant coat and breeches of blue velvet, greeted the hostess. Her wide skirts brushed by Nick in passing and she dragged her folded fan along his arm.

"Will you visit my boudoir later?" she asked in her purring voice, cultivated to please a gentleman's ear.

"No, Lotus—you're tempting me, but not tonight," he said, the memory of his prisoner's warm body weaving through his thoughts.

Nick watched two of the girls sitting in the laps of his friends, feeding them wine, grapes, and cheese. Another courtesan played the harpsichord in an alcove framed with gold curtains. The instrument's frail tunes added to the soothing atmosphere of the house, but Nick's feeling of well-being had disappeared upon the arrival of Ethan and Captain Emerson.

"Do leave me alone, Ethan," he said as he glanced at his stepbrother's scowling face. "I will not change my mind— ever. No matter how much you beg and cajole."

Ethan's expression grew dark and ugly. "You haven't seen or heard the last of me," he said. "I shall not forget your failure to support me in my time of need." He strolled to the table where delicacies such as roasted swan with currant jelly sauce, slices of boiled tongue, and smoked salmon had been laid out to tempt the guests' palates. He twined his arms around one of the smiling girls and kissed her hard on the red mouth. Nick sighed and turned away.

The captain saw Nick and his face lit up in a grin. He wore his sandy hair tied back with a satin bow and unpowdered. His sharp blue gaze scrutinized the assembled guests, and Nick knew that most of them called Emerson a friend. They had been a tightly knit group through Eton, and later Oxford. Friendships had formed that would last a lifetime. Nick missed Charles sorely, his favorite crony despite their rivalry over Marguerite, Lady Lennox.

"You're here then," Emerson said after he'd handed his hat to a footman and kissed Lotus's hand. "I sought your company yesterday at The Hollows after a singularly disappointing week of scouring Sussex for that damned highwayman." He sighed and accepted a glass of wine from one of the servants.

"What happened?" Nick asked, knowing very well what had occurred to ruin Emerson's temper.

"The militia were an inch from capturing the Midnight Bandit, but the scoundrel got away even though I had extra men on horses to ride him down. He and his accomplice robbed two coaches, then disappeared into the woods." Emerson swore long and profoundly in a low voice. "I will personally hang that villain when we capture him!"

Nick took a deep swallow of wine. "He has been your nemesis for many a month."

Emerson's eyes shot fire. "But it won't last."

"I believe that with your famed persistence you will catch him in the end. He might grow careless with his continued success."

"One error on his part and he will fall into my snares."

"His star will wane . . ." Nick said, sensing the danger ahead if he continued his reckless missions. Even a discussion like this was dangerous. His tongue might make a sudden slip.

"If only there were a witness—someone who has seen his face behind that black mask. By the way, we found his mask on the ground."

Nick said nothing, only felt a trickle of dread moving down his spine. He had purchased another mask in London, and if Emerson ever got wind of that . . .

Emerson continued, "The Duke of Atwood is thinking of issuing a big reward for the bandit's capture."

"That ought to get the locals talking," Nick said.

Emerson's eyebrows rose. "You think he hails from our area in Sussex?"

Nick shrugged, his limbs weak with dread. "I don't know, but many attacks have occurred in that part of the country. The smugglers might know something."

"We captured a group, but they do not speak of their criminal cohorts. Not much chance of finding out the truth from them. Besides, they might not know any more than we do."

"What *do* you know?" Nick asked casually.

"We suspect he has a secret refuge where he hides that great black brute of a horse. My men are searching the forest south of Haywards Heath even as we speak, but I had to come to London on business."

Nick had to set the glass down on a side table before Emerson noted his shaking hand. Noah might be in danger if they continued on to Cuckfield, and Pegasus had to be moved. Pegasus might not be noticed in London where every other horse was black. But his white stockings were famous in Sussex. He would ride down and bring Pegasus back to London.

My mission is not finished, Nick thought. Not until the orphanage was paid for in full. Only then would he be able to breathe easy and know that the children had a home that could not be taken away for lack of funds.

"If anyone will catch the highwayman, it will be you," Nick said and clamped a hand on Emerson's shoulder. "You should taste some of Lotus Blossom's delicious food. I'll have to leave before Ethan starts pestering me again with more demands for funds."

Emerson frowned. "I had hoped to spend a while talking with you. It has been some time since we last spoke."

"I shall visit your lodgings," Nick said. "That is if you'll be in any shape to receive visitors. Lotus's fine wine has serious effects on one's head."

Emerson laughed. "My head is hard as a nut and filled with iron filings."

"Iron corrodes when drenched in liquid," Nick said lightly. Emerson scrutinized him, and guilt washed through Nick.

He did not like to deceive his friend, but how could Emerson understand his motives to rob the coaches of the rich? Emerson would always be a staunch supporter of the law. "How are you, Nick? Your face is strained, and your eyes have the tired look of a man who has not slept well for weeks."

"I have my problems, like everyone else. Ethan is one of them. Frankly, I think he's about to ruin everything I've worked to protect."

"Do you purposely fail to mention Charles's and Marguerite's wedding? I noticed your desolation, as did everyone else. You can confide in me, Nick. Are you still pining for the fair Marguerite? Would you like to unload your heavy heart?"

The picture of Marguerite in her wedding gown flashed through his mind, then the face of the woman who had slept innocently in his arms last night. He'd never held Marguerite like that, tightly, intimately.

"I think I was in love with an ideal," he said at last. "I know I will never meet another woman like Marguerite. She nurtures the best in a man. I hope that one day I can be as giving to someone whose heart hurts more than mine."

Emerson's eyes gleamed. "Why, that's the most poignant speech I've ever heard from you." He slapped Nick's shoulder. "You are a good man, Nick. You would care for a lady in need, give of yourself unselfishly. You share that with Marguerite."

"What about you, Trev? I thought you had a soft spot for Marguerite as well."

"I did. I—do, but never love. I could see Charles's determination to win her. I have my military career, and that's enough. Soon I'll be able to afford a higher commission, when there's a vacancy. I inherited some funds from an uncle. That, my family, and my friends are my world."

Nick sighed. "You're content with the simplicity of life. By thunder, I wish I didn't *want* so much."

"Something or the care of someone will fill that gap, Nick. Trust me."

Nick felt another stab of guilt as he glanced into Emerson's kind eyes. They shook hands. "I don't deserve a friend like you, Trev."

"Plague take it, Nick. Don't get maudlin."

"See you soon." Nick strode toward the door before he confessed the whole to his trusting friend.

He glanced at one of the couples on a sofa, the man fondling a bare breast, tongue plunging into the courtesan's mouth as she lolled back in his lap. The orgies were in full swing, Nick thought with a vague feeling of dislike, and went in search of his hostess to say good-bye.

Sir Luther Hilliard rubbed his pendulous jowls and studied the landlord at the tavern Fish and Hound in Crawley. "You swear you've never seen the lady with such a description traveling alone with only an elderly coachman for company?"

"Naw, I've not seen such a fool 'ardy creature, guv. Not in the last sixmonth, or longer."

Irritated, Luther pulled down his tight waistcoat that had the tendency to ride up on his considerable paunch. Damn it, it needed taking out in the seams again; the buttons were almost popping. Too many cream sauces and too much rich wine. But who cared? Now that he held the deed to High Crescent, he could afford to satisfy any extravagant desire.

He adjusted the wide embroidered cuffs of his coat, clapped his cocked hat on his head, and strode out into the muddy inn yard.

The frustration that had dogged him since the moment she'd fled from his grip overcame him with renewed strength. He paced the yard as white-hot fury washed through him and roiled in his gut. He could barely contain himself, and every negative response he received from innkeepers along the road made him long to kill them, or at least punch their faces into bloody pulp.

He had sought Serena through the south of England, picking up the scent in Shaftesbury and following her into Sussex.

Why Sussex at all? he asked himself, puzzled by her direction that veered in strange detours. He was certain she'd aimed for London. The capital was a very large city. If he followed her trail in Sussex, he was more likely to discover more clues to her whereabouts.

She might have joined another traveling party or divulged her plans to the chambermaids at the inns. Serena was desperate, and she needed all the help she could get from kindly strangers. An innocent traveling alone to London was fair prey to all kinds of criminals.

Luther leered at the thought of her victimized by some scoundrel, perhaps even killed. That would take care of the one person who had witnessed Andrew's death.

His plan had worked; Andrew's death had been blamed on a vagrant lurking around the area. That vagrant would hang—it couldn't be too soon in Luther's opinion. He had spread around a falsehood that Serena had broken down in the wake of her father's death and had been sent away to stay with friends until she could deal with her grief and the disturbing memories of the murder.

Luther glanced north on the muddy hedge-lined road. She would have to die or he would hang for murdering his brother. Die she would. He would kill her with his own hands and take deep pleasure in it. Unless someone else . . .

He muttered, "If someone else has stolen the pleasure, I shall see justice done."

"Your carriage, sir," the stable lad said, breaking into his reverie. "A fresh team, an' I wiped the dust o' the coach." He expectantly held out his hand for a coin, but Luther only grimaced at him before swinging himself into the waiting coach. The conveyance swayed under his considerable bulk. The hatch opened and the coachman peered at him. "Where to, Sir Luther?"

Luther noticed that the driver's eye had swelled shut and turned purple where Luther had punched him earlier. It should show the dolt not to disobey orders in the future.

"To London, Tully, and don't spare the horses."

*   *   *

Serena woke up the following morning, rested but restless. She had not seen Nick since he left her bed. Not that she'd seen him then; he'd left before she awakened. But his scent had remained on the pillow and the sheets were wrinkled from his body. She had felt safe. For once her horrifying nightmares had left her alone.

She got up and stretched her stiff body, arms over her head and neck thrown back. She yawned but felt bright and fresh. As she crossed the room, through sunbeams slanting over the floor, she noticed that the door stood open.

Gasping in surprise, she tiptoed to the high threshold and looked into the hallway beyond. All she could see was dust on the floor. The windows were grimy but let through a golden autumn sun. How could anyone live like this? She listened for voices or movements that would tell her something about her jailer. Not a sound could be heard, only the muted creaking of a heavy wagon outside.

Excitement raced through her. What if her chance to escape had arrived? She hurried back into her room, flung off her shift, and washed herself in the basin. The water was icy and the air enclosed her in a cold and clammy embrace.

She dried off and hurriedly donned the dress that looked even more tattered this morning. She never wore soiled clothing and she loathed the greasy feel of her shift against her skin. As soon as she had the chance, she would find some other clothes to wear.

She went downstairs, cursing the creaking steps. Dust swirled around her ankles, and she wished she could close her nose. How could Nick live in such dreary, dirty quarters? Thrilled by the sudden opportunity for freedom, she listened for voices. Nothing.

On the first landing were three doors. She knew one led to Nick's bedchamber, the others to bare rooms. The door to her tormentor's room was slightly ajar, and she could not stop herself from peeking through the crack.

His bed was made, covered with a woven green and black blanket. Cravats and handkerchiefs lay in a stack on the carved chest in one corner.

A lute, a string instrument with a round belly, leaned against the chest. Boots had been flung on the floor, and coats hung on pegs beside the door. A wardrobe held waistcoats and shirts, but only a small collection that could not cover the needs of Nick, who dressed in the elegant manner of an aristocrat. Evidently robbing travelers was a lucrative business. The fine coats were proof of that.

She cringed as she recalled his attacks on hapless travelers. If only he weren't a bandit, she would find him maddeningly attractive. She still did, but the criminal aspect had to be a deterrent to any deeper feelings. It had to be. But there was something about him, a wonderful warm vitality that fascinated her. And his grin! It made her knees turn to water every time. If she didn't take care, her heart might become entangled with his, and that was something she dared not contemplate.

Unable to ignore her curiosity, she opened the creaking door fully and stepped inside. As she inspected a silver hairbrush and some buttons in a glass bowl, she threw surreptitious glances toward the door. She did not want to get caught snooping. Serena Hilliard had not been brought up to act in an unladylike manner, no matter what the circumstances, she thought. That did not stop her from putting her nose to his stack of cravats and inhaling the fresh scent of soap and starch, and the elusive fragrance that was Nick's. Her heart expanded in a strange way, giving her a sudden urge to cry. She moved away in haste.

She dragged a fingertip along the edge of the carved chest and the curved back of a wooden chair, finding her skin grayed with dust.

"This is disgusting," she said and grimaced. She left the room and closed the door behind her. Listening for sounds of Nick, she walked cautiously downstairs.

To her chagrin, a guard sat on a chair by the front door.

Keys dangled from a ring on his leather baldric, and Serena took note of the sword in its scabbard.

"Good morning, Miss Eve," the burly guard greeted her and touched his greasy black forelock. He was around twenty, she guessed, dressed in a coarse brown coat and breeches, grimy white stockings on his lower legs.

"I don't see anything good about it," she said haughtily. "I am still a prisoner."

"Aye, that ye are, but Mr. Nick will take care o' ye right fine."

"Where is he?"

"Went south, but 'e'll be back any time now. 'E said I might take ye for a walk as long as ye promise t' be'ave. Later. There's the vegetable-and-flower market at Covent Garden."

Serena eyed his beefy hands and coarse face and wondered if she'd be able to outrun him in the street. "That would be nice," she said, and left him, head held high.

To her surprise, she found food on the table and the tea kettle blowing steam on the trivet. She could hear someone muttering in the pantry.

"Who's there?" she asked, poised for a confrontation. It could not be the highwayman, or had he come back earlier than the guard at the front door had implied? Perhaps the dwarf.

A man, dark of hair and eyes, stuck his head around the pantry door. He was handsome in a brooding way, jaw square, and expression weary, as if he'd been awake all night.

"So, you're up then. There's hot coffee, or tea if you like."

"Who are you?"

"Rafe Howard. A friend of Nick's." He reentered the kitchen, carrying a crock of butter and a string of smoked sausages.

"Are you guarding the back door?" she asked suspiciously and drew herself up. She had to tilt her face back to look into his eyes. He was dressed in black; only his shirt and his elegant cravat were white.

"Right now I'm having breakfast. But don't try to escape. You won't get very far." He set his burden on the table, and Serena's stomach tightened with hunger.

"Can I help?" she asked, strangely humbled by her desperate need for sustenance. It seemed days since she'd had a decent meal—especially since she'd been forced to cook her own. Even the most loyal friend would not call her a fair cook.

"I hear you know how to fry eggs. I'd like two, and make as many as you want for yourself."

She set to work without delay, handling the frying pan like an experienced cook. "What is in the black pot?" she asked as she spied something bubbling over the fire.

"Beans and stew. Something I learned to cook while at the infirmary in Belgium," he said.

"You fought against the French?"

He shrugged. "Them and others—so I'm told." She could see the bitter grimace on his face and wondered what had happened to bring on such an expression.

"The war is over. You might not have to fight again."

"You're right. But if what my friends say is true, I killed many men. I can't remember any of it."

Intriguing, she thought, and intended to ask him more questions. Her plan came to naught as she dropped one egg in the fire, but pretended that it hadn't happened. He had seen and heard the mistake, but did not comment. She liked him for it. Biting her bottom lip, she concentrated on cracking the others and pouring them inside the pan.

"Do you work for Nick?" she asked.

"We're friends," he replied and sliced the sausage. "He is a good fellow."

She made a sound of disgust. "How can you be friends with a criminal?"

"As I said, Nick is a decent man."

Serena lost her concentration on the eggs and stared at the stranger. "Surely you are jesting?"

He shook his head. "Not at all. But I can understand if you have difficulty accepting that fact. Nick is fair and compassionate—always ready to help the less fortunate."

The increased sound of sizzling brought Serena's attention back to the eggs. They would be ruined if she didn't remove them from the pan. She forgot to probe into Mr. Howard's reason for calling Nick a good man as she managed to slide the eggs onto two plates. Then she watched as the stranger fried sliced sausage with confidence and brought a coffeepot to the table.

"At least Nick keeps a well-filled pantry even though he lives in a pigsty," she said. "I'm surprised he's willing to live like this." She glanced at the cobwebs in the corners as she bit into a forkful of eggs and sausage.

"I'm certain he keeps more than one residence in London. This was newly acquired due to the closeness to—" He clamped his jaws shut, his reluctance to communicate gossip about Nick intriguing her.

"Closeness to what? Brothels and gambling halls? I know about the existence of such places as my father was a gambler and a womanizer."

"Ladies are not supposed to speak about such vices," he said.

"Pooh, why pretend they don't exist? Those vices ruined my mother's life."

He stared at her, dark eyes full of contempt. "If she *let* her life be ruined."

Serena slammed down her fork. "She had no choice! Father made her life miserable."

"It takes two to quarrel."

He was right, but that didn't mean her father had been fair toward her mother when flaunting his lightskirts and gambling away parts of the Hilliard fortune. Her lips quivered as she remembered the screaming and the abuse. "I tried to make my mother part from him, but there was nothing left of her—only a dry husk of bitterness."

Steps sounded in the corridor outside, and Serena fell silent. Her gaze flew to the doorway. She sensed Nick before he appeared—as if his forceful presence walked a few steps ahead of him.

"Did I hear the word bitterness?" he asked as he stood on the threshold.

Serena's heartbeat raced alarmingly at the sight of his tall, attractive form—and that grin that had the power to touch her soul. His hair was tied back and he wore town clothes—a dark brown camlet coat with brass buttons, fawn breeches, and a dark green waistcoat that parted to reveal his strong thighs as he walked into the kitchen.

"It appears that your hostage's family life was not a happy one," Rafe said.

" 'Tis none of your business," she snapped and pushed her chair away from the table. "I wish I hadn't spoken. I think I'll go upstairs—though I'm loath to spend another hour in this filthy house."

"You're always welcome to clean. 'Twould make time pass more quickly. There are rags and a bucket in the scullery," Nick said.

Her anger rose in her throat. "I am not your servant."

"In that case, do not complain about the state of the rooms. Are you too snobbish to soil your white hands with dust?" He stood so close she could see the pulse beating in his throat, right above the band of his cravat, and she remembered how she'd pressed her nose against it and inhaled his male fragrance. Heat rose in her cheeks, and she could not maintain her anger.

"This has nothing to do with my white hands. I would think that a gentleman of your financial standing would be eager to keep a fine house full of servants, or at least a charwoman."

"Ah!" Nick said, his voice wry with humor. "But I am not a man of unlimited funds—no matter how many coaches I rob."

"I suppose you gamble the profits away, as befits a true gentleman," she said in a low voice. She could not remove her gaze from his throat, and it slowly traveled across the hard jaw up to the blue unyielding gaze. A teasing glitter sprang to life in its depths, and she could not find her breath for a long moment.

"I have been known to enjoy a hand of piquet or whist," he said, his lips curving upward at the corners. "But I do not play to lose." He went to the table and inspected the breakfast dishes thoughtfully.

Serena let out a long slow breath, and she had to lean against the door frame to regain her composure. What was it about him that threw her thoughts into confusion and made her heartbeat run away with her? She longed for company, for reassurance. She understood that feeling—having spent one night beside him feeling safe. But truly, she loathed gentlemen who pretended to be something they were not, like Father—gamblers and womanizers. She glanced at Mr. Howard. Warriors. Murderers.

A lady's life was always ruled by a gentleman, be it a father, a brother, a grandfather, even an uncle. A sob gathered in her throat and she thought she would choke on the anger and the old hurt. She swallowed her surging emotions and forced herself to forget the disturbing memories.

"The guard at the front door said I could go out today."

The highwayman served himself a plate of food and sat down. She waited anxiously for his next words. If she didn't get out of the house, she might choke on despair.

"Perhaps later," Nick said vaguely and poured a cup of coffee for himself.

Without another word, she hurried out of the kitchen and slammed the door behind her. She made an effort to open a window on the first landing. Mayhap she could try and shout for help again, but the frame had swelled in the damp air and she could not budge it any more than she could shift the second window in her prison. It had been painted shut.

She threw a glance over her shoulder to see if the front door guard had followed her. He was leaning against the door frame and leering at her.

Chapter 8

Nick had brought Pegasus back to London on the previous night, and had left the stallion at a stable in Southwark as the morning light arrived.

He'd worried about the horse in Sussex and would rather stable it where he could keep an eye on it. Having helped at the foaling of Pegasus, he counted the stallion as a beloved member of the family.

As darkness fell that evening, he rode across Black Friars Bridge to Southwark, paid the livery stables for Pegasus's keep, and led the horse into a dark back alley that reeked of the nearby tanneries.

He'd brought stove blacking and in the light from a weak moon, he rubbed the blacking over Pegasus's white stockings with a rag. He didn't like to take any chances, even if plenty of London horses had similar white markings. He unsuccessfully cleaned the black stains that smeared on his hands, then put the jar into the saddlebag.

Mounting his sorrel hunter, he attached Pegasus's reins to the pommel and rode onto the main road. He knew of a stable owned by one of the tavern-keepers in Cripplegate. No one would find Pegasus in those mean warrens.

The nightlife was slowly stirring across the bridge. Harlots offered themselves in shadowy doorways and street corners. Drunk young blades cheered and wove in and out of the crowds. Farmers were pulling their heavy carts and wagons out of London, clogging the entrance to the bridge.

Pegasus pranced nervously as a pack of dogs streaked across the street, and Nick pulled at the reins to calm the horse. He rode up Ludgate toward St. Paul's. Sedan chairs and elegant carriages became few and far between as he neared the meaner parts of the city. Low gambling hells and clubs existed along Aldergate Street, but he had no intention of becoming distracted by card play until he'd secured Pegasus's hiding place. Just as he passed the grand cathedral, he came upon a troop of militia-men led by Captain Emerson, herding a group of prisoners.

Damned rotten luck, Nick thought, stiffening. He threw a furtive glance at Pegasus and noted with relief that the white stockings were invisible under the blacking.

"Trev! What's going on?" he shouted and waved his hat.

Captain Emerson had already recognized him and separated from the group of soldiers. "What ho! Did you buy a new horse, Nick, old fellow?"

"Yes ... a big brute of a hunter. Might as well get him settled and used to my touch before the hunting parties begin." Nick got out of the saddle and watched with misgivings as Emerson circled the stallion.

Pegasus whinnied and pranced, hooves flashing.

"Spirited, by God," Emerson said. "Powerful hindquarters, a beautiful head, proud bearing." He slid his hand along the flank of the horse, feeling one of the strong front legs all the way down to the knee.

Nick fidgeted. "He's a sweet-goer. Sixteen hands easily." He tried to pull Pegasus aside.

Emerson stood staring at the horse's legs as if deep in thought. "Black as Satan," he commented absentmindedly. His head shot up, and Nick could feel his friend's penetrating stare. "What do you call him."

"Why ... Ebony Spirit, or Spirit for short," Nick temporized. "I can't very well call him Silver or Morning Thunder."

"Good name," Emerson said, and dragged his hand along the stallion's long neck. "He seems friendly enough."

Nick could barely speak. "He ... has a good disposition. Very quick, and responds to a feather touch on the reins."

As Emerson started touching the stallion's legs again as if searching for flaws, Nick stepped forward, crowding his friend. "I say, what are you doing here with your troop?" He threw a glance at the group of men waiting silently for their leader.

"Delivering three prisoners to Newgate. We're going back tomorrow. Let's go out to the clubs later tonight, Nick."

Nick nodded convulsively. "A splendid idea. I'll meet you at your lodgings in two hours."

After patting the horse once more, Emerson left, and Nick drew a deep sigh of relief. His hands trembled, and cold sweat rolled down his spine. What if Trev had noticed the blacking and questioned the strange substance on Pegasus's legs?

Clenching his jaw, Nick swung himself into the saddle. The sooner he could hide the horse the better. Next time, luck might work against him.

Serena could not stand the dirt and the dust. She went downstairs the next day to confront Nick. Her restlessness was such that she had to pace her room to keep from screaming with frustration. She'd do *anything* to make the time go faster.

There was no sign of Nick or Rafe Howard. Guards had been posted, though ... two burly servants that would not let her set one toe onto the street.

The dwarf was in the kitchen, eating a bun, but he only glared at her without saying a word. He pointedly turned his back on her.

"For a caretaker, you don't take much care of this house," she said.

He did not reply, only shrugged.

She could have shouted at him, but stomped into the scullery instead and found that water had been pumped into three buckets. For the dirty dishes no doubt. The plates were stacked in the sink, egg yolk and grease congealed on the pewter and ale sticky on the tankards. *Pigs!*

Still, it wouldn't be difficult to wash up, she thought. She dropped each plate and tankard into one of the buckets, and watched bubbles rise to the surface. Hmm, what now? Well, let the revolting dishes soak, she thought. She would deal with them later. She paused for a moment. Perhaps she needed warm water, but how would she manage that?

She looked at the kitchen hearth, finding embers still glowing. An empty black pot on three legs stood beside the fire. Was it for heating water? She had no idea.

Sighing in defeat, she decided she would clean her room. At least it was better than staring at the surly dwarf or the dust rats chasing each other in the slightest draft.

She hefted a bucket filled with clean cold water. In a corner, she found a hard brush for scrubbing. A stack of rags rested on the sink. At home, she had watched the maids scrub the floors on hands and knees, using a circular motion and dipping the brush into the bucket at regular intervals. How difficult could it be?

Her arm ached as she carried the bucket upstairs, and the guard did nothing to help her, only stared into nothing as if she did not exist.

In her room, she tied up her hair with one of Nick's handkerchiefs that she'd taken from the heap on the chest in his bedchamber.

"There!" she said. "I surely look the part of a scullery maid now. My fortunes have truly changed." She rubbed her hands on her skirt and studied the floor. If she started in one corner . . .

Twenty minutes later her knees ached and her hands were colder than ice. She dipped the brush into the water and scrubbed the planks, noticing that the dust turned into grime that fouled the water until it was brown as mud. And she'd only washed one small corner of the room! She stared uncertainly at the liquid wondering if there were some other trick to cleaning the floor. At this rate, she would have to use fifteen buckets of water to wash down every plank.

For a moment she felt sorry for all the maids that had cleaned High Crescent, but they'd had a knack for it. Scrubbing a floor usually did not take that long—if it were reasonably clean.

She cast back her thoughts and remembered brooms made from tough willow branches. The maids would have swept the floor first to remove most of the dust.

She stretched her stiff back. Her hands ached with the unfamiliar work and she grimaced at the red skin on her knuckles and her abraded nails. Perspiration trickled down her spine, and a feeling of defeat flooded her.

"There is no broom downstairs," she muttered, but despite that pronouncement, she went to the kitchen and searched every corner. She would not give up, not yet. She might have asked Lonny, but he had left. Thank goodness for that!

She laughed in triumph when she found a broom with a gnarled handle behind the scullery door. Within the hour she had swept up most of the dust. She sneezed, and her nose dripped deplorably.

Exchanging the bucket with the dirty water for another in the scullery, she managed to mop the whole floor and wipe the surfaces with one of the folded rags. The room smelled fresh, she thought as she straightened her tight shoulders. She did not have any strength left to carry the bucket and brush downstairs.

Wiping a hand over her face, she discovered that the skin was gritty with dust. She washed her face and neck carefully in the basin, and her arms all the way up to the elbows. Then she shook out her hair and sank down on the edge of the mattress.

She heaved a deep sigh, partly of exasperation, partly of contentment. Her restlessness was gone, and exhaustion had set in. A glass of wine would taste heavenly, then something to eat, and early to bed. Tomorrow she would tackle another area of the house.

* * *

Sir Luther Hilliard had discovered from the servants at High Crescent that Nurse Hopkins had a sister in London. Serena had been close to Nurse Hopkins. It was logical that she would visit Molly Hopkins in Haymarket and beg for room and board. Where else could she have gone? She had no one else.

Sir Luther peered through the window at the shop, seeing only the frills and frivolities that ladies liked to surround themselves with—the disgusting treacherous creatures. He slammed the door as he entered. Laces and ribbons fluttered in the draft.

A solid older woman came into the shop from behind a curtain at the back. "Good afternoon, sir, how can I help you?"

"I need some information. Are you Miss Hopkins?"

The woman nodded, suspicion now shadowing her eyes.

"I'm Luther Hilliard, Miss Serena's uncle. I know you're related to Nurse Hopkins, and I wonder if you've seen Miss Serena lately. Has she contacted you?"

"I don't expect Miss Serena to contact me at any time," she replied tersely and started rolling up ribbons. "What do you want with her?"

"I need to speak with her, that's all, to clear up a misunderstanding." He found a smile for the woman even though he disliked her penetrating stare intensely. He backed toward the door. "By the way, do you know of a livery stable nearby? I need to have my horses changed."

"There's one in Panton Street, just around the corner."

He bowed, hat in hand. "You've been most helpful." And she had, he mused as he closed the door. With any luck, he would find Roy Coachman and the High Crescent traveling chaise at one of the livery stables nearby, and Roy could be made to speak . . . Pain applied in certain places on a body always brought about a desired confession.

* * *

Nick found Serena sitting in a chair in the kitchen, so close to the fire that her ragged skirts might catch any second. Her head lolled forward, chin resting on her chest. He noticed her red hands and the bucket of unappetizing dirty dishes at her feet. An empty wine glass and a plate balanced on the brick ledge by the fire, and the wine bottle he'd brought home yesterday was half empty on the table.

He grinned, strangely pleased to see her peaceful form. The expression of serenity would not last long, however, only as long as he let her sleep.

He walked softly to her side and admired her hair that poured like an onyx river down her back. She looked more like a kitchen maid than the highborn lady she was. Her satin slippers peeked under the hem of her gown; the toes were completely ripped open, the stockings grimy and full of holes.

Pleased with his purchases, he eyed the brown package in his arms and placed it on the table. He quite looked forward to her smile of delight when she set eyes on her new garments.

He gently took her face between his hands and raised her head. She yawned and turned sleep-blurred eyes toward his. They widened in recognition and she pressed back against the chair, her expression that of a trapped animal.

"You!" she croaked, and wet her lips. She placed her hand to her forehead as if doubting her vision. "You're back."

"I brought something for you, and a meat pie from the coffeehouse on the corner since I suspected you had not cooked dinner for us."

"I'm too tired to cook," she said, her words slightly slurred from the wine.

"But you are hungry, aren't you?"

"I had bread and cheese, and an apple for dessert. That will tide me over 'til breakfast."

"Stubborn wench!" With a sigh, he turned toward the table, where steam rose from a covered crockery dish. "You make life very difficult for yourself. A little cooperation would make things go more smoothly."

She rose and walked toward him. He shot her a glance and

was taken aback by the desperation in those mysterious eyes that shifted from midnight blue to the deepest black.

"I thought I would go mad today," she said with a catch in her voice. "The dwarf treated me as if I were less than dust, and I had nothing to do."

"I understand your frustration, but don't get upset with Lonny. He treats all women the same. He had a wife who used to beat him. Fortunately she died before she had the chance to finish him off."

"Oh . . ." she said, trying to picture such a vicious woman. Mayhap Mother—after she grew bitter—would have relished taking the whip to her father if he had lacked in stature and strength like Lonny. No, Mother had not been that vicious.

She sighed. "As I said, I thought I would go mad today. Would you please let me leave? I promise I won't say a word to anyone about you. Not a word."

He crossed his arms over his chest and studied her narrowly. He had to admit that her eyes reflected honesty. "Why the sudden change from highborn lady who detests criminals to begging servant? It's rather difficult to believe you would change your character so quickly."

"What do you know about my character?" she asked. She flung out her arms in a gesture of frustration. "You know nothing about me. And I keep my promises."

"I am slowly learning all your quirks," he said coolly, "and your mood fluctuations do not inspire great confidence."

"You said I could leave if I swore not to reveal your secret to the law."

He grinned. "That tired of my company, eh?"

She flew at him, her gait unsteady. "You promised, *damn you!*"

"Gutter language does not suit you, Miss Eve," he drawled. He caught her wrists as she intended to punch him. Fragile bones, soft skin. Blazing eyes, the mystery of her soul consumed by the fire of her anger.

He held her close, smelling the wine on her breath and feeling her rounded form against his own body. He would like to hold her forever, if only to insure he did not have to spend his days and nights alone.

But if anything, she was dangerous as she might denounce him. He would like to make her his friend—or more. The thought disturbed him so much, he acted without thinking. Pressing her even closer, so close she cried out in protest, he crushed his mouth to hers, tasting the silken cave and her reluctant tongue.

Forgetting that she was an unwilling conquest, he dragged his hand the length of her back, finding the sweet curve of her backside. He pressed her hard against his swollen manhood.

His progress was cut short as her hands crept over his shoulders, found his earlobes, and tugged to get his attention.

"Damn your eyes! Why did you have to do that?" He gripped her wrists once more and pushed her away from him. Her eyes shone with triumph but also with deep turbulence, as if various emotions were at war in her chest.

"You mauled me without my consent," she retorted and struggled to free herself from his hard grip. He could not let her go as anger surged in waves through him.

"She-cat," he said and exhaled sharply through his nose.

"Cur!" she cried.

He loosened his grip abruptly and she stumbled backward, tripping over the chair by the hearth and falling onto the seat. Her hair flew forward at the impact, covering most of her face. He heard her mutter a curse, and a trembling sob broke from her lips.

"I'm sorry," he murmured. "I did not mean to maul you." He hadn't, but her alluring scent had befuddled his thoughts, inspired the urge to crush her in his arms. "Despite your volatile temper, you are a very beautiful woman," he said, meaning every word. "Very desirable."

"I'm sorry if I hurt your ears," she murmured, glancing at him quickly as she swept her hair back. "And I am not beautiful. You're only flattering me to get what you want."

He continued. "You truly are lovely, mysterious as a cat, and as lithe—elegant."

"My father once said I was nothing out of the ordinary—a *great disappointment,* to use his exact words."

"He must not have looked very closely at your exotic eyes, or sensed the mystery of your soul." He smiled and poured a glass of wine for himself. He offered her some, too, but she shook her head.

"There's no need to go on flattering me," she said with a glance riddled with suspicion. "In fact, I distrust flattery, as it is devised to gain certain favors."

"That is a very bitter outlook. Flattery, when honest, is meant to lift your spirit." He sipped his wine, his attention riveted to her face. His nostrils were still filled with her scent, that heady female fragrance that went straight to his head. He could barely contain himself from hauling her back into his arms and tasting that soft vulnerable mouth that now held a distinctly downward curve.

"Flattery is nothing but a vice invented by gentlemen to get their way. One doesn't too often hear ladies spreading flattery around as if it were corn for the chickens."

Nick rubbed one eyebrow to clear his thoughts. "I daresay you have not heard honest compliments—which makes me wonder how you've heard any at all."

"I'm not wholly ignorant. Father used to bring his mistresses to the house and ply them with wine and flattery. Then he would bring them upstairs ... right past my mother's door. His cruel actions finally killed her, you know." Her shoulders hunched as if she were remembering a hurtful past. "He killed her," she repeated.

"Some gentlemen have no sense of propriety; nor do they care whom they hurt with their actions." Nick clenched his jaw as he recalled his brother, who would not hesitate to bring home a mistress.

"Gentlemen are all alike," she said. "Only thinking of your own pleasures." Her face took on a haunted look, gaunt and white, her eyes enormous in the delicate face. "Mother wasted away. She could not eat; she could not sleep—"

"She must have loved him very much once," he said, and finished his wine.

"*No*, she loathed him. She hated him so much she died from her hatred. It ate away at her flesh until she was naught but skin and bones. And I . . . I felt so guilty for loving him a bit. He was my father."

He sensed that these secrets had weighed heavily on the mysterious Eve's shoulders for a long time and wine had loosened her tongue. Under normal circumstances she might not have talked about her family to him. "Couldn't she find a way to make peace with her husband's profligacy? She could have demanded equal freedom if theirs were a marriage of convenience."

"She would not stoop so low," she said, and wiped her eyes on the back of her hand. Nick was about to give her a handkerchief, but decided she would not look kindly upon his concern. "Even though she was full of hatred, she had high morals, and I admired her for it."

"Was his dissipation their sole bone of contention?"

She sat in silence for a long time, her chin trembling with suppressed sadness. He sensed that she was about to reveal something important about herself. One piece of the mystery that was Eve solved, perhaps.

"She let my brother die—or at least that is what my father blamed her for before he took up a life of debauchery."

Questions tumbled through Nick's mind, but he could not ask any, knowing she would not respond directly to probing.

"My brother was out alone in a rowboat on the pond. He was only five years old, but he knew how to swim. Mother was watching him because Nurse Hopkins was ill. Theo loved the water, always wanted to play around it. I was never very interested; besides I was seven years his senior."

"He drowned?" Nick asked.

She nodded. "Yes. Mother had been lying down on a blanket in the shade, reading. She fell asleep. All we know is that the boat floundered and my brother drowned. He was found later."

"A heavy blow to any family," he said softly. The air was

rigid with tension, and he could barely breathe as her agony came tumbling out.

"I loved Theo. Everyone loved him, especially my father. Theo was bright and friendly, a real charmer, and a promise for the future. I was someone who had to be married off in due course, at the cost of a dowry. Father loved me; I know that, but I was more of a burden than a promise. *His,* Father's, bright future died on the weedy bottom of the pond. He was never the same after that. I loathed him for his treatment of Mother—yet I loved him." Eve covered her face with her hands, and Nick's heart constricted with compassion. "How could I be so vile to love a man who destroyed my mother?"

"You're never vile for loving your parents."

"I wanted to save her; I tried so very hard to make her leave when the destruction of the family began. She could have gotten over her guilt, the corroding pain, but she had to flagellate herself, stay in the house and see herself whipped by Father's accusations every day—until she was no more than a shell. Such a waste of brilliance and vigor! My mother used to be everyone's darling—platonically, I mean. She drew love to herself and surrounded herself and us all with the best people, the kindest, merriest people."

Eve fell silent, and Nick said, "Your parents must have loved each other from the start."

She nodded. "I believe they did, but why is love unable to overcome the greatest tragedies? Why did it have to turn on itself and create hate that destroyed everything?"

"They did not have the strength to get over the pain of loss. Their world crashed, and there was nothing left to build on."

"I was still there," she said, her voice muffled with a bewildered sob. "I had to see it all—their sorrow for my brother, their inability to get over the loss. They forgot me. I felt worthless."

Nick thought of Ethan, feeling that his stepbrother represented a yoke he would have to carry all of his life. "Some people only think of themselves. I know someone who cannot rise above himself. He will always demand—never give anything in return. He always inspires guilt because he's part of my family and I cannot ignore him."

Nick sighed thinking of Sir James, who had been the finest person he had ever known. "My stepbrother—just by his presence and constant demands—fouls the memory of my father. I would like to turn my back on my stepbrother forever."

He studied her downturned head, but did not really see her as he looked into his memories. "One sibling is wasted for another. In that sense you and I have experienced the same. Sir James loved my stepbrother as he loved me, but he could never accept the darkness surrounding my sibling." Nick slammed his fist into the table so that she jumped. "I'm glad Sir James did not live to see the worst; and I pray every day that he does not see it now, wherever he is."

She raised her head slowly and looked at him. Nick's heart leaped to his throat and lodged there so that he could not breathe. Her face had lost some of its mysterious aloof quality, and he sensed a part of her reaching out toward him.

"You could have done nothing to change the course of your parents' married life, Miss Eve."

"My name is not Eve. I am Serena," she said without the usual hostile edge to her voice.

"Serena. 'Struth, a lovely name. Although I must admit I have not seen your serenity very much since we met. Only when you slept."

She grimaced. "The situation is not one that inspires serenity, is it? Anyway, I lived through the crisis of Theo's death, the crisis my mother could never overcome. She died from the weight of guilt and from a broken heart."

Serena turned her hands palms up. "I tried to make her see reason, but her life was a long downhill slide into death." Her voice broke once more, and she cried into her hands. "Nothing I did made any difference."

Nick did not know what to do. He hesitated. She needed comfort, but from him? Well, she only had him. There was no one else to place an arm around her shoulders and whisper soothing words in her ears.

He felt lighter after their easing of minds, but also concerned. Serena was no longer a nameless prisoner, but a person who demanded respect. Someone who deserved his support—not his punishment.

Nick groaned and fell to his knees, pulling her shaking form into his arms. She stiffened at first, then clung to him and whispered, "Thank you."

Chapter 9

Serena kept seeing the same thing over and over, the sea-weed-covered face of her five-year-old brother. Theo looked so pale, almost blue, but his features held a peace that permitted her to breathe, gave her a small measure of comfort. She lived; he did not. Cold as marble and blue-veined face. Almost forgotten.

She gasped, trying to wipe the image from her mind, but her hands could not reach her face. She struck out, but only touched air ... empty, cold air that would like nothing better than to suck the life out of her body and turn her into cold white marble as well. No! She would not die, not yet.

Anger like a red heat spread through her, shielding her, fighting for her against the threat of death. She gasped, running, running from the horrors until her breath seared her lungs and throat.

Someone cackled behind her, mayhap the specter of death, but it sounded strangely enough like her mother. That dry cinder-like cackle of bitterness that Mother had adopted toward the end ... It haunted Serena until she fought, her fists punching holes in the misty specter.

"Wake up, Serena!" someone shouted in her ear, and she swam to the surface of her dream. "You'll fall out of bed if you toss about in that reckless fashion."

"She could have lived, you know," Serena muttered and wiped her face. "She could have continued."

Warm arms encircled her and the fog of despair lifted from her mind. She recognized the bandit's male scent before she could actually see him. He was a dark outline against the faltering fire in the fireplace. She did not want to think about the situation; she did not want to worry. All she needed was comfort to dispel the terror of her dreams. She wondered if she'd ever find lasting peace or if the dreams would follow her for the rest of her life.

He brushed her hair back, and she noticed that her shift clung to her body from perspiration. Her insides, however, felt cold and shivery.

"There, don't cry," he whispered against her hair. "You're safe here. I will hold you."

"Oh God, Nick." She collapsed against his chest and wound her arms around him. She couldn't get close enough to his warmth and his comfort. His heart beat hard and steadily against her breast, and the rhythm soothed her. He wound his arms more tightly around her and muttered against her hair. Kisses rained on her head, his lips finding her ear and tracing its outline with the tip of his tongue. Bubbles of pleasure rose through her body at his sensuous touch.

She tilted her face to his, and his mouth caught hers in a soul-searing kiss. Unhurriedly, his tongue played with hers, sliding, licking, tasting—making her heart open up like a flower to sunlight.

His hands traveled up her back and cupped her neck, holding her head steady as he tasted his fill of her. Rivulets of pleasure danced through her veins, like wine seducing her mind.

"Ohh," he groaned as he finally lifted his face from hers. "Your taste drugs me, and your caress throws my thoughts into confusion."

Her hands found their way automatically under his shirt, the only garment shielding his hard muscles from her touch. She explored the smooth warm surface of his back, dragging one fingertip along the dip of his spine. She stiffened as she discovered that he wore nothing besides the shirt. She slowly pulled away, but he hastened to firm his arms around her.

"I heard you crying, so I came to investigate."

"You heard me all the way to your bedchamber?" she asked, her face pressed to his throat.

"Yes . . . it was clear you were having another nightmare." He rolled hanks of her hair around his hands as if unable to stop touching her. "It worries me. *You* worry me; you are seldom away from my thoughts."

His heartbeat escalated, slamming hard against her. She could feel him tremble. "Are you cold, Nick?"

"No, not exactly, but I'm ravaged with desire for your tempting body." His voice had turned hoarse, and his breath gusted against her hair. His words caught in her mind and stimulated her own arousal. It pounded between them, a thick current of sweetness that she could not dispel. Not now, not even if it meant taking tne risk of changing her life forever. It had already changed. She would never be able to go back to her old life anyway. Not as long as Luther lived.

She gripped his shoulders and slowly pulled him down with her into the mattress. Her face had softened, and she whispered, "Come to me."

He moaned, his lips kissing every bare surface of her body, the round knobs of her shoulders, the part of her chest that was not covered with her chemise. Every kiss ignited flares of desire in her blood, a fire that gathered in her abdomen and filled her with a raging longing for more.

She raised herself so that her breasts brushed against him, and he impatiently wrenched the chemise free of her shoulders and dragged it down to her waist. He cradled one breast in his hand, and she moaned with pleasure as he took one nipple into his mouth and sucked hard. Beneath the storm of pleasure, her heart opened up, softened, and grew warm. She looked into Nick's eyes, seeing a responding warmth. She gasped, heat filling her cheeks as something unusually tender vibrated between them. Was it all part of the game, or was it—love?

Nick gazed into her velvet eyes, seeing a wave of affection he'd not expected to see. His breath caught, and he stopped for a moment, his heart brimming with strange awe. Only when she turned her head aside did his senses once again take over.

His fevered mind filled with her scent, the satiny feel of her skin, the soft firmness of her breasts, the hard nub taunting his tongue until he thought he would burst with the agony of unfulfilled desire. He pulled his hand the length of her slim body, dipping into her waist and following the round swell of her hips. He managed to force the shift down over her hips, where it ripped. Impatient, he tore it from her body and cupped the silky mound at the apex of her thighs with one hand.

"You're so desirable."

Warmth spread from her, from her firm sinuous body that so ignited his lust until he could barely contain himself. He groaned out loud as he explored further and found the cleft hot and wet with desire.

"So are you." She lifted herself, curving one leg around his back. She caressed his chest and his stomach, and he guided her hand to his turgid member. She enclosed him, gingerly at first, then caressed him, gaining confidence as her own passion grew.

"My darling," he said, filled with visions of himself buried in her hot wetness. He slid one finger along her slick crevice, his head—his entire body—humming with lust. She writhed and arched against him as he teased the hard nub that centered on her passion.

Serena's blood was alive with the fire of yearning, her breath tortured as if it could not continue to flow into her lungs much longer, not until she could find a way to ease the sweet torment of her body. She wanted him, but without really knowing what that longing meant, what he would do to slake her thirst.

Her body strained to join with his, and as he eased himself between her thighs, she whimpered. Pleasure shot through her as the hard tip of him entered the opening of her female secret. He seemed to hesitate, but to quench her need, she lifted her hips and he pushed into her. Pain suddenly flared, then slowly receded with every heartbeat.

"Oh my God," he whispered hoarsely. "This is more than I can bear." He moved slowly, smoothly, finding a rhythm that had him groaning against her neck. All she knew was that pleasure spiraled ever higher with his every thrust.

Desire blossomed and exploded through her senses as he bore her over the edge of no return. She followed wave after wave of intense pleasure, their ferocity slowly dwindling to a gentle wash. Iridescent contentment filled her, but the fire was still burning as he rode her body, his powerful muscles brushing against her and his arms crushing her to him. He cried out, raised himself slightly on a crest of convulsions that went on and on. His ecstasy brought another release through her, her shudders echoing his.

"Serena," he groaned as he held her tightly. His breath slowly took on some semblance of calmness, and soon he started moving within her again, his manhood hardening as he kept murmuring her name.

To Serena it seemed that he loved her all night, never leaving her body and transforming her into a wanton who craved more with each new level of ecstasy.

Obsessed, Nick could not find the total ease he sought even though a release so strong he had to shout had just rolled through him. Her sinuous body that so willingly wound around him ignited a passion he had never known with another woman. She became a drug, a mystery, a challenge he had to take, to conquer, or forever long for her tight hot sheath. He had to ease his obsession, and tonight might be the only chance he had.

He explored her every graceful curve, laving her firm breasts with his tongue. Their thrusting shape with the large erotic nipples taunted him, ignited his passion over and over.

Feeble firelight danced over her flushed skin and lit the passionate glitter in her eyes. He nuzzled her flat stomach as a renewed need tightened his loins. Exhaustion mingled with desire in his blood, but he had to go on, drugging himself with her silky, alluring body.

"Ohhh," she moaned as he kissed the damp folds between her legs. He licked her, inhaling her perfume, wanting to steal all her secrets and hoard them within him. Worry rippled through him for a moment as he realized he wanted to break her, make her his until they were one, until there was no more rebellion in her eyes, no more distrust, only peace. And love.

He got onto his knees and turned her over on her stomach. He lifted her hips to him, her round buttocks pressing against him, arousing him further. He plunged into her hot wetness and wanted to cry with the feeling of oneness he had while resting within her.

He took her breasts into his hands and leaned over her back as he plunged himself toward another stormy release. She moaned and met his thrusts with her own until she arched and shuddered in wild deliverance. It brought on his own, and this time, he collapsed on the bed, totally satiated and so spent he thought he would be unable to move again. Finally. *Finally* . . .

He pulled her into his arms, holding her tightly as exhaustion overcame him. Dawn's gray light was already coloring the skies as he sank into deep, contented sleep.

Serena awakened, dazed. One side of her body was hot and sticky, the other side icy cold. She realized she was naked and pressed tightly against the bandit's body on one side. There was no sign of the blankets under which she usually slept.

Wanton. Wicked, her mind said, and in a rush, everything

flooded back to her memory. She had been wicked, as wicked as one of Father's mistresses, and she had not once chided herself for her lusty behavior; she had reveled in every second of the sweet desire he so tirelessly had inflicted on her. Her desire had burned as hot as his, and she blushed as she recalled her eagerness to have him inside her.

She lifted her legs from his and straightened them. Pain shot through her limbs and she groaned as she realized how stiff she'd become. She fumbled for the blankets, but saw that they lay out of reach on the floor.

Her lover stirred, groaning and yawning widely. She averted her face from him after seeing a glimpse of kiss-swollen lips and dark whiskers. He made such an intimate picture, his head on her pillow, his long hair tickling her chin, his body stark naked pressed to hers. She didn't even know his full name.

"Good morning," he greeted, his hand cupping her jaw and turning her head toward him. His eyes held lazy tenderness, and a soft response rose in her heart. "I take it you slept well, Serena. This bed is not the most comfortable in the house. You should try mine sometime."

"That would not be a wise move," she mumbled and leaned over him to drag the blankets from the floor. She knew by his chuckle that she'd presented him with a full view of her bare backside.

" 'Tis a lovely morning," he continued. "A fine view of hills and valleys. It is a picture a man could get used to, even obsessed with keeping in his line of vision at all times."

"Don't talk nonsense," she said and pulled the blankets to her chin. The bed was cold as she eased away from him. He raised himself onto his elbow and stared down at her.

"I'd say you have a prickly morning temper, my love."

He'd said *my love,* but did he mean the words? Or were they only meant to flatter her? She examined her own precarious feelings, the strange new tenderness making it difficult to speak. Love made fools out of perfectly sensible people, she reasoned. This was madness, and she would not repeat this night, not share a bed of intimacy with him again. Shame washed over her in a hot wave, and she could feel herself blush.

"It would be best if you leave," she said, not looking at him. "Last night was utter folly, and the faster we forget it, the better."

His eyes glowed intimately, penetrating her heart with ease. "I have no intention of forgetting the night of the best lovemaking I've ever experienced."

She averted her gaze, but her heart pounded madly. "Naught but animal lust. Rutting," she said, as if the word were a poisonous snake.

"There's nothing shameful in that. I recall distinctly that you found my presence in your bed highly to your liking. Your need was as strong as mine."

She admitted silently that he was right. She had needed him to ease her pain, to erase her disturbing past, even if it had been a temporary relief.

She threw a quick glance at him, noting the hunger on his face as his gaze traveled over her throat and shoulder, which were not covered with the blanket.

He gently inserted his hand under the cover and touched the triangle of hair between her thighs. She pulled away. "Don't! It's sore. I'm bruised all over."

"But your itch is thoroughly scratched," he said with that wicked smile that set her heart on fire.

"How vulgar. I'm embarrassed."

"Don't be. Even *ladies* have the right to make wild love with a gentleman of their choice. Somehow your innocence ignited me more fiercely than a courtesan with all her wiles."

"A lady becomes a fallen woman if she has no ring on her finger."

He stiffened beside her, his face all of a sudden serious. "You would be willing to marry me? I would not hesitate to make an honest woman out of you. Besides, a wife cannot give testimony against a husband, so my secret activities would be safe."

"I will not marry a criminal," she said. "It would be a great mistake."

He chuckled, then roared with laughter. She yearned to slam the pillow against his head to quell his mirth.

"But then we could make love every night; you need me to appease your hunger," he pointed out.

"You imagine my insatiable hunger," she protested. "I am not a wanton at heart."

"Your hunger has been awakened, and you won't easily be able to subdue it in the future. You'll see."

She glared at him. "You look very pleased with yourself."

"So should you, my darling. So should you." He paused, still staring at her. "Serena, don't you think it's about time you reveal something more substantial about yourself? I have communicated with you on a most intimate level, but I know nothing about you except that you're from Somerset and have a fierce temper and a suspicious mind."

She looked away, wondering if she dared to confide her difficulties to him. She had no idea if he would be willing to help her solve her problems, but she admitted that something would have to be done.

"I have noticed that you suffer from terrible nightmares, a fact that points to a disturbed past. Is there more than the quarrels of your parents?" He raised his eyebrows in inquiry. "I would be happy to lend an ear if that is what you need."

Serena sat back against the pillows, the blankets spread over her and his magnificent physique. It felt so natural and comfortable to have him lie beside her. Mayhap she could tell him something. She tucked her head onto his shoulder, and he held her protectively.

"I . . . well, I don't know where to start, really." She bit the inside of her lip, then continued. "When Mother died five years ago, Father threw himself further onto a path of deep dissipation. He quarreled with everyone around him, especially with my uncle. It could only end in disaster. I could sense it coming. He is dead now—died just before I left Somerset. I don't know if I should be happy or sad."

"There's no shame in loving his memory."

She nodded. "You're right. How can you fail to love your parents, no matter what they have done? You always seek their approval. I don't think we could have gone back to what we shared in the past. Father changed too much after Theo's death, and it was as if he looked at me through a veil, never quite seeing me—like an old piece of furniture. You know it's there, but you never notice it. In the end he cared for no one but himself—and the bottle. Deplorable!"

Serena clenched her hands around the edge of the blanket until they ached. The memories stirred up the old anxiety, and it nagged at her middle, a dull ache that nothing could soothe.

"Such memories would create nightmares." He gently pried her fingers loose from the blanket and held her hand. "You'll have to put the past behind you and go on with your life, look toward a positive future." He braided his fingers with hers, and the warmth comforted her. "What surprises me is that you're not married. You're lovely and ladylike, and evidently of a fine family."

"Mother was selfish. She did not want to lose the only child left to her. Besides, my parents were too busy fighting with each other to have the strength to plan my presentation at court." *There is more,* she thought. *Murder. How could she ever tell him about that? Would he believe her?*

"You lived a sheltered life that lacked the gaiety and entertainment of a young woman. You should have danced; you should have flirted and exchanged secret *billets* with young gentlemen."

"I don't regret my past," she said, and meant it. "I do miss my pastimes, painting and music."

"Ah! We have something in common then," he said. "I strum the lute and sing naughty ballads. Not that my voice is in any way exceptional, but singing cheers me." He let go of her hand, swept aside the blanket, and leaped out of bed. "Wait here."

Serena smiled teasingly. "Where would I go?"

He ran down the stairs naked and returned five minutes later carrying a big parcel and the lute she'd seen in his bedchamber. He placed the parcel on the bed. "This is for you."

She glanced at it in surprise. At first she was reluctant to accept anything from him, but her curiosity grew beyond control. He sat cross-legged against the headboard and tuned the lute while she tore the string off the package and unfolded the crackling paper. Inside reposed a stack of folded garments. She cried out with pleasure.

"Clean clothes! You don't know how much I've longed to wear something clean."

"I'm afraid none of the garments are of the excellent quality to which you're accustomed, but I think anything is better than the tatters you've worn these last few days."

"Yes," she whispered and held up a pair of white stockings. They were silk, but the rest of the clothing was fashioned of wool and rough cotton. She eagerly held up the simple chemise with lace at the end of the elbow-length sleeves, the sack gown of blue wool with a lace-up bodice to be worn over a boned stomacher, and a wide skirt that hung in pleats in the back.

"The hooped petticoat will arrive later today. I couldn't very well pack it with the rest. And I've ordered a pair of buckled leather shoes. Winter is coming soon, and satin slippers will not keep your feet warm."

"Thank you," she said simply, "but I can't help thinking that you owe me this much. If it hadn't been for you, I would be wearing clothes of my own choosing."

"That's true," he said, carefully strumming each string with a plectrum. "But now I'm trying to make up for your loss." The instrument gave out a full-bodied, mellow sound that caressed Serena's ear. Clothes crushed in her hands, she listened to him sing a sad ballad of a man who was going to the gallows for stealing a silk handkerchief.

Nick's voice was deep and strong, and it touched her emotions so much she felt an urge to cry. Evidently he sensed his influence as he raised one eyebrow and smiled. She slipped on the cool chemise and lay down, her head propped on a pillow.

She listened to his music as a deep relaxation came over

her. Time hung suspended in his voice. There was no tomorrow, no past, no worries. She closed her eyes as he sang another ballad and a lewd ditty that made her laugh.

"What instrument do you play?" he asked as he laid down the lute at the foot of the bed.

"The harpsichord and some flute, but my voice is weak. You sing with passion—like a minstrel."

His eyes glittered with pleasure. "Well, thank you for the lovely compliment." He leaned over her, touching his lips gently to hers. Her heartbeat raced as tension slowly rose between them, that by now familiar fire that demanded to burn bright before it went out. But she rolled over to her side, unwilling to play his game at the moment.

"I paint better than I sing," she explained. "Mostly landscapes, horses, and pets. I like to capture on canvas the bank of storm clouds moving over the horizon, or a ray of sunlight piercing the green mystery of the forest."

"*You* are the mystery here, a fey creature that is always perched for flight." His large hand enclosed her bare neck. "What are you running away from, my lovely? Besides your memories that is."

She wished she could blurt out the whole sordid story; but if she mentioned her last name, he would surely try to discover what she'd left behind in Somerset. "Nothing," she said.

"That is a lie. No young lady of breeding would hare along the highways of England alone at night."

"We've discussed this before, and I have no intention of continuing the conversation."

He kissed her shoulder, his hand dipping around the front of her body and cradling one breast. A golden sweetness streamed through her body at his caress and pooled in her womb. How easily he returned to her arms.

The morning went, the sun standing high in the sky before this new raging swell of desire had been appeased. He looked deeply into her eyes as he climaxed, his face contorted with a pleasure so intense he cried out. She melted as if part of his delight, deeply satiated from his expert lovemaking.

After a long silence, while her heartbeat returned to normal, she asked, "Do you trust me now—trust that I will keep your secret? Will you let me go? Will you set me free?"

He glanced at her, his eyes incredulous.

Chapter 10

"How can you think of separation when we've only just found each other? Did the lovemaking mean so little to you?" Nick asked.

"No, you have made me happy. But it is a temporary happiness. The problems won't go away with a shared hour of bliss, and our feelings only complicate the real issues." Serena looked at him imploringly. "I give you my word I won't contact the authorities." She was of two minds about leaving now after experiencing such tenderness, but it would have to be. The time would have to come sooner or later, for she could not contemplate sharing the rest of her life with a highwayman.

It would be best if she put this interlude behind her. The sooner the better, before her emotions became more firmly tied to him. Not only had he ignited her passion, but he'd touched her heart deeply as well. She was falling in love, and that frightened her more than the imprisonment had. Love made one vulnerable.

"If you care the slightest about my feelings, you must let me go," she continued when he didn't say anything.

"I cannot risk that," he said after a tense silence had stretched interminably. "Not yet." He sighed. "Soon."

"Why wait?"

His gaze traveled hotly over her until she cringed with embarrassment. "I can think of many reasons to keep you here, Serena. The only way I can ensure your silence is to discover something that will force you to keep my secret. I sense there's a mystery, a secret you are all too eager to hide."

"Are you alluding to blackmail?" She pulled her old chemise over her head to stop her rising temper. If he said another word, she would shout at him. It galled her that he was right—that she had something to hide.

"You'll never find out the whole truth about me unless I tell you," she said. "I hate to dash your hopes, but I don't hoard a mysterious secret that you'll ultimately hold over me."

She jumped off the bed and, riled, ignoring her new clothes, pulled on her old tattered dress that smelled of cooking fumes and perspiration. She might give up her freedom forever for a hot bath! She stood by the window, seeing a woman making a bed in the house across the street.

"Why don't you trust me after all we've gone through? I would not denounce someone to whom I've given my body," she said softly, but anger churned in her stomach. "Ultimately your motive is vile. You seduce me, but in reality you're trying to weaken me, to find something with which to hostage me."

He gave a derisive laugh. "I'm not as calculating as that, and I am not cold-hearted. I would not want anything dire to befall you."

"Did you expect I would blurt out my deepest secrets in the throes of passion?" she lashed out and paced the room. The iciness of the floor seeped into her bare feet. To keep herself occupied, she started making a fire in the grate.

"No," he said, "but I admit your nightmares intrigued me. You were shouting 'don't die, Father, don't die,' the first night I found you thrashing around in bed."

"Well, he died, but I don't see the significance of that dream. What would you make of it?" She blew on the weak flame produced by the tinder. Orange flames flared, and she piled shavings on top.

"Did you kill him?" His question had the sharp edge of a sword. "Is that why you had to flee head over heels?"

"You can believe what you will, Nick," she said, quickly voiding her voice of the outrage that churned within her. "Whatever I say will not appease your suspicion. The more I protest, the more you'll dig for clues—until you find something to use against me."

She looked at him over her shoulder. "I'm deeply disappointed that you are such an opportunist, Nick, but I should have known better than to think of you in a positive light. I loathe myself for my weakness, for my naiveté."

"Don't belittle yourself. I'm as much a victim of circumstances as you are. A gaoler should not get entangled with a prisoner or he might get too attached when the time comes for separation."

"You speak of separation, but I now doubt you'll ever let me go."

"After our night of lovemaking, I would be a fool to let you go. No woman has ever inspired such passion in me; and I fear that I would not find it again, should I allow you to leave."

She glanced at him in surprise at his candid confession. Warmth curled through her, cupping her heart. She longed to fall into his arms, to make peace, but there were too many unanswered questions between them. "That is a whole other issue," she said, steeling herself against her heart, "and I'd prefer it if you didn't bring your selfish desires into the discussion. But it shouldn't surprise me that you're only thinking of your own gain."

He got up and scooped the new clothes from the bed. He held them out to her as she rose from her crouching position. "Put these on."

"I will not." She tilted up her chin and stared him squarely in the eye.

"How can you return to your stubborn pride after what we experienced together?" he asked, anger clouding his eyes.

"In the bright light of day, I am full of shame for my behavior and your gifts are insults to me. Except for the hours of passion we shared, we have nothing. I am still your prisoner, and you are my gaoler. We are enemies."

"That's nonsense! I did not plan to take advantage of your body because you're my prisoner."

"What else? You had to slake your insatiable thirst—"

"—as I slaked yours, Miss Stubborn. It takes two to play."

She pressed her hands to her hot cheeks. "Oh, Nick, I'd rather forget that last night ever happened."

To her surprise, he laughed. "You'll have to come to grips with your deep capacity for passion, Serena. You might not like it now, but there will be a time when you'll crave more of the same. I'd like to be there for you then."

"How dare you taunt me so!" she shouted and ran out of the room.

Nick studied her slender back that he'd stroked so intimately and held so fiercely in the fire of passion. Her shoulders hunched, she rushed down the stairs, one hand pressed to her burning face. He filled with tenderness at the sight, feeling the emotional link to her even though he knew so little about her. Best leave her alone to calm herself. There was plenty of food downstairs, but he did not have any desire to taste her burned bacon and hard eggs.

He chuckled and stretched his sore muscles. Vitality rose through him like sap in a tree, and he felt exuberant and ready to take on the world—if need be. He fetched his shirt from the floor by the bed and straightened the wrinkled sheets, spreading the blankets smoothly on top.

Back in his bedchamber he washed himself in the basin and wished he were at the Leverton mansion in Berkley Square where he could have a hot bath to take the stiffness out of his muscles. He had no servants here to heat his bath water and scrub his back.

He looked out the window as he buttoned his yellow camlet

waistcoat. Dingy houses and the squalor around the corner assaulted the senses as one went outside. This had once been a respectable area, but the rookeries had moved ever closer to the worthy bastions of commerce. A merchant had owned the house before it fell into disrepair along with the rest of the buildings along the street.

He pulled on moleskin breeches, stockings, and boots. He eased a dark green coat over his shoulder and was ready to go outside.

As he placed a three-cornered beaver hat at a rakish angle on his head, he heard the slamming of cooking utensils and crockery in the kitchen. He had no desire to witness Serena's ineptitude, or be the target of her anger.

Somehow it really annoyed him to watch her work, no matter how honest and determined she was to manage a meal. It annoyed him in the sense that she'd grown up being waited on hand and foot by others, footmen who all bore the same name for simplicity's sake. Why bother to learn a footman's real name, when all he did was serve? Why bother saying thank you to a kitchen maid who carried a bowl of broth three stories only to be rejected on a whim when she reached the lady's boudoir? Things like that had always annoyed Nick, and probably always would. He had servants at The Hollows, but he always treated them fairly, almost like equals. They showed more common sense than all of his aristocratic friends, and if it weren't for them, The Hollows would not have prospered. After all, he was never a farmer, but he'd tried to learn, if only to feel the pride of making a go of something that might have defeated him from the start. He had succeeded with the help of his loyal people.

With the thought of checking on Pegasus, he stepped outside and closed the door behind him, locking it from the outside and slipping the key into his pocket. He went around the side and looked down over the railing to the kitchen steps and found that one of the guards had returned and was even now arguing with the prisoner through the open door. Nick grinned and whistled a merry tune as he headed down the street.

After seeing to Pegasus's welfare, he would make a quick visit to the orphanage with the gift of freshly baked buns, do some errands, and mayhap see a friend or two. He'd forgotten his appointment with Trev Emerson and would have to make his apologies. Then he would go back to confront the woman who had touched him more deeply than he liked. Only a week ago, he'd been sad at losing Marguerite to Charles, but the pain that his unrequited love had brought was only a pale shadow of its former strength. He was amazed at his quick recovery. Could it be that his love hadn't been true?

He would always cherish Marguerite, but from now on, he would put that period of his life behind him. It was strange how fast life could change.

A few more night raids and the orphanage would be paid for in full, he thought. Then the Midnight Bandit would mysteriously disappear from the roads, no one the wiser. It was only a matter of time before luck would shift to Trevor Emerson's side and Nick would be caught. Even if they were friends, Trev would have to see justice done.

Nothing in life came free of charge, especially not selfless creations like his orphanage in the poorer part of London. The poor always paid the most; they would hang for stealing an apple, while the justice who sentenced them might accept bribes without the fear of retribution. Such unfairness.

Nick's anger rose at the thought, and he pushed it aside before he started bubbling like a cauldron that boiled too hard.

As a carriage rattled by and the high-pitched cry of the chimney sweep offering his services echoed in his ears, Nick entered Broad Street. He went into a coffeehouse on the corner for a pint of ale, bread, and a bowl of stew. He realized the prolonged lovemaking had made him ravenous. After eating, he purchased the buns and headed west to the orphanage, not far from Bethlem Hospital, and from there toward Mayfair.

In the Strand, he bought thick paper for drawing, coal, stretched canvas, and some mixed paints. He knew artists liked to mix their own paints, but he had no idea what ingredients to buy. This would entertain his prisoner, and the thought made him light at heart.

He piled his purchases into a sedan chair and told the bearers to carry him to Berkley Square.

Delicia would have received his letter with the fabricated explanation of why he had not returned to The Hollows. He was sure she would follow him to London unless he returned home soon. She would stay at the Leverton mansion as she always did. She had an uncanny way of scenting trouble, and this would not be an exception. He disliked having to keep her in the dark, but one did not confess criminal activities to a stepsister.

Nick looked forward to seeing her, but should he keep Ethan's excesses a secret?

No, the truth could not be hidden indefinitely. Before long, Delicia would find out that her brother had thrown the family name into scandal. Nick sighed heavily as the sedan chair swayed back and forth with the quick stride of the burly carriers.

He got out and paid the men, then strode up the steps with his purchases in his arms. As he entered the hallway, he could hear Delicia's bell-like laugh from above. The stairs curved gracefully along one wall to the next floor, accenting a soaring ceiling that had been painted with bucolic country scenes that never saw the bleakness of winter. The white clouds moved in endless perfection across a blue sky that had turned rather dingy over the years from the smoke of many coal fires.

"There you are, darling!" Delicia cried as she beheld her stepbrother. She threw her arms around Nick's neck and hugged him hard. "I thought you had completely forgotten me. I so despaired in the country without you that I had to travel up to London."

"I hope you brought outriders with weapons," Nick admonished. "Evil might befall a lady traveling alone."

"I know that. I brought three grooms, and they all carried clubs and blunderbusses. And when we got here, Aunt Titania welcomed us. She is more hard of hearing every time I see her."

Aunt Titania Leverton had lived in the top part of the mansion as long as he could remember, but she rarely came downstairs to greet guests. Nick suspected she kept away from Ethan on purpose, and he didn't blame her. At least she would lend an air of respectability to the young lady's visit.

He gave Delicia another hug. She was blonde, her hair fine and flyaway, gleaming like spun gold. Her delicate features in a rather ordinary face were made extraordinary by a dazzling smile. She wore a cream silk gown over wide panniers. Her blue eyes sparkled with mischief.

"I brought a friend along for my stay in London." She gestured toward a young lady on a sofa, and Nick noted the friend's gazelle-like limbs and dark brown hair. She was looking at him with shy brown eyes. Sweetness lingered in every feature on her face as she smiled.

"Excellent idea, Delicia."

"This is Calandra Vine, an old friend of mine from before the time when we moved to Sussex. Callie, meet my brother, Nicholas Thurston."

"I think we've met," Nick said with a smile. "A long time ago when we were children."

Callie Vine blushed and lowered her gaze in a ladylike fashion. So different from Serena's frank stare.

"Callie has been staying with me for a week. It turns out that Ethan already knows her. He has been corresponding with her since they met at a ball in Surrey. He has paid special attention to her." Delicia clapped her hands together. "Isn't that exciting, Nick?"

Nick's spirits fell. He read the hope of a wedding ceremony in Delicia's eyes. Anyone who touched Ethan would become tainted with his wiles and debauchery. "Really? Well, how do you find my brother, Miss Vine?"

"Very much the gentleman. He is also amusing, tells many droll anecdotes to entertain me."

Lies, more likely, Nick thought. When Ethan put on his armor of charm, he usually had some vile scheme planned.

Nick wondered if Miss Vine were an heiress. He couldn't remember anything about her family.

"Are you visiting alone?" he asked, "or is a member of your family accompanying you?"

"My maid is here," Miss Vine said.

"And mine," Delicia chimed in. "We're chaperoned at all times, so don't worry. Then there is Auntie."

"Yes, there is Auntie. I hope you spend some time in her apartment. The old girl needs cheering up at times."

What would happen to Auntie if Ethan had to give up the mansion to pay his debts? Nick thought. She would come and live at The Hollows. No one would be able to pull Ethan out of the mire this time. The estate would have to be sold, and mayhap Leverton Court in Berkshire as well. Ethan would have to retire to a country cottage in disgrace.

Nick pulled Delicia aside and whispered, "Does Miss Vine have a fortune attached to her name?"

"Fie, Nick!" Delicia said and swatted him on the arm with her closed fan. "Are you looking for someone to boost your sagging finances?"

"You would draw a hasty conclusion as usual," Nick drawled. "But mayhap Ethan would not mind marrying into a family of funds."

Delicia tilted her head sideways and looked at him speculatively. "Callie is not an heiress."

"You'd better keep an eye on your innocent friend and our brother. I would not like to see the lovely Miss Vine hurt in any way."

Delicia's gaze probed his deeply, and he wondered if she could read his profound worry about the family situation.

"Does Miss Vine have anyone to take care of her—a brother, a father, an uncle?"

"Only a brother, and he is abroad on some pretext or other. Won't be back until Christmas at the earliest. That's why I asked her to come and stay with me."

Nick touched her soft cheek. "Always the kind and thoughtful friend. I wish you could find a gentleman to care for in the same manner. He would be a very lucky fellow.''

Delicia self-consciously patted her ringlets that were held back with jeweled clasps. She sighed, her eyes dark with some remembered event in the past. Had she been in love, and had he failed to notice it? He'd take better care of his stepsister from now on so that she did not end up like Serena, who had fled from everything she had ever known.

''I worry about you a great deal, sis.''

Her lips turned down at the corners and trembled in a distressing way. ''Are you afraid I'll become an old maid like Aunt Titania?''

''No, but I need to know that you're happy at The Hollows, not fading away with bitterness.''

''Nick!'' Delicia gave a trill of laughter and flapped her painted chicken-skin fan. ''What an absurd thing to say. What has gotten into you? I won't fade away, I promise.''

''I'm relieved.'' He touched her arm. ''By the way, do you know a lady from Somerset named Serena? I don't know her last name.''

Delicia wrinkled her brow and tapped a fingertip against her bottom lip. ''No . . . I have never met anyone by that name.'' Her eyes turned mischievous. ''Have you found the lady of your heart?''

Nick shrugged. ''You're prying, sis.'' He could not deny that Serena had touched his heart in a special way. He avoided his sister's keen gaze.

''Let's be polite and entertain Miss Vine,'' he said, planning to discover just how closely Ethan had gotten to the innocent young woman who beamed up at Nick's face in a such beguiling way. He kissed her hand and admired the rose silk gown and costly diamond pendant around her neck.

Ethan did not join the group until an hour later, early by his standards. He usually slept 'til late in the afternoon. Nick watched his brother saunter into the room impeccably attired in a full-skirted coat of green plush, a brocaded cream waistcoat, and tan breeches. If it weren't for the lines of dissipation on his face and the bloodshot eyes that no powder and rouge could conceal, he would be a handsome-enough man. Some females liked the air of debauchery, though, and Nick glanced at Callie Vine to see her reaction.

She smiled shyly at Ethan's murmured gallantry as he flourished an extravagant bow and kissed her hand.

Bile rose in Nick's throat as he witnessed his brother's superficial charm. Before his inner eye, he remembered Ethan once delivering a bruising slap to a courtesan's face at Lotus's house. Nick had ended up in a fight with Ethan for that atrocity, and he prayed he would not have to fight his brother again. How could Sir James Leverton have fathered such a snake as Ethan?

"Nick? I didn't see you skulking over there in the corner," Ethan said in a honeyed voice. Under that smooth tone, Nick heard the cold edge of dislike, and he set his jaw.

"I had to welcome Delicia to town. I've missed her sorely."

"La, you never told me, Nick." Delicia closed her fan, her lips drooping theatrically. "You left me to languish in Sussex while you drove to London without as much as a word of farewell."

Ethan's hard suspicious glance bored into Nick. "Why would you hare off to London in such a hurry, dear brother?"

"A business matter that does not concern any of you." Nick addressed Delicia. "I wrote you a note—"

"—saying you would return shortly. Well, it has been days and days. I would not want to be kept out of any of the entertainment with which you fill your life in London."

"Yes, you would," Nick murmured, embarrassed now as he glanced into the innocent eyes of the two women sitting side by side on the sofa. Callie Vine tilted her head with its elaborate hair arrangement to one side and stared at him curiously.

"I don't understand what you mean, Mr. Thurston. Would you explain, please?"

Nick felt heat rush to his cheeks. "Mayhap another time."

Delicia elbowed her friend discreetly, and Callie's gaze flitted to the window as red roses blossomed in her cheeks. "Oh, I see," she whispered. "I'm sorry I brought up the question."

"My brother does like to speak in riddles," Ethan drawled, and flicked the frothing lace of his shirt cuff back as he took a pinch of snuff from an enameled box. He flashed a seductive smile at Calandra, and Nick shivered as a premonition traveled up his spine. He would have a word with Delicia, warn her against Ethan and his deviousness.

Delicia more often than not chose not to see Ethan's flaws. She had the younger sister's admiration for an older brother and was too innocent to really see the dark depths of Ethan's soul. One day—soon—she would have a rude awakening. The thought pained Nick.

"I have a meeting this morning," Nick lied, "but I've been invited to a costume ball at Lady Hessler's house next Friday. I would be delighted to escort you both there. Meanwhile, you'll have to plan your costumes. I shall give you a draft on my bank, and I expect you to spend the lot at the bazaars."

Delicia flew to his side and kissed his cheek enthusiastically. "Nick, thank you! I knew you would cheer me up. You always do."

Nick laughed, his spirits rising. He noted the lethal glitter in Ethan's eyes and suspected that his generosity toward Delicia would have some retribution. He swiftly hugged his sister and kissed Miss Vine's birdlike hand. *If Ethan as much as tweaks a hair on this lovely creature's head, I will call him out,* Nick thought. This time, the fight would continue to a bloody death.

Chapter 11

Roy Coachman stared at the angry red face of Luther Hilliard. The door was closed, and he could not expect to flee through a back door since there was none in the cheap hostelry where he waited for Miss Serena to find him. If only he could run downstairs and mingle with the people in the yard, but the fat man barred the way.

Roy cringed under the glassy coldness of Luther Hilliard's eyes. "Honestly, I don't know where Miss Serena is. A pair of highwaymen attacked us in Sussex, and she's been missing since."

"Are you privy to the reason why Miss Serena left High Crescent in such a hurry?"

"No," Roy said, but he had his suspicions. "I thought she quarreled with Sir Andrew."

"Sir Andrew is dead. I am now Sir Luther as I have inherited the land and the title. You'd better show some reverence." He moved closer and Roy stepped back until he could not move any further. The rough wall stood between him and freedom. Tugging at his forelock, he bowed deferentially.

"Sir Luther."

"You must have some idea when she's coming to London *if* she isn't here already." He gripped Roy's wool vest and twisted it until the fabric ripped. "Are you lying to me?"

"No! I would not lie to you, Sir Luther. I would tell if Miss Serena had sought me out here."

Silence hung between them, and Sir Luther's puffy, red-streaked eyes narrowed. A foul smell came from his mouth and intensified as he started breathing harder.

"I don't believe you're telling the truth, Roy. How can you afford to stay here without Miss Serena's monetary support?" His grip tightened, and an icy wave of fear rolled through Roy Coachman.

"I have some funds, and I help with the horses around the yard. She has not come to London or I would have found her."

"You helped her escape, you dirty little rat," Sir Luther growled. He placed his large hands around Roy's neck and grimaced. "For that, you're to die. You would just spend the rest of your life working against me. I'm tired of opposition."

Roy sputtered, but he could not find his voice. *I would not! My life is precious to me. I would never speak against me betters.*

"You would always side with her, and accuse me of unspeakable crimes," Sir Luther went on, pushing his hands up under Roy's jaw.

Filled with panic, Roy fought to escape the madman's deadly grip, but Sir Luther was so much stronger. A strange light glowed in his employer's eyes, a wild mad light. The gent had always been peculiar.

Sir Luther started compressing his grip, and Roy fought for his life, but his strength soon waned.

He longed to cry out, to get away from the inevitable. The end. Waves of gray, then black swam in his vision, then red, as if every blood vessel had burst in his head, drowning his eyes. His heart beat so hard, the only thing left that spoke of life. That, and the roar in his ears. Suspended in slowly exploding panic, Roy crumpled.

Sir Luther squeezed until the body hung slack in his hands.

Then he dropped the stringy carcass of the man who had been coachman at High Crescent for twenty years. He kicked the lifeless body once, then strode out of the dingy airless room.

Serena arched her aching back as a rivulet of fear rolled up her spine. A premonition had touched her with cold fingers. She sensed that danger was coming closer every day. Even here she was not safe—nowhere, not as long as Luther lived.

In her memory she went over the scene, the one scene that would always remain fresh in all of its stark details. The purple rage on Luther's fat face, the red eyes of fury, the lifelong hatred. Father, once so proud and ruthless, now a broken mass of nothing except the well of blood that continued to spew out his life. A pool of congealing blood that had once been part of her parent.

She had stared, hidden behind the curtains in the library; she had witnessed the escalating fight between the two brothers over something so ridiculous as a strip of land by the riverbed that separated their estates.

Luther had finally erupted in an explosion of rage and repeatedly struck her father's chest with a knife. She had stood frozen in terror. Luther had found her, and she'd barely managed to flee through the window with her life intact. Nurse Hopkins had hidden her until Luther gave up searching for her; then Serena had sneaked into the main house and stolen the cash box from Father's desk and the key. The coachman had been only too willing to leave High Crescent behind.

Serena moaned and clapped her hands to her face. She'd forgotten that they were wet and cold from the water in the bucket. She cringed and stared at the grime under her broken fingernails.

She glanced at the stairs winding up past Nick's bedchamber toward her prison. The steps had the wet look of wood recently scrubbed, and the fresh scent of lemon filled the air. Soon every part of the house would be sparkling clean and her nails would be gone. Her knees were already rubbed raw and red from the hard floors. The imprisonment chafed against her, but she had to stop thinking of escape for the time being. She was sure Luther was searching for her. He might know about Nurse Hopkins's relative in London if he'd questioned the servants at High Crescent.

If Luther did not find her at the milliner shop in Haymarket that Miss Molly Hopkins owned, he would probably not return to search for her there later.

Even though her main reason for staying here without trying to escape was the threat of Luther Hilliard, she knew a large part of her wanted to explore the relationship with Nick further. Heat rose in her body as she remembered their night together, and longing stirred in the pit of her stomach. *Already*. It was only hours ago since she'd lain in his arms. The realization mortified her.

A door slammed in the kitchen below, and Serena suspected the guard had come in search of a cup of hot coffee or milk. The day had the cold bite of winter, a raw wind that whined through every crevice of the house. Cracks there were many.

She shivered as she realized how cold her back was despite her hard work. She could have put on the thick wool dress that Nick had bought for her, but that somehow meant unconditional surrender to his will.

She jumped as Nick's voice came from the hallway below. "There you are. I see that you didn't burn down the house while cooking breakfast this morning."

"I'm not surprised to hear that you expected the worst," she said and wrung out the rag hard, wishing it were his neck. She swabbed the steps vigorously so that she didn't have to face him. "For that I will not offer you any of my delicious dishes."

"Burned bacon and stone-hard eggs?" He leaned against the oak balustrade and she could feel his gaze on her like a hot caress. She concentrated on her work, swabbing harder and faster.

"I made a fish and potato pie, and it was quite delectable."

"Not as delectable as your kiss, I'll wager," he said, his voice a soft stroke on her raw nerves.

"But much more nourishing."

He did not say anything for some time; but he was still there, a large, threatening figure, yet so beguiling, so exciting because of that danger. She could not understand herself, as if some part of her were reaching out to his male presence with great eagerness.

"I brought something to make your stay here easier," he said at last, and she heard the crackle of stiff paper.

"You can keep your presents," she said rebelliously. "I won't accept anything from you."

Nick's heart raced, and he swallowed hard as a surge of desire raced through him, making him almost dizzy. He could not take his eyes from her rounded backside under the stained and tattered velvet skirt as she scrubbed the stairs. He clamped the parcel under his arm and slowly went toward that part of her that he yearned to touch.

His blood quickened, forcing him to take two steps at a time up the last flight of stairs until he was right behind her. He set down the parcel and knelt on the lower step and wrapped his arms around her from behind. She stiffened, her hands still buried in the rag on the step above her. He held her hard, pushing his aching need against her backside, the alluring cleft he remembered. He fumbled for her breasts, tightly laced under stomacher and bodice. The very severity of that barrier enticed him further, and he imagined what it would be like to slowly unlace the cords and discover her anew.

She stilled, tensing.

He closed his eyes and inhaled the heady fragrance at the nape of her neck, the elusive bouquet of roses and femininity. Soft curls tickled his chin, and he teased one with his lips, nuzzled her neck with his nose, and licked that tender spot where her neck ended and her hair began.

Her back stiff under him, her breathing agitated, he sensed

her outrage. He could have lifted up her skirts, opened his breeches, and taken his swift pleasure right there on the stairs, but he could not. He did not want to humiliate her, and her trust was too weak to accept such an assault unless she willingly offered her body.

He rose with difficulty, his gaze riveted to her narrow waist and flaring hips. The desire was like a swift rapier thrust in his gut, and he fought the urge to surrender to its savagery. "Aren't you the slightest interested in my purchases?"

She shook her head mutely.

He took her by the waist and lifted her away from the stairs despite her mumbled protests. He stepped over the bucket and prayed he wouldn't slip on the treacherous soap. Carrying her to his bedchamber, which was closer than hers, he laughed as she kicked out.

"Wildcat," he said as he set her down. "Stay here. Won't be a minute."

She fumed, her cheeks red, but she remained in the room. Mayhap curiosity had overcome her. He retrieved the large parcel and placed it into her reluctant arms. "Open it."

An expression of irritation chased one of eagerness across her sweet face, and he urged her on. " 'Tis not a snake or a poisonous spider."

"Snake," she echoed as if the word held a special horror. She ripped the paper as if she wanted the moment to pass quickly. He watched her closely, noticing the warm blush in her cheeks, and the widening of her eyes as she beheld the artist equipment.

"For you. You told me you enjoy painting, so I thought you would not be averse to a gift of materials." Something in his breast welled up, a strong surge of feeling that tightened up his throat and made it impossible to speak. He could not explain what was happening, but the feeling had been provoked by the expression of delight on her face. She could not hide that from him behind her stern mask of disapproval.

"Thank you," she whispered. "Very thoughtful of you."

"Even though I am a criminal, I am not an ogre."

She pressed her fingertips to her throat as if finding it difficult to swallow. "I know you are not." She was speaking so softly he could barely hear her. Her words, however, spoke of a great improvement in their relationship. He was surprised to realize how much it mattered to him.

An uneasy silence hovered between them, and Nick could not find anything more to say. He watched her touch the brushes, one by one, and drag a fingertip over the stretched canvas. "What are you going to paint?" he asked at last.

"A good question." She glanced toward the window, where the view was roofs and chimneys, and sighed. "I suppose, I'll have to find an intriguing chimney pot through one of the windows."

"Do you always paint natural scenes?"

"Yes, mostly. A flower, a tree, or a whole landscape."

"Well, I shall have to bring you a bouquet of flowers then. Would chrysanthemums of different colors suit the purpose?"

She nodded, her gaze warmly meeting his. "Yes, they are lovely." She bundled up the items and carried them upstairs to her room. Nick followed, feeling as if there were unsettled business between them. He noticed the pleasant change in the bedchamber.

"What have you done in here? The room seems almost hospitable now."

"I washed everything, even the walls, and I found some sheets, which I fashioned into curtains. Very plain, I'll admit, but they do soften the starkness and shield me from nosy stares from across the street. I never realized how close people live to each other in London. If I reach through the window, I can almost touch the house opposite."

Nick chuckled. "I don't think your arms are that long, but yes, people are used to cramped quarters in this area. In the more affluent parts west of here, the streets are more spacious and the squares on a grand scale."

"I would like to see the parks and the other areas of London," she said with longing in her voice.

Nick almost promised to take her on a tour in his eagerness

to please her, but he remembered the threat she represented. "Mayhap one day you shall see it all."

She faced him squarely. "I've abandoned my plans for escape for the time being," she said. "You were right when you assumed I was running away from something. I am, and I realize this is a good hiding place for me."

He stared at her for a long moment, sensing she was speaking the truth. "But that would not stop you from denouncing me if you had the chance to step into the street."

"If you were arrested, Nick, this house would be confiscated and my place of hiding lost."

"Yes," he said, and grinned. "You're speaking with great sense, my darling. You might have to hide here for the rest of your life. I like the idea."

Her gaze filled with scorn, and her shoulders stiffened. "If you think I will live here all my life as your mistress, you're deluding yourself. I will leave when the time comes, and you won't be able to stop me."

"As far as I can tell, you already are my mistress," he drawled and sauntered toward her. A deep need to hold her had come over him as he viewed her slender body and proud bearing. Her translucent skin and her fine bones gave her an ethereal quality, but he knew the strength underneath, the volcano of dormant passion. Her presence always challenged him to entice her and probe the depths of her character.

"I might have succumbed once to your wiles in a moment of weakness, but I can control my senses," she said, her old haughtiness returning. "I expect you to honor my wishes."

He stood before her, looking down at her lovely, expressive face. Her slanted, mysterious eyes returned his gaze with defiance.

"Do you believe in love, Serena?"

Her eyelids flickered and fell, and she averted her face. He could smell the sweet fragrance of her hair. "I don't know," she said at last. "I have never witnessed love between two people. I doubt love is a lasting emotion."

"You're truthful, and I appreciate that." He took her hand

and pulled her to the bed. He noticed her hesitation. "Let's sit down. I'm not going to attack you."

She obeyed, and stiffly they sat, one next to the other as if in a hard pew at church. He said, "I loved our neighbor's daughter when I was fourteen. However, that swell of unrequited love did not last longer than six months. Then I fell in love with the steward's wife." He noticed Serena's shocked glance and laughed. "Yes, how improper. She did thrive on secret love trysts, and she introduced me to the wonders of lovemaking. Yes—" He took a deep breath. "—there were others, but I've never truly loved selflessly until I met the woman destined to become my best friend's wife. She might have become mine, had I but really made the effort to woo her."

"Why didn't you?" Serena asked, her eyes round. "And what is it like to be—truly—in love?"

"I have wondered that myself—why I didn't make a wholehearted effort—and I could think of only one reason. I didn't think I was good enough for her, so I always held back. She was a viscountess, and I had no title, no fortune to offer her."

He squeezed Serena's hand. "You'll know when you're truly in love. For me it's like a deep pain but also a deep elation, and you're willing to do *anything* for that person. In a way, love turns people into complete idiots—but I wouldn't mind if only I could feel that depth of emotion. You know, mayhap I didn't *truly* love her." He glanced thoughtfully at Serena. "I don't know why I'm telling you this.

"But you"—he gave Serena a suggestive look"—you are a distraction. You keep me from brooding."

"I have always believed that true love should be strong enough to overcome all obstacles—even those of birth and fortune. Otherwise, it isn't love."

He let go of her hand abruptly and paced to the window. "I would not want to test that theory. Only a very foolish aristocratic lady would consider joining herself to a bastard who was raised as a nobleman."

"You sound as if you've always lived with a thorn of bitterness in your side."

"I cannot reconcile my two very different poles. At heart I am a thief and a street urchin; on the outside, a squire of elegance and wit."

"Why do you always speak of your upbringing with derision? You should consider yourself lucky to have received a fine education. Most poor people don't even know how to read and write."

"Mayhap they are happiest that way. Most gentlemen in the upper circles use their schooling for naught. They live wasted lives of debauchery and do not care that half of the population is starving."

She leaned back against the pillows and pulled up her legs under her. "You do?"

"How can I fail to be affected? The suffering is all around us."

"But what can you do about it? You can't save all of London's poor on your own."

He turned sharply and stared at her. He would have to show her the most important part of his life. He would have to trust her assurance that she had no desire to escape . . . and take her across to the orphanage.

Chapter 12

"Come, let me show you something. But first, please put on the new clothes while I find a cloak for you to wear."

Twenty minutes later, they were walking along the cobbled street, Nick's hand firmly holding hers. Serena inhaled the scents with pleasure, even the foul odor of muck. Her lungs swelled as a cold breeze blew in from the river, and elation rose in her like a heady bubble.

Outside at last. She wanted to stop and chat with the muffin vendor and examine his tray covered with green baize . . . or the newsprint seller . . . or the street sweepers. She hadn't realized how much she'd missed the company of others. She wondered what excuse Luther had put about to her friends to explain her absence from High Crescent. But why think about him now? He could not hurt her today.

Her new clothes felt good against her skin—even her stiff new shoes; and the heavy velvet cloak, which was a bit too long, protected her from the cold.

"I'm expiring with curiosity," she said, savoring the warmth of his hand around hers. Blissful at her sudden freedom, she smiled up at him.

"You grinned!" His face took on a dazed expression and he almost overturned a basket of apples as he bumped into a sturdy toothless woman dressed in a tattered cloak and an enormous mobcap. She swore a harangue of obscenities in a strident voice, and Serena flinched at the coarse language. Her bliss took on a hint of tarnish.

Children in rags darted among people on foot, drays, and farm carts. The crowds in the street increased as they walked into an area of narrower streets and more dilapidated buildings.

"This is the east edge of St. Giles," Nick explained. "We're almost at our destination."

He pulled her around a corner, and she came upon the doors to a large brick building that looked like an old warehouse. It had been extensively repaired, and fresh wood brightened up the grimy exterior. Scaffolding and building materials lined part of the front wall. Nick halted by the closed double doors. He faced her, holding up their intertwined hands between them.

As if part of a secret rite, he slowly let go of her hand and dropped his own to his side. It was as if she could read his thoughts, the suggestion of freedom, the testing of her statement that she would not escape.

They stared at each for a long time. Finally she said, "What are we waiting for?"

His face split in that delightful grin, and her heartbeat raced. She wished he were mean and callous so that she could more easily despise him. She could not. Rather the opposite.

Inside, there was a large hallway with a checkered floor, a long desk behind which sat a tall, exceedingly thin man. He stood immediately, his narrow face warming in a smile. The building with its tall ceilings echoed with the voices of children.

"Mr. Thu—"

"Good afternoon, Thornby," Nick said, and shook the other man's bony hand. "I've brought a friend to visit the children."

"They are at the dinner table at the moment, except the sick ones of course."

"Would you like to visit the infirmary, Serena?" Nick asked, his eyes sparkling with anticipation.

She nodded, unable to find her tongue.

"This orphanage is what I live for," Nick said as Thornby led the way up a set of stairs to a large cavernous area above. Nick whispered in her ear, "This is what the riches of my victims have bought; I haven't spent a farthing on myself."

Serena saw rows upon rows of small beds with white sheets and blankets. Order and cleanliness prevailed everywhere, and the air smelled of soap and starch. She noticed several maids in uniforms of gray roundgowns, white aprons, and mobcaps. A haven in the midst of chaos, she thought. A home for the children. Her heart squeezed painfully, and she knew she could not view Nick as a vicious criminal ever again.

Another room had been divided into alcoves. Thin white curtains fluttered as a maid carrying a tray hurried along the path between the alcoves.

Nick peeped behind a curtain, and a delightful giggle from the occupant rose toward the ceiling. "Hello, Mr. Nick, did ye bring me a sugarplum today?"

Nick pulled the curtain aside and Serena came eye to eye with a fair-haired child with fever-glazed eyes. The body under the white nightgown looked frail and undernourished. "No, not today. This is Birdie Jones," Nick introduced gravely. "And this is Miss Serena."

"A real leddy?" Birdie's eyes grew round with awe.

Serena smiled. "No, not a titled lady." She wished she had something to give the child.

"You look better, Birdie. Can you breathe without coughing?"

"Yes, Mr. Nick. Sometimes."

"Well done!" Nick reached into the pocket of his coat and pulled out a silver coin. He flipped it into the air. The child squealed with delight and caught it.

"Next time I visit, I hope to see you downstairs with the others. Do we have a pact?" He held out his hand, and the tiny girl solemnly shook it.

"Aye—upon me dead granny's body as Mr. Thornby says."

Serena swallowed the lump in her throat. Despite her weakness, the child maintained a cheerful spirit. Serena's own spirit lifted further as she could not be immune to such inspiration.

She glanced at a sleeping boy on another cot and noticed the clean linen and sparkling window above his head. Everyone took great pride in this orphanage.

She flinched in surprise as she recognized Rafael Howard. He was sitting on a chair holding a pale girl who could not have been more than four years old. She had the translucent look of someone who already had one foot on the threshold of death.

Serena went to him, and he nodded in greeting. "I'm sorry I can't rise to give you a proper bow," he said with that grave look she'd noticed before.

"Think nothing of it, Mr. Howard. I did not know you were working here."

"I am not," he said, and she wondered if she could pry further. He smoothed back the blond curls from the child's forehead. "Only trying to give some comfort, but I don't even know if she recognizes me."

Serena didn't know what to say. Nick joined them and bent over the child. "How is she, Rafe?"

"No change. She's fading away." His voice cracked on the last words, and Serena bit her tongue to prevent herself from crying. She slowly retreated as she was loath to intrude on his evident grief.

Nick took her hand, his warm squeeze giving her comfort. "Come along."

"He is so sad. I feel sorry for him."

"Rafe sits most days and nights with her. She is his daughter. That's all I know, so don't ask me any questions. He just came to the orphanage with me one day and found his daughter. I have a sneaking suspicion he was sent by Fate the moment we met in the woods."

"I sense his heart carries a heavy burden of sadness," she said.

"Yes, more than some." Nick led her to another ward, where smaller children were being fed. "Some of these infants were abandoned in the gutter, but they shall have a decent life—learn to read and write and become apprentices in the trade of their choice. We've already gained quite a few influential sponsors. Tradesmen mostly.''

Nick's face had taken on an animated look she'd never noticed before. ''It is true, you really live for this,'' she commented.

'' 'Tis my sole reason for going out at night robbing coaches,'' he whispered. ''It's the only way the rich will give any significant amounts to the poor.'' He glanced into her eyes. ''I truly don't condone criminal acts, but the meager alms given will not make a dent in the appalling poverty of the city.''

''No, they won't,'' Serena said. ''But why such a desperate act as robbing coaches? You might lose your own life in the process.''

He shrugged. ''One life is insignificant compared to the many I've saved. Besides, the only person who would truly miss me is my stepsister Delicia, and mayhap some of my friends.''

''How many children are there here?'' Serena asked and realized she would sorely miss him if he were hanged.

''One hundred. Some of the older ones are about to leave. Once they have found lawful work, there's no reason to keep them; but they come back and help with the other children. They form attachments—we're one large family.''

Mr. Thornby joined them. ''Would you like to see the dining hall, miss?''

''Yes, that would be interesting.'' She wound her arm through Nick's and they followed Mr. Thornby downstairs. The din rose to a jubilant salute as they entered the vast room. Lines of long tables and wooden benches filled with children stretched from one end to the other.

Nick laughed and waved as the young ones cried his name. ''They never fail to cheer me up,'' he shouted to Serena over the noise. He led her through the room, tweaking tiny noses and caressing heads. The children beamed. They looked well cared for in neat homespun dresses and sober coats and breeches.

At the other end of the hall there was a long passageway which ended in the kitchens, a series of rooms with stone walls and stone sinks. An enormous hearth provided heat and fire for the cooking. Large pots hung on hooks over the flames, and half a pig had been skewered on a spit. The contraption was attached with straps to a wheel high on the wall and a cage on the floor. A dog turned the spit by running inside the cylindrical cage.

"Mr. Nick!" a young maid exclaimed in delight. She wore an apron liberally spotted and streaked with food and a mobcap that covered all of her hair except one brown saucy ringlet that fell over her shoulder. "Are ye 'ere to sample me food?" She turned to Serena with twinkling nut-brown eyes. " 'E's always 'ungry."

"Not one to cook for himself," Serena said with a meaningful glance at Nick.

The maid wiped her hands on her apron and patted her round freckled face with one corner. "Sit yerselves down, and I'll serve up a bowl of rabbit stew and turnips. 'Tis today's fancy offerin'." She laughed, and Serena could not stop herself from joining in.

Nick showed Serena to a small table under the window where the servants evidently ate their portions. A stack of clean bowls stood by a tray of spoons, knives, and forks. Everything had been scrubbed clean; not a speck of food remained on the tabletop. Maids and menservants flitted in and out of the kitchen, two of them carrying a large pot suspended from a pole between them. "Stew," Nick said as he noticed Serena's stare.

"How many people work here?" she asked, in awe of all the activity.

"It varies. Around twenty-five people. Sometimes there are volunteers from the parish. Two curates volunteer their time for teaching in the morning. As I said, the orphanage has attracted many sponsors since it was founded three years ago. It is almost debt free by now; and if only I could pay off the mortgage on the buildings, I should be at liberty to stop my illegal activities." He was speaking for her ears only, and

Serena suspected that he would not have confided his secrets to her if she hadn't seen his face on that fateful night when he abducted her.

" 'Ere ye are then," the maid said, and placed two steaming bowls in front of them. She fetched a basket of coarse bread from a nearby table.

"This is Mavis Cork, the chief cook," Nick explained. "I've told her she should apply for employment at King George's court—her cooking is that good." He winked at the young woman, and Serena experienced a stab of jealousy.

"I'd rather work wiv th' nippers. They are that easy t' please, and I doubt King George—bless 'is soul—would 'ave such acceptin' taste." Her laugh tinkled toward the vaulted ceiling, and Serena found it contagious.

She tasted the steaming stew gingerly so as not to burn her tongue. Simple fare, but anything would be better than her own meager cooking. She closed her eyes and savored the rich taste of the meat sauce. "Delicious," she said, meaning it, after the first swallow.

The cook bobbed a curtsy. "Thank you, miss. I take great pride in me cookin'. Th' li'l mites should not 'avta starve."

Serena ate the whole bowl and then another one. The bread tasted grainy, but not much else. Dipped in the sauce, it was a pleasant complement to the meal. Replenished and happier than she'd been in a long time, Serena leaned back with a sigh. She watched Nick finish his meal, and he gave her a knowing look.

"The first time your belly has been full since you left home."

"Ladies do not have bellies," she said tartly.

His eyebrows rose a notch. "Of course. I am forgetting that you are a lady to your reddened and rough fingertips."

A flare of anger fizzled and died in Serena's chest, and she had to laugh. "You're incorrigible."

"And you are lovely when you laugh," he said, and raked an intimate gaze over her face. "You should do that more often."

She looked away as heat rose in her face. "I have little to laugh about, but this meal was superb."

"You have changed a great deal since you came to London. I'd say the spoiled lady has humbled herself."

"Mayhap the lady was not as spoiled as you claimed. You are not always right."

He pushed aside the bowl and leaned back in his chair, his hands braced behind his head. "I have always trusted my instincts."

"Even the best instincts can be wrong at times," she said, and raised her chin in defiance.

"Not about you, though. I'd say we already mean a lot to each other. We didn't just meet by chance; our paths were destined to cross."

"I don't know anything about that; but we did meet, and the encounter certainly changed my life." She grew hot and breathless from the storm of desire in his eyes and the lazy grin on his lips. "*You* turned my life over."

"You changed my life, too. Changed the very course of it. I'm glad you did." He stood. "Let's continue our walk."

Serena found the offer to her liking. She watched Nick pile the bowls and carry them to the scullery, a dark room two steps below the kitchen. She shuddered as she remembered her own adventures with buckets and water back in her prison.

Mavis waved, then continued stirring in the pot by the fire. Serena wished she would've had the time to ask some questions to increase her level of culinary knowledge, an art that had been a complete mystery until she became Nick's prisoner.

They walked down to the Thames and lingered by Black Friars Bridge. A fresh breeze blew over the ruffled brown water, fluttering the debris on its shore and pulling at Serena's hair. She lifted up the hood of her cloak to cover her head from the cold.

Barges glided slowly up the river, and small sailboats bounced like seagulls on the waves. A boatman offered to row them across to Southwark, but Nick shook his head. "Not today, mate."

Serena watched a cloud of pigeons rising above the bridge and swirling on the wind before heading back into the city. She couldn't get enough air; and if the sun had dared to show its golden face, the day would have been perfect.

"I'll show you St. Paul's Cathedral some other day. It is at walking distance from here. Then there's the Tower, farther east."

"Where they beheaded prisoners and incarcerated kings."

"The same. The Tower has a bloody history, alas."

Serena shuddered as if someone were walking across her grave.

"Are you cold? Mayhap we should go back." Nick steered her down a narrow side street that converged at a larger thoroughfare. She found herself swallowed by a surge of humanity bundled up in rags or fine cloaks, depending on the person's standing.

Carriages and farm wagons jostled down the street, coachmen shouting and cracking the whip. Horses tossed their heads and whinnied as if throwing a greeting to another team. A cart of coal lay overturned at one corner, and an argument was underway between two drivers.

Serena's mind filled with the cacophony of sounds and smells as she tried to see and hear everything going on around her.

Nick bought a bag of sugarplums from a vendor and veered away from a swaying sedan chair. The sturdy carriers ran past Serena at a sharp clip. She glanced at the occupant in the window and gasped in fright. In a flash, the moment was over, but she could have sworn she saw her uncle, Luther Hilliard, inside.

"You look pale, Serena. Are you chilled?" When she nodded numbly, he continued. "Let's return home. You've had enough adventure for one day."

Dazed, she followed him. If Luther were in London, she was not safe anywhere but in her prison. She broke into a run.

Chapter 13

Nick caught up with her at the end of the street. He gripped her arm hard, almost pulling it out of its socket as he jerked her to a halt. "What are you doing? You said you weren't going to run away. I trusted you!" His face was red with anger.

She gulped down a wave of panic and pulled herself free. "I wasn't running away, you idiot. I was running to your house." She pressed her fingertips to her burning eyes and, despite her struggles to keep her composure, tears made a hot trail down her cheeks.

"How was I to know that?" Disappointment mixed with anger on his face. "You just ran, didn't give me a word of explanation."

"Not an ounce of trust in that big body of yours. I *said* I wasn't going to run away, but you have to doubt it at the first opportunity." She dashed away her tears, but they kept coming as the horror of her nightmares came rushing over her. Unease and worry rolled into a hard ball in her stomach, and she desperately tried to shut out the memories.

"Why are you so afraid?" he asked, and slid his arm around

her shoulders. People jostled them on both sides, and the steel-clad wheel of a cart almost crushed her toes.

She rubbed her eyes, wondering if she dared to reveal her secret. Mayhap he would help her in some way, but possibly he would rush off in a temper to confront Luther, and then she would never be safe again. Luther had killed once, and he most likely wouldn't hesitate to kill again. "I thought I saw someone I recognized," she mumbled.

"That someone must mean a great deal to you if your fear is any indication."

"Yes, so much so that he would like to see me dead."

"Dead?" Nick quickly led her away from the crush of humans and down a side street. Soon she realized that they were almost back at the house that she'd loathed but now saw as a safe haven. He unlocked the door and pulled her into the shadowy hallway.

In the kitchen he sat her down on a chair and untied the ties of her cloak. "I shall make some tea for you and heat water for a bath. There's a hip bath in the closet under the stairs."

"You would do all that for me?" she asked, surprised and pleased at his concern.

"It distresses me to see you so disturbed," he said and pulled off his cloak and coat. He flung them over the back of a chair and went to stir up the glowing embers in the hearth. Soon a fire blazed, spreading warmth into the room.

Serena slowly relaxed, and she smiled with gratitude as Nick placed a cup of steaming tea before her on the table. "I think you should tell me the whole story, Serena."

"So that you can rush off and slay the dragon for me?" she asked and wiped her nose on a handkerchief.

"Not necessarily, but I'd like to help if possible."

"Your concern is my undoing, Nick."

He kneeled beside her and took her hand into his. "We have been closer than friends, yet I am still trying to build that lacking friendship. We are strangers, yet I know you better than I've known any woman. 'Tis a rather strange relationship."

She nodded and put her hand against his cheek. Feeling

blazed between them. "Yes, but I don't consider myself a prisoner any longer."

"I think we have gone past that; but if you decided to leave, I would have to live with the nagging worry of the lawmen arriving on my doorstep." He did not wait for an answer, but went to the hallway and came back lugging the hip bath. Then he set to pouring water in the large black pot on the hook over the fire. He was doing this for her, and her heart warmed even as the water heated in the pot. Nick was not as she imagined a real criminal. He was far from callous and hard. *Oh, Nick,* she said silently.

"For many reasons, I'm not interested in talking to the authorities," she said. She shuddered with apprehension at what would happen if she reported Luther to the law. He had the knack for playacting, and he was powerful. He would find a way to blame her for her father's death. She wondered what he'd done with the body, what he had told the servants. Even though she hadn't been very close to her father, he still deserved a decent burial.

"Don't you have any male relatives who could help you, protect you?" Nick asked, shattering her thoughts.

She shook her head. "I lived alone with Father and the servants after my mother's death. We had few friends since Father's temper scared most of them away."

"The servants will wonder what happened to you," Nick said and poured a cup of tea for himself. "They'll report you as missing, and the local authorities in Somerset will be searching for you."

"They will do what my uncle tells them to do," she said coldly.

Nick's keen gaze bored into her and she had to look away. "You're running away from him, aren't you?" he concluded and took the cup from her hand. He stood over her. "Now tell me the whole."

She nodded miserably. "He killed my father. Stabbed him to death. I witnessed the murder as I hid behind a curtain. I was taking a breath of fresh air on the terrace before going to bed, and the window was open—one of those tall windows that you can easily step through.''

In a flash, Nick pulled her into his arms. He hugged her protectively. "You'll have to do something about it! Report the crime, at least."

"No one will believe me. I am a mere woman, and my uncle is a powerful man. He will twist the truth to suit his own purposes."

Nick caressed her hair, and some of the misery lodged in her chest dissolved. All at once, she felt tired and weak.

"I could mayhap help you bring the murderer to justice."

"I don't want you to get involved, Nick," she said with finality. "When our roads part, as they will someday soon, I don't want to owe you." She glanced up into his eyes, seeing the emotions crossing his face—surprise, suspicion, and disappointment.

"I would not charge you a groat for my assistance," he said. "I would like to help you."

"I would be beholden to you. Anyway, I don't think there's anything you can do, not now. I shall find a way to avenge my father's death, but I'll have to be more devious than my uncle. I know I fall short, but I shall find a solution—even an underhanded one."

He held her face between the palms of his hands. "Sounds as if you're eager to join the legions of criminals to avenge your father's death. Revenge is dangerous, and you might end up losing your life."

"My uncle will lose his life first," she said, but realized as she said the words that she would not have the courage to kill Luther even if he deserved death for his crime. Should truth be known, she had difficulty stepping on spiders and swatting flies, let alone killing a human being. She now wished she hadn't brought up the subject. Nick had a calculating look in his eyes.

* * *

Nick shook his head and eased her back down on the chair. From the start, he had sensed that she'd brought with her a deep mystery coupled with danger. It appalled him to find out that she'd lost a parent to a killer. *Murder.* The word sent an icy shiver down his spine. He pressed the teacup into her hands and found them as cold as marble. She trembled as she clutched the cup between her stiff fingers.

"You really haven't had time to grieve for him, have you, Serena?"

"I threw myself into the world right after his death, and I am still reeling from the changes. I don't have time to grieve."

"But it's unhealthy to keep it all inside."

"I can't think of Father now; I don't know what I feel, both hatred and love. Grieving him won't be easy. I will have to find my legs in the world before I can think of what happened at home."

She sounded so full of despair and looked so lost that Nick's heart softened. He quenched an urge to force all the details from her so that he could make her revenge his. He sensed her reluctance to speak. She lacked trust as much as he did.

Steam curled out of the pot, and before it grew too hot, he ladled water into the hip bath. "After a bath by the fire, you'll feel a great deal better," he said. His lace cuffs grew damp and hampered his movements, so he detached them and rolled up his sleeves. This reminded him of his childhood, when he'd helped fill the bath for his mother—before they had lost the hovel they had called home. The stark memories were as clear as if everything had happened yesterday.

"Why are you doing this for me?" she asked softly.

"You can use some friendly care, that's all," he said and tested the water. "I'll go upstairs for some soap while you get out of your clothes. And don't worry, the doors are locked and we are alone in the house."

She smiled, but the smile did not reach her eyes. "Really? Should I be afraid of you?"

He chuckled and pinched her red nose as he passed her. "Mayhap."

When he returned downstairs, he found her naked in front
of the fire. Her back looked slender and defenseless, her hips
gently swelling and tapering into long, luscious thighs. His
manhood swelled with instant desire, and he set the soap on
the table and went to stand behind her. He slowly wound his
arms around her waist and held her tight for a moment. Her
hair fell from its precarious arrangement on her head and smoth-
ered his eyes with a silky web.

He shook his face free and leaned forward over her shoulder
to get a better view of her firm breasts. He cradled their weight
in his hands and rubbed his fingertips over the tightening crests.
She did not flinch away.

Growing hot all over, he could barely contain himself from
ravishing her then and there. It seemed much too long since
he'd held her naked body in his arms and brought them both
to the shuddering brink of ecstasy. He would now. He had to,
and he sensed her arousal in the musky smell emanating from
her body and in the hardening of her nipples. He slid his hands
over the distended pebbles, reveling in the sensation against
his skin.

Every part of her seemed to ignite an erotic response in every
part of his body. He lost his breath as a desire so powerful he
could barely remain standing washed through him and ate at
his control until he felt dizzy. She began to tremble in his arms,
and a deep sigh passed her lips.

''The water is getting colder by the minute,'' she whispered.

He had to force himself to release her silky body. Her skin
glowed like mother-of-pearl in the leaping orange light of the
fire, her nipples brown-gold against her pale flesh.

He closed his eyes and tried to gather his composure as she
stepped into the water and eased herself down into the tub. The
water only reached to her waist, and he could not take his eyes
off the round impudent swell of her breasts. They seemed
engorged with desire, and her parted lips gleamed, wetly
inviting.

''The soap, please,'' she said, those maddening lips turning
up at the corners in a teasing grin. She held out a graceful

hand, and he had to obey. He was glad he had bought a French rose-scented soap of the finest quality during his latest foray in the shops.

She worked up a lather as he watched, and rubbed her soapy hands over her chest and around her breasts. Soap bubbles glided over the smooth round forms, and Nick groaned. He fell to his knees beside the tub.

"Please, give me the soap," he said.

Serena noted the dark glow of desire in his eyes and the red flush in his cheeks. Without a word, she obeyed. His irresistible smile flashed, and a sense of purpose settled in his wide shoulders. Serena gasped as he lifted one of her legs and propped it on the edge of the tub. He creamed lather on his hands and inserted his fingers between her toes. She laughed and squirmed, but he held her foot firmly, as firmly as he could with soapy hands, and caressed the sensitive arch and the slender ankle. His hands slid over the curve of her calf, and sweet thrills rolled up her leg and settled in her womb as he advanced ever higher.

Heat filled her entire body, and passion quickened her blood.

His hands worked magic on her thigh, a long finger sliding up to her secret place. He touched her, slipping his fingers along her crevice, and she cried out with longing.

Had cutting the strings with her former life changed her so completely or had this wanton she did not recognize lived inside her the whole time?

She gasped with pleasure as he worked his magic on the other foot, each toe getting his undivided attention, and each curve his caress.

"Such perfection," he said hoarsely. "Such seductive lines made for a man to love."

"I wouldn't let just *any* man touch my toes," she said with a shaky laugh. His hands and arms were buried in the water, sliding up over her hips in a demanding caress. He spanned her waist like a belt and glanced deeply into her eyes. His face diffused with hunger, he pressed his lips to hers in a demanding kiss that stole her breath away.

His tongue mated silkily with hers, giving her the essence of him, making her heart race like a demented horse in her chest. She wound her wet arms around his neck and pressed her breasts against him, not caring that she soaked his shirt.

"Oh, Nick," she whispered as he finally lifted his face. The kiss had devastated her, and all that filled her head was the need for more.

He chuckled as if understanding the smoldering depth of her desire. "You have the most kissable mouth I've ever tasted."

"I don't fall for such blatant untruths," she said, but she had fallen and was eager to continue the exploration into the mysterious realms of love.

He cradled her neck in his hands and kissed her again, his tongue thrusting deeply into her mouth and demanding a rousing response. He tasted of lemon, and the rose scent on his hands floated on the steam and curled into her nostrils.

He finally threw his head back and groaned as if frustrated beyond endurance. As he released her she laughed and touched one set of toes to his chest. "You sound like a wounded bear."

"I am one—until you find the mercy to heal me," he said, and captured her leg. One hand slid down her thigh, and the other cradled one slick breast. He explored the wet cleft with a thoroughness that left her gasping for more, and his hand kneaded her breast. Her body ached with a dulcet need so great she could only moan. Pleasure bloomed from the center of her being at his clever caress and spiraled hotly up her spine. She rose on a peak; but before she could fall into the abyss of mindless delight, he withdrew, leaving her aching and desperate.

His shirt was sopping wet, and she dragged her hands over the broad expanse of his chest and untied the stubborn lacings of his breeches. She pulled them down over his hips, and his manhood sprang swollen into her hand. She kneaded the velvet length, sensing his raging desire. His cheeks held a deep flush and his eyes glittered dangerously.

"You'll be the death of me," he said in a tortured voice. He pulled up his breeches and lifted her out of the bath. Water streamed on the floor, but he didn't seem to notice. He ran through the house and up the stairs to his bedchamber.

She shivered in the cool air, but he shoved the covers over her and joined her naked under the blankets a short while later. Their arms twined around each other, her slick body rubbing against him, her hips grinding against his as she sought to slake the frenzied desire in the core of her being.

He pushed his velvet hardness into her silken sheath. She moaned against his neck as he started moving, slowly, tantalizingly at first, then faster until every thrust brought such intense pleasure that it swelled into a peak that erupted into a surge of ecstasy. She cried his name.

He clutched her to him so hard she couldn't breathe and thrust convulsively into her in a great wave of release. He shuddered in her arms, his mouth fusing to hers in a kiss that made every second sweeter than the previous one.

Another powerful ripple rolled through her, dissolving every bone and heating her blood with delight.

A sea of softness engulfed her, mellow, golden, her life hanging suspended in a mist of eternity. Slowly, with every heartbeat, she returned to the present, noting the creaking timber of the walls, the subdued din of London outside the window.

The afternoon sun splashed blessed autumn light over the blankets and gave her lover a gilded aura. Nick looked young and carefree, and infinitely appealing. Reborn, renewed in their love.

"I so enjoy your company," he whispered, and touched the tip of her chin with one fingertip.

She smiled. "And I enjoy yours."

He leaned over on his side and thrust one thigh over hers. He propped his head on one elbow. "There's something about you that inspires my passion; and when I'm not touching you, I'm filled with the yearning to touch you, to hold you, to drink the honey of your love."

"It is called *lust*, Nick," she said, and stroked his hard cheek.

It felt slightly raspy against her fingers, and the sensation sent a thrill through her veins.

"How callous of you to mention the word *lust* and my name in the same sentence." His voice sounded muffled as sleep wove its web around him.

"The sheets are wet from bathwater," she said and moved closer to him. He rolled over on his back and pulled her on top of him. She snuggled against him and thought there were worse places in which to go to sleep.

Chapter 14

The next morning Serena found herself alone in Nick's bed. The sun already stood high in the sky. Pressing her hands to her hot cheeks, Serena remembered their long evening of lovemaking . . . and how his kisses in her most secret places had spun her into spirals of such bliss that she even now felt like crying for the beauty of his wizardry.

She wondered where he'd served his apprenticeship, but quickly pushed away that thought as a niggling feeling of jealousy started destroying her happiness. Happiness was like the finest crystal bowl, radiant and pure, but which would shatter easily if dropped on the floor. She'd better hold on to it with caution.

The house brooded in silence, and she wondered where Nick had gone. She pulled a sheet around herself and went downstairs to the kitchen. He was not there, and the fire had died. The bathtub had been emptied and removed. A piece of paper leaned against the wooden fruit bowl on the table.

Sweet Serena,

> *I had to go out on an errand. Go back to bed and
> dream of me. I shall wake you with a kiss when I return.*
> *Nick*

Serena smiled and hugged the note to her chest. This must
be love, this dizzying explosion of feeling that made her heart
race and her blood pound hotly through her head. This dangerous swell of emotion that ruined her reason and made her fling
caution to the winds.

She found the clothes he'd bought for her folded on one of
the chairs. After clamping them under her arm, she ran lightly
up the stairs to her room. She washed her sore body and brushed
out the tangles in her hair. In the mirror over the basin, she
saw a pale face and eyes languorous with contentment. Her
hair hung in wild disarray, as if she'd spent the night in a
windstorm.

She dressed and arranged her hair under a mobcap to look
more like a servant girl than a highborn lady. This area of
London was not the place to flaunt one's origin. Luther might
spot her. That thought pulled a veil of unhappiness over her
exhilaration.

She went downstairs to await Nick's return, but she didn't
feel like making a fire and cooking a meal. Hungry, she piled
bread and cheese on a plate. To end the simple meal, she
polished an apple and bit into its juicy tart flesh.

Tired of waiting, she tried the back door. It was unlocked,
and there were no guards in sight. Nick had chosen to trust
her. The thought brought tears to her eyes, and she cursed
herself for her precarious emotional state.

She could leave and never come back.

The possibility haunted her, but she could not leave for good.
Not now, perhaps later. She could not abandon Nick at the spur
of a moment. The thought niggled at her, making her realize
her mounting weakness for him. Soon would come a day when
she would be unable to leave him, no matter what.

She sighed, pushing away the disturbing thought.

She could always visit Mavis in the orphanage and mayhap offer her services there. Elated with her plan, she wrote a note at the bottom of Nick's message with a goose quill and ink pot she found in his room.

The day was cold, the wind brisk. A newspaper fluttered along the cobbles and rose on a gust of wind like a large bird of prey ahead of her. Clutching her painting material under one arm, she hurried along the street, suddenly feeling insecure and worried that Luther would wait around the corner of the next building.

She hastened past a coffeeshop. The scent of roasted meat and freshly made coffee came from the open door, and her mouth watered even though she'd already eaten.

She arrived at the orphanage safely. The workmen were hanging the large carved sign over the door. "Sir James's Orphanage," she read aloud, savoring every word. It was kind of Nick to place his uncle-father's name instead of his own over the door. The gentleman who had cared and pulled Nick out of miserable poverty. She almost sensed Sir James like a benevolent ghost beside her as she walked into the cavernous hallway.

There was no one at the desk in the corner. She walked through the empty dining hall, her steps echoing in the vast chamber. A small group of children sat along one of the walls, and a clerical man was reading to them from a book, which she assumed was the Bible. She could only hear his murmured voice. Two of the children waved recklessly at her, and she waved back, grinning.

The kitchen was a beehive of activity, kitchen maids scurrying back and forth with platters of meat and trays piled with loaves. No one paid any attention to her. Serena recognized Mavis standing by the fireplace and went to speak with her. For some strange reason she felt shy, an intruder, an impostor.

"I would like to help," she said when she'd greeted Mavis. "Is there anything I can do? I'm not trained to kitchen service, but I learn quickly."

Mavis's nut-brown eyes lit up. "We are shorthanded, Miss Serena. Ye can 'elp peelin' the turnips, if ye don't mind." She led the way to a wooden bench on which stood a half barrel filled with muddy water. Serena noticed the pale round shapes of the turnips on the bottom.

"Ye scrub them 'ere, then rinse them in clean water in that bucket and dice them on th' choppin' block."

Serena viewed the large knife with misgiving and wondered what *dicing* meant. Washing and peeling could not be too difficult, she thought, and put her brown parcel on a table. She pulled off her cloak and hung it on a hook by the back door.

" 'Tis not often Mr. Nick brings 'is friends 'ere, and this is th' first time any of them 'as come back to work in th' kitchens. It warms me 'eart, it does."

Serena nodded and worried about the task at hand. "Just to come here makes me cheerful," she said, realizing it was true. The children filled the house with happiness and—life. This was such a change from the vast empty mansion in which she'd spent most of her life.

She lowered her arms into the cold water and eyed the turnips suspiciously. A stiff brush rested on the edge of the tub, and she managed to scrub the first vegetable clean and rinse it. Now for the *dicing*. The knife was sharpened to a honed edge, and the large turnip looked hard as marble, its skin tough as horsehide.

Serena threw a sideways glance at Mavis, who was directing the emptying of a large cauldron into buckets. Maids threw curious glances at Serena, but did not acknowledge her in any way.

The back door slammed as she turned the turnip over in her hand and tried to decide where to start peeling. A cold gust eddied around her ankles, and she shivered.

"Need help with that?" a male voice asked so close to her ear that she jumped with fright and dropped the turnip. It rolled under a bench filled with stacks of bowls.

"Nick! You startled me," she said, and looked into his keen blue eyes.

"I'm sorry, but I could not resist offering my assistance as I saw your quandary." He held up his hands, palms out. "Don't stab me with that knife!"

A chorus of voices greeted Nick, and he nodded to everyone after taking off his hat and cloak. "I am going to show this maid how to peel a turnip," he said to Mavis when she asked if he wanted a cup of tea.

He winked at Serena, and she took a firmer grip on the knife, thinking she ought to peel off the tip of his nose while she had the chance.

Nick retrieved the turnip from under the bench and rinsed it in the bucket.

"Where did you go this morning?" she asked, and handed him the knife.

"Did you miss me?" he countered, ignoring her question. He gave her a smoldering, suggestive glance and deftly cut the turnip in four parts. "This will make it easier to peal."

"No, I didn't miss you. I was glad you were gone when I woke up," she lied, huffy when he wouldn't reveal where he'd gone.

"I'm glad you didn't abandon me for good, Serena, even though I left the door unlocked. I worried when I returned home to find you gone, so worried that I ran all the way here, wondering if your note were a ruse."

"You don't seem the least bit out of breath," she said gloomily.

"I'm used to running," he said, the double meaning of the words reminding Serena of his criminal activities. The thought depressed her. Despite his noble goal with the money stolen from wealthy travelers, he still was a bandit—a man of the lowest kind. She suspected she had only one choice, to quell her growing love for him.

"Your downfall will come one day," she said as she watched him peel one large wedge of turnip. When he was finished, she took it from him and rinsed it in clean water. He handed her the knife and she felt awkward under his scrutiny. Biting the inside of her lip, she applied the unwieldy knife to the tough skin and prayed that she would not slice her own hide off. She didn't; the vegetable skin came off with a certain flair, she thought.

"You relish the idea of my downfall?" he asked, one hand braced on the edge of the table. He stood so close she could feel his every breath on her cheek.

She sensed the rising tension between them and glanced at his face. He wore a faint scowl.

"No . . . in truth, I don't relish the thought, but—"

"Splendid!" He gave her that heart-stopping smile, and his eyes held a suggestion of intimacy.

"But I believe that criminals should be brought to justice," she added, and set to work on another wedge of turnip. "Don't you?"

He stood silent for a long time. "Yes . . . but many do criminal acts for causes in which they believe—Jacobite spies, for instance. The poor steal to eat."

"The end justifies the means?"

"I would not kill a man to get his purse, but he does not know that as he stares down the barrel of my pistol."

"The pistol might accidentally go off, and then you would be guilty of murder," she said, and wished she'd not brought up the sensitive matter. She could feel his withdrawal from her. It might be for the best, she thought. There simply was no future in store for her with a highwayman. The realization put a leaden weight of sadness on her chest.

"I don't always load the pistols," he said in a cool detached voice. In silence, he set to work on another turnip, and half an hour later, they had all been peeled.

Serena dried her hands and picked up the bundle of artist materials.

"Where are you going?" he asked.

"I thought Birdie Jones might enjoy a painting lesson," she said, and left the kitchen after waving to Mavis.

She hurried up the stairs to the sick ward. Birdie was awake, sitting up in bed. She brightened as she recognized Serena.

" 'Tis the leddy," she said in a breathy voice, and coughed. "Miss Serena."

Serena laughed. Birdie's face held a pale frailness that tugged at her heart. Every blue vein in her forehead and on her eyelids could be seen through the thin skin. "How are you today? You look much better."

"I coughed all night, miss." Her head tilted upward on the thin stem of her neck. She gave Serena a long inquisitive glance. "I'll be dyin' soon; I know I will. Do ye think God will make me into an angel?"

Tears filled Serena's eyes as she looked into the earnest face of the child. She sensed there might not be much time left for this little girl; but that Birdie would know, and so readily accept the inevitable—that was more than she could bear.

"I'm sure he would, *if* you would die, which you won't. You'll be well soon."

"No, I won't." She changed the topic. "The nurses are ever so kind t' me, an' I can eat as much puddin' as I want. I've niver seen so much food in me life. 'Tis 'eavenlike. D'ye think God serves meat on golden plates, miss?" Birdie clutched Serena's hand. "Do say 'e does."

Serena caressed the feverish dry skin of the bony hand. "You won't need to eat in Heaven, methinks. Angels drink Heavenly nectar, and from what I hear, it tastes better than lemonade on a hot day."

Birdie beamed with pleasure. "I saw an angel once by my bed, an' she looked that 'appy. 'Twus me mum."

The child's honesty almost made Serena believe in smiling angels. She pulled the artist materials closer to the girl. "I thought you might enjoy painting with me. I wish to see what your angel looked like."

She propped the pillow behind Birdie's back to support the frail body. Her heart cried at the pitiful sight of the little girl, but an aura of contentment surrounded the child.

Part of Nick's gift had been thick parchment paper and coal sticks. She put one into Birdie's grip and the girl formed, with unaccustomed fingers, squiggles on the paper in her lap. Her large eyes expressed pleasure. "I've niver done this afore."

"Did she have wings?" Serena took another piece of coal and sketched an angel in flowing robes and huge wings from her memory of church paintings.

"Aye . . . white like the swans in th' park." The tip of Birdie's tongue rode across her upper lip as if it would help to steady her hand. "Me mum 'ad blond curly 'air they say."

Serena touched the child's limp blond curls. They were as soft as silk. "Yours is the color of gold, Birdie."

"Me father 'ad black 'air. 'E wus killed, but I know 'e wus ever a good man."

Serena's heart brimmed over with sadness, but at the same time, she felt blessed to witness Birdie's firm belief in goodness. Despite the fact that she was a child of the rookeries, she had kept the unsullied views of childhood. Just watching Birdie was like touching something that could not be explained.

Serena wondered when she, herself, had lost her childhood faith in goodness and begun to only see the dark side of existence. Impressions of family strife and bitterness had slowly permeated her views and changed her life.

Steps sounded on the wooden floor, and Serena looked up and found Nick at the end of the bed. As always, her heart made a somersault as she watched him. "How is my favorite patient?" he asked and delved into his pocket for a cone-shaped twist of paper that held sugarplums. He extracted one and gave it to Birdie, who chirped in delight.

"Thankee, Mr. Nick. I'm paintin' an angel. Miss Serena 'as niver seen 'un, she says."

Nick stood close to Serena to get a better view of the picture. "Maybe not, but she's seen a lot of devils," he murmured for Serena's ears alone. He raised his voice. "I didn't know you could draw so well, Birdie."

The child giggled in gratitude, and Serena smiled at Nick for his kindness. Birdie's angel was no more than a series of disconnected lines and swirls, but still an honest effort.

Serena could not pull her gaze from his. Love simmered, a

hot trembling current between them in this moment of perfect stillness.

"Do ye think angels can whistle, Mr. Nick?"

"Mayhap," Nick said and rubbed his chin. His lips twitched with mirth. "Why not. Angels can do anything they want."

"When I be an angel, I'll eat a 'undred sugarplums every day."

"Do you know how many that is?" Nick asked, cupping the child's chin and tapping her nose.

She shook her head so that the blond curls bounced.

"So many they won't have room in your stomach all at once."

Birdie patted her scrawny middle. "In 'Eaven, the stummicks are bottomless—like Fleet Ditch."

Nick laughed and wrinkled his nose in distaste. "Fleet Ditch should not be mentioned in the same sentence as Heaven. That sewer is the entrance to Hell, Birdie."

"I know," said the child. "Mavis says her neighbor, Mr. Dobbins, fell into it when 'e wus bosky and disappeared, niver ter be seen agin. She said Dobbins' be offerin' the Devil a bottle o' gin." Birdie lay back against the pillow, her cheeks red with fever. "I'm feelin' poorly. Want t' sleep now." She coughed weakly and turned her back to her company.

Serena's breath caught in her throat as she stroked the downy head until the girl fell into a fitful sleep. She got up quietly from her perch on the mattress and collected the artist materials.

Nick followed her along the passage. She wiped her eyes discreetly. "She told me she's dying," Serena whispered.

"She has pneumonia. There's no cure, alas, except for rest and a strong physique. That, Birdie has not, and she has no family to stand by her side.

"She speaks of death as a journey of adventure. I wish I could die with such an unsullied outlook."

Nick slung his arm over her shoulders protectively. "You have lived longer, and you had a disturbing childhood. Your memories are bound to be sullied."

"No worse than hers. After all, she grew up among the

poorest of poor. Birdie expects *nothing*. I want so much from life before I die."

Nick halted her between two empty alcoves. "What exactly do you expect from life, Serena?"

"Why, to be happy, of course," she said without hesitation.

"Does that happiness include me?" His earnest gaze bored into her until she had to look away.

"Not as long as you continue your criminal activities. Anyhow, happiness will not find me until the man who murdered my father is brought to the gallows." Her gaze was irresistibly drawn to Nick's. "Only snatches of happiness," she added as she recalled their lovemaking.

"I wish you would let me help you," he said, and pushed back an errant curl from her face. "I wish you would let me love you—forever."

"You are a remarkably sanguine man. I have said no, and I won't change my mind, even though I admit to having strong feelings for you."

"To create an orphanage in Hell's Kitchen, you have to possess a large amount of confidence and gall," he said. "At least I don't live a wasted and useless life like my brother, the baronet." He took her arm and turned her around so that she was forced to look down the passage. "Come, let's speak with Rafe. He looks like a wagonload of bricks just fell on him."

Serena did notice the dark rings around Rafael's eyes and his expression of hopelessness. Her heart overflowed with pity. "He's sitting with the little blonde girl."

"His daughter."

"Has he discovered how she came to be here?"

Nick shook his head. "Not that I know."

Rafe looked up from where he was sitting holding one small hand in his. The child lay like a gray shadow against the white linen.

"Is she any better?" Nick asked, and sat down beside Rafe. He clamped his hand in a comforting gesture on the slumped shoulder of the other man.

"The girl's dead," Rafe said in a savage whisper. "She died half an hour ago."

Feeling the blood draining from her head, Serena sat down on the hard chair by the bed. "Isn't there something we can do? Where is her mother?"

Rafe looked at her with dark eyes filled with despair. A mixture of ferocity and bewilderment poured from him, and Serena feared he would bellow with pain and frighten the children. "She's dead, damn it!" he snarled. "There's nothing anyone can do—least of all her mother."

"Where *is* the mother? Why isn't she here?"

Rafe's face twisted in a gargoyle grimace. "She left the child here so that she could go off to the Continent with her lover. All I know is that a nurse who once worked for my family said she'd recognized my fiancée when she brought the child here. She recognized me, too." He dragged his hand over his face, and Serena noticed the wet silver trail on his cheek. "I don't remember a damn thing! If I did, I would kill the person responsible for starving my child and keeping her locked in an attic since she was born."

Serena glanced at Nick in surprise. Nick shrugged as if saying he was at a loss. "You don't know where you live, Rafe? The nurse couldn't tell you?"

His voice was hoarse with tears. "She says I'm the oldest son of the Marquess of Rowan, which makes me an earl . . . and this waif, Lady Bridget—now the deceased Lady Bridget. But according to the nurse, I died in the war and Bridget was locked up in the attic with her nurse." He clutched his head in a gesture of utter anguish. "If the marquess sent Bridget here, I shall kill him. I swear I will."

"I don't blame you for feeling that way," Serena said, "but you need to discover more about your past before you act."

Rafe massaged his neck with both hands. "If the news is more of this kind—" He gestured toward the dead child. "— I'd rather not have any more."

"Understandably," Nick said. "But you won't know for sure until you investigate."

"It was a mistake to return to England," Rafe said in a choked voice. "It would have been easier to start my life over in Flanders."

"Yes, but when is life ever easy?" Nick pulled the other man away from the corpse. "One step at a time."

He could have spoken straight to her, Serena thought, as she realized her life had no future, only "one step at a time." In many ways, the thought comforted her.

Chapter 15

"Isn't there something we can do for Rafe to help him?" Serena asked as they left the bereaved man beside the crude coffin in the enclosed yard behind the orphanage. "I mean, after the funeral."

"I offered to help him find out the truth about his past, but he says he doesn't know what to do next. He isn't sure if he ever wants to go back to his family." Nick sighed. "I'm not sure I would, if they had starved my child to death."

"I fear he will seek revenge."

Nick took her arm as they stepped into the street. "I'm rather certain he will, but he's bound to hang if he kills his sire." Nick gave her a keen look. "You should know all about the desire for revenge, Serena. Isn't that your first wish in the morning when you wake up?"

"Mayhap," she said, and averted her face. Memories of her father's death flashed through her mind. "Even though my father was a cruel man, he did not deserve to be murdered."

Nick hailed a hackney cab outside Bethlem Hospital. "I'd like to cheer you up, my darling." With a theatrical bow, he assisted her into the dilapidated coach.

Filled with curiosity, she entered. "Where are we going?"

"To a modiste I know. She shall fashion a costume for you to wear at a masked ball next week. You shall come with me and mingle with your peers in London. 'Tis a pity they don't know you are in town, but you will attend incognita as my mysterious friend."

A thrill of anticipation went through Serena at the thought of attending a merry gathering. It had been a long time since she had danced and laughed.

A week later, Nick watched Serena come downstairs, dressed and ready for the ball. A warm feeling rushed through him, and his breath grew erratic. Surely he had never seen a lovelier woman or a woman who could touch his soul like this—making him weak and filled with longing to close his arms around her and move aside the white silk veil and kiss her slender neck. Again and again.

She wore a wide bliaud in the fashion of the Middle Ages, a full-length tunic of deep blue silk that complimented her slanted dark eyes and was held together at her waist with a gilded metal mesh girdle. The trumpet-shaped sleeve billowed around her slender arm as she lifted her hand in a greeting. A brass crown that reminded him of queens from a distant time held the filmy veil in place by circling her forehead.

"Forsooth, a regal queen comes to mind," he said, and kissed her hand gallantly even though he wanted to sweep her up and smother her with kisses.

"I don't have enough height to be regal," she said, and dazzled him with a coquettish smile.

His heart seemed to skip a beat. He helped her put on the white silk half mask, tying the cords at the back of her head under the veil. Her hair, hanging loose, moved over his hands like liquid satin. He closed his eyes and inhaled her fragrance, an exotic blend that was purely her.

"You look rather dashing yourself when dressed as a Cavalier.'' She closed her velvet cloak at the neck and gave him a seductive smile.

He twirled his wide-brimmed plumed hat in an extravagant arc before settling it atop his long curly wig that had been fashionable at King Charles II's court. Lace at his wrists fluttering, he held his hand to his heart. His eyes glowed wickedly. He gave her an elegant leg, then offered his arm.

"Shall we depart, lady of the silver smile? Our gold chariot awaits us," he said with an affected lisp.

Serena laughed in delight, and Nick's heart swelled with warmth. His plan to take her along to the masked ball had been a stroke of genius. For one night, she could forget her problems and enjoy herself as if the nightmares or her father's death had never occurred.

She leaned back against the squabs of the best Leverton coach, which Nick had appropriated for the occasion. Ethan would escort Delicia and Miss Vine. Nick doubted the prudence of that arrangement since he didn't trust Ethan with Miss Vine, but he wasn't going to lose his chance at an evening of enchantment with Serena.

By letting her move about as she pleased, he constantly feared he would lose her. He still harbored a fear that she would not hesitate to denounce him should the opportunity occur, but he chanced that she would not run to the authorities and divulge his hiding place in London.

She hadn't, not yet, perhaps never. Clearly he had made a deep emotional impression on her, and the thought made his blood sing. She had somehow crept into his heart, and he knew she would stay there for a long time. He gripped her hand, removed the glove, and caressed the soft inside of her wrist in a slow circular movement.

"Nick—"

"I can't keep my hands to myself, alas. You have bewitched me in the deepest way."

"Nick, I think we should not dally in such a wanton manner in public." She gently withdrew her hand.

"I despair," he said, slapping his gloves against his thigh.

"For a week now, you have deprived me of glorious loving, and I am a starving man." He caught her hand anew, and she did not resist him.

Serena chuckled ruefully. "Somehow you managed quite well before you captured me. I'm certain you can manage in the future." She flapped her vellum fan—a gift from him— agitatedly, as if the discussion touched her more than she wanted to admit.

"Fie! How can you speak so cruelly, my fair? Everything has changed, the whole course of my life has changed. I have found the true lady of my heart."

"You cannot have forgotten Marguerite so quickly."

"Your star outshines hers on my personal horizon," Nick said simply, caressing her fingers. "I'm sure my friend Charles would argue the point, but then he's truly besotted with Marguerite. Would kiss the ground upon which she walks."

He sighed. "Anyone could see that they belong together. I knew that then, and I know it now." He turned toward Serena, overcome with an urgency to speak in earnest. "You have shown me that love can bridge any sort of gap. I don't even know your last name, but I don't feel the need to know it. I care not whence you come, or about your past. I care only for *you*. For today, and for tomorrow. 'Tis very important to me that you stay in my tomorrows. Life without your presence would be a world without the sun rising every morning, a sphere of darkness."

Her fan flapped rapidly, sending puffs of her scent across his face. He could barely contain himself from gripping her and kissing her until she lay limp in his arms.

"I am surprised you have thoughts about tomorrow, Nick. You live each day as it comes, methinks. I cannot risk to tie myself to you. If a child would come out of our union, I would truly despair as I have no home to give it."

"You would have one if you but married me."

"Nick, I do not want to discuss marriage with you, and I do not want to carry your child."

"My seed might already be sprouting in your womb," he

said, and felt a stir of tenderness, of wonder, wonder he hadn't felt for a long time.

She snapped her fan closed. "There's no use discussing this further. We might as well face the hard truth. I have quite made up my mind. Our liaison shall go no further, and the day is coming when I will leave you behind."

"How cruel, how cold! Has our time together meant so little to you?"

"No, it has touched me a great deal—more than I can say; but I will not permit myself to be attached permanently to a highwayman. If you halt your criminal activities and show that you can support a family by honest means, we might speak of this again."

He searched her face, reading the sincerity in her eyes. The rash words evidently pained her, but she could not permit her tenderness, her growing love for him to overcome her, not until she felt they had a future together. He envied her control, when all he wanted was to keep her beside him forever.

He stiffened, piqued that she would judge him after the pinnacles of love they had shared. "You know I cannot stop until the orphanage is secured. I need only a few more thousand to pay off the mortgage, and pay it I shall!"

She said nothing, and he disliked being put in a position where he had to choose. Anger rolled through him, a quick fury that burned every emotion in its wake and left him drained and cold. If she could act contained and indifferent, so could he. He dropped her hand, closing himself into a shell. But longing for her still burned in his blood, damn it all.

The iron gates of Lord Hessler's mansion along the Strand loomed ahead, flambeaux on each side lighting the way. The main building had three stories topped with a cupola and two short wings projecting forward as if to embrace the visitors; but there was nothing welcoming about the grinning stone gargoyles in the niches set between the windows, which blazed with candlelight.

The wide steps held a cluster of guests in costume: Caesar in a white toga and a laurel wreath, Queen Elizabeth in a farthingale and curly red wig, a gypsy and his lady, a group in silk dominoes and masks. Some guests wore garb reminiscent of the Middle Ages with steeple headdresses and hats with dangling liripipes. A court jester jingled a cluster of bells, his face painted half white, half black.

Still seething with wounded pride, Nick felt isolated in the sounds of animated chatter and carefree laughter. With Serena on his arm, he entered the glittering mansion. To maintain the anonymity of the guests, there was no major domo to announce their identities. The masks would be taken off at midnight.

"It is splendid," Serena whispered, her eyes glittering with curiosity behind the mask.

She had never seen such opulence. Her gaze traveled over the gilt moldings, the wall panels of watered silk, the pastoral scenes painted in the ceiling, the chandeliers reflecting the light of the plentiful candles. "I have never before entered such a magnificent palace."

"Surely you must have visited estates in the country that equaled this in elegance."

"No . . . we live on a smaller scale from where I come. This is the height of splendor."

"Since you've been very closemouthed about your actual address, I have no way of comparing the grandeur," he said bitingly.

She spread her fan and started fanning herself nervously. Her fingers tightened around his arm. "Do not chide me, Nick."

"Your lack of trust in me is an insult, Serena. As I said before, I don't really need to know—not right now, anyway; but why would it hurt to divulge your last name and the address of your family seat?"

"With your hot temper, you might rush off and challenge my uncle if you knew his name. I do not wish your temper to interfere with my future. Uncle shall pay in due time, but I won't ruin my chances at apprehending him with some evidence that will declare his guilt."

Nick faced her, his face dark with wrath. "You think *I* would do anything to ruin your chances? Your lack of faith astounds me, Serena. I would follow the code of honor, demand satisfaction, and if he didn't die of the wounds, I would deliver him to the law. But he won't hang unless we manage to find an impartial witness. You don't have a witness, so the murderer will go free if I don't run him through with my sword.''

Misery filling her, she removed her hand from his arm. "I do not want to talk about this any longer, Nick. I already have another plan. I have decided to contact a powerful friend of my father. He will help me. He might even be able to arrange an audience with King George."

Nick laughed incredulously, and she wanted to sew his lips together. "You actually believe you'll get to plead your case with His Majesty?"

"I don't know, but 'tis worth a try. He, if anyone, can bring my uncle to justice."

"Your naiveté is a source of constant wonder, Serena, but it also has a special allure in this city where innocence is a rare gem indeed."

"Your compliment sounds like an insult," she said, feeling a cold shiver inside. Something had changed between them since they'd arrived, but she couldn't put her finger on it. The attraction flowed as strongly between them as before, but they had reached a crossroads or a wall that had to be scaled. On the other side waited a different world. The thought made her uneasy. He was giving her that keen stare that peeled away all her defenses.

"I am thirsty," she said to break the tension.

"Come, let us find a glass of wine. And we'd better pay our respects to our hosts, *if* we manage to recognize them."

Serena glanced at the milling guests and laughed with sudden delight. "I have stepped into the pages of the history books which I so despised as a child."

Nick's lips turned upward in a faint smile. "A masked ball gives you some freedom of movement, license to flirt with a stranger."

"I do not make a habit of flirting," she said, and smiled at him, her blood heating.

"Only with me."

She tilted her head to her side as that bittersweet ache of love rose in her heart. "Only with you."

"Let's drink champagne, Serena; then I want to dance with you." He guided her to a chair and went in search of wine.

Nick sought his sister in the crowd. Delicia had said she would attend as a Spanish noblewoman wearing a black lace mantilla and matching fan. He spotted her by the door to the ballroom and decided her companion in a red domino must be Callie Vine.

Ethan stood right behind them, dressed as a harlequin in a suit of triangular patches in bright colors, a neck ruff, a soft-brimmed hat, and a half mask. Nick would have recognized that rouged and supercilious mouth anywhere.

A shiver of unease traveled up his back. Carrying two glasses of champagne, he joined them. He gave the ladies a gallant bow and offered them the glasses of wine. "I see you have arrived, and looking both lovely and secretive."

Delicia flapped her fan languidly. "I would not miss this ball for anything. I will seek my secret admirer."

"Secret admirer, Delicia? You have not confided in me," Nick said, and glanced around the room as if to see if some gentleman was lurking to pounce on Delicia as soon as her escort's back was turned.

She slapped his arm playfully. "No need to look so worried, Nick. I was only jesting. But I would not be averse to a gentle flirtation."

Nick's gaze drifted to Ethan, who had bent over Miss Vine's shoulder and whispered something in her ear. Miss Vine laughed softly, and Nick sensed her excitement. What had Ethan said to induce such an intimate laugh? He felt an urge to separate his devious stepbrother from the young innocent lady, but before he could act, Delicia spoke.

"I'm disappointed in you, Nick. You don't visit us in Berkley Square, and you don't take me out driving or riding. What holds greater interest than riding with me in the park, pray tell?'' She gave him a penetrating glance, and Nick felt heat rush to his cheeks. ''Hmm, methinks you have met a lady.''

''Mayhap, sister dear, but I fear there is no solid base on which to build the relationship.'' He lowered his voice. ''But you're right, I have met a lady who has captured my entire attention, and I'm not ashamed to confess it.''

''I wish to meet her,'' Delicia said excitedly.

''You shall, but not today. When I bring her home as my intended bride, you shall meet her. I had hoped to make her my wife in short order, but she has other plans, alas.''

''She must possess a muddled perception if she cannot see your fine qualities.''

She knows something about me that you don't, he thought. *The identity of the Midnight Bandit.* ''She is not befuddled, but she trusts me not.''

Delicia pursed her lips. ''Hmm, I can't say I understand. You are a solid rock of dependability, Nick. I have always trusted you and leaned on you, and so did Father.''

''A loving relationship is different from that of a family, Delicia, as you're bound to discover in due course. When you find the gentleman of your heart.'' He kissed her cheek. ''Enjoy your evening, and don't let Ethan patronize Miss Vine.''

''Callie is quite taken with Ethan, you know. My brother would be lucky if he could attach her affection. He could not hope to find a kinder wife.''

Her words chilled Nick. He lowered his voice. ''I doubt that Ethan has any plans of matrimony in the near future. I urge you to remember that! Please do not encourage Miss Vine to accept his advances.''

Delicia glanced at him, her eyes narrowed with suspicion in the slits of her mask. ''You do not wish Ethan to find a good wife? Why?''

''I wish him all the best, but I doubt he's seeking a wife at the present time. You should hint that to Miss Vine, or I will do it. You don't want her to suffer with a broken heart, do you?''

"No." Uneasy silence hovered. "You sound quite serious, brother. What has Ethan said or done to make you believe he's not planning to wed?"

"Nothing that you should worry about tonight, sweeting. Besides, I don't think Miss Vine is his type. You have to admit he's always been drawn to more . . . mature ladies." *And women of loose morals,* Nick added silently. He wished Delicia could see the true character of her older brother.

Delicia eyed Ethan speculatively. "I shall endeavor to keep an eye on Callie, but she's so happy; she's enjoying herself hugely in London. I would appreciate having her as my sister. Surely, she would make Ethan a splendid wife. He has been so attentive. The perfect host."

Nick gripped her arm. "Do as I say. One day you will understand why I'm warning you. Not today, but soon you will find out the whole truth. I shall tell it to you myself if Ethan doesn't."

Delicia turned her trusting gaze on him, and Nick felt a stab of guilt that she should have to suffer the humiliation of her brother's excesses. But he simply could not carry Ethan any longer financially or hide his vices.

"I will leave you now, Delicia, but remember what I said." She squeezed his arm fondly. "I will."

As the hours flew by, Serena enjoyed herself royally. She danced the minuet and the quadrille; she drank wine and—contrary to what she'd told Nick—flirted shamelessly with kings and knights without knowing who hid behind the masks.

The wine was rising to her head, and she decided she could use a glass of lemonade to slake her thirst. A cool breeze from an open window fanned her cheeks.

"La!" she cried in surprise as an arm enclosed her shoulders. She looked up at Nick's smiling eyes. "Nick, you're no longer angry with me." Her heartbeat pounded harder, and that honeyed attraction she always felt in his company had returned with renewed force. Their earlier tension had completely evaporated. Tenderness lay like cotton around her heart. He'd said once that love was painful. He was right; it lodged a bittersweet ache in her chest, but she would not permit herself to *feel* too much.

"I wish I could stay angry with you, but I've been fighting a losing battle while watching your delight. Will you take a walk with me in the portrait gallery? We shall admire the dour ancestors of Lord Hessler, or make derogatory remarks about his siblings," he added from the side of his mouth.

"That would be uncouth," she said, but gladly linked her arm to his. Carrying glasses of cool lemonade, they stepped up the long curving staircase. The dome above was topped with glass, and she could see the twinkling stars against the crystal black sky. "What a grand house," she said as they walked the red-carpeted length of that gallery that held tiers upon tiers of portraits, even paintings of horses and dogs. Candles in sconces at intervals on the walls filled the area with a muted golden light.

"That Roundhead looks like he just swallowed a frog," Nick said with a chuckle as they stopped before an imposing portrait against a dusty brown background.

Serena laughed. "And that Elizabethan lady had her lips stitched together to get that perfectly pinched look."

"You are a cruel woman, Serena," Nick said with a chuckle.

"The pleated ruff seems to chafe terribly against her chin."

"I'm glad those are out of fashion nowadays," Nick said. "It would be very difficult to kiss a lady with that stiff collar sticking out several inches." He turned to her. "I much rather prefer the style of the Middle Ages. At least a man could easily kiss his beloved." He leaned toward her, and Serena closed her eyes in anticipation.

His mouth found hers, his tongue invading and courting hers in a silky dance of seduction.

"Begad," he groaned against her mouth, his grip tightening convulsively around her shoulders.

Her hands moved over the hard muscles of his back. She wished he would discard the velvet coat and the stiffly embroidered waistcoat so that she could feel the warmth of his skin against hers.

He pushed aside the veil and buried his hand in her hair. Her brass crown tilted over one eye, and she laughed as his kisses tickled her skin along the jaw and the neck.

He righted her crown and took her hand. "Come, there are some private alcoves further down the passage. They are meant for private conversations, but everyone knows what they are truly for."

"For?" Serena asked in a teasing voice.

"For trysts of a romantic nature," he whispered in her ear, and pulled her behind a heavy red curtain.

"You cannot mean it," she said, and looked around the area swathed in velvet darkness. The tall latticed windows above let in a faint light. "This is not an alcove for trysts, 'tis only a window embrasure."

"We can make it into whatever we want," he murmured, sitting down on the long cushioned seat. He pulled her onto his lap.

Feeling giddy with love—somewhat laced with wine fumes, she laughed and wound her arms around him.

"Are you enjoying your evening of entertainment?" he asked, nuzzling her neck with his nose and exploring with his lips.

"Oh yes, very much. I am glad my father had the wits to hire a dancing master to teach me the various figures."

"Mayhap he expected to bring you out in society and see you married to some pimply fop with a lisp and a lantern jaw." He cupped her neck, kissed both cheeks, and sucked on one of her earlobes.

In one dizzying moment she realized how deeply she'd come to love him. She had never dreamed of meeting someone like him. As he'd said, her father would have chosen someone of whom he approved. Her feelings would never have come into consideration. The forbidden fruit of Nick's love—his grinning, expectant face—made her sad, as she knew she could not go on like this. They could not keep playing with fire or both of them would be burned badly. At that moment she had the insight that she had to make up her mind. She would have to leave tonight, and the thought made her infinitely sadder.

Chapter 16

She loved him.

Now more than ever, but she had not dared to say the words. The words would have bound her to him, like wedding vows. Serena had read the question in his eyes, but she had not given him the words he most wanted to hear. A confirmation of her feelings. She could not let her lips form that confession.

She saw him across the ballroom talking to a lady wearing a Spanish mantilla. Serena would remember his smiling face, the proud figure in the dashing costume of a Cavalier. She would remember his hands, hotly caressing her body into a frenzy of delight. He would always be part of her anywhere she went.

The depth of feeling they had shared was beyond comprehension. Mayhap if she threw caution to the winds and lived for each moment, she might find that theirs was a relationship made in Heaven. But she was afraid of the encroaching tarnish that mundane life brought, or even bitterness if their love did not prove lasting. And as she had said to him, if theirs were true love, she would die if anything happened to him.

She glanced toward the ballroom door. It stood wide open

and she could glimpse the front entrance at the end of the stairs. No one was guarding it to prevent her from leaving. She could do as she pleased.

Without further thought, she ran quickly through the door and downstairs. The last thing she'd seen was Nick's kind smile upon the lady in the mantilla.

The lackey at the door went in search of her cloak while she hid behind a pedestal that held a large flower arrangement.

The cold air enveloped her outside, and the breeze whipped her cloak as if trying to force her to return inside.

No. Her spirits lifted at the thought of freedom. She was grateful to Nick. She had grown stronger in his love, in his house, and now she felt she could deal with the difficulties ahead. One day she would have to confront Luther about her father's death, and this was her first step in the direction of dealing with her past.

She walked quickly through the tall iron gates and headed west on the Strand. Haymarket lay rather close to Covent Garden, according to Nurse Hopkins, and they had crossed the square to reach Lord Hessler's house.

A carriage rattled past her at a fast clip, and only the occasional torch or oil lamp on a post lit the dark street. There had been no lamps to light the way in the poorer sections; and here, in the more fashionable part of town, she still felt uneasy walking alone. Fear skittered up her spine, and she shivered.

Hurrying along, she threw glances into the dark corners of doorways and courtyards. A cat slunk along the wall, startling her, and every shadow concealed something—at least in her imagination.

She started running and almost collided with a night watchman at the street corner.

"Aw, miss, watch where yer walkin'! Ye stepped plumb on me aching bunion." He shook his wooden staff at her and lit her face by holding up his lantern.

"I'm sorry," she said, "but, *please,* can you point me in the direction of Haymarket?"

"Is 'at where yer runnin'?" He peered closely at her with shrewd eyes.

Serena flinched at the word *running*. "I'm seeking employment with a relative in Haymarket. Hopkins' Milliner Shop."

He nodded his head thoughtfully. "Aye? I know 't. Go up this street, then right at the first crossroads, left—aw, I don't know 'xactly. Let me show ye."

Ten minutes later, Serena waited tensely as the watchman pounded on the door next to the shop. A window opened abovestairs, and a head wearing an enormous mobcap leaned outside. "What's all the ruckus about? Is the street on fire, watchman?"

"No, 'tain't. A young lady t'see ye, Miss Hopkins."

Serena glanced up at the old woman who must be Nurse Hopkins' sister. "I'm Serena Hilliard."

"Well! You're alive then. Thank Heavens for that!" The window slammed shut, and heavy steps sounded on the stairs inside.

The watchman saluted Serena and went on his way, lantern swinging.

Serena held her breath as the door opened and she came face to face with her nurse's younger sister Molly. The older woman's gaze swept over Serena's cloak and stopped at her head. Serena recalled the metal crown. She touched it and blushed. "I'm coming directly from a masked ball."

"You'd better come in. Not safe on the streets at night." Carrying a lighted candle, she led the way into a shadowy hallway that smelled of cabbage and old furniture. Her nightgown trailed on the floor under the plain wool wrap. Serena could not see the color of her hair under the mobcap.

"Miss Hopkins, did my coachman come to see you?"

"That he did, and I've been worried sick about you." She clasped her hands to her bosom as if to still her agitation. "My sister had the vicar write three letters, wanting to know your whereabouts."

"I wonder what Uncle Luther told the people at home—about Father's death, I mean."

Molly Hopkins gave her a hard glance. "What do you mean? According to my sister, your father was attacked by a vagrant. That is what the local lawmen are saying."

Serena gave a mirthless laugh. "I'm not surprised to hear that. Well, Nurse Hopkins would not write to you about my secret, but you might as well know the truth. My father was murdered, and I was the only person who saw Luther Hilliard stabbing him to death."

"Lawks! I am shocked. You are sure about this?"

Serena nodded. "I did not dream the events. Luther saw me, and he's looking for me. Has he been here?"

Molly nodded. "A gent by that name asked for you last week. Big and burly with heavy jowls and small shrewd eyes. Dark bristly hair, elegant clothes."

"Yes, that's him." Fear coursed through Serena as she thought of the narrowly missed danger. "What if he comes back?"

Molly's shoulders squared, and her face took on a militant scowl. "I shall tell him that I haven't seen you, but I doubt he'll return. You shall stay concealed here for a time." She held out her hand for Serena's cloak. "You look like you could use some food. Too slim and pale for health."

Serena relaxed, feeling exhausted. "You're most kind. Nurse Hopkins was right. She said you would help me."

"You can work in my shop for your keep while we see to bringing your uncle to a court of law. If you have any artistic skills, I could use help with the ladles' fans. So many orders, and I am always behind."

She beckoned to Serena, who followed. They walked down some steps and into the dark kitchen where a fire had been banked in the grate. Molly lit more candles and went to the larder, muttering.

While Serena warmed herself in front of the fire, Molly returned with a platter of cold meat, a wedge of cheese, and bread. She held a tankard of ale in one hand.

"It isn't much, but should be enough to see you through the night. 'Twill soon be dawn, the time when I usually rise."

"I didn't realize it was this late. I . . . I was at a gathering," Serena said reluctantly. She instantly regretted bringing it up as Molly gave her a calculating stare. How could she give an honest answer to Molly's questions?

"If you have been in London all this time, I am surprised that you did not come here earlier," Molly said, her voice hinting that she wanted to know more. At least she was too polite to ask directly.

"I was captured by a . . . criminal and kept prisoner," Serena explained, holding back some of the truth.

Molly's eyebrows rose. "Criminal? Why, you should report him to the law! What's his name?"

"He did not harm me in any way. In fact, I feel he gave me strength to face the difficulties ahead." She steeled her voice. "I have no intention of reporting him to the law, Miss Hopkins."

Molly pursed her lips in disapproval, but she only said, "I see."

Serena studied her nurse's sister, finding the sturdy square form and strong-jawed face reassuring. *Capable* was a word that came to mind when she watched Molly Hopkins move, and *self-assured*. No air of servitude there. Not that Nurse Hopkins had ever shown an obsequious trait, even though she'd been a servant in a grand household. They were proud sisters.

The Hopkins family was of superior merchant stock, Londoners for generations, and it was obvious that Miss Hopkins managed a prospering business. Just by the set of her jaw, Serena could tell that Miss Hopkins would succeed at any enterprise she embarked upon.

Serena's old nurse had sought employment in the countryside when her young man broke her heart and wed another woman. So long ago, long before Serena was born. Nurse Hopkins had raised many children during her lifetime, but none of her own.

"I am grateful you would take me in, Miss Hopkins." Serena meant every word, feeling as if she'd found a safe harbor at last. "So very grateful."

Molly urged her to eat, then went off with the promise of returning in a minute. She did, carrying a metal box.

Serena put aside the bread and cheese and chewed quickly to empty her mouth. "That is my box!" she said after washing down the food with ale.

"That it is. I doubt a penny has been extracted. At least you could count on your coachman, an honest fellow by any means."

"Is he here?" Serena sought the key which she'd started to carry on a string under her shift.

Molly shook her head. "No. He said he would go visit a sister who serves at a grand house in Surrey, but I'm sure he's back by now. I put your nags in the livery stables. Didn't have room for them in mine. You'll probably find the coachman in the hostelry nearby. He said he would stay there until you arrived."

"I knew he would not abandon me. Thank you for arranging lodging for my horses." Serena opened the lid and found the heap of sovereigns and smaller coins her father had kept in the box. "I will be able to reimburse you for the cost of their keep." She clasped the older woman's hand spontaneously. "Thank you again. You have lifted a load off my shoulders."

"Don't mention it," Molly said gruffly. She fluttered her eyelids as if unaccustomed to any show of emotion. "Least I could do for one my sister's beloved charges." She sat down on the other side of the table and pushed the food toward Serena. "Eat your fill, and then I want to hear everything about Alice."

"Alice—or Nurse Hopkins—the name by which I always call her, was spry when I left Somerset. Her blindness is progressing, but that won't stop her from gardening and helping the vicar with his work for the poor." Serena sighed and thought about the orphanage. "I wish I had taken some more interest in that kind of work while at home. I was bored and lonely," she said, more to herself than to her company. "Work might have made me less bitter, but I never thought of it. It isn't healthy to dwell on past horrors."

"Work I have aplenty here. You can start tomorrow. When you've finished eating, I shall show you to your bedroom.

Seeing as you are a lady, you shall have the one next to mine. Otherwise you would sleep in the attic with the wenches."

Serena smiled. "That would do, you know. Without your generous help, I would not last long in London."

The next morning, Serena slept late. No one awakened her, and she felt filled with energy and relief. Her only regret was leaving Nick without saying good-bye, but he would have argued endlessly, perhaps even stopped her from leaving. She might write him a note later, but she had no idea on which street his refuge was located, only that it was close to Black Friars Bridge.

She dressed in a pale gray serge gown that Miss Hopkins had offered her. It was too large and too long, but anything was better than the bliaud. Serena did not want to be the target for crude jests if she were to work in the shop wearing the costume from the night before. She would have to find a seamstress to sew some new gowns for her.

Downstairs, a maid in a brown homespun dress and a snowy apron and modesty piece crossed over her bosom met her. "Good morning, miss," she said with a curtsy. "When ye've eaten, I'm to take ye next door t' the shop."

Serena ate and sent a note to the hostelry summoning her coachman. Half an hour later, she stepped through the door of the millinery shop. Her first impression was that she'd stepped into a cave of frivolity. Ostrich plumes dyed in all colors nodded in the draft; hats of velvets, silks, and lustrous taffeta; bonnets; straw hats with satin ribbons, and frilled muslin caps filled every wall and stand in the room. Laces and ribbons spilled out of drawers and baskets.

Gilt mirrors and chairs for the customers occupied the corners, and a glittering chandelier in the middle of the plastered ceiling lent an air of gaiety to the room.

Serena had difficulty imagining the stern-faced Miss Hopkins the owner of such a shop of pure frivolity. Mayhap she harbored a romantic heart under the brusque facade.

On a table was a large wooden tray of painted fans. Serena went to look at them as she waited for her benefactress. There were vellum fans, lacquered ivory brisé, silkboard fans, and fans with carved sticks inlaid with mother-of-pearl. Some were made of ebony sticks and chicken skin; and some were feather fans, mounts adorned with jewels. She admired the dainty paintings on the vellum fans, wondering whose clever fingers had fashioned them.

A door slammed and hurried steps sounded behind her. "Aren't they beautiful? The sales of fans are brisk because I have an excellent, if overworked, artist designing them. Did you know that some of the wealthy ladies hire their own artists to decorate their fans? That way they can secure an original design since the printed fans are becoming more and more popular."

"No, I didn't know," Serena said with a smile, "but I am not surprised."

Molly looked at her shrewdly, and a half smile softened her stern face. "My sister wrote that you are a superb artist and that I should put you to work to make my fortune in fans." She pointed toward a door at the back concealed by a gold velvet curtain. "No need to tarry as I don't know how much longer I may keep you."

Filled with curiosity, Serena followed Molly. They entered a large room where seamstresses were sewing at a long table. Scraps of lace littered the surface and the floor, and bits of muslin spilled over the rims of baskets.

"They are sewing caps and fichus. I even have lace-makers upstairs, but the French and Italian laces are the ladies' choice today—and there's a shortage since the war." Molly sighed as if sad that the French had won the war of laces, if not the real war. "Come along, Miss Serena. My fan designer is upstairs."

Serena entered a room under the eaves. Autumn sunshine streamed through the only window onto a wide table. The air held the tree-sap scent of turpentine and the odor of chemicals used in mixing the paints. A young woman with graceful thin limbs and a crown of pale gold curls under a tiny frilled cap was bending over a piece of work on the table. She wore a light blue gown with lace at the elbows and edging the modesty piece crossed over her bosom.

"Andria, this is Miss . . ." Molly threw Serena a cautious glance. "Miss Hillman. You will teach her to paint the vellum fans and how to use your materials. Miss Hillman, meet Andria Saxon. I'll leave you now to get acquainted." Smiling briskly, she left, closing the door behind her.

Serena drew a breath of relief that Miss Hopkins had chosen to keep her real name a secret. Servants might gossip.

Andria gave a warm smile, but Serena sensed a lurking sadness in her light blue eyes. Andria held out a frail hand. "Welcome to the place where ladies' dreams are created," she said.

Serena was charmed by the unusual expression. "Please call me . . . Serena."

"Then, please call me Andria." She brushed her hand over her eyes as if to ward off fatigue. Serena noticed a smudge of gray paint on her chin.

She studied the delicately painted landscapes, a bird in flight, cartouches of cherubs, bouquets of roses, silk ribbon garlands that looked so real she expected to feel the silk under her fingertip as she touched it.

"You are very good," Serena said. "I have never seen such a deft and light touch."

Andria smiled, an expression that held a hint of bitterness. "Yes . . . when there is nothing else to practice but one's artistic skills . . ."

"Mayhap Miss Hopkins demands that you work too hard. Not good for your back and your eyes."

"She is a kind and fair woman. Took me in when I had nowhere to go, and she pays me well."

Serena sensed an underlying story, but it was too early in their friendship to pry further. Each of them had something to hide, she thought, and it was for the best not to delve too deeply into the past.

Serena spoke. "I don't know how long I will stay here, but I could certainly paint the backgrounds with the skills I possess today. You will have to show me the procedure."

Andria stood immediately and said in her cultured subdued voice. "It shall be my pleasure."

Serena thought the morning would have been perfect if she for one moment could forget the looming threat of Luther Hilliard and if her longing for Nick could stop nagging her middle. But the memory of his wicked smile would not fade; she wondered if it ever would.

In the afternoon, a reply to her note arrived from the hostelry landlord.

The man you're seeking is no longer alive. He was attacked and killed in his room. The lawmen suspect he was robbed and strangled as he fought back.

Serena dropped the note and staggered to the nearest chair. Sorrow sank through her entire being. She *knew* that Roy Coachman had not been killed by a common robber. Sir Luther had found him before she had.

Chapter 17

In the saddle, Nick spent a week combing the streets of London. Not riding the magnificent Pegasus with his two white stockings; no, only a commonplace sorrel hunter he used when traveling down to Sussex. Pegasus was too notorious to bring out in the middle of the day, even in London.

Grief and hurt ate away at his heart like acid. Bursts of unrestrained anger at Serena's desertion churned in his stomach at even intervals, and he promised himself that he would strangle her when he found her. Find her he would. There was no question about that.

"Damn her to hell," he swore as he thundered across London Bridge after a sleepless night. He'd spent some time with Lotus Blossom; but he could not bed her or any of the other courtesans, feeling that if he did, he would sully everything beautiful he had experienced with Serena.

He passed the street on the edge of St. Giles where his refuge was located and went to an alehouse frequented by the neighborhood thieves.

The alley was dark and cramped, the odors foul from the rubbish heaps. This was a place where one might expect to be knifed in the back for a silk handkerchief. He didn't carry one in his pocket, and he always kept his wits about him.

He went inside the smoky tavern that smelled of rancid fat and sour ale and filth. The landlord had greasy strands of hair hanging over his face and a chin full of black bristly whiskers. He wore an apron over a soiled white shirt and leather breeches.

The barmaids had the frowzy coarse looks of those that had never seen the outside of St. Giles and rarely spent any time in the sun.

The customers were already deep into their cups even though it was early in the day. Nick grimaced in distaste. There were better ways to spend a morning.

To his surprise, Nick found Rafe at one of the crude tables, a plate of food and a tankard of ale in front of him.

"S'faith, I didn't expect to see you here," Nick said, and sat down on the bench beside his friend, his back to the wall. "Not exactly a congenial place to have a meal."

"I don't feel congenial, Nick. Besides, the ale is good."

A barmaid brought a tankard to Nick and gave him an inviting smile and a wink. He ignored her.

He looked closely at Rafe, noticing the haggard look and the haunted eyes. Rafe wasn't drunk, but not completely steady as he lifted the vessel to his mouth. "Burying your sorrows in ale, eh?"

Rafe wiped his mouth. "Yes . . . I suppose you're right on that score. Foolish of me, but it does dull the edges of my pain."

"The business with the child at the orphanage—"

"—and the fact that someone wanted me dead! I've been thinking about it, Nick, and it makes sense. Someone in my family spread the word that I had died in the war. That same person put the child in the orphanage, probably wishing Bridget would just disappear in the masses of the poor. She would have, except for the fact that the nurse recognized me." Rafe gave him a probing stare. "Do you think she's right? That my father is the Marquess of Rowan?"

"The only way to find out is to ride up to Yorkshire and

confront the old man. There ought to be portraits of you in the house.''

Rafe kneaded his eyes with his thumbs. "I'm afraid of what I will find. Where is my daughter's mother? What happened to her? Were we in love or did we part on hostile terms? Or did I toss her into a haystack to make merry for one night only, an act that created the child?''

"I doubt you would easily toss someone into a haystack and make her with child.''

"You know me the way I am now, but what if I were a reckless blade in the past, a libertine who cared for no one but himself?''

Nick braided his fingers together, clenching them tightly. "That I cannot answer. But if you want, I shall ride with you north, and we shall ferret out the truth of your past.''

Rafe brightened at his words. Nick worried about the hollowed cheeks and the dark rings around his friend's eyes. The problems were wearing Rafe down, and Nick knew that Rafe had truly cared for the dead child. Sometimes a bond formed immediately with another person—as it had between him and Serena.

"That friendly offer might give me the courage I seek,'' Rafe said.

"What happened in the war to take away your memory?''

"They said I was kicked in the head by a dying horse. The surgeon stated it was a miracle I survived. I suppose the horse lacked strength. A swifter kick would have sent me to the other side. It might have been for the best.''

"Dammit, Rafe! I won't hear another word from you. Instead of moping about in this filthy pit, you can help me find Serena.''

"Still no luck with your inquiries?''

"Not a clue.''

Rafe downed the rest of his ale. "Let's speak with the Charlies at the watchhouse on the Strand tonight. They might have seen her.''

As darkness fell, the two men rode along the thoroughfare, to the watchhouse closest to Lord Hessler's mansion. "She might have walked this way," Rafe said and slid out of the saddle by the open door.

Light spilled from the building and *Charlies,* watchmen carrying lanterns, stout sticks, and a rattle that would summon reinforcement, were filing out of the interior and heading west.

Nick halted one of them, a squat muscular fellow with suspicious eyes under the brim of his three-cornered hat.

"I'm looking for a lady who might have come this way last week. She would be easy to remember as she wore a veil and crown reminiscent of a queen of the Middle Ages. She departed from a ball at Lord Hessler's without leaving a message."

The watchman looked him up and down, and Nick longed to shake the doubting man. Evidently Nick's fine cloak and hat convinced the Charlie he was telling the truth.

"Ye mean Lord Hessler's costume ball?"

"Yes, precisely."

The watchman waved his arm and shouted. "Come back, jacks. We've an inquiry 'ere, 'bout a missin' mort."

Some of the Charlies straggled back, their homespun brown cloaks flapping like wings in the cold breeze off the river.

Nick repeated his description of Serena. "Has anyone seen her?"

One of the watchmen stepped forward and shone his lantern into Nick's face. "Aye, 'tis possible. A mort fittin' that description stepped on me bunion somethin' fierce. Could barely walk all night after that."

Nick longed to shake the placid man's hand. His heartbeat pumped with excitement.

"I took 'er where she wanted to go. To 'Aymarket, and Miss Hopkins' millinery shop. Th' ole girl took 'er in. That's all I know."

A spurt of hope and happiness rushed through Nick. He fished in his leather purse for a coin and gave it to the Charlie. "Thank you, my good man."

Rafe and Nick returned to their horses. "Why didn't I think of the Charlies?" Nick asked. "Let's go." *I shall close my arms around Serena tonight and convince her to come back to me,* Nick thought, eager to find her, yet filled with apprehension about her reaction when she laid eyes on him.

Serena heard a series of thumps on the front entrance below, and the serving wench muttered as she stomped past Serena's room and down the stairs. Who could be visiting this evening? Molly had said nothing about visitors. Besides, the old woman had gone to a dinner party at the wine merchant's house down the street.

Serena stood and stretched her aching back. She had worked all day bent over the fans she had been allotted. They were in various stages of completion. She found the work challenging and absorbing, but also tiring. She had never realized what everyday labor entailed.

It had humbled her to watch the frail Andria working from sunrise to sunset without a word of complaint. Andria had a room in the attic and had evidently also heard the commotion downstairs. When Serena left her room, Andria stood on the landing right above the front hallway.

"Miss Serena!" the maid yelled up the stairs.

Serena joined Andria on the landing. "What's amiss?" she asked the maid.

"Nothin', miss. A gent ter see ya." The maid gestured with her head toward the door, and Serena immediately recognized the two tall men. Nick and Rafael.

She sensed Andria stiffen beside her. "No need to be afraid, Andria. These men won't hurt us. I shall talk to them alone. You go back to bed."

Andria stood as if rooted to the floor, her eyes huge and filled with agony. Serena wondered why. Nick and Rafe stepped inside, hats in hand. They both lifted their gazes to her, and then to Andria. Silence hung for a long unbearable moment. They did not show any expression, as if this were nothing but a boring social call.

Knowing why Nick had come, Serena joined them in the

hallway. Andria's footsteps pounded the stairs as she disappeared into the upper regions of the house.

Serena steeled herself against the wave of longing that threatened to overcome her. "I wish you hadn't followed me," she said to Nick. "How did you find me?"

Rafe muttered that he would wait where he was.

"I need to talk to you, Serena." Nick took her arm and coaxed her toward the front parlor. Still holding her, he went inside, closing the door. The room was dark except for the weak flame of a candle on the windowsill.

"How could you, Serena?" he growled. "How could you leave me without saying good-bye? Did I mean so little to you?" His voice lowered to an angry whisper. "We made love; we were as close as two beings can be, our souls mating even as our bodies joined together. How could you treat me like a man unworthy of the simplest courtesy?"

Serena braced herself against his emotional onslaught—and her own. "Yes, it was wrong to leave you without a word of farewell. I knew you would argue, Nick—as you're doing now. And you would have tried to stop me. I don't—"

"I am shocked that our love means nothing to you!" he shouted, and she flinched as if slapped. "You discarded it like a dirty shirt and moved on." His eyes were dark unreadable pools, and she could see frustration and bewilderment in every line of his face.

Distress filled her, making her weak. "You're wrong, Nick. It meant too much. With you, I would have worried every day of losing you. I do not want to live the rest of my life like a fugitive from the law, and you very well know that." She took a deep breath to steady her trembling voice. "I severed our relationship before it was too late."

" 'Tis already too late for that. You will never forget what we shared, Serena. The memories will haunt you for the rest of your days."

"Yes, you're probably right. And I'm sorry I hurt your feelings." Serena's hands trembled so much she had to seek the support of a chair.

" 'Tis too late for forgiveness, Serena."

"Please don't say that," she whispered. "There must be hope." Faintness rolled through her at the thought of never seeing him again. He looked so handsome, his virile presence immediately turning her into a shivering mass of longing. Had she been wrong to leave him? No, she would not allow that thought to fill her mind and divert her from her purpose.

"How can you sever yourself from me like that, as if by the quick slash of a knife?" he asked, holding out his arms in a gesture of confusion.

"My feelings for you are pure, but I cannot live with you. Nothing has changed since our last discussion of the matter." She somehow found the strength to walk to the door. "You'd better leave now. I am safe here, and I shall not need your protection any longer."

He took two long strides to her side and caught her shoulders in a hard grip. "You cannot mean this, Serena. A love like ours comes only once in a lifetime."

She hung her head, feeling his heat through the wool of her gown. "Yes, mayhap you are right. But I'd rather die at a ripe old age than hang at the gallows with you a year from now— or sooner."

"I would risk anything for you," he shouted, shaking her. "But you won't risk anything for me. Not a moment of your life."

"I am a coward, perhaps, but I have a mission of my own that has to be accomplished. Please don't judge me too harshly." She looked at him beseechingly. "I give you my solemn promise that your secret is safe with me. I shall never approach the authorities to denounce you," she said, ignoring his hurtful accusation.

It was true; she dared not risk anything for him, not as long as she had to bring her father's murderer to justice. "This is not the time for love; it's the time for hate, for revenge," she said and wrenched the door open. "You'd better leave."

He dropped his arms to his sides. His eyes had darkened with misery and hurt, and Serena's heart twisted with pain.

When she hurt him, she hurt herself, but she believed that a swift blow would be easier to bear than a slow deterioration of their love. The tension of his illegal activities could not live together with love.

"I'm so sorry, Nick."

He clapped his hat on his head and his mouth hardened. "If you can't see beyond your desire for revenge or beyond my work to who I really am, our love was misguided from the start." He strode to the door, Rafe a silent shadow behind him. He slammed the door so that the walls shook.

Serena crumpled onto a settle by the door and cried until her head ached. Her heart had been torn to pieces, and she doubted it would ever mend. Had she made the wrong choice after all? She remained frozen in the spot for a long time. An arm finally wrapped around her shoulder, and Andria's sweet voice penetrated her misery.

"Come along, Serena. A good night's sleep will make you feel better. There is always tomorrow and another day and another. The pain will be easier to bear."

"I doubt I'll ever be able to sleep again," Serena replied in a thick voice and wiped her eyes on her sleeve. She walked upstairs with Andria's help. "How is it you know about such pain?"

"I have once lost everything and everyone I ever loved. I thought the pain would kill me, but here I am, still alive. My past is a bitter memory now, and I learned that everyone in this world is not good."

I am one of those people, Serena thought as she remembered the hurt in Nick's eyes. But it was too late to take back her cutting words, or change the course of her life.

"I was once married," Andria said. "I had found a man who loved me beyond reason. We had the most adorable child together. We actually had two . . ." Andria's voice took on an edge of steel. "We also had a powerful enemy who would not allow our happiness to grow. He—or she—destroyed us. I lost my husband and my child. I nearly lost my life, but I have not found the strength to discover why." A sigh trembled on her tongue. "I live only one day at a time, one moment after the other, most of them filled with work. It is the only way I can live."

Crying, they clung together. "Why is love so painful?" Serena asked against the other woman's shoulder.

Andria shook her head as if in wonder. "Because there is deep pleasure as well."

Nick and Rafe rode out of London without saying a word to each other. As if in a silent agreement, they headed for the familiar haunts of Sussex. This was a night when a highway raid was necessary to force unwanted thoughts aside, a night to feel the tension of the moment as a pistol was held to the head of a coachman, Nick thought. A dare. A snap of the fingers at Fate. An opportunity to once again prove that the mission of securing his orphanage was more important than a broken heart.

Nick swore, the longest and foulest string of curses he'd ever invented, as his and Rafe's horses ate up the miles at the south edge of London. Rafe was riding next to him, his head low over the neck of his stallion.

"Heard of any great festive gatherings in Surrey, Rafe?" Nick shouted.

"No, not a one, but there should be some excitement in Crawley or Lewes. If we hang about the outskirts there's bound be a carriage coming down the road."

"If we're lucky," Nick said, feeling exceptionally unlucky. "Too bad Pegasus is still in London."

"I don't want to go back to London," Rafe snarled. "Nothing but misery and unwanted secrets."

"Foul odors, crowded streets, thieves, and murderers," Nick filled in.

"And faithless women."

Nick's heart ached until his throat filled with tears. He swallowed hard, cursing himself for his weakness. *She* had made him weak, made him forget that he was not a gentleman a *lady* would choose to marry. He was still an urchin from Hell's Kitchen.

He had neither fortune nor fame to offer, and to Serena, he had even less. Only his sordid past as a highwayman, and memories of poverty and pain.

She knew nothing about Nicholas Thurston, Esquire. It was for the best. Mayhap she had done the right thing—kept her feelings at bay and left him to protect herself. If she died on the gallows with him, she could not pursue her revenge against her uncle. Still, her rejection hurt worse than the kick of a horse.

"I don't want Trevor Emerson to catch us," Nick said, more to himself than to Rafe. He hoped that he could return to Serena in due time, his tools of the trade—pistols, face mask, and white gloves—dug into Noah's turnip garden. But the orphanage came first. He would not veer from his goal, not for anyone.

"Why do you mention Captain Emerson?" Rafe asked as they slowed down to a trot.

"The man is a nuisance even if he's one of my friends. He can smell me, and I can smell him nipping at my heels. A few more raids, and the legend of the Midnight Bandit will be no more."

"I will miss the danger and the suspense, but I don't like the idea of hanging, not when I managed to survive the war."

"Yes, it would be foolish. I don't understand why you keep coming with me, risking everything."

Rafe adjusted his hat that a gust of wind had tried to dislodge. "I am always loyal to my friends. You were the only man who would help me when I did not know where to turn."

"I can't imagine what it's like to lose one's memory."

"It's like being newly born already a grown man. The doctor said my memory might return." He snorted, and Nick sensed his confusion. "I'm not sure I want it to come back. Somehow I know that my past was not very happy. My life was filled with strife."

"Very likely—if you're related to Rowan. He's known for his hot temper and dubious morals. He was also involved in a scandal where he called out his mistress's husband and ran him through the heart.''

Rafe leaned farther down over the stallion's neck. ''I shudder to think what my past involved. Mayhap more scandals.''

''No. I don't think so. I would have heard the rumors.'' Nick held up his hand. ''Listen, there's a carriage coming this way. Why waste the opportunity?'' Nick turned his steed off the road and in among a clump of trees. He dug into the saddlebag for his mask and gloves. ''The Midnight Bandit will strike closer to London this time. Lewes can wait.''

As Nick rode out on the road, his neck hair prickled. He knew he was taunting Fate, and this time might be the last.

Chapter 18

Two weeks later.

Serena came downstairs after a night of tossing and turning in her bed. Exhaustion weighed down her every muscle. Her eyelids still resembled lead as she stepped through the door connecting Miss Hopkins' home with her shop.

The storage room held crates and boxes, some filled with bolts of fine materials. She heard voices through the closed curtain and wondered who was in the shop. Staying hidden as she had done for weeks now only made her more curious about the outside world. A life in seclusion was not easy.

The gentry usually didn't venture out this early in the day. A male voice. How unusual, she thought, her attention sharpening. She stepped closer to the curtain, and instantly recognized her uncle's voice.

"No, as I've said twice before, she is not here," Miss Hopkins said. "I haven't seen her or I would've sent word to your club, Sir Luther. I think she's left the country or you would've found her by now."

"Why would she do that?" he asked silkily. The hairs on Serena's neck rose. She was well aware of the steel underlying that smooth voice. "What reason would she have?" he pressed.

"I don't know, but sometimes young people get preposterous ideas. She might have taken fancy to a young man she met and followed him abroad."

"I would have known if she had!" Sir Luther said, and a fist against wood made Serena jump with fright. "She wouldn't leave without her inheritance or her clothes."

No, *you*, uncle, know why I left everything behind, Serena thought. He's playing games, pretending to be the worried relative.

"If you don't mind me saying so, Sir Luther, you did not live at High Crescent. You didn't know whom she met, or didn't meet."

Sir Luther growled something, and Serena could see his red jowly face in her memory. If she pushed aside the curtain and took four steps she would be in his power. How delicate her freedom! She had felt safe here, hoping that her uncle would not return to seek her in Haymarket, but she should have known better than to lull herself into false security. She could wait no longer; she had to act out her plan. Sir Luther would not give up until he found her.

Serena looked up at the stately Palladian facade of the Leverton mansion in Berkley Square. Soot had darkened the pale stone walls, but the tall windows glistened as if newly washed. The front steps had been swept, but autumn leaves were even now clustering along the base of the bottom step in the brisk breeze. The house held the sad air of neglect.

With a trembling hand, she applied the knocker. An eternity seemed to pass before a bewigged footman in livery opened the door. He did not say a word, only stared at her disconcertingly.

She took a deep breath. "I'm here to see Sir James Leverton."

"Who may I say is calling?" he asked in a nasal voice.

"Miss Serena Hilliard."

He gave a small sniff and let her enter, then motioned her toward a small anteroom that felt cold and damp, as if never used. The brown fabric on the furniture looked cheerless in the shadow-laced autumn light. A vase of wilting flowers added to the drabness.

Mincing steps sounded in the hallway. She expected to see a thin old man wearing high-heeled shoes and an old-fashioned wig, but instead she met a tall slender man who was slowly going to seed. Dissipation marred his otherwise handsome face, and the bloodshot eyes held the weary look of someone used to looking deeply into the bottle. Her father had often exhibited that same expression of exhaustion and paleness of skin.

The man wore a coat that dazzled her eyes with its gilded buttons and intricate embroidery. His hand trembled as he brought hers to his rouged lips.

"I am enchanted at such a lovely vision on this dreary day," he said, lisping affectedly.

"Sir James Leverton?" she greeted, her spirits plunging. This man would not help her. He would not have the energy.

"Miss Hilliard, I recognize your name. Your father and mine were close friends. I am surprised that you don't know that Sir James is dead. I am Sir Ethan, the head of the Leverton family."

"Sir James dead?" Serena echoed, icy disappointment filling her body.

"Yes, some years ago. Not a recent demise. How can I help you?" He glanced critically at her simple cloak and the wide-brimmed hat that had effectively shielded her features from prying eyes, a gift from Miss Hopkins.

"I had hoped to see your father since he might have offered to help me in my time of difficulty."

A cloud fell over his face. "If you need money—"

"*No,* no such thing."

He motioned her toward a sofa in front of the fireplace where no fire brightened the day. "Tell me the whole."

Feeling slightly uneasy, but deciding she had no other choice, she told Sir Ethan of the murder, and Uncle Luther's part in the crime. "I am the only witness, and I won't stop until my uncle has been punished for killing my father."

Sir Ethan placed one beringed hand limply over the armrest and rubbed his jaw with the other as she finished her story. Silence fell in the room, a heavy, brooding kind of silence that made her uneasy. She found it difficult to breathe as she waited for his reply.

"What exactly do you want me to do, Miss Hilliard?" he asked at last, his voice noncommittal.

"I thought that mayhap you could put in a word with the authorities. Leverton being a respected name, you must have powerful connections. You could help me see justice done, Sir Ethan." Despair overcame her and she placed her hands over her face. "I don't know where to turn. I have no one to help me—no one in power that is."

Ethan patted her hand awkwardly, and she drew back at the cold clammy feel of his skin. He reminded her of a reptile, and she almost regretted coming to Berkley Square. "I don't know if I have the power my father possessed, but I shall certainly make some inquiries on your behalf, Miss Hilliard."

She stood as she heard his dismissing tone of voice. He rose with some difficulty and swayed back and forth as if already inebriated.

"I am very grateful to you, for your willingness to respect our fathers' friendship," she said.

"Where can I reach you in case I get one of the judges or Sir Henry Fielding interested in the matter?"

Serena decided on the spur of the moment not to divulge her address. "I will call here again in the near future, Sir Ethan."

" 'Twill be exceedingly difficult to bring Sir Luther to justice if you have no proof of his crime."

"I realize that, but I have to try or—die. My uncle will not rest until he has tracked me down and silenced me. He cannot risk—" She let the words hang.

Sir Ethan gave a theatrical shiver. "That is a very dark possibility. I assure you, it won't happen."

He walked with her to the door. She left, not feeling the relief she'd expected. Sir Ethan did not strike her as a person who might have great influence anywhere.

Choking down a wave of tears, she could not help but compare Nick with the painted and trembling aristocrat, finding the criminal a gentleman of superior strength. If Sir Ethan could not help her, she was truly alone.

Ethan studied her slender back as she hurried across the square. He had been touched by her beauty, but too tired and sick to pursue her with flowery compliments and seductive smiles. That might come later, he thought with a smile. A few promises, a lie or two about lawmen he'd approached would soon make her feel obligated. The hope of one day possessing that lithe body gave him a thrill, but his stomach ached too much for him to pursue passion—mayhap later in the evening.

He beckoned to an empty sedan chair passing his door and ordered the men to follow the young lady hurrying along the street. He would find out where she lived, then have the men carry him back to the square.

Miss Hilliard would be a pleasant amorous challenge with her slanted cat eyes and supple body. He had tired of Callie Vine the very first time she gave herself to him. Such a watering pot, such a timid little flower to pluck. A violet. He liked his women decadent and vigorous, not a pale shrinking violet in his bed. Then again, to pluck the maidenhead of an innocent had its special rewards, like absorbing a ray of sunlight. It had given him strength, if not deep carnal satisfaction. It had temporarily filled his soul.

The sedan chair swung back and forth, making his head spin and his stomach protest. He was carried across the busy Piccadilly, the conveyance weaving between carriages and carts. It turned down Haymarket and halted abruptly as the men set it down. Ethan parted the curtain to one side with a beringed hand and observed Miss Hilliard throwing furtive glances in both directions of the street, then entering Hopkins' Millinery shop.

He smiled at her transparent efforts of secrecy. He had found her refuge. He tapped the windowsill with one long fingernail. The knowledge might prove valuable in the future.

Miss Hilliard would prove to be a born courtesan, he hoped, not a shrinking miss like Callie Vine. As he thought about Callie, he wished he hadn't been filled with the ungovernable urge to deflower her. When all was said and done, it had been an unnecessary mistake. The worst blunder had been to promise Miss Vine marriage to get his way. She had taken it so damned *seriously*. She'd been nearly hysterical when he explained that there would be no wedding. No wonder she'd been involved in that accident afterwards. The twit had absolutely no sense.

The lawns at The Hollows lay under a blanket of red and yellow leaves. They rattled and danced in lazy circles as wind swept along the ground and shook the trees surrounding the old knot garden at the back of the mansion.

Inside, Delicia bent over her friend Callie and spoke earnestly. "You'll have to get out of your bed now; try that wheelchair. I've plumped up the pillow to support your back. Each day, the pain shall be less, I promise you."

"I'm an invalid, Delicia. I would rather die than learn to live the rest of my life in a wheelchair."

"You don't have to spend the rest of your days in a chair." Delicia's heart ached for her friend, noting with dismay that the trust, the openness, the customary sweetness of Callie's expression had disappeared. Only a pale ghost of that youthful beauty remained amidst the hollow cheeks, lackluster hair, and dull eyes.

Delicia cursed Ethan in silence, burning with anger and humiliation since the time when the coaching accident had happened ten days ago. Guilt also ate away at her composure, and every day she felt more despair as Callie's injured leg did not show much improvement. It was healing, but healing crookedly, just as the surgeon had predicted. The bone had been broken in more places than one and it was a miracle that Callie still had a leg, he'd said.

"You can't remain lying here all day. Don't feel so sorry for yourself," Delicia said with deliberate cruelty. She would plead or bully, anything that would get her friend out of bed. But she was tired, and the shock of Ethan's perfidy had been eating away at her thoughts. Her own innocence and trust had been replaced by horror and repugnance at the same time as Callie had been ruined by her beloved brother. *Beloved.* Curse him, she thought. She had known that Ethan was prone to excesses, but she'd never thought of him as repugnant and dishonorable.

"You have to fight, Callie. Get back on your feet."

" 'Tis easy for you to say. You don't have to lie here knowing that your life is in ruins." Callie clapped her thin hands to her face and cried.

Delicia bit down hard on her bottom lip to prevent herself from expressing her deep-felt sorrow and guilt. Her *brother* had done this to her best friend. 'Twas too much to bear.

"Come now, Callie. Nick is waiting for us downstairs. It's time for breakfast. You know you like your eggs warm."

"Nick should have killed Ethan when he had the chance," Callie said, as if she hadn't heard anything that Delicia had said.

"Nick is furious, but he knows Sir James would turn in his grave if he learned that brother had killed brother. If Nick had not remembered Father's love for Ethan, he would have killed Ethan after the accident." Delicia sighed. "Ethan's downfall will come. He has acted abominably and he shall pay; don't you fear."

Callie finally made an effort to get out of bed. In twenty minutes she had been dressed in a loose sack gown of striped sarcenet and placed in the wheelchair by two maids. Delicia wheeled her into the dining room.

Nick's face held a dark brooding look, a look that suggested he was turning over the facts of the events of these last weeks. So much had happened, but Delicia wondered if Ethan's scandalous behavior was the only reason for Nick's lack of enthusiasm. Like Callie, he seemed a shadow of his former self. She wondered what had transpired between Nick and Ethan in the past.

"Good morning, brother," Delicia greeted in a falsely bright tone. She felt as if she were the only one holding the specters at bay at The Hollows. The darker and shorter the days, the more closely the specters crowded the house.

Nick rose, greeting both ladies with a bow. He ordered his butler to place eggs and toast in front of the invalid. His heart twisted with guilt as he viewed Callie's pale face. She seemed slightly more than a skeleton now, and it was all his fault. Not only was her body broken, but her heart as well.

He had *known*. If only he'd kept a closer eye on Ethan at the time, but he'd been so involved with Serena that he saw nothing else, thought of nothing else. A wave of fury still went through him as he remembered the day of the infamous coaching accident.

Right after the last daring attacks that had brought almost enough loot to pay off the orphanage mortgage, he'd gone over to Berkley Square to find solace from Serena's rejection in his sister's company. His heart broken with longing for a love he could not have, he hoped that Delicia would make him laugh again.

Instead, catastrophe had struck. He had entered the mansion and handed his hat and gloves to the lackey by the door. He recalled every detail and feared the memories would haunt him for the rest of his life . . .

Delicia had run toward him in the hallway, her face as pale

as the sheets in his bed. "Nick, you got my letter. You know the worst."

"Know what? I have no idea what you're talking about."

She pressed her trembling hands to her mouth in agitation. "You don't know that Ethan and Callie eloped this afternoon?"

He shook his head as icy dread flowed through his veins. He'd known what was coming next.

"They had made an assignment in the park. Aunt Titania took me for a drive with one of her old friends. Callie complained of a headache and stayed at home. Evidently Ethan arrived half an hour later and she drove off with him. She left a note behind that they were off to Scotland to get married in Gretna Green. Callie is not of age."

Nick swallowed his rising bile and unclenched his hands. The joints ached as if he'd pressed them together too hard. "I'm going after them. That snake will ruin her."

Nick returned to the present and swore under his breath. He hadn't found the runaway couple, only Callie on the following day, a Callie who had already given herself to Ethan, a Callie who had been broken by his brother. Ethan, the heartless worm, had disappeared after the night of lovemaking and left Callie to fend for herself. She hadn't managed very well.

Nick could still remember her distraught face when he'd found her overturned carriage, the coachmen helpless beside her injured body on the ground. Nick had taken her back to London and consulted the best surgeon, who'd informed them that the leg had been broken in such a way that it would never be right again.

Not only had Callie lost her virginity, she had lost her health, her good name, and her self-worth. She had lost everything except her life.

He recalled how he'd gone in search of Ethan, finding him in bed with two courtesans at Lotus Blossom's house. He could still hear the rapier sing against the scabbard as he pulled it free and challenged Ethan right then and there, still naked, still grotesque with his flushed face, his glazed eyes, and his erection.

Nick flexed his hand, remembering. He could have run him through without a gentlemanly challenge. The only thing that had prevented an outright slaying was the memory of Sir James and how much he'd loved Ethan.

The fight had been fought—without seconds, without pride, without honor—in Lotus Blossom's parlor. One day Ethan would die, Nick thought. Nick had given him a deep flesh wound in the shoulder, but it did not pay for Calandra's ruined life. Nick could have forced Ethan to marry her, but he did not wish such a tedious, even horrifying, fate on sweet Callie. She deserved better. Too bad she didn't have any family close by.

Nick finished his breakfast without really tasting the food. He watched his two companions—Delicia, picking at her food, and Callie, a constant reminder of his own failures. He pushed back his chair and stood.

"Callie, I would like to speak with you in the library after breakfast. Please come, it is very important that we have a private discussion."

She looked up at him, her brown eyes empty and bleak, like the moor in midwinter. He didn't receive a reply, not even a nod of her head. Nothing. He would have to do his damndest to bring the merry sparkle back to her eyes.

He exchanged a knowing glance with Delicia. Her lips turned downward at the corners, trembling and pale. She was obviously blaming herself for her friend's dilemma, but the fault was his alone—for never quite dealing with Ethan and stopping the demon's progress. How did one kill one's brother? Only death would successfully stop Ethan, who dirtied or ruined everything in his path.

Half an hour later, Delicia rolled the wheelchair into the library. She settled Callie in front of the blazing fireplace and draped a shawl over her shoulder, and another one across her legs.

"Please leave us alone for a moment, dearest sis." Nick

gave Delicia a long searching look. She whirled away, but not before he'd seen the tears in her eyes.

He kneeled by Callie's chair as soon as the door closed. He took her cold bird-claw fingers into his own and held them tightly. "Callie, please look at me."

She obeyed, but there was nothing in her eyes.

"I feel a desperate need to make things right, to atone for what Ethan did to you." He looked intently into her eyes and held her fingers to his lips, feeling an urge to warm them. "I would like to marry you, to try to make your life bearable again. I have to repair the damage my brother did to you."

"I will never walk again. At least not without a limp. You can't change that," she said tonelessly.

He could feel her hands trembling. He blew on them, keeping up his effort to warm her. "I know. All I can do is try to make your life as comfortable as possible. I could force Ethan to marry you, but he would make you miserable."

"I'd rather be dead. Ethan ruined my trust, my belief that gentlemen are honorable. He destroyed my life and my pride."

"He forced himself on you—didn't he?—before the coach accident. You didn't comply with his wishes—"

She nodded, her facade suddenly cracking and revealing the searing pain in her heart. Tears trembled on her eyelashes. "No, I did not give myself voluntarily. *He* would say that I did, though."

"I have to be honest with you, Callie. I don't love you; but I like you. For you, I harbor the same feelings as I have for Delicia. I promise to cherish you forever if you only say yes to my proposal."

"Yes," she whispered, and clutched his hands as if he were her only hope.

His life crumpled. All his dreams lay in ashes, but what did it matter what he desired? Not only had Ethan scandalized himself and Callie, he had scandalized the Leverton name, his filth smearing Delicia's reputation. It was now well-known that Ethan hovered on the brink of bankruptcy. No suitors were beating down the door at The Hollows, and Nick had noticed Delicia's silent suffering.

He squeezed Callie's hands kindly. "Thank you. You have helped me put some order to my life." And she had. Mayhap he could now concentrate on completely forgetting Serena.

Chapter 19

Serena heard nothing from Sir Ethan Leverton. In fact, from a customer in the milliner shop, she learned of the scandal that had ruined his name and Calandra Vine's, whoever she might be. Serena also heard the ugly gossip about his uncontrollable gambling and his vast losses. In a way she was relieved she didn't have to meet him again. She'd felt soiled by his touch. But at the time, she'd had no choice but to pursue the avenues open to her.

She had only one other option, to visit the other brother, Nicholas Thurston, and mayhap solicit his aid in her mission to bring her uncle to justice. *Nick*. Nicholas. Strange that the two men would have the same name. Wherever she turned, she encountered reminders of her erstwhile lover. To think of him intensified the nagging ache in her heart. However hard she tried, she could not forget him, and her body longed for his embrace. Most of all, she needed to feel close to someone, especially since her problems had not been solved. She had never felt lonelier, and if her visit to Nicholas Thurston in Sussex didn't get results, she didn't know what to do.

She traveled down to Sussex on the stage after telling Miss

Hopkins she needed some time away to solve her problems of the past.

"Good luck to you, Miss Serena. You'll need all the luck you can get," the store owner said grimly. "I wish I could help in some small way."

"You have already helped me. You've protected me and shielded me, and I cannot ask for more."

South of Cuckfield, she jumped off the farm wagon that had brought her to The Hollows, the Thurston home. The tall iron gates stood open, and there was no one at the gate house. Apprehension agitating her mind, she walked up the winding drive. The estate lay in a valley surrounded by woods and backed by a gentle slope of the South Downs that rolled inland.

In the hollow of a palm, she thought as she studied the large red brick house with its latticed windows and two shallow wings that flanked the main building on both sides. Ivy covered most of the front facade, and she noticed the ornamental foliage of a formal knot garden, the box hedges now covered with a mantle of dry leaves. The grand house had an air of peace, and oil lamps gave the downstairs windows a golden glow in the cold overcast morning.

Feeling strange, as if she'd traveled for years, she had found the destination she'd always been looking for—without even knowing she was searching. Like coming home.

She applied the knocker. Made of brass, it had the shape of a grinning lion head.

A footman opened the door, and she met the butler in the hallway. He was old and bent, but not haughty like the London servants.

"I would like to see Mr. Thurston if he's in. I'm Serena Hilliard."

"Certainly, miss. Come this way." He showed her to a seat that was attached to the dark paneling that went halfway up the wall. A stained-glass window over the door let in a faint multicolored light. Portraits and landscapes adorned the walls, a rather informal procession of faces, horses, and meadows.

The butler returned. "He will see you in the library now, Miss Hilliard."

For some reason, Serena's heart hammered uncontrollably. It was as if she'd felt the feeling of this house before—as if she knew the occupants who had put their stamp on the dwelling.

The library shone with light. A fire blazed in the grate, and two branches of candles cast a mellow glow onto the desk. Books lined every wall, and an old worn Oriental rug added green and red color to the otherwise rather brown room.

First she saw a young woman in a wheelchair. Standing beside her, his hand on the tall back of the invalid chair, stood Nick. *Her* Nick.

She stared. Her ears started to roar. She hadn't connected Nick to the Thurston name. She had never discovered his last name.

He stared, his mouth a grim line.

The butler turned to her. "Miss Serena Hilliard to see you, Mr. Thurston. Will you require refreshments?"

Nick nodded in a distracted manner, and the butler left, closing the door behind him.

"Please find Delicia, Nick. I'd like to return to my room," the woman in the wheelchair said, as her dull gaze traveled over Serena once.

"Serena," he said between stiff lips, his color returning to his face, two waves of angry red. He ignored the invalid's request. "Hilliard . . ." he continued, as if testing the word on his tongue. "Yes, I have heard that name before."

The woman in the wheelchair put her hand on his arm, and Serena noted the thinness, the despair on the pale face. "Please, Nick. I need my rest."

"I would like you to stay a little while longer, Callie. This won't take long, I'm sure."

Calandra Vine, the woman Sir Ethan had ruined. Serena felt a stab of compassion for the young lady. She returned her gaze to her former lover.

Nick took on a brisk demeanor, and he looked at her as if

he didn't know her any longer. He walked toward a leather armchair in front of the desk. "Will you please sit down, Miss Hilliard, and state your business."

She obeyed, but only after throwing a reluctant glance at their spectator by the fire. Better pretend she'd never laid eyes on Nick before. Evidently that was the way he liked to play the game. "My father, Andrew Hilliard, and Sir James Leverton were very good friends. I didn't put Sir James's name in connection with you. Anyhow, my uncle, Sir Luther Hilliard, murdered my father, and I wondered if you could see it in your heart to aid me in my quest to bring him to justice. I asked your brother, Sir Ethan, for help, but he has not come forth with any remedy to my problems at this time."

The woman in the wheelchair gasped in shock, and Serena glanced at her. Murder was not a polite word, by any means. Serena's heart hammered so hard and fast she thought it would bring about her collapse. Every feeling she had ruthlessly suppressed since her last meeting with Nick rushed back, pressing like a spring flood on her senses and drowning her mind in confusion. God's bones, but she wanted him. Needed him more than she thought possible, needed his love.

"He would not," Nick replied, his voice thick, as if he, too, experienced a welter of emotions. "My brother is not keen on helping anyone but himself."

"I have to find someone powerful who could bring my uncle to a trial by his peers, someone who is not afraid to confront him. I don't know any justices or lawmen in London. At home, Luther pays the local authorities to comply with his wishes. I am sure of it, or the investigation into my father's death would not have been so slipshod. I have word that Sir Luther blames a vagrant for the murder."

Nick scratched his chin and viewed her with those sharp blue eyes that made her insides melt with longing. "To convince a jury consisting of your uncle's peers, you need another witness, someone impartial, not related to the Hilliard family."

"There is none," she said. *As you well know*, she wanted to add. Nick looked so handsome in a dark gray velvet coat and a paler gray waistcoat with pewter buttons. His hair was brushed back and tamed with a ribbon, but one curl had escaped and fell over his forehead. She longed to brush it back and kiss the harsh planes of his face. She longed to lean against his warm broad chest and feel his strong arms around her.

The door opened, and another woman entered. Nick stood politely. "Delicia, meet Miss Serena Hilliard, Luther Hilliard's niece."

"*Luther Hilliard?* Father's worst enemy?" The woman's eyes widened in shock, and she took a step back as if Serena brought with her the taint of her uncle.

"Yes, but her father was Sir James's good friend."

"Andrew Hilliard," the woman named Delicia said.

Nick held out his hand toward Serena. "Meet my stepsister, Delicia Leverton, and"—he motioned toward the fire—"my fiancée, Miss Calandra Vine. Only minutes ago, she promised to marry me."

Serena thought that this time she would surely faint, but there came no darkness to soften the blow to her heart. Nick must have slept in her bed while already plotting, or knowing, he would marry another woman.

"My felicitations," she said weakly. "I pray you will be happy for many years to come."

Delicia threw her arms around her brother's neck. "Ohh, what a wonderful idea, Nick! Was that why you wanted to see Callie alone, to propose? I'm so happy for you both." She rushed to the wheelchair, and Serena could see the bony profile of the bride. The young woman did not look overly happy, but somehow that did not ease Serena's feeling of dread. Nick was forever lost to her. He would soon marry another.

"Callie gave me her 'yes' not half an hour ago, and I think we will be very happy together." Nick looked straight at Serena as he spoke, each word a sword tip spearing her heart.

She felt an urge to rant and rave, but no one would benefit from a scene of jealousy. Yes, her entire body brimmed with that vile emotion mixed with a sensation of futility. She had arrived too late—as always.

She arrested her thoughts as they flew in ever wilder circles. Too late for what? For his proposal, for his promise of undying love? She had already discarded his love weeks ago, and she couldn't expect him to moon over her.

"Miss Hilliard has come to ask for help in the matter of her father's death," Nick said to his stepsister, not describing any details. "I'm sure Sir James would have wanted me to help her any way I could."

"He would have helped her, had he been alive," Delicia said.

"I did not know that Sir James was dead," Serena said, looking at Nick. "Having spent all of my time in the country, I knew nothing about the Leverton family, but Father always spoke highly of Sir James. I never met him, though." She looked from one to the other, so secure in their elegant home and their fine clothes. So secure in the family circle. She had lost all that, but mayhap found out more about herself . . . and her limitations. She had also found strength.

"I might be foolish to expect help, to bother you now that you have a wedding to plan," she added. "I should return to London. I'll think of something else to solve my problems." She slowly walked toward the door.

"Wait!" Nick said and marched toward her, his determination closing around her like an invisible mantle. "Of course we want to help you any way we can—no question about that." He looked down at her face, his eyes dark with pain. "I would like to speak with you in private for a moment. If you don't mind."

The scene froze before her, Delicia's eyes caring and worried, Calandra's flat and dead. This was Nick's world—and the other world, where he became a reckless highwayman and hid in the poor parts of London—was nothing more than a distant memory. "Very well."

She stepped into the hallway and he followed. He showed her into a parlor and closed the door. They were alone. She filled with the haunting pain of longing as she realized how deeply she'd missed him.

He stood so close she could touch him, but she clasped her hands in front of her to prevent them from reaching out spontaneously. But the scent of him enveloped her, making her senses spin.

He crossed his arms over his chest as if to protect himself. "I was surprised to see you walking into my life again," he said coolly. "You so vehemently pointed out at our last meeting that you did not want to see me. That your decision to break with me was final."

She lifted her chin proudly. "It still is. I was startled, too, to find you here. You never introduced yourself as Nicholas Thurston. You were always Nick, or Mr. Nick. And you never informed me that you had a large estate in Sussex."

"It is not as large and prosperous as you might think. It barely pays for itself, but I have never used the, er—funds— from my other activities to pay for the bills accumulated here."

"Hmm, I daresay Miss Calandra's dowry will take care of those," she said coolly.

"No need for sarcasm, Serena. You made your choices; and if you are bitter, you can't blame me. I offered you my name, and you threw the proposal in my face. At least I did not propose to get my hands on your fortune. I offered from the depths of my heart. Love was all I had to offer, and that is still all I have."

A dreary feeling, like a gray ceiling of clouds, filled her. "I had no other choice. Besides, you are still a criminal," she whispered. "Nothing has changed."

He looked hard at her for a long moment, and she was aware of his chest rising and falling with rapid breaths. He shared her agitation, and now guilt mixed with the other feelings racing through her.

He had said he loved her. Hadn't she once told him that she believed true love would overcome any obstacle, including the lack of funds and a low birth?

She took a step toward him, but checked her progress. He took a step toward her, but an invisible barrier stopped his progress. They stared at each other for a long time, and Serena could not think of anything to say until he held out his arms, inviting her.

"You are soon to be married, Nick. Do not forget that."

"I had to protect the family honor, try to reverse some of the damage my brother has done. I cannot stand by and watch Miss Callie die from a broken heart."

His compassion warmed her. "You're a gentleman, Nick. It was too late for us anyway. Mayhap you can find happiness with Miss Calandra. I hope you do."

Nick dropped his arms to his sides. A flush deepened in his cheeks, and Serena sensed his agitation. "Had I but known that you would come here today, I would not have offered for Callie. I would have asked you again to marry me."

Serena did not know what to say, so she kept silent.

He sighed deeply, as if finally giving up a struggle. "Very well, I know your answer. Still, I will help you with Sir Luther. I offered before I knew about Sir James's and your father's friendship."

"As I pointed out in the past, I don't want you to rush off and confront Sir Luther. We must find a more subtle way to bring him to justice."

"You're right. My temper ran away with me when I witnessed your nightmares, but I'm quite calm now."

Serena smiled in relief. "What do you suggest that we do now?"

"I need to find out more about Sir Luther and his life in Somerset. Do you know where he is now?"

"He might be searching for me. He came to the shop to ask for me twice, but he has not shown up lately. I believe he hired men to watch the millinery shop. I spend all my time inside, only going out when absolutely necessary."

"If he suspects that the shop owner is lying, he might lie in wait for you when you leave the premises next time. You're not safe in Haymarket. While I speak with Sir Luther's friends in London, I want you to remain here until the matter is cleared up."

She lifted an eyebrow. "So that you can keep an eye on me?"

"No, don't be sarcastic. Just let *me* decide what's best for once."

Serena sighed, realizing she would have to trust him, or else the whole idea of asking for his help had been for naught.

"Very well, I gracefully accept your invitation to stay here for a few days." She gave a forced smile. "I take it I don't have to cook my own meals?"

His eyes lit up for the first time since she'd arrived. "No, I suppose my staff can handle the cooking for now. But you never know. If the cook takes sick, you might have to substitute for her."

"I'm sure my welcome will be curtailed at such a time. Your family would not like my cooking."

"Talking about food, are you hungry?" He took her arm as if to lead her to another room. A hot current flowed through her at his touch, making a blush bloom all over her body.

"Yes . . . no," she said, filled with confusion.

He dropped his hand as if burned, and she experienced a sense of loss, as if she craved his touch and couldn't live without it. *Nonsense!* She did not need him other than in the difficult matter of her father's murder.

He showed her into the hallway. "If you didn't pack for the trip, you can always borrow some things from Delicia. She's the soul of generosity." He turned as if to leave, but Serena placed her hand on his arm. He glanced at her as if irritated by the delay.

"Thank you," she whispered through stiff lips. "For everything."

"No need to mention it. I'm only doing what my father would have done." He gave her a cool smile and left.

Serena discovered the truth of Delicia's generosity later in the day when Delicia brought an armful of dresses to the guest room that had been allotted to Serena. She knocked and stepped inside, a sunny smile on her face. "I'm glad I can be of some help in your moment of need," she said.

Serena got up from the bed where she'd been resting. She felt slightly awkward in Delicia's company, remembering her wanton nights in Nick's arms. A gentle lady like Delicia might not want a fallen woman in her house.

"Nick said you were to rest, and then be shown around the estate." She laughed and dropped the gowns on the bed. "We all obey Nick's commands—as long as they make sense. Anyhow, I'm delighted to have a guest in the house."

"It's a lovely house." Serena already liked the other woman, who was about her own age. Delicia looked lovely in a gown of brown wool pulled back to show the quilted yellow underskirt. Her lustrous blond hair had been pulled into a knot at the top of her head. She wore pearl earrings and a simple strand around her neck.

Delicia pursed her lips in thought. "Hmm, I'd say I'm somewhat taller than you, but not much. My gowns should fit you without too much difficulty." She held up one fashioned from pale blue velvet and another, a deep rose wool with a detached bodice and a very wide skirt that would be held up by panniers.

"Your brother is kind to let me remain here while he investigates in London."

Delicia eyed one gown thoughtfully. "Yes, he always had a weak heart for people brought low. Nick is the most compassionate man I know." She smiled ruefully. "But mayhap my opinion does not count since it is highly subjective."

Serena did not know what to say. Delicia was right, but did she know the full extent of Nick's compassion? Serena almost mentioned the orphanage, but at the last moment recalled that the secret was hers to keep. Nick hadn't asked her to keep it, but Serena was sure he didn't want his sister to know the truth about the Midnight Bandit.

She regarded the painted wall panels, scenes of bucolic meadows, blue skies, and the occasional angel riding on a cloud; the fine curtains of cream silk fringed with gold; the cream brocade bedhangings, and the fine rugs on the floor. "I believe his generosity complements yours. You must have put me in the finest chamber of the house."

"My motives are purely selfish. You might stay longer if I pamper you. Aunt Titania, whom you will soon meet, is rather a bore—if a kind bore—and Callie's situation has threatened to break me." Delicia sat down on the bed, her brow furrowed in anxiety. "I have to keep her happy, for I'm afraid she will fade away to nothing if I don't. Nick's offer to marry her will surely cheer her up. Her disgrace will be nullified."

"You seem strong to me, but I shall do my best to help you with your burden while I'm here."

Delicia bounced up and gave Serena a warm hug, a thoughtful gesture which elevated her rather low spirits.

"I think we will become friends," Delicia said. "I hope you don't mind my calling you Serena."

"As long as I can call you Delicia."

A scratch sounded on the door. "That's my pet dog, a whippet named Sunshine."

Serena let the slender animal in and patted the light gray velvety coat. The dog wore a gentle expression. She nuzzled Serena's hand with a long nose.

"Her sister Moonlight won't be far behind. They follow me like shadows."

Another dog wearing a red ribbon tied around her long neck entered, whining. Serena could not have told the two dogs apart.

"When I ride, I take the dogs with me. They like to run, fast and furious." Delicia hugged her pets as Serena watched. Delicia glanced up. "You do ride, don't you?"

"Yes. I like to ride very much."

"Then it's settled." She smiled. "I think our lives changed for the better when you arrived."

Serena hoped that Delicia would not be disappointed. Not if she could help it.

* * *

Nick rode toward London as fast as his sorrel hunter could carry him. He could not forget Serena's stricken expression as he'd announced that he planned to marry Callie Vine. If only she had arrived ten minutes earlier! Fate worked in strange ways. Hadn't Sir James always said that?

Feeling torn inside, he recalled her dark blue, mysterious eyes, her rounded curves and hidden valleys. A sinking feeling filled his stomach and desire flared in his blood. He wanted her more than ever. But he might never wrap his arms around her again.

In the end, he wasn't good enough—never had been for a lady like her, always used to the best, expecting nothing less. She had the right to expect the finest. Still, while under his roof in his refuge in London, she had not voiced many words of complaint. He'd toyed with the idea of taking her there again, but to what purpose? That period of his life was over, and she would not submit to lovemaking now that she had gained her freedom. Unless she yearned for their union as much as he did, and, of that, he wasn't sure.

Nick muttered his plan aloud as cold rain started falling, shortening the already short day. "I'll frequent the clubs until I come across Hilliard. He's bound to attend one if he's in London. He won't talk to his enemy's son, but he might let something slip, some clue that could be used against him. I might confront him, but I won't provoke a quarrel."

Nick had every confidence he could help Serena find a way to bring Sir Luther to justice. He pulled the cocked hat lower over his eyes and wrapped the cloak more tightly around himself to prevent icy water from running down his neck.

Late that evening, he rode into London. He decided to stay at the Midnight Bandit's refuge. The rooms seemed empty and sad without Serena. He had no desire to stay here where everything reminded him of her.

Nick dressed in a full-skirted coat of dark red velvet adorned with gold braiding, dark gray knee-breeches, a lace-edged cravat. He placed two rings on his fingers and dropped an enameled snuff box into his pocket. Offering snuff was an excellent way to initiate a conversation. It was time to spend some hours on the town with his friends.

He had dinner at the Cocoa Tree, a popular coffeehouse, where he ran into Carey McLendon, Charles's oldest friend.

"I'm happy to see a friendly face," Nick said, sitting down. "What brings you up to London?"

"Business. Despite my preference to spend my evenings with my lovely wife, I sometimes like the company of my male friends." He ordered a bottle of wine. "Would you like to join me in a card game at the Crimson Rooms in Covent Garden?"

"The infamous Letty Rose's establishment?" Nick pondered for a moment, thinking the gambling hell might be as good a start as any into gathering information about Luther Hilliard's life. All gentlemen visiting London gambled somewhere. "Sounds like a splendid idea, McLendon."

"Are Charles and Marguerite back from their honeymoon trip to the West Country?"

"Yes . . . but I haven't seen them."

Carey, whose dark gray eyes always saw too much, said, "I understand why you're reluctant to see them, but I know you'll forget Marguerite in due time."

"Yes, as a matter of fact, I barely think about her any more, but it'll be deuced embarrassing to see her."

A sad shadow crossed Carey's face. "I'm glad Charles is so happy. I predict they'll have many children, and I envy them that."

"Why?"

"Francesca and I seem incapable of having our own. We're thinking of adopting a child. I've been visiting the orphanages."

"I'll take you to a good one near Bethlem Hospital while I'm in London." Nick sighed. "At least you have a wife you love. Not everyone is that fortunate."

"You sound bitter," Carey said, sending a probing glance at Nick. "You could have any lady you choose to court."

Nick shook his head. "No, I can't. You might as well know

the truth since it'll be common knowledge soon enough. The announcement is yet to appear in the newspapers, but I have asked Calandra Vine, one of Delicia's friends, to marry me. I haven't formally asked her brother for her hand, but he's not available."

Carey slapped Nick's shoulder. "Congratulations, old fellow! Ecod, I knew you would succumb to Cupid's arrow sooner or later."

Nick grimaced as he remembered Callie's wounded expression and painful injury. "I don't love her, but any gentleman in his right mind would offer to save her reputation after what my *dear* stepbrother did to her." Nick told the story about the sham elopement and the subsequent carriage accident. "The reason for my hasty proposal is between you and me, mind you. I don't want any rumors to start."

"Ethan's wild ways have started a great deal of rumors already," Carey said, his expression dark with anger. "Why should you have to suffer for his sins? You should force him to wed her."

"For one, I can't force Ethan to do anything. He would rather die from a sword's wound than marry a woman he cares nothing about. Ethan doesn't *care* for anyone or anything; that's why he does anything he pleases. Second, I would not want Miss Vine to suffer unduly under Ethan's command. He has hurt her already, and he won't stop there. I wouldn't wish his tyranny on my worst enemy."

Carey leaned back and pushed his hand over his wavy dark hair as if deep in thought. "Ethan will eventually dig his own grave, but I understand your aggravation."

"Every time I see him, I feel like running him through. Not a very brotherly sentiment. I always believed brothers should love each other."

"Envy can eat away at the best family relationships. Ethan mayhap feels that Sir James treated you too much as a real son, usurping Ethan's rights."

Nick nodded, accepting the filled wineglass from the landlord. "Yes. He as much as told me that himself. He feels he should have The Hollows and that The Hollows should pay for his horrendous gambling debts. Damn him to hell!'' Nick swallowed the wine in two gulps and refilled his glass.

"You have been put in an awkward position. I'm not sure I could offer to wed a lady who had been compromised by my brother. I'm not that noble.''

"Like me, you were born on the wrong side of the blanket, but your family disowned you completely. You don't have the same sense of responsibility.''

Carey nodded. "You're right. I have no contact with my family in Scotland.''

A serving wench brought a platter with roast fowl and a bowl of beef soup, which she set in front of Carey. Nick tore a leg off the fowl and chewed it hungrily. He wished he could unburden his pain concerning Serena Hilliard, but then he would have to reveal secrets that he had told to no one.

He could at least try to find out more about the death of her father.

"Did you know that Andrew Hilliard is dead?''

Carey nodded, chewed, and swallowed. "Yes. He was killed by a blasted vagrant that was passing by the estate in search of valuables. Evidently helped himself to some silver, too.''

"How do you know all this?'' Nick's heart beat harder.

"I read about it in the newspapers. I think the vagrant has been hung already. Justice is swift at times—especially in the provinces.''

If it suits the man who wields the power in the court. Nick thought, and went on fishing for information. "Andrew Hilliard had a brother, didn't he?''

"Yes, Sir Luther. I have seen him in London. Last night he played deeply at Boodle's. He was losing heavily.''

"Were you fleecing him?'' Nick asked with a laugh, and helped himself to more meat.

Carey took on an innocent expression, but his dark gray eyes glittered. "Me fleecing my fellow men? Hardly. He just did not play whist very well.''

"I wouldn't mind gambling with him tonight if I could leave

the Crimson Rooms with a heavier purse,'' Nick said, gnawing the last of the meat from the bones.

"He visits the various hells regularly. We can always find him somewhere tonight if he's still in London."

Nick drank the last of his wine. "Let's go."

Chapter 20

The hostess of the Crimson Rooms, Letitia Rose, greeted the guests by the door wearing a crimson brocade gown draped over enormous panniers. She always wore crimson, and every piece of fabric in the gambling rooms sported the same color.

Letty's hair had been coiffed and powdered into ringlets that coiled over plump white shoulders. A star-shaped beauty patch adorned one cheek, and another, this one heart-shaped, drew attention to her rouged lips.

She flapped her painted vellum fan languidly. "Well, it has been a long time since you entered my establishment, Carey McLendon. Evidently marriage suits you. What has become of my erstwhile hostess?"

"Francesca is well and happy at Burgess Hill."

She patted his arm coyly. "You're starting to stray from her side already?"

"Nothing like that, Letty," Carey said impatiently and greased the palm of the doorman. Nick followed suit. He glanced around the large hallway, seeing no one he knew.

"Is Luther Hilliard here, Letty?" Carey asked.

"No, not yet, but he was here last night. He'll be here later if he comes at all." She smiled at Nick. "Nicholas Thurston, you don't come here very often. I hope that will change."

"I don't have any money to lose," Nick said with a wink and a smile, and followed Carey into the gambling halls. The first one had a faro table, and other rooms had tables for other types of card games. They went to the inner sanctum, which had been set aside for the hazard table. There, rolling the dice in a leather cup, was Sir Ethan.

"Damn his eyes!" Nick said between clenched teeth. "What is he staking—borrowed money?"

Carey threw him a glance filled with concern. "That bad, is it?"

"Worse." Nick clenched and unclenched his hands, feeling powerless as he watched his stepbrother. " 'Struth, I don't know if I can stop myself from killing him if I stay here any longer."

"Don't let your temper ruin your good judgment. Let him ruin himself. He can't take what is yours."

"In a way he did. He took my freedom of choice when he put me in a situation where I felt I had to marry the woman he ruined."

Carey crossed his arms over his chest. "There is that, of course." He gripped Nick's shoulder and urged him away. "I think we'll go to another room."

A meeting with Ethan was inevitable as long as they stayed at the gambling house. Nick's path crossed with that of his brother as he went from one room to the next.

Ethan's eyes flashed cold fire. "Well, well, if it isn't my saintly brother."

Nick automatically gripped Ethan's fall of lace at his throat and twisted until the lace ripped. "I'm not at all surprised to see *you* here, Ethan, squandering someone else's money."

Ethan pried Nick's fingers from his throat. "Be that as it may, you have nothing to say about it that I want to hear." He looked down at the ruined tatters of lace on his chest and grimaced. "And you owe me ten guineas for the damaged cravat." He held out his hand, palm out.

"Ten *guineas?* Plague take it, you must be out of your mind."

They stared at each other for a long suspended moment. Hatred oozed from Ethan, and Nick felt the familiar storm of cold anger gather in his stomach. He barely managed to curb the urge to pull out his sword right then and there and challenge his brother.

"If you don't remove yourself from these premises, Ethan, I shall rip every button from your waistcoat and slice your coat to ribbons. And if that isn't enough, I shall run you through in as many places as possible without actually killing you. The pain should be enough to drive you to suicide."

Ethan paled under the rouge, and his mouth thinned into a grim line. "I might choose to leave the Crimson Rooms this time, but I think London is too small to hold us both. One of us will have to leave—permanently."

"Are you challenging me to see who will have to abandon the capital?" Nick said, making his voice drip with sarcasm.

"If you provoke me deeply enough, I shall look beyond our family connection and make an end to your miserable life."

Nick threw his head back and laughed so loud that several gamblers halted their gambling and looked up from their cards.

"I mean it, Nick."

"You're always drunk. If we were to meet at dawn, you would not know which Nick to shoot as you're bound to see two or more of me." Nick gave another laugh, this one quiet but mocking. "Just give me an excuse to call you out right now, little brother." He knew Ethan hated the epithet *little* as he'd always envied Nick's position as the older brother.

Ethan's bloodshot eyes narrowed. "You shan't have the satisfaction of killing me." His beringed fingers clawed at Nick's sleeve and Nick shook him off in disgust. "I shall kill you first." He flung out his arm in a gesture of exasperation and stalked off as fast as his high-heeled shoes would carry him.

Nick stared at the narrow back and calculated exactly how many inches Ethan's heart was located above the waist-high gold buttons. A futile pleasure, but an act that brought a small sense of satisfaction.

Carey came to stand beside him. "Not an exchange of eternal devotion, I gather."

"Rather the opposite. I suspect one of us will die if our life-long animosity is to be extinguished. If I have any say in the matter, it shan't be me."

Carey looked toward the front door, where more gentlemen had entered to try their luck at the tables. "He's here. Sir Luther, I mean."

Hilliard wore a pale yellow waistcoat that strained over a sagging paunch. His sparse hair had been pomaded and powdered and was held back with a large silk bow. He had a jowly face and cold shrewd eyes that took in the assembled people in the hallway with one sweeping glance. He walked with a slight waddle, holding his back straight and proud.

Nick stared at the older man as he crossed the room toward the doorway where Nick and Carey were standing. *Unscrupulous,* was the word that came to Nick as he watched Hilliard's progress. Sir James had always maintained that the man had no conscience. Greedy, to boot. Hadn't he, after all, killed his brother over a strip of land between the two estates?

Hilliard stopped right in front of Nick, his black gaze sweeping the younger man from head to foot. "I recognize you. You're one of Sir James's young pups. The adopted one. I recognize that proud tilt of your head, as if you're always ready to face a challenge about your humble ancestry." He clucked his tongue. "Your mother acted so very foolishly when she ran away with that traveling actor. She could have done so much better for herself." He smiled coldly, revealing a set of decaying yellow teeth.

Nick suppressed a wild urge to accuse him of murdering Andrew Hilliard. He stood back, folded his arms with deliberate slowness, and rubbed his jaw as if coolly appraising the man before him.

"My low birth did not hamper my appearance, whereas your highborn ancestors did not give you any feature of which to be proud, Hilliard. I daresay no *lady* has ever looked at you twice.''

Silence hung heavy in the room as gamblers clustered around the small group.

Sir Luther's eyes glittered with hatred. ''A proud bearing and a plump pocket more than adequately compensate for any other deficiency, and no lady has ever accused me of lacking *manhood.*''

''Again, I doubt you've ever had a lady, only women. A well-filled purse cannot buy affection, only temporary relief of your carnal itch.''

Sir Luther sputtered, his hand raising as if ready to slap Nick's face. Letty Rose intervened.

''I will not permit raised voices in my establishment,'' she said, her gaze darting suspiciously from one face to the next.

''A challenge can be delivered in a whisper,'' Nick said, giving Sir Luther the opportunity to offer his ultimatum over the head of Letty Rose.

Only silence filled the room, then Sir Luther snorted and elbowed his way through the throng toward the faro table.

Nick found that he was trembling, and anger churned in his stomach. ''That lying, conniving fool!'' he said under his breath to Carey. ''I should have called him out when he didn't issue the challenge.''

Carey shrugged. ''Why bother with worms like Hilliard? Let's find a club with a better odor.'' He bowed to Letty Rose and Nick followed his lead.

They headed toward the door, and Nick saw from the corner of his eyes that Ethan stood partly concealed behind a leafy plant in an urn. No doubt—if his smug expression were an indication—he'd been listening to the conversation with Hilliard and gathered every insult like precious pearls.

Nick did not find out anything of importance about Sir Luther in London. Hilliard had a spotless reputation, and a fortune behind him. Without solid evidence, anyone would be hard put to bring a peer to the gallows. Nick stood on the front steps of the Cocoa Tree coffeehouse, thinking that Somerset was the next step. Mayhap the people still at High Crescent would have some light to shed on the mystery. It did not look promising, however.

Nick glanced down the street. A sedan chair came toward him and he crossed over to the opposite side. The evening sun was powerless to warm the icy autumn air. The houses cast long shadows. Before he left London, he would visit the children at the orphanage. He strode down the street, hoping to reach his destination before dark.

Ethan watched him from the interior of the sedan chair. Filled with a sudden need to discover Nick's destination, he ordered the men to follow his stepbrother. He wished he could find something to hold over Nick's head. Extortion was not a pretty word, but would take care of his debts nicely, Ethan thought, gnawing on a fingernail.

Nick hailed a hackney, and the men started running to keep up with the faster horse.

Darkness had crept over the city when the hackney finally stopped and let out its passenger. Ethan parted the curtains and glanced up and down the street. *Filth, thieves, and whores,* he thought. A sewer. He did not like to spend time in this Hell's Kitchen, but something caught his attention. Nick walked through the doors of a large building over which hung a carved sign with the words Sir James's Orphanage. Surprise flowed through him. *Sir James's Orphanage?* Had his father founded this? He beckoned one of the sedan carriers.

"I'll give you a shilling if you can discover who founded this orphanage."

"That I can do." The burly man licked his thick lips, a gesture of greed, and headed toward the door. He returned two minutes later and said, "An ole toff at a desk said many patrons provide for th' orphanage, but that some nob, Mr. Nick, is th' man who made a go of it." The bearer snorted. "The ole man wanted to know if I wanted t' make a contribution." He held out his beefy hand, and Ethan placed the silver coin reluctantly into the palm. "You have been a great help." Mr. Nick, indeed. Where had Nick gathered the funds to support such a vast project? Ethan could not wait to get to the bottom of the matter.

Nick arrived at The Hollows two days later to find Charles's new traveling coach, which he'd had made before the wedding, parked in the drive. Nick's heart took an involuntary leap as he thought of seeing Marguerite again.

Birdie Jones, whom Nick had brought with him from the orphanage for a spell of bracing country air, chirped with pleasure as she saw two squirrels frisking around a tree trunk. Against all odds, she had recovered some of her strength, and Nick was proud that she'd survived her bout with lung fever. The girl had pluck.

Charles met him in the hallway. They embraced, and Nick was relieved to have his best friend and neighbor back.

"S'faith, I've missed you, old fellow," Charles said, his eyes bright with humor.

"Judging by your wide grin, I take it the honeymoon was a glorious success."

"More than that," Charles whispered. "Marguerite is in the family way."

The sinking feeling of dread that Nick had expected at such an announcement did not happen. Instead, delight filled him. "This is great news," he said, squeezing Charles's shoulder. "The proud father. I can see you dandling an infant on your knee."

"Never thought the idea of fatherhood would bring such joy. Marguerite is happy, and her happiness is mine."

"After the ordeal with Montagu Renny, you deserve every ounce of happiness you can get."

They walked together through the house and out on the terrace. Women's laughter reached Nick's ears, Delicia's and Marguerite's. Nick expected a shock when he laid eyes on the woman he'd loved; but when his gaze found Marguerite sitting next to Serena on a bench, he only felt a gentle pleasure, pride to call himself Marguerite's friend.

She looked radiant, her golden red hair like a curly halo around her head and her freckled face blushing. He grinned, running to hug her, but it was Serena's troubled face and sad slanted eyes that caught his attention.

Her darker presence obscured Marguerite's happiness, and it nagged at Nick's conscience. He wanted to remove the sadness. He watched her over Marguerite's shoulder, and she averted her face as if loath to meet his gaze.

Marguerite had filled out somewhat. As far as he could tell, her waistline had not increased, but there was a sweet ripeness about her and her lush lips held a secret smile.

"Charles told me the wondrous news. Congratulations are in order. Well done, Marguerite."

She gave him a pleased glance and squeezed his hand. "We would be honored if you would stand as godfather to the child. Will you, Nick?"

"Of course! The honor is wholly mine. Children should all have godfathers and godmothers."

He exchanged a glance with Serena, her mysterious dark eyes making him swallow hard. A charged current sprang up between them, vibrating in the gentle warmth of the autumn sun. Secrets. He held so many secrets, and she shared more with him than most.

"How are you, Miss Hilliard?" he asked, holding her cool hand to his lips and studying the stubborn line of her lips.

"As well as can be expected," she replied tonelessly. "Everyone has been very kind to me here."

"I take it your trip to London was successful," Delicia said after going back inside and returning with Birdie. The girl looked so much better, pale pink roses in her cheeks where there had only been whiteness before. He kissed Delicia's forehead and hoisted the child high into the air. "I took care of urgent business, but failed in certain matters." He could almost feel Serena's questioning glance at his back.

"Did ye buy sugarplums in Lunnon, Mr. Nick?" asked the child.

"See if you can find any in my pocket." He set the child down and she slid a slim hand into his coat pocket, immediately extracting a bag of sweets.

"You're spoiling her," Delicia said, but she eagerly shared the bounty with Birdie and offered the other ladies the rest of the sweetmeat.

"Where is Callie?" Nick asked, his high spirits crumbling as he remembered his fiancée.

"Still abed," Delicia said, her animation fading. "She refused to get up this morning."

"We were surprised to hear about your sudden wedding plans," Charles said cautiously. "Plans made in haste, methinks."

Nick nodded. "The only possible solution to an unbearable situation."

"Very noble," Charles said, but his voice held a note of disapproval. "You're throwing away the rest of your life for something Ethan did? You're not responsible for his acts of dishonor."

Uneasy silence fell over the assembly, and Nick's stomach turned over as he thought about his bleak future. "I've chosen, and my decision cannot be changed. I stand by my offer to Miss Vine. At least she shall not suffer further."

Delicia touched his arm. "Your choice might have been a mite hasty. Once her broken heart is healed, she will see the world more favorably—"

"—but her name will always be in ruins thanks to our brother, the heartless libertine," Nick said scathingly.

"Yes . . . I'm so very disappointed in Ethan." Delicia stepped away, her attention flitting away from him. Not only Callie, but his sister had suffered as well as she came to grips with Ethan's true character. Her innocence had been rudely destroyed, and Nick held that against Ethan. There was nothing that Ethan hadn't done to destroy the fabric of their lives.

Feeling suffocated, Nick jumped down from the terrace. "Excuse me, but I need to stretch my legs before dinner."

He went along the brick path to the knot garden, kicking up mounds of leaves as he walked. He noted the box hedges needed trimming next spring and mayhap he should consult with the gardener about planting new perennials in the borders.

Rapid steps sounded behind him on the gravel. He sensed Serena's elusive female perfume before he turned around to confront her. He would recognize that anywhere.

She wore a stiff expression, her cheeks pale and her eyes shadowy with anxiety. "I wanted to thank you in private for helping me, Nick. I truly appreciate your support. Did you discover anything about Uncle Luther that will aid my cause?"

"No word to say how happy you are to see me?" he chided, devouring the view of her slender figure in a simple blue sack gown with velvet bows on the stomacher. Her throat looked white and vulnerable above the lacy shawl slung over her shoulders. A cold breeze fluttered the curls that had escaped the simple knot on top of her head. He longed to take her into his arms and crush her mouth to his. He *needed* her. To find strength he needed to hear her words of love, needed to bury himself in her, feel her response, hear her sigh of pleasure, of surrender, of approval. He could not bear to see the barrier between them, invisible yet as strong as a wall of steel.

"You know I'm happy to see you," she whispered, her eyes softening. "But it's too late for declarations of love, Nick."

Sighing, he pulled himself together. Yes, it was too late for them. He had to think of Callie. "Hilliard was gambling in London. As you said, the publicly accepted explanation to your father's death is that a vagrant killed him. We will have to prove otherwise, and the only way to do that is to learn if one of the servants happened to witness the murder. Sometimes they do see things they are reluctant to admit."

"Did you see him personally?" she asked, her arms cradling her middle as if trying to relieve a wave of pain.

"Yes, we exchanged insults at one of the gambling houses. I'm sure he has not forgotten his enmity toward Sir James. He has transferred it over to me.'' Nick gesticulated in frustration. ''I wanted to confront him then and there, but managed to curb my temper at the last moment. He must not know anything about our plans for revenge. 'Tis better if he believes that you're hiding somewhere, frightened for your life.''

''I am hiding,'' she said.

''Yes, but not for very long,'' he said, hoping he could help to set her free. ''I visited my banker and he could tell me that Sir Luther's finances are in order. He did not kill just to get his hands on High Crescent and the land adjoining his estate.''

''He killed father because he hated him. Sir Luther has always possessed a violent temper, and that time, he did not bother to control it.''

Nick longed to wrap his arms around her, but he could sense her rejection if he tried to comfort her. He walked along the straight hedgerows and she fell into step beside him. ''Have you accepted your father's death, Serena?''

She nodded. ''He's gone, and there is nothing I can do to change that. I also find it difficult to grieve such a cruel man as my father.''

''His death threw you into a sea of uncertainty.''

''Yes . . . it has forced me to seek self-knowledge. I have more strength than I realized.''

He stopped behind a cone-shaped juniper. ''You have everything a gentleman would ever wish for in a woman—compassion, honor, and passion. Irresistible allure.'' He gripped her shoulders and pulled her toward him. ''I wish you could admit that to yourself.''

''Oh, Nick. Why do you always prod me?''

''Because you don't appreciate yourself as you should.''

He could not stop himself from kissing her luscious lips that so easily could bring him to the edge of no control. He sucked on the plump curves, his tongue delving into the silky moistness of her mouth. A hunger rose in him, a raging beast of discontent. He squeezed her breast through the soft material of her gown, felt its familiar thrusting firm shape and went weak at the knees.

He groaned deep in his throat, yearning to rip off her clothes and take her on the first hard bench he came across.

"It can't go on like this," he said as he subdued her struggles to get away and held her tightly. "You belong with me. I need you, Serena—even if you're a terrible cook."

She sighed forlornly against his cravat. "I wish we could have a future, but you are to be married soon and I have no desire to stand between you and Miss Vine. In a way, I feel sorry for her. *She* doesn't know she's marrying a highwayman."

Her words brought him back to reality, and he loosened his grip enough for her to push away from his embrace.

"Do you truly believe you can have everything, Nick? Travelers' purses, children's gratitude and adoration, a pleasant wife, a doting sister, fawning servants, and a mistress." She pushed against his chest so that he had to step back.

"You know I'm not that calculating, Serena."

"Well, I won't become your mistress. I can't. Whatever happened in your sanctuary in London is forgotten and buried. You shan't make me with child and set me up as your mistress somewhere. I shan't be at your beck and call every time your hunger stirs. You'll marry, and then you can love your wife to your heart's content."

"Damn you, Serena! Have I asked you to become my mistress?" He closed his hand around her arm. "No. I want our relationship to be sealed in the church, and if that cannot be, then we will have to learn to live without each other."

She nodded. "I succumbed to your seduction in moments of weakness, when I had nothing but the comfort you could give me. You gave me great comfort. In a way, you taught me that I could do more than simply be a *lady*. I could *live,* choose my own path."

"You have uncommon strength. All you had to do was recognize it."

"But am I a fool to place my burden at your feet? Am I heartless for expecting you to help me since I have rejected you? Should I confront Uncle Luther with a pistol in my hand?"

He smiled. "That would be foolish, Serena. Only cold planning will bring Hilliard to justice, and that involves your staying on here for some time. I can't leave Callie while she's in a dismal state; but as soon as she has regained a particle of her crushed pride, we shall travel to Somerset and take care of your problems. You can count on that.''

She eyed him with worry. "I don't wish to give you anguish.''

He touched her cheek with one finger. "I suspect I am not the only one who shall suffer from unrequited love," he said with a wry smile. "But nothing can ruin the memory of the love we shared." He could not trust himself to speak further. He turned away from her abruptly, feeling as if he had torn part of his heart out of his chest.

Chapter 21

Serena watched him leave. This time, she had lost him for good. Something had happened, an invisible battle where her heart had been trampled and torn asunder—all by her own rejection of him. She doubted herself, feeling as if she'd turned away her only hope of happiness.

She wished she could crawl into a hole and nurse her bleeding heart, but there was no time for self-pity. She had to solve her problems, and until they were solved, she needed Nick's help. If she could find a way to make Miss Vine return to life, he would be ready to go on the journey to Somerset. After that, she could lick her wounds in solitude.

After dinner, an awkward affair since the tension between her and Nick was such that it filled the room, she excused herself and went upstairs to Miss Vine's bedchamber.

Filled with reluctance, she nevertheless knocked on the door. A maid admitted her, and Serena found the young invalid propped against the pillows, eyes closed. Her face had the marble grayness of someone dead. The whippet dogs lay sprawled across the cover, long noses resting on Miss Vine's thighs and brown eyes trained on her face as they sought to comfort her. Serena patted Moonlight's silky head, and the dog nuzzled her hand.

She sensed that Miss Vine teetered on the very edge of expiration. Serena had spoken to her during the time she'd spent at The Hollows, but only in passing. She'd resented that this wraith of a woman was going to marry the man Serena loved, but now she could only see the urgency of saving a fellow human being from death.

Serena sat down on the chair next to the bed and took the thin cold hand on the coverlet into her own. "Miss Vine? Are you feeling very poorly?"

The large brown eyes opened, and Serena could only feel compassion for her rival. She squeezed the hand, hoping to convey her support. "Do you want me to read to you?"

"You may call me Callie. *Miss Vine* sounds like the stiff name of a governess. It suits me—becoming a governess with a name to match." She sighed. "That is if I ever get back on my feet again."

"You don't really want to, do you?" Serena said, sensing Callie's inner struggle. "To be betrayed by someone you love is most difficult to accept."

Callie gave her a glance full of doubt. She did not reply, and Serena was at a loss for words. She patted the hand, looking around the room for some diversion. All she saw was a heap of gowns tossed carelessly onto the back of a chair and the welter of shoes on the floor, all of them broken, the satin slippers cut to shreds.

"Did you do that?" she asked.

Callie nodded, pinching her lips tight.

"Why?" Serena asked, but she knew why. Despair, pure and simple, the end to a world once known. Serena shuddered at the destruction and wished she could say something that would soothe Miss Vine's tormented mind.

"I have no use for shoes any longer." Callie stared at Serena. "Have you ever been betrayed?" she asked in a small voice.

"Yes, in a way. My parents did not care what became of me, and that is one kind of betrayal. All they ever cared about was themselves . . . and their private battles—which destroyed them in the end. Father cared deeply about the brandy bottle, and Mother cared only about getting revenge for Father's slights—real or imagined.''

Serena sighed, feeling something give in her chest, a dam opening, flooding her with pain. Tears welled into her eyes and she could not stop them. Callie was a stranger, but a woman adrift just like herself. Between bouts of blowing her nose, Serena told Callie about her father's death and how she longed to bring her uncle to the court of justice. ''Only then will I be able to rest.''

Callie wiped her eyes with the back of her hand. ''I'm sorry to hear all that you've gone through, the heartache. I'm so ashamed of myself,'' she whispered. ''I was so weak, gave Sir Ethan everything; I was foolish to believe his declarations of love.''

Serena shook her head. ''No, don't blame yourself. 'Tis not wrong to trust. Sir Ethan behaved abominably. The blame lies wholly with him.''

Callie pounded the mattress with her fist. ''I can't help but berate myself. He seemed to care, and he spoke in such romantic terms about our future together. I *believed* him.''

''Sir Ethan has lived in the metropolis for a long time and is practiced in the ways of the world. He would know what kind of words would impress your innocent heart.''

Callie covered her face with her hands. ''I'm mortified. I don't know if I'll ever manage to leave this house, to face the world again.''

''Your leg was broken badly, but it could have been your neck.'' A flame of anger stirred in Serena's chest. ''Besides, you don't want to give Sir Ethan the satisfaction of knowing you're grieving for him.''

Callie punched the mattress anew and one of the dogs jumped down. ''I am not grieving for *him!*''

''He will construe that explanation. Since you're going to marry Nick, your path is bound to cross that of Sir Ethan more often than you like. You need to hold your head up and look at him in defiance. Don't give him the satisfaction of watching you turn into a shadow of your former self. He will only gloat."

Callie looked at her for a long moment. "I can't walk."

"Not right now, perhaps, but one day you will, if you work at it."

"No man in his right mind will look at me now. I'm crippled. The doctor said my leg won't heal straight."

"You'll be a married lady. Nick cares about you; you won't need the admiring glances of other gentlemen."

Callie grimaced. "Nick only offered for me out of pity and shame over what Ethan did to me, and I leaped at the chance to escape from my guilt."

"He did the right thing, trying to honor Ethan's promise to you. What exactly happened? Sometimes it really helps to talk about a problem; it make it easier to bear."

"Ever since the moment we arrived in London—Delicia and I—Ethan paid me compliments. He took us out on the town, seeing all the sights. We went to small supper parties and other gatherings. He took me riding in the park." Callie crossed her hands on the coverlet and looked intently at Serena. "Did you know he dresses like royalty and has a very fine manner?"

"No—but sometimes fine clothes and polite words mean very little."

"I thought he drank too much wine at the dinner table and his eyes were uncommonly red. But I could only see his sophisticated manner and elegance."

"You're not the first woman who has been taken in by the smooth charm of a libertine. And you won't be the last."

Callie flung her arm over her blushing face. "Then he proposed. I knew Delicia would tell me to wait, not to give my answer until my brother returned to England. Ethan convinced me we should get married immediately, in Scotland. I agreed, and in the coach ..." She sobbed. "... in the coach, he whispered love words, then seduced me at the inn, saying we would be man and wife before the week was out."

She wailed. "Such shame! I so enjoyed his embrace, thinking I had arrived at the gates of Heaven."

"You were in love; you trusted him in everything." Serena sighed, feeling uncomfortable as she thought of her torrid love-making with Nick. "You're not the only woman who has fallen for the virile spell of a gentleman."

Silence filled the room, and Serena sensed that Callie's despair had lessened somewhat. She walked to the window, feeling that her own life had taken on a new course, part of her past put to rest.

Looking at the blazing autumn colors and the sapphire blue sky, she said, "Why is it that women so readily take the blame unto themselves? Are we of less worth because we're not allowed to make monetary decisions or speak against our husbands? Are we lesser creatures and thus have to take the blame for the excesses of the gentlemen?" She straightened her tense back. "I think not, even though the law says we are nothing more than chattel. In London I came to meet a woman, Miss Hopkins, who has never been married and owns her own millinery shop. She does not bend to anyone's will, and she makes every decision concerning her sales and purchases. She has women who work for her, and unlike her male peers, she does not take the whip to tired backs. She pays fair wages and encourages her workers to take pride in their skills."

Callie had heaved her splinted leg over the side of the bed, the end of the bandages dangling on the floor. "You're right, Serena. We're only worth what we think we're worth. Mayhap I can find a place for myself where my disgrace won't count. I would not mind doing something with my hands. Embroidery is one of my special skills." Animated now, she swung herself into her invalid chair, her voluminous nightgown trailing.

Serena watched in surprise.

"Please push me to the window seat at the other side of the room, Serena."

Her spirits lifting, Serena complied. One of the dogs followed and jumped up on the seat. The sunlight slanted golden through the windows. Callie pulled a satchel of yellow brocade onto her lap and extracted a wooden frame over which a canvas had been stretched. An intricate motif of a peacock with his tail gloriously spread, trees in the background, dazzled Serena's eyes.

"You are an expert needlewoman, as much is clear," she said. "You will never be bored as long as you have a canvas close by."

"You're right." Callie smiled for the first time since Serena had entered. "I designed it myself." She gave Serena a probing stare. "You really think it is good?"

"It's more than good; it's superior."

Callie clutched the frame to her chest tightly. "Mayhap I should work on it before the daylight is gone."

"An excellent idea. I'll fetch your wrapping gown, and you can sit right here by the window."

"Will you stay and chat some more?"

"It will be my pleasure," Serena said, meaning it. In the place of a rival for Nick's affection, she had gained a new friend.

Two weeks later, Callie walked for the first time with a stick. Her leg would always be crooked, but at least she'd found the strength to move from the bed to the wheelchair and then to walking. Serena took Callie's progress as a personal triumph, a feeling she evidently shared with Sunshine and Moonlight, who followed Callie everywhere she went.

Admittedly, she had approached Callie out of selfish motives since Nick had claimed he would not leave The Hollows until Callie was out of danger, but her motives had changed from that first day in Callie's bedchamber.

Then Rafael Howard arrived one night, and Nick announced that he and Rafe would ride with her into Somerset to search for a way to prove that Luther Hilliard had murdered his brother.

An old and dour maid kept Serena company and lent an air of respectability to the expedition as the traveling chaise set out early on the following morning. Rafe and Nick rode beside the carriage, and Serena leaned out the window to wave at her new friends on the front steps, Delicia and Callie, who was leaning heavily on her stick.

Serena fell back against the velvet squabs and looked out the window. An uneasy feeling filled her as she watched Nick's stern profile as he rode beside the carriage. She hadn't seen his infectious grin for a long time; she hadn't heard him really laugh for weeks. Not that she'd spent much time in his company during the last few weeks, only at dinner. He had avoided her since their last confrontation in the knot garden. An uneasy barrier had risen between them, one of anger and disappointment. She had to remind herself it was all for the best. He would marry Callie when they got back from Somerset.

She was going home, and the thought sent her spirits plummeting. Her stomach filled with anxiety about returning to the place that held so many bad memories. She wished she could've had Nick's support. He was present, but not really with her.

They stopped at a hedge tavern for luncheon. The tavern consisted of a taproom that smelled of sour ale and roasting meat. Nick led Serena toward the fireplace, where a fire sent out warmth, to thaw her frozen toes. The day had turned chilly, with a stiff breeze from the north. Snow flurries danced in the air.

"Wait here. I shall order some food from the landlord," he said tersely.

She sat down on a wooden bench by the table nearest to the fireplace and watched Nick's broad back as he spoke with the landlord.

She wished she would have the opportunity to speak with Nick again, to feel his support, but he avoided her at all cost.

The landlord, wearing a long waistcoat and breeches of brown homespun and rough gray stockings, carried over a bowl of steaming stew, a basket of bread, and a plate of roast fowl. He finally polished an apple with a white towel and placed it cautiously beside her plate. "There, my lady. 'Ope that'll please yer palate," he said with a series of bows.

"Thank you." Serena could not help but smile. Clearly, he did not get many guests besides the local farmers. She ate, finding the stew tasty and the bread fresh. She wished Nick would sit beside her, but he shared another table with Rafe. He glanced at her once, and as their eyes met, the air crackled with tension. She coughed as a piece of bread stuck in her throat. He would have noticed her discomfiture.

Her appetite appeased, she patted her mouth with a napkin. She exchanged another glance with Nick, and this time he did not turn away. She read both wrath and hunger in his expression, exasperation as well. Her heart hammered, and her limbs went weak with longing. No matter what he had done and said, he still had the power to stir her blood. Heat rose in her cheeks, and she had to look away.

Without as much as a word or a movement, he'd undressed her and held her in his arms. Her body seemed to open up toward him, like a flower to sunlight. It took only one glance.

"Are you ready?" he asked gruffly.

The double meaning of the words made her tremble. "I'm ready to move on," she replied. "I don't like to stay in one spot forever."

"So I've noticed," he said, holding the door for her.

"I resent your cynical tone," she said.

"At this point, I don't care what you like or don't like. I'm only here because I promised to help you, but my disposition is none of your business." He slanted a cool glance at her. "You've shown your contempt for me in many ways, and I would be foolish to leave myself open to another rejection from you."

They came to the carriage door, and Nick stood so close she could see his chest rising and falling in rapid breaths. Physical attraction, as thick as syrup, moved between them, and Serena's breath faltered in the magnetism of his stare.

Remember Callie, a voice chanted in her head. *She's your friend now. Don't give in to the attraction. You will only get hurt.*

"If you let love rule your life, you'll be weak, vulnerable. You're bound to get burned," she said out loud, then clapped her hand to her mouth, shocked that she'd spoken her thoughts.

He shrugged as if he cared naught for her views. "A path for cowards," he scoffed. "Those who dare not love are dry and empty beings."

He opened the door and handed her inside. His touch burned through her kid glove, and she breathed deeply to calm her emotions. The farther away from Sussex they rode, the more she was reminded of the times that they had spent alone at Nick's refuge in London. There had been no tomorrow, no promise for the future, no Callie Vine. They had loved as if nothing else mattered. Loved too much in haste.

Nick slammed the door so that the coach rattled. Serena jumped in surprise, wondering if she'd turned down the only chance at love she would ever have. No, *no!* She had to hold fast to her principles, no matter how desperate she longed to feel whole and loved again.

They stopped at the Bell and Gander outside Winchester for the night. Stiff, and with an aching back, Serena got out. A sheet of icy rain enveloped her, and she pulled the cloak tighter around her as she dashed to the front door.

Behind her, Nick and Rafe shouted something to the ostler, and the carriage creaked on its way to the stables. All she could think of was food and a warm fire.

The closer they came to Somerset, the more grief rose within her. More memories. In London, far removed from the place where the murder had taken place, she had been able to suppress her reactions to some degree; but now the horrors were slowly seeping back, and with them the feeling of helplessness.

In London, a new woman had started to emerge, one who was breaking out of the shackles of her bitter past; but now, here, she had to step down the long staircase to an inner purgatory and meet all the ghosts she'd banished from her thoughts.

On the verge of tears, she looked around the dim taproom filled with acrid smoke from the fire and the oil lamps. Her eyes stung, and it would have been enough of an excuse to cry; but where would it end if she opened the flood gates? She forced herself to get a grip on her emotions. The room with its low-beamed ceiling had about ten customers, local farmers drinking ale at the tables.

As she shook out her damp cloak, the landlord, a small weasel-faced man with red curly hair, came forward and greeted her.

At the same time, Nick and Rafe entered, their cloaks wet and their hats dripping with rain.

Nick pulled off his gloves, his expression closed and grim. Serena sensed his hostility, and it fueled her premonition of doom.

"My good man, give us three rooms for the night, a private parlor, and a hot meal," Nick ordered.

"Yes, sir. Would turbot in a white sauce and a leg of mutton boiled with capers suit you? Plum pudding for afters."

"To a famished man, it sounds delicious," Nick said.

"In the parlor at the back, sir." The landlord bowed and scurried through a door through which delicious cooking aromas emanated. Serena recognized the woodsy scents of onion, thyme, and basil.

Nick took her arm brusquely and led her across the room. She shook off his grip. "I can walk perfectly well on my own," she said under her breath.

"As I know 'twill rile you, I'll always find an excuse to touch you. And I don't like the locals ogling you," he said.

She returned his irate glance. "I'll embrace any excuse that takes you away from my side," she shot back.

"I think hunger has ruined our tempers," Rafe said, having overheard their conversation. He brushed back his long hair with his hand, securing the loose ribbon at the nape of his neck. He had dark hollows under his eyes, and Serena noticed his utter exhaustion. She was not the only one who had suffered a deep loss.

Rafe held out her chair, and she sat down as she glanced around the room. A maid was putting platters on the sideboard. Two serving wenches entered with earthenware bowls, plates, and wineglasses.

Nick ordered a bottle of claret, and tankards of ale for himself and Rafe. "What do you want, Miss Hilliard?"

Serena could feel his gaze resting on her, and a slow heat started in the pit of her stomach and spread to all the parts of her body. For a moment, she could have given anything to have his arms around her, but she pushed aside the disturbing thought. "Wine, please."

She swallowed and found that the swell of emotion had dried her mouth. Nick kept staring at her, his eyes now chiding her as if he could read her every reaction.

She spread her fan—one she'd painted herself at Miss Hopkins'—and started flapping it in front of her face, but it didn't lessen the heat in her cheeks. She studied the design, gilt framed cartouches depicting flowers and cherubs carrying satin banners with the words *Truth, Love, and Honor* painted in spidery letters. She took strength from the knowledge that she had fashioned this exquisite article. *She* had made it. No one had made it for her.

Nick must have noticed her close scrutiny. He said, "Judging by that self-congratulatory smirk, I'd say you're admiring your work."

"No need for that kind of ungentlemanly sarcasm," Rafe said quietly. He held out his hand toward Serena, and she gave him her fan. He spread it out, staring at it thoughtfully. "I remember something—I don't know what. A woman who spent a long time painting, both fans and pictures. The design seems familiar somehow."

"Similar to the church paintings you might have seen. Cherubs, flowers. Angels are missing, or else the motif would be a religious one. I personally like the flowers—any kind of flower," Serena said, grateful for the break in the tension between her and Nick.

Rafe rubbed his eyebrows back and forth. "I recall a flash of thin fingers working, a deft flick of the wrist, pots of paint. Then there was sunshine streaming through a window onto a table."

Serena immediately pictured her friend Andria at work.

Andria had fleet fingers and a deft wrist, but so did every other artist. "It is popular among the gentlewomen to paint their own fans if they have the smallest skill. You could be remembering a sister or a cousin, even an artist who did the work for your mother."

Rafe's face took on a look of frustration. "You could be right. I don't really remember anything of substance." He leaned his elbows on the table and pressed his fingertips to his temples. Serena's breathing grew shallow as she felt his pain; he was on the verge of breaking down, or giving up the thin hold on his life.

She instinctively laid her hand on his arm and squeezed reassuringly. "Don't despair. You are very kind to help me in my time of need, and I shall find a way to repay your patience and generosity."

Rafe's chest heaved in a deep sigh, and she saw that he'd gained a grip on his despair. She gave Nick a long look, and he nodded as if understanding her silent plea for reassurance.

"I have already promised I'll ride north with Rafe after this adventure. We'll confront Lord Rowan together."

I would like to go, too, Serena thought, but she didn't speak the words. Her road would have to part from Nick's after their trip to Somerset. She had her work now, and she would return to London as soon as the matter of her father's death had been cleared.

"That was the kindest thing you have said today, Nick." She gave him a smile. "I'm glad your friends don't have to taste your vitriol—the one you have reserved for me."

"They have not acted in any way to provoke my ire," Nick said, his voice a whiplash of anger. "A man has only so much patience and tolerance."

"Yes, I can tell. But what you lack in one area, you have in others—irascibility, stubbornness, and restlessness. Stealth and cunning. The list is endless."

"And a list only you would consign to memory. You pounce on my smallest flaw and it builds into unbearable proportions."

Serena looked away under his onslaught. Rafe stood, pushing

back his chair. "I shall make sure the horses are safely sheltered from the rain before dinner." He left, and Serena's spirits sank.

"Nick! See what you did? You pushed Rafael from the room with your careless speech. We should not quarrel in public. 'Tis very rude."

Nick sighed and leaned back in his chair. "You're right, but I can't help my baser instincts from emerging in your presence."

"Find a way to control yourself," she spat.

He gave her a lingering look that promised revenge and punishment. A shiver went up her spine, but her heart beat with excitement, and desire flared hot and tempestuous between them.

"I challenge you to accept the truth about your feelings," he said in a low voice. "Let nature takes its course and stop denying your heart and your physical longings for me. We can't hobble along like this much longer."

His words made her skin tingle and passion leap to life in her heart. His gaze made her think of a forest fire that burned down everything in its wake.

Chapter 22

Serena tossed and turned on the lumpy pillow, unable to sleep until late in the night. She rested uneasily, going in and out of oblivion. Her thoughts raced interminably even though she'd drunk wine with her dinner to deaden the disturbing memories of her past. Horrible dreams of her father's death filled her sleep.

Gagging, she sat upright in bed, her senses swimming. At first, she had no idea where she was. Then she remembered and was grateful for the weak gray light coming through the only window of her room at the inn.

Clammy sweat covered her body. She wrapped her arms around her knees as the latch lifted on the door. Someone slipped into the room, and she stiffened in fear.

"Who is it?" Was that thin and breathless voice really hers?

" 'Tis me, Nick. My room is next door, and I heard you scream and thrash about in bed." He sat beside her on the mattress, and she sensed his reluctance to hold her.

She sobbed and held out her arms toward him. "You came."

He pulled her up against his bare chest and tightened his glorious embrace until she could barely breathe. She felt safe.

"You still suffer from the nightmares, don't you?"

Feeling shattered and vulnerable, she could only nod. He shouldn't be here; she shouldn't be in his arms, but she could not pull away. She craved his comfort as a bee craved nectar. If he removed his arms, she would collapse into a boneless puddle.

Slowly she became aware of his hard muscles and the velvety skin stretched so tightly across his broad back. A contrast of softness and strength. Rough virility tempered with refinement. Her hands traveled of their own accord along the indentation of his spine. He groaned against her hair, his hands plucking aimlessly at her curls and sliding over her back to cup her neck.

He wore only breeches, the waistband tight and hampering her caresses. She ought to stop. Protests erupted quick like mushrooms in her mind, but for a moment, just for a moment, she longed to savor his embrace, exchange pain for pleasure, for a short spell pretend that he was hers and that she was not alone in the world.

She could not betray her new friend, Callie. She couldn't . . . but even as the warning flashed through her head, it faded.

His embrace soothed her better than a warm bath would soothe her tired limbs. She reveled in the strokes of his demanding hand over her back and the way his other hand rubbed the nape of her neck where muscles pulled like tensely knotted cords.

He crooned in her ear. "There, there, sweetheart. Hush. The dreams cannot harm you. I'm here now."

She turned her face toward his neck, kissing his soft skin— the most natural act, then finding the whiskered jaw and kissing its hard contour. She waited breathlessly. He tilted his face down and finally sought her mouth, even now whispering, "Hush, hush."

He seemed to hesitate, as if debating the rationale for kissing her, then ground his mouth against hers in desperation. She responded in kind, wondering how she'd lived without his loving for so long. Drugged by his nearness, she held on to him as if drowning and moved her hips against him in a silent plea.

With his knee, he parted her thighs and pushed his turgid member against her femininity. A wave of desire, thick as honey, poured through her.

"Plague take it, but I want you, Serena," he said roughly, pinning her wrists over her head on the pillow. With the other hand, he pulled her nightgown up over her hips and buried his fingers in the curls at the apex of her thighs and slid one into the wet folds, leaving hot aching longing in the wake of his caress. He repeated the teasing stroke, and every time, she arched against him, now frantic for his love.

He nipped her breasts through the material of her gown and sucked one crest into a hard pebble. Pleasure waves surged through her, gathering ever more yearning in the core of her being.

"You are lovely," he said against her neck. "I've wanted you since the moment you left me. I haven't been able to sleep for wanting you." He continued caressing that most sensitive nub, and urgency made her push against his hand. He murmured, "In you, I forget myself. I feel that I'm home at last when I join myself to you in that place that gives me erotic daydreams."

His warm breath stirred her skin, and she touched him, rubbing his hardness through his breeches. "I want you, too," she whispered, knowing she could say that every day of her life. Before she could fall over the edge into the sea of bliss, he lifted himself from the bed and hastily discarded his breeches.

The proof of his desire sprang forth as if bursting with need. He leaned forward, and she took him into her mouth, licking and teasing the velvety length until he trembled and groaned. He gripped her shoulders and squeezed convulsively as if the pleasure were too explosive to contain. He finally pulled away, coaxed her up onto her knees on the mattress, discarded her nightgown, and lifted her into his arms. He stood, holding her so tight in his arms she could barely breathe. Skin against naked skin, breasts against the hard wall of his chest. She wrapped her legs around his waist as he drove into her slippery sheath.

Her hard nipples rubbed against his chest, adding another dimension of desire to her already aroused state. She lifted her hips and bore down on him. He staggered, then held her still in ever-mounting anticipation.

"Ohh," he moaned as she rubbed her breasts against him. He carried her to the hard-backed chair and sat down on top of her dress. Straddling him, she rode his shaft as he kneaded her breasts. She rose on a convulsive peak, and as she shattered in a shower of ecstasy, he buried his face against her heart. She held onto his head as wave after wave washed through her, leaving her limp with satisfaction.

Nick tasted the soft flesh of her swollen breasts, their very shape, their firmness, their hard crests making him mad with desire. He gripped her round buttocks, driving himself toward the edge of frenzy. Her dulcet core, so deep inside he thought he would drown, beckoned him, teased him with its honey until he could only cry out her name in desperation and pump his seed into her.

At first he could not catch his breath; it finally returned—a ragged groan of wonder. A golden wave of satisfaction rolled through him, but also the faint voice of need. He had to have more, had to find a way to slake his thirst for this woman who seemed more elusive than the stars. Either he would have her forever or she would destroy him.

"I want to make you mine," he said out loud, feeling himself stiffen anew as if her very scent, her soft skin, her sweet tight sheath were a constant challenge to his manhood.

She tried to pull away at his words, but he held her fast, nibbling at her neck and stroking her back.

"It's growing cold," she said finally, and for the first time, he felt the icy draft along the floor.

"My lovemaking shall keep you warm," he replied, and carried her to the bed.

She did not protest as he pulled the blankets over them both and started playing the instrument of her body again. He had to make her remember this night forever.

Serena awakened very early the next morning. She had not slept much; she'd spent most of the night in Nick's arms, knowing she had become the mistress of a betrothed man despite her strong resolve to keep away from him. One part of her reveled in the bone-deep satisfaction. Another side cringed, aghast at what she had done. The inner war robbed her of whatever rest was left that night.

Sighing, she stretched in catlike contentment, wondering what would happen next.

Nick flung one arm across her chest, pinning her down. He lifted his face, dark with stubble. Unruly hair hung over his brow, and his eyes glittered with delight—tempered with caution. He gave her a long, searching stare.

"You look tired, Serena. Did sleep fail you?"

She moved up, pushing the pillow into a mound under her head. "Yes, it failed me." She twisted a strand of hair around her finger. "Mayhap my conscience would not let me sleep," she added thoughtfully.

He groaned, and buried his face against the side of her throat.

A well of sorrow—she did not know where it came from—opened in her heart. "I never act correctly! By loving you, I have ruined myself. Have I so little self-control that I had to give in to the first temptation that came along after I left my home?"

Nick's head jerked up. "No one is perfect, Serena. Love plays by its own rules. I, for one, am happy that I had the chance to meet you."

She wound her hair so tight around her fingertip that it turned cold. "Yes, you were always ready to slide into my bed," she teased. Inexplicable sorrow from deep within filled her throat with tears. She tried to swallow the pain; she had no reason to start crying now after such a glorious night with the man she loved.

He stroked her hair. "You'll have to learn to trust your feelings and to trust me. I have told you in the past how special you are to me and how I've wanted to make you my own. You shut me out of your life, even as we were happy. I know we lived on borrowed happiness in London. My life is not the most stable kind, but our love was true then, and it is true now. Our love has nothing to do with my 'profession.' "

She fought the river of tears. The last thing she wanted to do was make a fool of herself in front of him. He gathered her into his arms while leaning his shoulders against the rough headboard.

The gate burst, and she could not stop it. She despised herself for her lack of control. A wave of bitterness, a part that she had carried so close, that had become *her,* poured forth. She had a vision of a dark river, thick-flowing and odorous, as she cried into the hair on his chest. His arms comforted her, and he didn't say anything. She had expected him to pull back in horror or reject her in her moment of utter weakness, but he only tightened his arms further. I am a haven, safety, his embrace seemed to say.

The bitterness slowly drained, leaving emptiness and a limp feeling in its wake. She wiped her face with the corner of the sheet. "I'm such a watering pot."

"You have the right to grieve, to get rid of your bitterness, darling. This trip is bound to bring up the bad memories of your past."

"My parents must have been happy once," she said to his chest hairs. "Why couldn't they keep the happiness? When did they start to hate each other? Will we start hating each other one day?"

"I don't know, my love. You can speculate until the end of time about your parents' past, but you'll never get the whole picture. At some point, one of them hurt the other so deeply that it set the course for the rest of their lives."

She looked into his face, uncaring of the picture of red-eyed despair she must present. "Who's to say that any relationship will succeed? Ruin will come along and crush the finest love."

"It's a gamble, but if your love is very strong from the start, there is something to build life upon. Most people of our class marry for the sake of fortune and property. If love is not there from the beginning, they won't have a chance to build a life of respect and intimate sharing." He sighed. "There are exceptions to the rule, but how many are fortunate to find true love even once in their life?"

He pushed back her damp hair, and Serena floundered in a sea of uncertainty. The fabric of her life had been torn once by her parents; who was to say it wouldn't happen again? What was there to anchor her—except herself? "They were so unhappy," she muttered.

"They chose to be unhappy, to stay rooted in the bitterness and let it color their every action. With a little understanding and compassion, most problems can be solved, even the most difficult ones. You are not part of your parents. Not any more; not since you chose to think for yourself and find a way to live with their animosity. A weaker person would have blamed them for everything, would have turned her back on the problems; but you loved your parents and tried to help them."

Nick tilted up her chin. "They were not worthy of your love. It's about time you cut your bonds with their ghosts and stopped doubting your worth. You can make the choice of not living like them, sharing their narrow-minded opinions. You're strong in your own right, Serena. You can make a complete success of your life."

She threaded her fingers through his long hair. "How do you know that for certain?"

"I have lived it. The glory of finding myself living in a fine home was rapidly tempered as Sir James got his legitimate offspring. Ethan has always resented me, and he always will. I, on one hand, found happiness and a full stomach and a fine sister, but Ethan will never forget where I came from. He will never let me forget either. In the early days it almost broke me, but I found a way to rise above his constant slurs and gestures of contempt. Sir James gave me the base to create a happy life, and I have—at The Hollows."

"But you live a secret life besides."

Nick squirmed uneasily. "Yes . . . I suppose part of me is still doubting that what I have is real. Ethan has always pointed out that I carry the odor of the rookeries, and part of me will always believe him. Living the dangerous life of a highwayman is one way to thumb my nose at Ethan. I'm bringing something better to the filthy area that once was my home. Part of it is due to his goading, which then pushed me to serve the children. Sometimes a negative influence can help to bring out the best in you."

Serena nodded.

Nick gave a mirthless laugh. "That's probably the reason why I haven't killed him, even though I've been close to running him through the heart many times."

She listened and truly understood Nick for the first time since she'd met him. She knew his strength, but she had never understood how he could have chosen a path of danger and destruction deliberately. She had thought his choice was wholly due to a reckless streak that didn't feel any consideration for the people touched by his brash behavior.

"Anger can eat away at a person," he added. "It has to find a way out, something constructive, not destructive."

Serena nodded. "Yes, you're right. I see now that my parents had no desire to rise out of their misery. If they'd had it, their lives would have turned out differently."

Nick held her jaw, forcing her to look at his face. "You will choose a worthwhile path on which to travel, won't you, my dearest?"

She nodded, her throat clogging up anew. "I will make the right choices. Starting now."

His eyes narrowed as if he sensed what she was about to say.

"I'm sorry, Nick, for all the hurtful things I've said to you in the past. I respect you, and in doing so, I can't go on living a life of stolen moments with you."

Chapter 23

Serena got up from the bed. "Nick, you came to me, comforted me in the night, but this has to be an isolated interlude. To respect myself, I cannot succumb to the temptation of becoming your mistress. We must not repeat this past night. I won't be able to look into Callie's eyes without feeling a great deal of guilt."

A dark cloud fell over his brow. She sensed his disappointment and frustration, but he only played it out in the savage flinging aside of the blankets.

"You're right," he snapped. "I could never ask you to become my mistress. I cannot treat you in that shabby way, not if you are to find your own path of dignity. I would like to beg and tempt you, but I know it would be for naught."

He looked at her, his eyes bleak. "Just as I can't break my engagement to Callie. It would rob her of the thin veil of dignity that my proposal has given her. She is so frail that my rejection might bring on her death."

The gray dawn filled the room, bringing in the air of finality. They had come to a crossroads where all arguments had been spent and where only new plains lay ahead for their exploration—in the opposite direction.

"I pray to God I haven't made you with child," he said, touching her cheek. "If I have, rest assured it shall have the best of everything. I would always love any child of yours, and I won't leave you to suffer alone."

Serena swallowed the salty tears rising in her throat. "I know you wouldn't." She averted her face, praying he could not read her hopelessness.

She heard him pull on his breeches. He touched her head in a quick caress, then slipped out the door.

Sir Ethan Leverton rode through the forest bordering The Hollows. Dense oaks and ash would make a tidy sum if Nick had the forethought of cutting them down, which he didn't. He never had any idea how to liquidize his assets, always mumbled on about preserving the forest to provide a wind shelter against the north wind. As if The Hollows didn't sit snugly at the foot of the Downs.

Ethan swore as a powerful wave of hatred rushed through him, leaving behind a sensation of helplessness. He could barely stand the squalling emotion. He tightened the reins on his mount so hard, the equine reared on his hind legs as the bit sawed at his tender mouth.

"Blast and damn! Get down, you big brute," Ethan snarled as tree branches clawed at his face. He recalled his humiliation at the front door of The Hollows. Nick would pay for it, as much was certain, dammit all. Aunt Titania had given him a hard stare out of her small pig eyes and told him he was not welcome on the premises.

"If Nick were here, he would throw you off the property immediately; but as you probably know, since you dare to show yourself here, he's gone away to help Serena Hilliard. I don't understand how you have the nerve to come here after what you have done."

"I came to apologize to Miss Vine," he'd said, but in reality he'd come to find some silver or gold to hawk. He had to pay his most pressing debts. He'd heard through the gardener drinking at the local tavern that Nick had driven into Somerset and would not be back for a week, or longer.

But he'd been unable to set foot on the threshold of the blasted estate, and furthermore, guards had been placed on the premises with the orders to turn him away. He would rather leave with his life intact than be shot if he tried to break into the dashed house.

He cursed loudly as a broken twig tore his sleeve. Kicking his heels into the horse's flanks, he rode up onto a hill on top of which he had a good view of The Hollows. Tonight he might find a way to sneak into the house under the cover of darkness. It was his only chance. He had to pay part of his debts or flee the country. Or lose his life.

He stared at the mist-shrouded hollow that held what he most coveted, but also that which he most hated in life. The estate and Nick. Sir James had bought The Hollows especially for his bastard nephew, taken funds that should have rightfully belonged to the Leverton estate. He had showered them on the bastard from the Spitalfield rookeries. The Leverton name had been sullied forever from the moment Sir James decided to take in the fallen-from-grace aunt's child. Her name was never mentioned, but Ethan had known that Sir James had loved his sister. And he had loved Nick. Always Nick.

"How many times did I fall short in Father's eyes?" Ethan asked himself. "Every time he looked at great handsome Nick, did I fall short?" *Always second best.* Ethan sighed, feeling the aching, invisible thorn in his side. Sir James had many times said he loved all his children equally, but Ethan had always doubted. Father had always looked to Nick for advice, that pillar of virtue! That leech! Nick had ruined his life. It was no more than right that Nick should pay the gambling debts.

Ethan clenched his hands so hard that his long nails made bloody crescents in the palms of his hands. He licked the small wounds, all the while muttering to himself.

The sun rose over the mist, and before noontime, the haze would be gone. Best to find an inn and rest before the adventures of the night.

He remembered the old path through the woods, a path he'd ridden many times in his childhood. The sunlight slanted through the trees and would have made the ride pleasant if it hadn't been for his dark thoughts. Birds twittered in abandon, and he felt like raking his whip over the branches. Squirrels scaled the tree trunks and looked at him curiously. He could have stoned them, had he carried stones in his pockets as he had as a child. He had an accurate aim, better than Nick's.

He contemplated shooting Nick, even in the back. Who cared where he shot Nick, as long as the bastard disappeared from this world? He would . . . he would. Ethan's spirits rose as he chanted those words to himself.

He came to a clearing and smelled wood smoke. Behind a curtain of saplings, he glimpsed the gray cottage walls. Old Noah's cottage, he thought. The damned groom had always doted on Nick, taught him to ride his first pony, and comforted Nick when he fell out of the saddle. Noah might have been Sir James's stable groom, but he'd always been Nick's slave, ready to follow his master's smallest command. Probably still did.

Ethan's horse halted, pricking his ears. Ethan glanced in the direction of the horse's head and stiffened as his gaze found a great black brute of a stallion. What was it doing here?

Ethan remained motionless in the saddle, thinking. The stallion had been tethered to a pole in the ground, and it walked in slow circles, chomping at the dry grass as it went. Ethan noticed the two white stockings on the forelegs. *Two white stockings.* By God, it might be the legendary Pegasus, the horse of the Midnight Bandit, who operated in these parts of Sussex.

Ethan curbed the urge to rush forward and steal the horse, but to what purpose? It could not be Noah's horse. He did not have the funds to pay for such a fine animal. Noah still worked for Nick. God's bones, the horse belonged to Nick. If the notorious highwayman owned the horse . . .

Thoughts rolled through Ethan's head quickly. What if Nick

were the Midnight Bandit? That would explain how Nick had acquired money to fund the orphanage. He called out softly, "Pegasus."

The stallion lifted his head and turned his dark eyes on Ethan as if waiting for a command. The damned brute harked to the name *Pegasus*. He repeated the name once more, and the horse whinnied.

A shiver of excitement traveled up Ethan's back. If his calculations were true—which they had to be—he had a way to force Nick to pay the gambling debts, or better yet, see Nick hang for the scoundrel that he was.

Then The Hollows would be his, Ethan thought. Even if Nick had left the estate to Delicia in his will, there had to be a way to wrest it from her grip.

He threw a furtive glance toward the cottage, but there was no sign of the old groom. *He must not see me,* Ethan thought, and wheeled his mount around. Noah should not have the opportunity to report his presence to Nick.

He laughed soundlessly and rubbed his hands together. Soon Nick would have the surprise of his life. But first, Ethan would make what money he could from the secret. He knew who would be willing to pay to get his hands on a certain damsel. Luther Hilliard. They could both benefit from a deal.

Ethan could already hear the jingle of gold in his pocket.

Sir Luther had spent a long night at the clubs gambling and drinking and had barely started his breakfast even though the last of the afternoon sunlight slanted through the windows. In half an hour it would be dark and another night of gambling would evolve.

Sir Luther did not sleep well since the death of his brother, and he dared not close his eyes at night lest a devil rise from the Underworld and carry him off to the Realm of Darkness. Sir Luther shivered as if catching a sudden chill. Brandy was the only thing that could make him forget, keep the nightmares at bay. He drank thirstily straight from the bottle.

His body jolted as the fire spread through him, and his heart started to race. Deuced uncomfortable, but he had nothing else with which to ward off the specters of his past.

Ethan found Sir Luther in his room at the club, a meal barely touched on a tray and a brandy bottle already half empty even if the evening was young. The old man sat slumped in an armchair. Ethan noted the stooped shoulders and the heavy paunch. Purple veins traced his pendulous jowls and nose; his coat looked unbrushed, and his breeches sagged on his scrawny thighs. It looked as if Sir Luther had lost weight since he had last visited his tailor.

"Who are you?" Sir Luther barked, and peered at Ethan with hostile eyes. "You seem slightly familiar."

"Ethan Leverton."

Sir Luther flinched as if slapped. *"Leverton?* Don't say that name in my presence! It is a curse."

"I know that Sir James and you were bitter enemies, but I have no quarrel with you, Sir Luther. I have come to offer a proposition—concerning your niece."

"Serena? How do you know her?" the older man asked suspiciously, and fumbled for his brandy glass.

"She approached me some weeks ago in the hope that I would help her. She claimed you had murdered her father and that she needed someone to help her bring you to justice." Ethan felt a spurt of triumph and sat down without being bidden. He had all the trump cards in his hand.

Sir Luther's stertorous breathing filled the silence. The stale air in the room pressed upon Ethan, and he glanced with distaste at the man before him. Sir Luther had a cold smile that made the hairs stand on Ethan's neck.

This man was capable of killing his kin, and for that strength Ethan envied him, but he also feared the murderer. Ethan wished he'd had the nerve to shoot Nick in the back, but to tell the truth, he was not a killer. Looking into Sir Luther's eyes, Ethan realized that. He could always hire someone to ambush Nick some dark night in London—later, when the business with Serena Hilliard was over.

"Is my niece in London? Have you seen her while I have failed?"

Ethan nodded. "She was in London, Sir Luther, but she has traveled back to Somerset with my brother. He, not I, offered to help her make the truth of Andrew Hilliard's death public."

Silence hung in the room, a silence alive with menace. Ethan inserted his finger under the tight cravat to breathe more easily. His hand trembled, and his palm was damp with sweat.

"How much do you want?" Sir Luther asked, his voice deadly soft.

Ethan moved uncomfortably on the hard chair and fingered the hat in his hand.

"You have come for money, haven't you?"

"Yes, Sir Luther, I am in a financial hole and I need your assistance. You shall have your niece back, and not a word about the past shall pass my lips as long as you pay my demand."

"How much?" Sir Luther leaned forward, his whole body sagging as if filled with liquid. The old man smelled putrid.

"I know you're very well off, Sir Luther." Ethan took a deep breath. "Twenty thousand pounds."

Ethan sensed that if Sir Luther accomplished his mission to silence Miss Serena, he would not hesitate to silence Ethan as well. That was a problem of the future, and now, what pressured most were the heavy debts. He would deal with the danger later.

"It's an outrageous sum!" Sir Luther grumbled, rising slowly, ponderously.

Ethan flinched at the wave of foul odor emanating from the body as Sir Luther moved. "Not a penny less, alas."

Sir Luther stood over him, a decaying ship that had sailed foul waters too long, Ethan thought, losing his nerve. He was about to rise and rush out as the older man spoke.

"Very well. Twenty thousand you shall have. I shall see you to the bank and pay you half—right after you've explained where I shall rendezvous with my niece."

"I have already formed a plan. I shall kidnap her. It won't be difficult to discover her when my brother returns from Somerset; and no matter the outcome of their mission, I shall deliver her here or send you a message where she can be found."

Sir Luther grabbed his arm with a pudgy hand. "You know that if you don't deliver her as promised, you are a dead man."

Ethan nodded, swallowing hard. He had no intention of failing this mission. He knew where Miss Serena worked. He would offer to help her. "You can count on me, Sir Luther."

Serena inhaled the familiar salty smell from the sea. Oh, how she had missed it. She had forgotten the wonderful memories of this land that she called home. Her mind had been fully occupied with the awfulness of the recent past.

Over the mountainous ridge, behind which lay the moors, the land rolled down toward the sea, the dry grass moving in the breeze around rocky outcrops. Autumn leaves rattled and danced on the trees and scuttled across the lane on which they traveled. She hung outside the window, eagerly looking for the familiar drive that led up to High Crescent on the outskirts of Williton.

There were the tall stone gate posts set with lion heads. Her heart squeezed. Home. Yet not quite like the home she remembered. High Crescent had always seemed enormous, but now it had shrunk, looking more like a manor house than her childhood palace.

Nick rode up beside her. "How do you feel? Do you want me to ride up and inquire inside for the servants who left after your father's death?"

Serena was grateful for his offer. Ever since their night of lovemaking, he'd behaved like a correct and supportive friend, something that worried her but also gave her strength. They would never be a couple under the circumstances, so why think about it?

"No, I want to go inside," she said.

Five minutes later the carriage came to a halt in front of the house, shaped as the Elizabethan E and made of bricks and gray stone. There was no sign of life in the silent yard, and the house held an air of abandonment.

Serena got down before Nick could help her. She couldn't trust herself to touch him lest she throw herself into his arms.

She tried the front door, which was locked. Big drifts of leaves skirted the bottom. Rafe and the coachman waited in the drive while she and Nick went around to the side to try one of the back entrances.

"There's someone in the kitchen," Nick said. "Smoke is coming out of the chimney."

Serena stepped into the dim hallway, then into the kitchen. Dry herbs hung from the ceiling beams, and a broom leaned against one corner. A fat female servant sat at the long table drinking tea. Her mouth fell open in surprise, and she stumbled to her feet.

"Miss Serena! Yer back then. Sir Luther said naught about ye coming back so soon. Said ye were stayin' with friends."

"Yes, Mrs. Whipple." She turned to Nick. "This is our cook. She has worked here longer than I can remember." She introduced Nick to the cook.

Nick nodded in greeting, peeling off his gloves. "Is Sir Luther in residence?"

"No," said Mrs. Whipple, bobbing a curtsy. "He's in Lunnon on business. We haven't had words when he's likely to return."

"I should have been here at Father's funeral."

"You should go up, Miss Serena, and I'll serve up a cup o' tea in the dining room."

"I'd rather not make any trouble. We'll drink it here. I will take some of my clothes later."

The cook, wearing a homespun gown and a white apron, gave Serena a look of surprise and waddled to the fireplace where a kettle steamed on a trivet. It was clear she couldn't imagine Serena drinking tea in the kitchen. *But I've changed,* Serena thought.

"The funeral was ever such a sad event, and we all understood how the master's death must have frightened ye." The cook rolled her small eyes. "I don't sleep too well meself, thinkin' 'bout vagrants that might stab me while I sleep."

Serena and Nick sat down, and Mrs. Whipple offered them a plate of newly baked yeast cakes. As she chewed, Serena said, "Are you sure that's how Father died, Mrs. Whipple?"

"The new master said so. We cain't very well doubt his word, now can we?"

"But do you *believe* him? Truly?"

The cook's round red cheeks puffed out as she evidently turned the thought over in her mind. "I don't know, Miss Serena. I thought at first the death was a mite strange, but the cash box disappeared that same night. It had to have been a vagrant who needed funds." She placed earthenware mugs on the table and poured the tea.

"Does everyone share your opinion, Mrs. Whipple?"

The cook shook her head so that the mobcap moved down over her brow. She gave it an impatient push. "I don't know what got into the other servants. Most of them left, sayin' they didn't want to work for Sir Luther. There isn't any work to have in the area, so I don't know what they were thinkin'— leavin' like that. They will starve."

Serena and Nick exchanged glances, and Serena felt a glimmer of hope.

"I wouldn't know what to do wi' meself if I wasn't workin' here," the cook added huffily, and placed a crock of butter on the table.

Serena broke apart one of the cakes and spread it liberally with butter. "Are any of the other servants working anywhere close by or did they all leave the parish?"

"No, some of the grooms got work at the liv'ry stables down the village, and the others I rightly don't know. Ned Nelson works wi' his brother at the alehouse in Williton. That I know."

"I wonder what made them leave so abruptly," Serena said, and sipped the hot tea.

"Were they angry for some reason?" Nick inserted.

The cook shook her head. "No . . . there warn't any grumble

that *I* heard, but then I've always kept meself to meself. There were some who din't like the new master. Sir Luther is not a soft touch, rather the opposite. He whipped the grooms occasionally.''

"Father never did that," Serena said. "I can see why the grooms might resent Sir Luther's discipline."

"Aye, there is that. Sir Luther cut their wages as well, but not mine, seein' as another cook is hard to find."

"Why would he do that?" Serena thought aloud. "He's a very wealthy man."

"There are some that don't like to part with their coin," the cook said, pursing her mouth in disapproval.

Serena finished her tea. "We'll be leaving now, Mrs. Whipple."

The cook's eyes opened wide. "Why? Ye've just come back." She studied Nick suspiciously. "Besides, it isn't seemly that a young unwed lady—"

"Say no more, Mrs. Whipple. A maid is traveling with me in the carriage. I shall return here in due course, but I need to solve a pressing problem first." She beckoned to Nick. "You might as well take a look at the house while I pack some things."

They went through a long corridor which ended in the large hallway. The air had a musty, unused smell. The curtains had been pulled across the windows, closing out the spiritless daylight.

"By Jupiter, this is a grand house," Nick said, staring at the painted ceilings.

"It might be grand, but it is without a soul. It's just that I never noticed it before." She led him through the salons downstairs with their silk walls and stiff furniture. Old carpets softened the rigidity, but even with sun-yellow silk curtains, the rooms had a gloomy air.

A curving staircase led to the next floor. "My room is up there," she said, pointing to the dark passage. She ran up the red-carpeted steps and he followed. She showed him the gallery and the large, echoing music room. Dragging a hand along the harpsichord, she realized she would not play it for a long time.

She smiled at Nick. "Mayhap we'll play together one day. You on lute, me on harpsichord."

He nodded, his mouth curving faintly. "I would like that."

They entered Serena's bedroom, and it looked just as she remembered. Gold bedhangings around the four-poster, a sofa, and an armchair covered with striped silk. A window seat dressed with velvet cushions, and beside it, a table piled high with books she hadn't had the time to read.

She started pulling out dresses from her clothespress. "Nick," she said, "you've never told me about the animosity between my uncle and your father. Do you know what started it?"

Nick sat down on the window seat and faced her. "Sir James told me about it once. He was married twice, first to a lady who could not produce children. She died of lung fever one winter." Nick scratched his ear as if embarrassed. "He found me that year, when he discovered the whereabouts of his sister. He took me in, never thinking he would marry again. I was to be his heir."

Serena folded the gowns without looking very closely. Nick's story had captivated her. "What about Sir Ethan and Delicia?"

"Sir James met a lady—Sara Miles. He fell in love, but their future looked bleak. She was from a very religious family, and they didn't want her to marry anyone not connected to the Church. She rebelled against the rules—that's what Sir James told me," Nick inserted. "Sir Luther also fell in love with Sara, and when she chose my father, Sir Luther ravished her one night. A duel ensued, and Sir Luther almost died from the wounds inflicted by my father. After that, James and Luther were mortal enemies."

"That's understandable," she said, and placed a stack of handkerchiefs on top of her bundle.

"The enmity between the families is still strong. Isn't it strange how one can inherit the problems as well as the material things?'' Nick rubbed his neck, as if telling the story had made him tense.

"Yes ... it was envy, pure and simple, the same as has created the conflict between you and Sir Ethan.'' Serena folded everything into a square fringed shawl. She looked at Nick. "I wish you didn't have such problems with your brother. Family feuds act like acid; they eat away at your life and prevent you from moving forward strong and free.''

He nodded and stood abruptly. "You're right.'' He hoisted the bundle into his arms. "Are you finished?''

She glanced around the room, seeing very little she wanted to take along. Scooping up her small jewelry case that didn't hold much of value, she smiled. "Yes, let's go.''

The cook put her fat hands on her hips, and an air of curiosity came over her face as they returned to the kitchen. "Nurse Hopkins has been worried 'bout ye. Some think ye didn't go north to see yer friends. Some think ye didn't take any trunks on yer trip.''

Serena brushed lint off her skirts. "Be that as it may, Mrs. Whipple. You shall know the whole in due time.''

She went outside, and Nick followed, closing the door firmly behind him. "How does it feel to leave, Serena? Will you miss your home?''

Serena shook her head. "This is no longer my home. In my mind, I only see the crime that was committed here and a dark shadow hangs over the whole house. Even if Sir Luther is brought to justice, High Crescent will never be the same. It belongs to my past now. Besides, if Uncle Luther is convicted, the Crown will confiscate the estate.''

Nick stood so close she could feel his breath wafting across her cheek. Many emotions flashed through his eyes—compassion, worry, understanding, and melancholia. He was there, but they had already parted. There was no question, no hope springing up between them, only a mood of resignation.

"Let's find Nurse Hopkins. I won't leave before seeing her,'' Serena said.

The old half-timbered cottage with its steep thatched roof

was exactly as Serena remembered it. Flowers grew everywhere in the summer, and a tidy vegetable garden showed some cabbages still forming on the ground.

"Nana," Serena greeted her old nurse at the door. Nurse Hopkins studied Serena's face very closely, straightening her bent back as much as she could. Her blue eyes were covered with a gray veil that seemed denser than Serena remembered, and the old woman had lost weight. Her shoulderbones stood out like pegs, and the face had sunken into dark hollows and grown sharp ridges.

Serena's heart constricted with distress at the changes. This was the one person who had truly loved her without asking for anything in return. She hugged Nurse Hopkins, worried by the bony fragility of the woman.

"Nana," she repeated.

"Yer back then, but ye won't stay," the nurse said. "I can feel it in me bones. They ache and ache, and 'twon't be over 'til the dark clouds are lifted over High Crescent." She shivered as if cold and wiped at her eyes with a corner of her apron.

"I know," Serena said. "Justice shall be done."

Nurse Hopkins walked down the cottage brick path that was lined with late chrysanthemums and Michaelmas daisies. "See these flowers, Miss Serena? They are brave; they will flower even as the frosts come. They don't complain, and so won't I. When the great frost comes, I shall bend my head down and accept my fate graciously."

"It won't come for a long time," Serena said.

"But I won't go until I know yer happy."

Nurse Hopkins stood very close to Nick by the stone fence and studied his face through her wire-rimmed spectacles. Serena introduced them.

She placed a protective arm around Nurse Hopkins' shoulders that were covered with a moth-eaten shawl. The white hair had been combed back and covered with a plain cap. "You don't eat enough," Serena said. "Are you out of funds?"

The old woman shook her head. "No, me friends keep victuals on me table, and I tell them stories of the past in payment."

Serena pulled a leather purse with money out of her pocket and pushed it into Nurse Hopkins' apron pocket. "This is for when the stories run out."

The nurse laughed, a soft cackle that brought memories back to Serena. "I don't need anything more from this world," said the old crone. She took Nick's hand and held it tightly.

Serena was grateful that Nick did not try to pull away in disgust from the paper-thin fingers. They stood in silence as Nurse Hopkins seemed to read his heart through the feel of his hand.

"Ye are a good man, Mr. Thurston," the nurse said at last. "Yer heart is in the right place." She took Serena's hand and joined it to Nick's. "Ye have me blessings, children. I sense that ye'll bring happiness to each other."

Heat rushed to Serena's face, and she didn't dare to look at Nick. He did not protest, only held her hand in a comforting grip.

"Now go and find Ned Nelson in Williton. He shall help ye. He has told me sommat ye need to know. He has no other choice if he wants to go to his grave with a clean conscience."

"Something about Sir Luther Hilliard?" Nick asked.

The old nurse nodded. "Sir Luther claims he was not at High Crescent the night Mr. Hilliard died, but I know better and so does Ned."

There was hope, Serena thought. A new urgency filled her. She could almost smell the success of her mission.

Chapter 24

Ned Nelson, brawny and towheaded, carried a large keg of ale across the muddy yard where carriage wheels had dug deep trenches. Serena watched him from the window of the coach, and Nick addressed him while still in the saddle. "Ned Nelson?"

"Who wants ter know?" the stalwart young man asked suspiciously. He shifted the keg farther back on his shoulder and gave Nick a hard look.

"Your former mistress, Miss Hilliard," Nick said, motioning toward the coach.

Ned turned slowly and touched his forelock as Serena waved at him. His face did not brighten as he recognized her. An expression of panic came over him, and his gaze darted from one end of the yard to the other. "What yer want, miss?"

Serena got down, daintily stepping through the mud until she reached a dry spot near the front steps. "I need to talk to you, Ned. There's no reason to be afraid, but I must ask you for help in an important matter. I think you already know my errand here."

The groom threw a glance over his shoulder as if expecting

someone lurking behind him and ready to attack. "I don't know, Miss Serena. I know naught that would help ye."

"I think you do." She looked at him steadily, and the young man scratched his neck, then set down the keg on the steps.

They waited until two farmers had walked through the door, soon followed by Rafe, before continuing the conversation.

"I think you know more about the night that Father died than you've told anyone."

"Nurse Hopkins has been talkin' to ye. Ye should not listen to her wanderin' mind." He tapped his head. "She's been tryin' to convince me I saw sommat I shouldn't have. As if I would make a habit of starin' at me betters through the winders! I did not." His mouth took on a mulish set.

"Mayhap you did something unusual that evening when my father died," Serena suggested. "I did. I hid behind the curtains in the library, and I saw something that ruined all our lives." She glanced at Ned's worn fustian coat and patched breeches. "I'd say it made your life a lot heavier to bear. You never wore patched clothes at High Crescent, not as long as Father controlled the purse strings."

Ned's craggy face reddened with anger. "Well, he ain't holdin' them any longer, is 'e? I had to leave when the pay would not keep food on me family's table. We have ten mouths to feed."

"I thought you might have left because you saw something, because you wanted to protect yourself and your family."

Ned gave her a fierce look, his light blue eyes filled with agitation. "What's it to ye, Miss Serena? I don't mean to be rude, but why dig up the past? Nothin' but trouble will come out of it."

Serena decided to be blunt. "Sir Luther killed my father, and I think you know that. You saw the fight, didn't you?" She stepped forward and touched his arm. "Please, don't deny it! It is very important. I hope to bring Sir Luther to justice, but I cannot do it without your help." She shook his sleeve to impart the urgency of her request. "I promise you shall have a better job, and more pay. If Sir Luther goes to the hangman's noose for murder, you shall be rewarded—for stepping forward and telling the truth."

Ned pulled off his cap and scratched his thick thatch of hair. "Are ye sure, Miss Serena?"

"She would not lie," Nick said behind him as if settling the matter.

"No ... I would not lie. Please tell me, Ned, what did you see that night?"

"I wus going 'ome to me wife when I 'eard the ruckus up at the big 'ouse. The winders were open. 'Twus dark, and I'd been workin' late in the stables cleanin' the tackle. Light came from yer father's library, and at first, I thought he was workin'. But anyone crossin' the yard that night could not have missed hearin' the angry quarrel atween yer father and Sir Luther."

Ned looked around suspiciously, but no one had entered the muddy yard.

"I worried, so I stopped by the winder to see if I could 'elp. I saw ye, Miss Serena, hiding behind the curtain, and yer face was as white as a sheet."

"Did you see the knife, the one Sir Luther used on my father?"

Ned nodded, his Adam's apple bobbing convulsively. "He struck yer father in the chest many times. I could not move; I stood there starin' like a bloody coward."

"There was nothing you could have done after Sir Luther started stabbing my father. Who would have guessed he would go to such extremes to end a quarrel?"

" 'Twas always bad blood atween those two. Sir Luther hated yer father, if ye don't mind me sayin' so."

"He hates everyone. He's always been a bully and a miser ... and now, a murderer."

Nick gripped Ned's shoulder. "Would you be willing to testify in court against Sir Luther?"

Silence fell as Serena anxiously waited for the groom's answer. He wore a hunted look, as if filled with a keen desire to run away.

"I don't see 'nother way if we're to put to rights what's

wrong at High Crescent," he finally said. "And I would dearly like a better job."

Serena curbed an urge to fling her arms around him in gratitude. "I knew I could count on you," she said instead, beaming a smile at him. A weight had lifted from her shoulders. She addressed Nick. "Should he return with us to London?"

Nick shook his head. "He'd better stay here until Sir Luther has been arrested. No need for Sir Luther to find out there was another witness besides you. Not that it's very likely he'll learn what transpired here today, but we'd better be cautious."

Ned nodded. "I won't breathe a word o' this talk to an'one, and I'll keep workin' 'ere until ye contact me."

"I'll send my carriage for you when the time comes," Nick said, and squeezed Ned's brawny shoulder reassuringly. "You shall have secure employment at my estate in Sussex. If that suits you."

"I'm ever so grateful," Ned said, smiling for the first time.

Nick held out his hand toward Serena. "Come, we've accomplished what we came here for."

Serena smiled. "And much sooner than I expected. Nurse Hopkins said you would help me, Ned."

"Aye? That old woman knows more than what's good for 'er I always thought. She might be almost blind, but she 'as eyes in 'er neck."

"Yes, that's true," Serena said. "There's no telling what she has seen over the years. I would not want her to be my enemy."

"The master surely gained an enemy when he halved her pension," Ned said, his Adam's apple bobbing anew. He looked at Serena with fondness mixed with fear. "I shall stand by you, Miss Serena. 'Ave no doubt."

With those comforting words, Serena let Nick aid her into the Thurston traveling chaise. The coachman turned the four horses eastward, and Serena mulled over ways to confront her uncle. As the carriage reached the ridge high above the village, the coachman halted to meet a farm cart wide with a mountain of hay.

Serena leaned out the window, inhaling the salty breeze with nostalgic pleasure. The sea was covered with a milky haze, the view achingly familiar. The memories of her childhood tugged at her heart, but she had changed. She had walked a narrow plank across a chasm, and she could never go back. She had changed, as everything changed over time, even High Crescent. New people walked its hallways and cleaned out the stables. Her memories would always remain the same, but the place— never.

Heaving a deep sigh, she realized that her past was finally over, buried in the soft layers of time. A warm peaceful feeling came over her, and she knew that she would win, would come out of her difficulties an enriched person. No longer the pampered Miss Hilliard, but Serena, who'd had to find herself when all the outer trappings of her life had been torn away. She was still learning, but now she could put the past behind her, put it to rest.

When Uncle Luther had been apprehended she would return and visit Father's grave. She would take her final farewell of him, and he would truly rest in peace.

On the following day as they stopped on the outskirts of Basingstoke to change horses and dine, Nick took Serena aside. They walked on a narrow lane bordering a cow pasture. The grass verging the ditches was flattened with recent rain. The air was humid and cold, and water puddles glistened on the path. Nick took her arm and guided her past a particularly large puddle.

"You don't have to worry about your uncle again," he said. "Sir Luther is as good as caught. I shall notify the magistrates in London, and all you have to do is wait for word that he's been arrested."

"You would do that for me?" she asked. "Put yourself in jeopardy with the law?"

"I'm the law-abiding Nicholas Thurston. I see no danger to myself. Very few people know about my other persona." He halted and took her face between his hands. A sweet longing sprang up between them, and Serena wished she could throw herself into his arms and be certain they had a future together. But Callie stood between them, an invisible barrier that was as effective as the thickest stone wall.

His hands lay warm against her cool skin. "I'd like you to go down to The Hollows and wait there," he said softly. "I need to know that you're safe."

She shook her head and sought to look anywhere except into his eyes, but she could not avert her gaze. His keen blue eyes held a hint of pleading. "No, I cannot do that, Nick, not now. Not after what transpired between us. You're a betrothed gentleman. I cannot face Callie and pretend to be her friend while I secretly covet her fiancé."

A wave, so bittersweet it made her tremble, went through her as he caressed the contours of her face with one fingertip. His strength, so masterfully held in check and transferred into that one finger, made her weak with longing. His blue gaze, darkened with passion, lingered on every feature as if memorizing every detail.

"Here I stand, holding you, holding the woman I love, and yet you are unreachable, as distant as a star, and as achingly lovely." He dropped his hands in frustration. "Are our paths never going to join into one?"

Serena looked across the mist-shrouded meadow, seeing the dark forms of grazing cows. "I doubt it. I am, however, deeply grateful to you even though I ranted and raved while being your prisoner. You have helped me a great deal in my quest for myself and forgiveness of the past."

He gripped her neck beneath the hood over her cloak. "Serena, do you love me?"

Her heart leaped to her throat, then settled back, beating wildly. "Yes . . . I have to admit my love for you."

"Then nothing should stop us from being together."

"Mayhap," she said with hesitation, "but the memory of Calandra jilted most cruelly would always stand between us.

You cannot reject her as Ethan did; nor can you live with me knowing you failed in your duty.''

His shoulders slumped, and a muscle tightened in his jaw. ''You are right. I've been filled with a vain hope that our problems would just evaporate. But you're so matter-of-fact. Everything is stark black and white in your world, no diffused areas.''

''More than you think. My life is a complete muddle. I get tired thinking about it, but I shall remain true to myself from now on. I cannot change the past, and neither can you.'' She touched his hard jaw. ''I've put my pain behind me and will now look toward the future.''

He seemed on the verge of taking her into his arms, but fought to remain passive. ''No more nightmares that will make you cry out for my comfort? No more dark spells of sadness?''

She sucked in her breath as she remembered the disturbing images. ''I wish that were true, but I can't say what will happen. I'll struggle through somehow, even if the dreams fill my nights with terror. They will weaken in due time.''

''You say I changed your life. You changed mine as well,'' he said. ''I no longer feel the desperate urge to put my life in danger.''

''Then you have also put your past behind you, Nick. You can let the Midnight Bandit rest. He cannot save the entire world.''

''You're right, he never could, but he sought something worthwhile.''

''Something that Nicholas Thurston, Esquire, could not find?'' she interjected.

Nick laughed then, his face creasing in a way that took her breath away. ''That part of me is much too frivolous to search out a serious mission. Then there was always the question of funds.''

''You said you have almost enough to pay off the mortgage on the orphanage.''

His eyes brightened with pleasure. ''Yes.'' He took her arm, and they resumed walking. "One more mission, and I shall be free of debt."

She took his hand, clasping it firmly. "I would like to give you the amount once the matter of my uncle has been taken care of. Father's solicitor shall release my inheritance—"

"No!" Nick exploded.

"My money isn't good enough?" she asked incredulously and dropped his hand.

He wore an expression of dread. "Of course it is, but there's no reason for you to pay my debts. I won't accept your offer, and that's the end of it."

"Are you too proud to accept a donation?" she asked, her anger stirring in the pit of her stomach. "The children will benefit."

"Yes, but paying the mortgage is something I have to accomplish on my own. I set up the goal for myself, and only I can fulfill it."

Serena sighed with exasperation. "Is it your way of justifying living the life of a squire while your old friends expire in their filthy dens or on the streets?"

She could see that she'd touched a sore spot in him, and his eyes blazed. "It's my way of thanking Sir James, of paying back what he gave me. At least I am in a position of spreading my good fortune, and I will never forget that."

"I think you'll feel the need to pay all your life. You will never be able to set that street urchin part of you aside."

His jaw set defiantly. "With a future I might. A wife and children would give me a reason to accept my place at The Hollows. The estate has much to offer a child." He stopped, looking down at her face. "I would like you to carry my children and anchor me to my place in the world. You know me better than anyone, know all about me. I need you at my side."

She blinked away her tears. "I think you're already firmly ensconced in your place, Nicholas Thurston. You're strong; you're attractive, kind, and—you sing well. I know you'll make Callie happy. That's the end of it."

The shadow of defeat darkened his face. "S'faith, I stumbled again, pleading with you to reconsider even though I know better." He sighed. "You have reduced me to the beggar I swore I would never be." He took her arm and turned her around. "Let's not linger here; let's conclude our mission."

Chapter 25

Sir Ethan laughed, thinking how easily he would trap Nick. A great ball celebrating the betrothal of a Sussex heiress and a young earl would happen at an estate outside Cowfold in West Sussex, at a comfortable riding distance for the Midnight Bandit. All Ethan had to do was to make sure Nick found out that the wealthy lady and her father would be traveling from London with the trousseau and other valuables. The Midnight Bandit would not be able to resist such a lucrative chance to line his pockets.

Ethan had already hired the equipage and a dubious character to drive the team when the time came. All he had to do now was kidnap Miss Hilliard and approach her distasteful uncle one more time, and his problems would be over for good! He would also get rid of the thorn that had festered under his skin all his life, *Nick*. The stepbrother who always lectured him, told him to mind his manners, show respect; who punched him mentally and physically. The brother who would dangle from Tyburn Tree with only ruffians and harridans cheering raucously as his air intake was cut off. His last view would be the toothless gap of a vicious crone. Serves him right, Ethan thought.

"I shall be there in the background to witness my ultimate triumph," he added to himself as he arranged his cravat to his satisfaction. He looked critically in the mirror. With a hare's foot, he dabbed rouge onto his pale cheeks and pondered the magic of a future no longer containing Nick Thurston.

Ethan smacked his lips, then outlined them with rouge. He was so close to victory he could almost taste the sweet ambrosia on his tongue. He sat down and let his valet Shepley throw a protective sheet over his shoulders before brushing his hair and powdering it. Shepley tied it back with a velvet bow and helped Ethan on with his coat, a new velvet acquisition from his tailor—who had threatened to withdraw his credit if the bills weren't settled within the month.

Without my tailor, I will be nothing, Ethan thought, and admired the padded shoulders in the mirror. The wound in his shoulder that Nick had inflicted at Lotus Blossom's ached like the devil, but for some reason Ethan savored the pain. He brushed a sprinkle of powder from his sleeve with his gloves. Soon he'd be able to pay his bills. All of them. Life would start over; he would be the master of his future once more.

But first he had an anonymous letter to write, to Captain Emerson. Then he had a kidnapping to accomplish. He chuckled and admired the shine of his shoes with their new silver buckles. All in due time. The chess pieces were falling perfectly into place.

Nick had decided to seek help from the powerful Chief Magistrate at Westminster, Sir Henry Fielding; but to secure a successful arrest, he first wanted to make sure that Hilliard was still in London.

He delivered Serena at the Hopkins' shop in Haymarket, making sure no one in the street witnessed her entering the premises. He already missed her so much his heart was slowly tearing apart.

"I don't want this to be the end," he said in a last effort to bring her back to him. But the barrier between them did not crumble.

She turned her dark blue, mysterious eyes on him, eyes he longed to explore for the rest of his life. Solemnly, she shook her head. She stood on her toes and kissed his cheek. "Good-bye, Nick. You have been a great help to me, not only as my protector but also in making peace with myself."

She melted away, an elusive wraith that bore with it his longing, his very heart.

"Good-bye," she said once more and ran up the stairs to be swallowed by the shadows in the passage above.

All that remained was a feeling of hopelessness. Somewhere, a clock ticked away the seconds heavily, ponderously, as if time was a great burden to bear. On days like today, it was.

He returned to the street, where darkness had fallen, and asked the coachman to take the maid and the carriage back to Sussex. Climbing into the saddle, he said to Rafe, "Let's find out if the lion is still in his lair."

They found the club in St. James's where Hilliard was staying, but discovered that Sir Luther had not been in residence for the last two nights. The staff had no idea if, or when, he would return.

"Damn it!" Nick swore as he joined Rafe outside. Rafe glanced at him calmly. Nothing could stir his anger quickly; he looked upon life with patience, but Nick also knew that Rafe was only partially involved in life due to his lack of memory.

"We can visit the gambling hells. If he's still in London, we'll find him there," Rafe suggested. "The night is young."

They visited the seven most popular gambling salons, but Hilliard was not present in any of them. Nick made discreet inquiries, but the doormen had not seen Hilliard; nor had any of Nick's friends.

"Just my blasted luck," Nick said, gritting his teeth. He clapped the three-cornered hat onto his head and flung himself onto his horse. "Where the deuce has he gone?"

"The only way to find out is to wait outside his club. If he's in London, he'll return there in due time."

Nick agreed, but did not look forward to lurking in the shadows waiting for his enemy.

Ethan sent around a note to Serena on the following morning which stated that he wanted to see her since he had some important news about her uncle. He had discovered something about Luther Hilliard that would benefit her case, a witness.

"How did he know I live here?" Serena said out loud and crumpled the note in a flurry of agitation. She wasn't safe here any longer.

Mayhap she should hear what Ethan had to say. She had learned that he wasn't worth the dust in the street, but she'd better not make him her enemy. She was curious to learn what he'd found out about Luther Hilliard. Secrets unveiled would make a stronger case against her uncle.

"Are you going out?" Molly Hopkins asked as Serena put on her cloak shortly after breakfast. She put the letter in her pocket.

"Yes, I am to hear something useful in my case against my uncle. I'll be back shortly."

"Be careful. Don't let anyone see you. Sir Luther might still have spies posted outside."

A chill traveled through Serena and she dreaded leaving the house, but she had no other choice. She no longer had Nick to lean on.

"Don't worry," she said and left through a side door that led to a narrow alley. Keeping her head down and the hood pulled deeply over her face, she hurried along the street, turning west at the corner, She paid for a sedan chair and was taken to Berkley Square at a brisk clip.

The butler ushered her into the parlor in which she'd met Ethan once before. She waited anxiously, and he appeared two minutes later dressed in a cloak and carrying gloves as if planning an outing.

"Miss Hilliard," he said with an ingratiating smile. "I'm delighted that you cared to call on me as I suspect that Miss Hopkins would not have let me visit you."

"How did you know where to find me?"

He pursed his lips, his eyes twinkling. Evil imp, she thought. "I saw you on the street one day and followed you. Harmless curiosity, I assure you."

Feeling uneasy, she only glared at him.

"I want you to meet someone, a witness who saw your uncle murdering your father. Come, let us hurry so that we can accomplish the rendezvous before 'tis too late."

"I don't understand," Serena said, suspicious now of his secret. "I really shouldn't go anywhere with you unchaperoned."

He tilted his powdered head to the side and his red lips parted in a small smile. "Why, you are here already, unchaperoned, and you would not be so foolish as to turn down my offer of help. Not when I can lead you to someone—his former major domo—who will speak of other crimes and see your uncle to the gallows." He tilted his head to the other side, a sly bird with feathers of brocade and velvet. "You will have to trust me in this as you need to build a solid case. The testimony of a major domo will carry a lot of weight."

"I don't know—"

"What in the world has made you doubt my word?" he asked impatiently and pulled on his gloves, wiggling every finger like thin worms.

Serena thought of Callie Vine and her ruination, but surely, Sir Ethan could not have plans for her downfall. Unlike Callie Vine, she was more experienced and knew how to defend herself. She would have to learn what she could about her uncle.

"I wish you would tell me where we're going," she said, her shoulders aching with tension. If Luther's major domo would testify . . .

"To a livery stable near Covent Garden, my dear, where the man is staying at the moment."

With a heavy sigh, she swept through the front door which he held open. She should not have come alone, but it was too late to fetch one of her friends from the Hopkins' shop.

Sir Ethan had only smiles for her as he kept to his side of the seat in the lavish Leverton coach. He oozed good nature and high spirits, treating her with utmost gallantry. Not a lewd word, no indecent suggestions passed his lips.

He twirled his walking stick with its carved ivory knob and twitched the lace dripping from his shirt cuffs. The coach traveled east toward the seedier part of town. Serena recognized the square of Covent Garden with its fruit and flower stalls.

The coach turned down a narrow alley.

"We're almost there," Sir Ethan said with a half smile.

I shouldn't have come, Serena thought, but as the coach stopped, she got down. It was too late for regrets.

There was the unmistakable odor of horse and a stable, a long dilapidated building, with piles of manure on the floor and tackle on wooden wall pegs. Sir Ethan had not lied. She walked toward the stable, almost expecting her uncle to appear, but all she saw were empty stalls and a rough staircase going through the low ceiling to quarters above.

She turned around to ask Sir Ethan for more information. To her surprise, he stood right behind her, aiming a dueling pistol at her stomach. The world started to spin as she realized that he'd laid a trap for her. She should have listened to the warning bells in her mind. She grabbed hold of a wooden post to stay upright.

"Go upstairs," he hissed, his gaze darting around the room, "or I will shoot, relieving your uncle of the task of putting an end to your life."

"How? . . . When?" she gasped, fighting to keep breathing. Fear ran through her, an icy river, familiar from that night when her father died.

"You don't need to know the details. Let's just say that you've conveniently played into my hands. *I* don't personally want to hurt you, but you have given me the perfect opportunity to start my life anew." He pushed the barrel of the pistol into her middle, and she flinched, stepping back, then stumbled up the stairs. He followed her footsteps.

Upstairs, mounds of hay waited to feed the absent horses and a door led to a windowless room—the groom's quarters, Serena thought, as she eyed the narrow cot with its filthy mattress. The room smelled of stale food and wine, and the greasy table held dirty dishes and a loaf of moldy bread covered with flies. She recoiled, but Sir Ethan forced her inside by pushing the pistol into her back.

"You shall stay here until tonight, my dear. Don't fret; you're perfectly safe here."

"Safe?" Serena groaned, standing rigid in the middle of the tiny room. "You are using me as a pawn, and I can only guess at the gruesome outcome." She sought for a way to attack her captor, but his attention did not stray and his hand held steady on the pistol.

"You accompanied me voluntarily, Miss Hilliard. More the fool you." Before she could reply, he left, closing the door behind him and pushing home the iron bolt on the other side.

I am a prisoner yet again, she thought, filled with self-loathing. Her eagerness to bring about Sir Luther's downfall had brought about her own.

She glanced around the room, now swept in semidarkness as the door had been closed. Without looking too closely, she knew there was no way to escape from this prison. Her captor would not show an ounce of Nick's compassion.

She sat on the edge of a chair after pushing aside a heap of clothes stiff with mud and other unspeakable substances.

Holding her breath, she tried to force her mind to still its riotous thoughts—a fruitless endeavor. She had let herself be trapped by a person she *knew* was a villain of the worst kind.

Nick and Rafe waited all night, but Hilliard never returned to his club. At dawn, Nick's temper had frayed to tatters and he snarled a response to every comment Rafe made.

"You'd better try to find out where Hilliard went and go

after him," Rafe said as he urged his friend into a coffeeshop for a hot meal and hotter coffee. " 'Tis possible he returned to Somerset while you were on the road."

"Without a word to the staff at the club? No, methinks he's still in London." Nick sank down at a long table covered with a wine-stained tablecloth. Bone tired, he ordered food.

The serving man brought plates of grilled ham, kippers, and eggs, then returned with coffee and bread.

"I am at the lowest point of my life," Nick said, leaning his head into his hands. "I don't know what to do next." The food did not inspire him, but he drank the coffee, trying to clear his weary mind. A sleepless night had left a feeling of cotton wool stuffed into his head.

He listened to the early morning patrons discussing the latest items in the news sheets spread over the tables, but he couldn't concentrate on their chatter. Most of them were merchants from the City. The scent of frying fat made him slightly queasy.

He massaged the tense muscles in his neck as the door opened, letting in a stream of cool air. He needed to sleep, but a restlessness ate at him. Something was very wrong. A sensation of darkness, evil, dogged his every footstep; but if he told Rafe, his friend would scoff at such fanciful fears.

"La!" came a familiar voice. "If it isn't my stepbrother trying to put the pieces back together after a late night on the town," Ethan said, his lisping voice airy.

Nick shot him a dark look. Despite the hectic red in his cheeks, Ethan looked unusually sprightly. He seldom left the mansion in Berkley Square before noon. His arm was linked to that of another man, a fop of the first order wearing a pink satin coat crusted with silver embroidery and a powdered tie wig. He had not spared powder and rouge at his morning primping, and three velvet patches adorned various parts of his face.

"This is Pollock Fortescue. Polly, meet my stepbrother Nick and his unknown friend." Ethan gazed narrowly at Rafe, but Nick did not introduce them. He wondered in what low gambling hell or bordello Ethan had struck up a friendship with the weasel-faced Polly. Nick had no intention of speaking with his stepbrother. He started to rise, but a look from Rafe halted him. *Something.* There was something in the air. He sat back down and struggled to find a neutral voice even though he yearned to strike Ethan's face.

"You sound too cheerful, Ethan. Did you have a good run at the gambling tables?" Nick asked tersely, loath to even look at his brother.

"Egad, you could say I struck an ore of great fortune," Ethan said, gesturing extravagantly. He ordered breakfast and sat down opposite Nick and Rafe. Polly joined him, lisping something about a cold draft that was bad for his chest. "The wind in my sails has turned," Ethan went on.

"I doubt you can dig yourself out of the pit you dug. It goes deep, to the rims of Hell, where you shall one day join the devil himself."

"No need to get nasty. Too early in the morning for that."

Nick grimaced. "I can get a lot nastier than that, and you're the last person I wanted to see this morning. In fact, it riles me so much I'm of a mind to call you out just for the satisfaction of doing it."

Ethan waved a languid ring-adorned hand. "Don't cause an uproar, much too early in the morning for that. You're not even drunk."

"But you are—on your own importance. Besides, we have unfinished business on the dueling field." Nick glared, but fatigue was taking its toll on him, more with every minute. He slowly lost interest in arguing.

Polly spoke, smiling with importance, "I won two thousand pounds at Watier's last night."

"And drank champagne out of Lotus Blossom's jeweled slipper, didn't you, Polly?"

Polly's soft hissing laugh wafted across the table. "I did— with greatest pleasure, but my interest is gambling. There are deep pockets to fleece out there. Like those of the Marquess of Allard. He enjoys deep gambling."

Their breakfasts arrived, and Ethan ordered a bottle of wine to go with the meat.

"Allard is a nasty fellow. Does not like losing at the tables," Nick said. "You'd be wise to stay away from him."

"Well, I heard a rumor last night," Polly said in an ingratiating whisper, and sipped the steaming coffee placed before him. When no one answered, he continued.

"Did you know that the Marquess of Allard is marrying off his daughter Daphne? They don't live too far away from your estate in Sussex, do they? Invited guests are streaming out of London to attend the ball. 'Pon rep, I'm going to angle for an invitation."

"Allard's a pompous fool. He has no regard for anyone but himself." Nick looked at his brother. "Just like you, Ethan."

Ethan sneered. "Well, I thought the groom, Viscount Burford, is a lucky man. Daphne is a great heiress, and I've heard her trousseau is worth a king's ransom. I know a sprightly girl at the modiste where Daphne ordered her things." He sighed theatrically and slanted a calculating glance at Nick. "I think I shall befriend Burford. He might not be above lending me some money in a pinch—unlike some people I know."

Nick gritted his teeth. "I doubt Burford will remain your friend for very long once he hears about your excesses. I shall tell him about them myself."

"Devil you will!" Ethan glared and spilled his coffee.

Polly went on gossiping. "Burford's coming up to London to escort his bride-to-be back down to Sussex tomorrow afternoon. He's bound to carry home some grand jewelry, a wedding gift to Daphne I would dearly like to see. His family seat is south of Crawley, and the Burford diamonds are famous." He paused, flipping his beringed hand theatrically. "Mayhap I should befriend Daphne instead. What do you think, Ethan? Will she bestow a gem or two on me?"

"Who knows what she might be persuaded to do?" Ethan said, dabbing at the coffee stain on his chest. "Give you her innocence."

Nick jerked up from his seat and gripped Ethan's waistcoat in one fist.

"Don't! You're jarring my wound," Ethan whined.

"Curse you! If you touch one hair on Daphne's head, I swear I will kill you! I can only stand so much nonsense from you. I warn you! Even though you are my stepbrother, I will not spare your life."

He snarled in anger, and Ethan paled under the thick layer of powder.

"Heed my words or I might loose the slender hold I still have on my patience," Nick added. He abruptly let go his grip, and Ethan slumped as if all air had gone out of him. "You make me want to throw up!"

Nick swore and left the table. He drew deep steadying breaths of the cold autumn air outside and fought to get control over his fury. A red haze simmered in his mind and buzzed in his ears.

Rafe joined him in the street. He threw a coin to an urchin who had watched their horses and handed the reins to Nick. "Let's go. Don't let Leverton get your goat. He thrives on stirring up your anger. Concentrate on the important issue of capturing Hilliard."

"You're right," Nick said, letting out an explosive curse.

They spent the rest of the day searching for Sir Luther, but when the evening came, they had not found him. No one knew of his whereabouts.

Chapter 26

Cold night air seeped through the cracks in the walls and chilled Serena to the bone. She refused to wrap the filthy blanket on the cot around her; but toward morning, after sitting stiff and waiting for something to happen, she got up and pulled the blanket over her shoulders. If she caught pneumonia, her planned escape would be for naught. She could not die before Sir Luther had been brought before the court of justice.

Hunger gnawed at her stomach, but no one came with food. All through the night as sleep claimed her in fits and starts, she did not hear any movement below. The stables were deserted.

Only the muted sounds of the city wafted up to her prison. She dreamed, the horrors returning, vivid flashes of color and destruction.

She awakened, at first not knowing where she was. Dawn had crept through the cracks, lending a murky light to her cell. Her neck ached from being tilted forward at an awkward angle. She rose and groaned at the stiffness of her muscles. Misery filled every corner of her being, and her spirits had fallen so low she could barely find the strength to move.

Even though he wasn't there, she could feel the powerful

menace of her uncle. Most likely he was behind this scheme, and Sir Ethan was only a pawn in his game. Mayhap she had only days left to live, even hours . . . A shudder went through her, and she cried out in anguish. Why had she been so stupid? She rattled the door, but it did not give.

Later that morning, steps pounded on the rough stairs outside. Serena gripped an earthenware bowl in which something had congealed to a gluey substance. Her only weapon, and she would use it. She stood next to the door as the bolt was pushed aside. Her hands shook and her lungs labored as if the air was no longer fit for breathing.

The door flew open, but before she had a chance to slam the bowl at the visitor, the muzzle of a blunderbuss pointed at her face. She slowly lowered her arms and set the bowl on the table.

Behind the blunderbuss came a bent old man and a mouse-like woman all dressed in patched gray homespun. Even her mobcap looked gray with wear. She did not once lift her gaze to Serena, only placed a basket of food on the table and scuttled out.

The old man kept pointing the weapon at Serena's face. "Eat, miss."

"Please let me go," she pleaded. "I have done nothing to you, my good man. A murderer is coming to find me. Do you want that on your conscience? Please, let me go."

He shook his head in denial, sidestepped out the door, and pushed home the bolt. He hadn't even had the decency to speak to her.

Serena kicked the door in a fit of wrath, but the steps of the man receded rapidly down the stairs. She longed to fling the basket against the wall, but hunger ruled her judgment.

She tore pieces of bread and chewed rapidly. She found cheese, a chicken leg, and a jug of warm ale in the basket. If she would ever find a chance to escape, she had to keep up her strength, she reasoned. Eating all of the food with grim determination, she tried to form another plan since a surprise attack with a heavy bowl clearly would not surprise her gaoler.

Her head seemed frozen, unable to form any coherent thoughts at all. She wasn't certain of the reason for her incarceration, but common sense told her that it wouldn't be long before she stood eye to eye with her uncle.

The day passed, and Nick slept part of it away in his hiding place at the edge of St. Giles. Late in the afternoon, Rafe awakened him, bringing a mug of tea.

"It's likely Hilliard went back to Somerset," Rafe said, staring out the window.

"I sent Noah to investigate. He'll be back tomorrow night. Before that, we can only keep an eye on Hilliard's club. I've put Lonny on that, so we can only wait for word." Nick leaned back against the headboard and drank his tea. He'd found a piece of red ribbon that Serena had left behind, and he twined it around his fingers, remembering the satiny feel of her skin.

"You'll go mad, waiting," Rafe said.

"I was thinking about what Polly Fortescue and Ethan said. If Allard's daughter is bringing her trousseau to Sussex, we might make another raid. We'll catch the coach as darkness falls at some secluded spot along the road. Allard is wealthy, and I don't mind robbing him of some of his riches. We won't take Miss Daphne's gowns, only her jewelry. The haul might be enough to pay off the last of the mortgage, and then I'll say good-bye to the Midnight Bandit for good."

Rafe sighed deeply. "I shall miss the adventure."

"You will have to find out the truth about your life, Rafe, not live in this twilight domain forever. If you continue to rob the travelers on your own, you'll end up in the noose sooner or later."

Rafe's face darkened, and Nick wished he could read the thoughts behind that calm facade. He sensed his friend's continuing inner struggle despite Rafe's unperturbed exterior.

"I'm not sure I care much one way or the other," Rafe said, leaning his shoulder against the window frame. "I doubt anyone would miss me if I were to hang."

"I would, damn it!" Nick flung aside the blanket and started dressing. "We'll do the raid tonight, and that will be the end of both of our careers as thieves of the road."

Rafe pushed away from the window. "Yes . . . you're right, Nick. One last raid. Our career should end in glory. Otherwise it will end in our downfall."

"Don't even think it!" Nick wrenched on his waistcoat and buttoned it quickly. "Let's get ready."

Sir Luther Hilliard had spent two days in the decadent arms of a courtesan. In her bed, between its crimson sheets, he'd spent most of his strength but also gained the satisfaction for his aching needs. He realized, though, that nights of lovemaking took their toll upon his physique—so much, in fact, that he could barely walk up the steps of the Leverton mansion in Berkley Square.

Leverton had left a message at his club, and Sir Luther had hastened to change his linen and ordered a sedan chair to convey him toward the source of good news.

"I have her," Leverton said, meeting him in the hallway. "Caught her yesterday, but I could not find you to deliver the exciting news."

"Very well done, indeed."

Sir Ethan ushered him into a gloomy parlor where the curtains had been drawn against the mellow autumn sun. He offered a glass of excellent wine, and Sir Luther felt that his world had tilted back onto the axis of good fortune. His only witness had been caught and was even now awaiting his decision of what to do with her. He sat back on a plump sofa and awaited his host's next words.

"Sir Luther, I believe it would be best to take her out of London. I know a secluded cottage in Sussex where you might deal with her quietly and dispose of her body. No one would know. Besides, you're a stranger in those parts, whereas I know all the secret lanes and paths.''

Sir Luther pondered the younger man's suggestion, finding it solid. ''Very well, I believe you're right. When you've taken me to Serena, I shall pay you the rest of your fee. I do expect you to provide a guide for the expedition.''

Sir Ethan went to the fireplace and pulled a folded paper from the mantelpiece. ''I have made a detailed drawing of the road to the cottage, but I shall ride with you to the turnoff. From then on, you don't need any witnesses.''

Sir Luther felt a flurry of excitement. ''God's bones, this is coming together splendidly. You are a resourceful young man, Leverton.''

Ethan preened, feeling he'd earned the twenty thousand pounds already. He sensed, though, that Hilliard could not be trusted. Once Serena had been disposed of, Hilliard might seek to silence the only person who knew of his plans for his niece.

Ethan wanted to rub his hands in glee. He was one step ahead of Hilliard. He would get rid of his stepbrother for good, and then he would get rid of Hilliard with the help of Captain Emerson. Ethan was sure Nick would pursue such a rich catch as Lady Daphne . . . even if *she* had no idea of the plan. She was probably sitting at home embroidering chair covers and dreaming of the day when someone would be foolish enough to ask for her pudgy hand in marriage. Stupid females! Polly's help in telling the story about Daphne's betrothal had been a stroke of genius.

What happened to Miss Hilliard was not his problem, Ethan thought; but most likely, that capable fellow Captain Emerson would take care of her—if she escaped with her life in the great confrontation.

Ethan wished he would be present to see it, but he had already set up an evening of card games, and he would not miss that for anything in the world. He would read about the good news in the sheets tomorrow morning.

He bowed deferentially to Luther Hilliard. "I think you shall find my plan highly satisfactory." His hand trembled as he tipped the glass to his lips. "I shall take you to Miss Hilliard at dark."

Captain Emerson had gathered his thirty militiamen and some extra hands in Cuckfield, outside the local inn. He drilled the plans for the evening into the men. "This time we shall catch the nefarious bandit. I have gotten a sure tip that he's about to strike this evening south of the Burford estate. We'll spread out, two and two, and make a pincer move. There's no way he can escape this time. We shall all march to glory and reward once that scoundrel hangs from the highest tree."

He divided the men and dispatched them to Crawley by wagon. Every quarter mile of the road would be guarded by soldiers carrying muskets and bugles which would be used to summon the rest of the troop.

Emerson placed his cocked hat squarely on his head and went to mount his horse. This time he could taste success. He couldn't wait to clap the elusive bandit in irons, the man who had mocked him with his daring and given him nightmares for a year. He checked his pistols in the saddle holsters. They had been primed and loaded, waiting to hold up the man who had held up others and spread terror on the heaths. It would soon be over, and for once he would be able to rest easy at night.

Serena watched the wall as the room grew darker and darker. She had surveyed the same knotted wall for hours, memorizing every swirl and bump in the rough wood. It was one way to keep herself from thinking about her predicament, but her body constantly reminded her of its needs. She abhorred the thought of lifting the lid of the chamber pot in one corner and using it just as much as she hated the thought of stretching out on the bed. She could not hold out much longer. Her capitulation to her needs would be her final mortification.

She sighed, a long slow exhalation, and stood. Her backside ached from sitting for hours on the hard chair. Her leg muscles stiff, she walked the length of the small room, then back. She longed to scream, but that would only shatter her tightly held composure.

An hour later, she had to capitulate and use the filthy chamber pot in deepest defeat. Only the end of her life remained, and she prayed it would come quickly.

When the room had grown completely dark, the sound of steps came from below, heavy, muffled steps. At first she thought she had imagined them, but they grew louder, closer. Under the crack below the door, she saw the light of a lantern. It swung back and forth, and she tensed, sensing danger.

Her muscles encased in icy fear, she watched as the door slowly opened. Two figures stood in the yellow glow cast by the lantern. Gentlemen in cocked hats over shadowy faces. She flinched as she recognized her uncle.

"There you are, m'dear. I am glad that our paths have crossed at last. I've missed you sorely."

"I have not you," Serena said with more hauteur than she felt inside. "I wish I never had to lay eyes on you again, Uncle Luther. Not after what you did."

He lifted his eyebrows in mock surprise as he entered the room. "Did? What have I done to earn your scorn, dearest niece?"

"Do not speak to me in terms of endearment. I am no longer your kin." She moved away as he held out his hand to take hers. "And don't touch me."

His smile flickered on and off, and he moved slowly—menacingly—toward her.

"Don't pretend that you did not murder my father. I know better than that, and the truth will out one day. Even if you get rid of me, there are others who will see that justice is done."

"Don't be ridiculous!" Sir Luther snarled. "There's no proof that I had any part in your father's death."

Sir Ethan stood silently by the door. Serena sent him a

pleading glance, despite knowing full well that Ethan had arranged this meeting.

"Come along, Serena," Sir Luther said harshly. "If you don't want to believe my innocence, there's only one thing for me to do."

"And what is that?" Serena asked coldly, and straightened her back until she achieved a regal stance.

"Convince you," he said, gripping her arm so hard that pain radiated up to her shoulder.

Fear trickled through her. She knew he had to kill her to "convince" her. Where had it all gone wrong? Was it only a few days ago she and Nick had returned to London ready to confront Sir Luther with the law on their side? What had happened to Nick? Had Sir Luther—if he knew about her friendship with Nick—"convinced" Nick already? The thought filled her with despair, but she did not voice her fear.

"Do not fight or I might have to stop you most forcefully," he said tersely, and gave her a push toward the door.

"No—oo—oo," she cried.

Sir Ethan tied a neckerchief folded lengthwise over her mouth even as she fought to get away. Her uncle held her in a powerful grip; despite his paunch and flaccid limbs, he possessed the formidable strength of a bully.

"Ecod, she fights like a tigress," Sir Ethan said, chuckling. "I like spirit in a lady."

She stumbled down the stairs, her legs still stiff after her long hours of sitting down. She glanced around the gloomy stables, not seeing anyone who might help her. The alley lay in darkness, and a distant raucous laugh made the sense of her desolation more acute. No one there to help her.

Her uncle pushed her into the waiting carriage and slammed the door. She noticed through the window that he gave Sir Ethan a heavy pouch. "The rest is waiting for you at my bank, Leverton. You kept your word." He spoke to the coachman, heaved himself into the coach, and pulled the leather curtains across the windows.

"This is your last journey in this life, Serena. Prepare yourself to meet your Maker."

His words pierced her, bringing dread and hopelessness. But as long as she had breath left in her body, she would fight.

Chapter 27

Nick and Rafe found a perfect copse for their ambush south of Crawley. Before long, the carriage holding Daphne and her fiancé, and their riches, would trundle south toward the Burford estate.

"What if the coach has already passed?" Rafe asked.

"We've been here since before dark; there's no possibility the coach has gone by without our noticing," Nick said, slowly filling with impatience. He did not like to sit atop his horse—not Pegasus this time—and wait for the travelers to cross his path. He disliked the inactivity, and the waiting made tension rise in him like a ghost.

"I have a bad feeling," Rafe said thoughtfully, "as if one robbery will be one too many. This might be it."

"You're fanciful, Rafe. The raids are what we make of them. And we've never been careless. This won't turn out differently."

Rafe sighed, pulling his hat down farther over his eyes. "I hope you're right, but I have a strange feeling. After my injury, I seem to have a keener sense of everything around me. It is strange, and I don't like it." He tilted up his face and sniffed. "Even the air has a bad odor today."

Nick studied his friend's profile. "S' faith, this is the last raid we do together. My last raid at any event. I wish you would show a small amount of excitement."

Rafe gave him a long, thoughtful look. Nick could not see it in the gathering darkness, but he felt the intensity. "I would, if I truly felt it. I can't pretend, my life is beyond pretension." He paused.

"But you shall stay alive. You must create new memories to replace the old ones. Every day adds more."

"You're right. But I always thought my life was a collection of memories—of childhood, of my parents, of school, of my first love, but it isn't." Rafe laughed mirthlessly. "I must have had a first love even though I can't recall it."

"I am certain you did," Nick said with a laugh. "Mine was a kitchen maid when I was seven. She had dimpled cheeks and merry eyes and the softest hands that ever stroked my head." *Except for Serena's.*

He held Rafe's attention. "What was her name?" Rafe asked.

Nick thought for a moment. "Blast it, I can't remember. Sally or Nellie or some such ordinary name."

Rafe drew a raspy intake of breath. "Begad, I do remember something! I had a bitch called Nellie. Some type of hunting dog if I recall rightly. She had one brown and one dark green eye."

"You do surprise me, Rafe. One of these days you will remember everything."

Rafe held up a finger. "Shhh, I hear something. A carriage approaching."

Nick tensed, also hearing the steady *clip-clop* of running horses. "This is the moment we have waited for. Heigh-ho!" He kicked the heels into the flanks of his horse, and it pressed through the thicket and jumped the water-filled ditch. Rafe followed suit, and together they barred the road.

Nick pulled his pistol from the saddlebag. "If I'm caught, you know what to do, Rafe. Save yourself."

"What if it's not the carriage we're waiting for?" Rafe asked tightly.

"Then we shall rob two coaches tonight."

His heartbeat pounded, blood singing in his ears as the horses arrived at a fast clip. Rafe had lifted aside one of the black-painted panels of a lantern of the kind smugglers used to signal the French luggers in the bay. He swung it back and forth to alert the coachman to rein in. The horses slowed, and the coachman swore long and loud.

"Stand and deliver!" Nick shouted and touched his mask to make sure it was fastened securely.

Rafe rode up to threaten the driver with a pistol, and as the passengers did not alight immediately, Nick slid off his horse and approached the carriage. As he opened the door, a horseman appeared at a spanking clip on the road and shot at him. It happened so fast.

The bullet grazed his arm, and he staggered back as an excruciating pain coursed down his arm and into his hand. He dropped his pistol, and he could feel the carriage move against his back as the horses pawed the ground in fright.

"In the name of King George, you are arrested," the new-comer shouted.

Nick recognized Captain Emerson's voice immediately, and as he pressed himself into the shadow of the coach he frantically looked for other soldiers. He didn't see any. Had Emerson been so foolish as to come alone or had he happened upon the robbery by chance? Thoughts swirled wildly in Nick's head, and he could not seem to gather his wits as his arm throbbed viciously.

He sidled toward the driver's box as the soldier circled his horse around and came bearing down upon Nick. Probably holding another cocked pistol.

Nick jumped onto the step and jerked the coachman from the box. "Go!" he hissed at Rafe. "Go now! See you at the usual spot."

Rafe seemed to hesitate, but Nick drew a sigh of relief as his friend wheeled his horse around, jumped across the ditch, and crashed through the thicket. It had all happened in seconds, but to Nick every movement seemed sluggish and ponderous. *Get away, go . . . get away, go . . .* The words danced incessantly through his mind.

He held the coachman in front of himself as a shield and shouted, "Don't shoot an innocent man!"

"Nick?" Emerson's voice held a note of uncertainty as if he didn't quite believe his ears.

"Yes, 'tis me."

Emerson got down from his horse and marched up to the spot where Nick was standing. The captain pushed aside the trembling coachman and gripped Nick's coat. "Damn you to hell, Nick! Don't tell me you're the blasted highwayman." He looked at Nick's white gloves, the Midnight Bandit's emblem, and swore a long string of curses.

The carriage door opened and a fat man stepped down. Nick gasped in surprise. "It's Luther Hilliard," he rasped as Emerson gripped his cravat and tightened it. "Let me go."

"What is going on here?" Hilliard asked, his voice harsh with annoyance.

The lantern on the side of the coach sent out a weak flickering light, and Nick stared into Emerson's angry eyes. "Don't arrest me yet," he pleaded. "You must hear me out. I won't pretend that I've never heard of the Midnight Bandit, but I have never murdered a man, as Hilliard has."

Emerson's eyes widened, and his gaze flickered to the fat man standing beside them.

"I know you're itching to arrest me, Emerson, but please hear me out," Nick wheezed.

Emerson groaned and loosened his grip. "Where are my men when I most need them?"

"Lost in the woods?" Nick suggested flippantly as he righted his cravat.

"Have you caught the vermin of the roads that calls himself the Midnight Bandit?" Hilliard asked, prodding Emerson's arm with one fat finger.

Uneasy silence fell as if Emerson were reluctant to give

away the highwayman's identity to a stranger. "Mayhap," he said. He gave Nick a wrathful look. "Mayhap."

Nick strode to the door and looked inside the carriage. He saw a bundle on the long seat, a bundle that made choked noises as if eager to speak. He touched her, moved his hand to her face, and instantly recognized Serena.

"What in the world are you doing here?" he asked, and quickly untied the neckerchief. "Serena," he said as she cried out. He gathered her into his arms and swore in anger. "He found you before we found him."

"Oh, Nick, I thought I was going to die tonight," she said against his shoulder. "He was taking me somewhere to kill me."

"Well, he shan't take you away." He gently untangled her arms from his neck and set her back on the seat. "Wait here. Don't say a word until I've discussed the matter with Captain Emerson."

She nodded, her face pale and drawn. "Your luck has finally run out, Nick."

"The game isn't over yet. We shall see what we can gain." He turned toward the captain, who stood right behind him as if expecting him to escape.

Nick clasped Emerson's shoulder and coaxed him away from the coach. "Let's discuss this matter now—before it's too late."

"You've taken the words out of my mouth," Emerson said angrily. "Not that I believe there is much to discuss."

They faced each other in the darkness as Hilliard muttered something by the coach. The moon came out from a bank of clouds just as Emerson pulled back his arm and delivered a punch to Nick's jaw. "Damn you to hell, Nick! Double damn!"

Pain exploded through Nick's head and he staggered back. He lifted the arm that throbbed from the bullet wound and touched his jaw gingerly. "I suppose I deserved this."

"And more. I've been your friend for years, yet you deceived me, talked about the Midnight Bandit as if he were someone you yearned to see captured. How you must have laughed behind my back." He pulled back his fist once more, but Nick took Emerson's wrist in a firm grip and they wrestled, each eager to get control of the situation.

"Please, no more pounding. I'm already steeped in pain," Nick said, breathing hard as he fought to control Emerson's arm made strong by fury.

Nick held the captain's shoulders even as his arm throbbed so much he wanted to howl with pain. He stared hard into his friend's eyes. "I robbed coaches to finance an orphanage in London. It now houses and feeds a hundred previously destitute infants and children."

Emerson breathed hard through his nose, shaking his head.

"You might not believe me, but you have to. I shall prove my statement to you later—if you don't arrest me right now."

Nick waited tensely as an ominous silence hovered. He noticed from the corner of his eyes that Hilliard was slowly walking toward them. "Do you need help, captain?" he asked. "I brought loaded pistols for just this kind of situation."

To use on Serena, Nick thought, blinded by wrath. He longed to throttle Sir James's enemy, but first he had to assure that his own life was not hanging in the balance.

"Trevor," he said urgently. "You owe me for saving your life when Montagu Renny tried to shoot you on the beach. I'm calling in the favor now. Please don't turn on me, not now, not when I'm so close to finishing off the business with the orphanage. The Midnight Bandit shall never ride again, I promise you that."

Emerson bent to retrieve his hat. He raked his hands through hair that hung in tangled hanks around his face. His shoulders sagged, and Nick already sensed his capitulation.

Emerson's face twisted in a grimace of defeat. "I shall never understand you, Nick. But consider my debt paid in full."

He moved aside as if about to leave the scene. Other militiamen came running along the road, circling the coach. Bugles blared, but Nick noticed that Emerson had not used his.

Nick remained in the shadows, took off his mask even though his wound made him faint with pain. He tossed it away. He stuffed his gloves into his pockets and ran to catch up with Emerson, who was ready to swing himself up into the saddle of his horse.

"Trevor, you may arrest a murderer instead," Nick said in a low voice. He motioned with his head toward Luther Hilliard. "That man murdered his brother and has now abducted his niece, who is a witness to the murder. She claims he has plans to kill her, too. Tonight."

Emerson's eyes widened in surprise, and he stepped toward the coach, where Hilliard waited by the open door. "Who is he?"

"Sir Luther Hilliard. His brother Andrew's death has been reported in the news sheets. The magistrates say he was murdered by a passing vagrant, but there are witnesses—"

"*Are* witnesses?" Emerson asked. He gripped the door and peered inside.

"Can we go now?" Hilliard asked peevishly. " 'Tis the first time I've seen the law in deep discussion with a highwayman." He eyed Nick closely. "I should have known 'twas you. Let's just say I'm not surprised to find you—"

"There has been a mistake," Captain Emerson said stiffly. "Mr. Thurston is working for me in my efforts to capture a certain gentleman who goes by the name of Luther Hilliard. Mr. Thurston says he attacked your coach with the purpose of freeing your niece, whom you allegedly have imprisoned."

Good explanation, Nick thought, feeling that he didn't quite deserve such a loyal friend as Emerson. Trevor always was good at getting control of a difficult situation. He would not reap the rewards of bringing in the Midnight Bandit, but if Nick could help it, Emerson should have all the glory of capturing a murderer and bringing him to justice.

"My niece and I are traveling to the country house of a friend," Hilliard said haughtily and started climbing into the carriage. "Until he stopped us," he added, pointing at Nick.

Emerson whistled to his men, who pulled their swords and closed in on the man. "Sir Luther, please step away from your coach."

Swords' points prodded the heavy man to move aside, and he stared in silent wrath as Emerson helped Serena to alight. She ran to Nick, and he closed his arms around her.

"Serena, tell the soldiers what you saw at High Crescent that night."

Serena trembled in his arms, but straightened her back proudly and gave an account of the night when her father drew his last breath.

"It'll be her word against mine!" Hilliard cried in outrage. "The local lawmen are on my side, having already decided who murdered my poor brother."

Emerson's face hardened, and he pointed at Hilliard's heart with his sword, ruffling the lacy ends of the fat man's cravat. "Methinks the matter needs a thorough investigation. One witness saw you holding the knife that killed Andrew Hilliard, and that is good enough for me. I'm taking you to the Duke of Atwood's estate, and he may well contact the authorities in London for a thorough investigation. He is connected to the highest officials."

Hilliard spit on the ground. "You would take *her* word over mine? A woman's word?"

"A witness is a witness," Emerson said, unperturbed. He moved to put manacles around Hilliard's wrists. The prisoner struggled.

"Don't you dare put your hand on me, soldier!" Hilliard bellowed, and Serena cringed, moving into Nick's arms once again.

"There is another witness," Nick said, watching the undulations and awkward kicks of the prisoner.

Hilliard went still, and the night breeze seemed to stop; all sounds receded. He stared at Nick, a hard reptilian glance, yellow lantern light glinting off his eyes. "Another witness?" he repeated. "What do you know of this?" he spat at Serena. "And how does Thurston know anything about our family business?"

Nick put his finger to Serena's lips and replied for her. "I heard the witness speak, and I can vouch for his cooperation. He has promised to witness at the trial."

Emerson finally managed to clinch the manacles around Hilliard's wrists. "If this is true, Sir Luther, the hangman will soon have an appointment with you."

"They are lying!" Hilliard shouted. *"Lying!* There was no one in the house that night."

He fell silent abruptly; and again, the night had hushed as if shocked by his unwitting confession.

"So you were there, despite your claim to being far from High Crescent that night," Nick said. "Well, well." He turned to the tense soldiers. "You heard him say those words, and if ever asked in court, you will be able to repeat them."

The soldiers nodded, and Serena pressed herself against him in a gesture of affection and gratitude. "Nick," she whispered. "I think justice will be done."

"The truth will always out," Nick said, and held her head protectively against his chest.

"I think I will faint with relief."

She didn't, but Nick held her more tightly. He exchanged a glance with Emerson as the soldiers moved the prisoner toward the coach.

"The night was not wasted, was it?" Nick said to his friend.

Emerson rubbed his chin in thought, and a small smile played around his mouth. "No, not wasted at all."

"You will gain fame out of this," Nick said.

Emerson nodded, now grinning widely. "Fate works in mysterious ways." He pushed Hilliard into the coach and got in behind him. He ordered his men to take positions on the outside of the carriage and to tie his horse behind.

Nick watched the equipage make a difficult turn and head back toward London.

"What about us?" Serena asked. "Are we going to walk back?"

"No. I'm taking you with me to The Hollows." He looked down at her face, a milky oval in the weak moonlight. "I will not be separated from you again. We shall find a way to be together.''

Before she had a chance to reply, Rafe rode out of the thicket.

"S'faith, you didn't leave as agreed."

"I could not leave, Nick. I planned to help you when an opportunity presented itself."

"Let's all of us go home together," Nick said, and lifted Serena into the saddle of his horse. As he joined her, curving his arm around her waist to keep her pressed against him, he asked, "How did you get to be in the coach with Sir Luther this evening? There are parts that I don't understand."

"I received a note at Miss Hopkins' from your brother. He offered to help me and said he had found an important witness to the murder. I was curious, but foolish. He brought me to a stable near Covent Garden where he locked me into a room. My uncle came to fetch me two days later." She flung out her arm in a gesture of exasperation. "I should have known better than to listen to Sir Ethan. I knew he was dangerous after what happened to Callie Vine."

Nick gritted his teeth while suppressing a howl of anger directed at his stepbrother. "I shall find a way to deal with Ethan, but first we'll have to lure him down to Sussex. If he suspects that I'm searching for him, he'll go to ground somewhere in London and we won't be able to find him." Nick groaned, chilled at the thought of what might have befallen his beloved. His wound throbbed like the devil, stirring his temper to a boiling pitch. "This time, Ethan went too far. He shall be punished accordingly."

Chapter 28

The following day, Sir Ethan Leverton sang a tune off-key as he left the bank in the City. Hilliard's bank draft had covered his pressing debts, and he no longer had to hide from his creditors behind drawn curtains. He would settle with his tailor and get measured for some new coats. He liked the new silver lace that the tailor had imported from France. Shirt cuffs of the material would not come amiss. Mayhap he'd consider ordering a shirt of silver cloth . . . The possibilities were endless.

A new life had opened up, a vista so grand, so golden with relief, that Ethan felt lighter at heart than he had in years.

Even now, as Ethan walked through the City, Nick would be locked away in a cell somewhere. The thought gave him a dizzying sense of bliss. He twirled his walking stick in the air, almost removing a cap from a flower seller's head at the street corner. Her angry shout could not ruin his sense of well-being. He was free, free from that rookery urchin Nick Thurston, who dirtied everything he touched with the legacy of his low birth. The news sheets would tell all about his arrest and degradation.

Ethan hired a sedan chair at a stand to take him across town to Berkley Square. Home for luncheon, then a much coveted visit to his tailor. Maybe an afternoon at Lotus Blossom's would slake a different kind of desire.

He arrived home to discover that a letter from Delicia awaited him on a silver salver in the hallway.

"Came this morning, sir, by special messenger," his butler informed him.

"I wish she wouldn't hole up in the country," Ethan said, more to himself than to his butler. "She's probably begging me to let her stay here now that Nick is arrested. She should not have shown so much anger when I left that dimwit Callie Vine," he added under his breath and hastened into the study.

Sitting behind the desk that once had belonged to Sir James, he broke the wax seal and spread the stiff paper before him.

Dear Brother,
   You must come immediately to The Hollows. Something terrible has happened, and I cannot write about it in a letter. Oh, please, please come. Let us make peace. Let bygones be bygones. I beg of you. You have to help me now as I have no one else to ask.
               Y'r Most Obedient Sister, Delicia.

Ethan reread the message, mentally rubbing his hands in glee. Delicia was distraught to have learned about Nick's arrest, and she needed male support.

"There's only me left to ask," Ethan said to himself, slowly filling with a sense of power and purpose. He would truly be the head of the family now, not that upstart from Spitalfields. Until Nick's arrest, he'd been the head of the family in name only. It was right that he finally received what was due to him.

He folded the letter and pushed it into his coat pocket. Then he went into the hallway and gave orders to have his trunk packed and his traveling chaise brought to the door.

Serena sat in the bright drawing room at The Hollows, dressed in a borrowed gown of rose silk that was too long for her and laced too tight over her breasts. But it was better than her old, soiled gown, and Delicia's maid had washed and arranged her hair into a braided bun on top of her head. Errant curls fluttered in her vision as she read aloud from a poetry book to Callie, and she pushed them impatiently behind her ear.

Her heart did not brim with poetry, but with worry. It sat like a clump of bile in her chest, slowly eroding her composure. Before long, Sir Ethan would arrive, and Serena feared that Nick would kill him as he set foot on the threshold.

Nick had walked around the house in a foul mood, unable to sit, unable to eat, only staring out the windows that faced the front drive. She had tried to talk to him, but he could not concentrate on her—or didn't want to. He turned away every time she approached him, and she knew he could not find peace until Ethan had been removed from this world.

The thought saddened her. She did not see more bloodshed as a good solution. Unfortunately there was no cause for Ethan to be imprisoned. If Nick went to the authorities and accused his brother of her abduction, Nick most likely would have to reveal his own secrets. No, the law could not be brought in.

"You've read the same verse twice now, Serena. Your mind is elsewhere," Callie said kindly. She shifted her weight around in the invalid chair as if the inactivity were chafing her nerves. "Let's take a short walk along the hallway," she said and reached for her walking stick.

It gladdened Serena's heart to see her friend's progress from wheelchair to crutches, and now walking stick. Her leg had healed crookedly as the doctor had predicted, but no flaw was visible under the gown of bright yellow satin.

Serena sensed Callie's nervousness. Callie knew Ethan was coming to The Hollows any minute. Two red spots glowed on her delicate cheekbones, and Serena wished she could find something to say that would soothe the pain in Callie's heart.

"Yes, a good idea to stretch those stiff muscles," she said absentmindedly and put aside the leather-bound book of sonnets.

They slowly walked the length of the fine Oriental carpet with its swirling pattern in rust, red, and gold. The curtains of rust silk barely obscured the lovely autumn day outside. The sun splashed bright gold over sofas and settees and framed the marble mantelpiece in a checkered pattern of shadows. With difficulty, Callie skirted a round rosewood table holding a gilded candelabra. She grimaced, but her mouth was set in a line of determination.

She stopped to admire a silver candle snuffer with a long twisted handle. Touching it, she said, "Serena, I had a letter from my brother yesterday. He says he's coming home any day now."

Serena's breath stuck in her throat. "Does he know about . . . about your accident?" she asked when she could find her voice. She worried how the brother would take the news of Callie's ruin.

"Adam knows nothing. He has a very hot temper, and I could not bring myself to tell him the truth."

"He will know something is wrong the very first moment he sees you."

Callie set down the candle snuffer. "Yes . . . and I admit I'm afraid of his reaction. He will be so very angry with me, and furious with E—with Nick's stepbrother."

Serena felt that Adam had no right to be angry with Callie. "Adam should have been here to protect you instead of leaving you in the care of a young friend."

"Adam left England in a desperate effort to forget a deep wound inflicted upon his heart. I don't blame *him* for what happened. I wanted him to leave so that I could have him back whole and sound again."

Silence hung in the room, bringing with it a sense of futility. The prisms of the chandeliers tinkled in an unseen draft, and golden autumn leaves, whipped by an unseen hand, scuttled past the windows.

"Yet *you* ended up broken."

Callie turned large brown eyes on her. Serena read both pain and wisdom in their clear depths.

"I have made peace with myself," Callie said. "What is done is done and cannot be changed. My life will be adjusted to accommodate my infirmity." She looked away, but Serena had noticed the light of embarrassment in her eyes. "It could be worse. At least I am not in the family way," Callie said, so quietly that Serena barely heard her words.

"That is a relief," Serena said, and felt that the world had all of a sudden turned brighter. Nick would not have to pretend to be the father of Ethan's bastard offspring. For a moment she could forget her own pain and rejoice with her friend. "You'll see, it will all come right in the end, Callie."

Callie gave her a searching glance, then traced the intricate carving on the back of a mahogany chair. "But not for you, Serena."

Serena bit down on her bottom lip to suppress a wave of sadness. She felt Callie's gaze searching her face. "What do you mean?" she asked when she dared to trust her voice.

"You are in love with Nick, aren't you?" Callie questioned softly.

Serena immediately wanted to scream *no,* but she could not hold up the pretense any longer. "Is it that obvious?"

Callie nodded. "I don't know what happened between you and Nick in the past, but I can see that you have shared something profound together. Every time Nick looks at you, his heart is in his eyes, full of yearning."

Serena dropped her gaze to the intricate pattern of an embroidered pillow on the sofa. "Something did happen, I cannot deny it, but that doesn't change the future. Nick will not break his word to you."

Callie touched Serena's arm. "I know. He's an honorable man, and I think I could learn to love him. But can he learn to love me?"

Serena glanced quickly at her friend, noticing the thoughtful expression. "He will honor you, and respect you," she said. Feeling trapped in the moment, she looked toward the door. "I think I shall go upstairs to rest. Will you manage on your own, Callie?"

"Of course. There are always servants if I need help later on." She balanced on the walking stick and kissed Serena on the cheek. "Thank you for your friendship. Without you, I don't know how I could have gone on. In a way, you saved my life."

"Nonsense," Serena said, and wiped the corner of her eye with a handkerchief. " 'Twas only a matter of time before your spirits returned."

Callie flashed her a smile of singular sweetness. "Nevertheless, thank you."

Serena rushed out of the room, unable to stem the flow of her grief at losing Nick.

Nick knew there was only one thing left to do. He would kill Ethan, even if it would cost him his own life. He waited impatiently, striding from one window to the other. As soon as the carriage arrived, he would go and meet it in the drive. Better get this unpleasantness over with as soon as possible. He had put his affairs in order, leaving the estate and all its holdings to Delicia.

Serena would be offered to always have a shelter at The Hollows, but she would have her own inheritance even if the Crown seized High Crescent when Luther Hilliard was found guilty of his brother's murder.

Brother killing brother. Here he was, Nick thought, in the very same predicament, his dark fury aimed at the person who had always made his life difficult. Nick did not believe in bloodshed, but it was the only way to stop Ethan from perpetrating more atrocities.

His arm throbbed. It had been cleansed, stitched, and tightly bound, but the wound bothered him more than he liked. He strode from the study, across the checkered marble floor of the foyer and into the blue salon, whose cool colors reminded him of ice and always made him feel cold. It was only a pleasant refuge at the height of summer. He hoped Callie would have the inclination to redecorate, to mark a new start for him and the estate itself.

It should have been Serena, he thought. She should have chosen the colors and the fabrics that would change this house into their home. The start of a marriage, the start of a life.

No, he would not think about it further. Despite his sickness of heart, he could not go back on his promise to Callie.

The servant he'd put on the lookout for Ethan's carriage waved frantically by the row of poplars that lined the drive. The moment had come. Thank goodness the ruse of Delicia's letter had lured Ethan to The Hollows. Had he come to rule— at last—over his family?

Nick compressed his lips and marched to the door. He went outside and stood in the middle of the gravel drive as the coach pulled up. Arms crossed over his chest, he faced his brother. Ethan was staring out the window, and his jaw dropped in surprise as his gaze landed on Nick.

"Quite a shock isn't it, dear brother?" Nick spat and tore open the carriage door. "Did you think I was locked up in a foul-smelling dungeon awaiting death, mayhap?"

Ethan opened and closed his mouth, but no words issued forth. He paled visibly, and his gaze darted from one side of the curved drive to the other as if searching for a way to escape.

"There is nowhere to go from here, Ethan, except to the grave. You have no choice this time. It'll be me or you." Nick pulled Ethan out and twisted his cravat, nearly choking him. His arm throbbed. The pain fouled his mood until he saw his stepbrother through a red fog. " 'Twill be you, Ethan; so prepare yourself."

He slapped Ethan across the face twice with the back of his hand. "Name your weapons and your seconds. This time, we shall fight in an honorable manner, a meeting at dawn."

He released the cravat and Ethan staggered back.

"Go down to the village and take a room at the inn. My men shall accompany you and prevent any attempt at flight. You shall not get away this time. This world isn't large enough to hold us both."

Rafe had evidently heard the commotion and come outside. He stood beside Nick. "Count on my support, Nick," he said grimly.

Ethan took one look at the two men and scrambled back into the coach. His jaws snapped together and a dangerous light came into his eyes. "I choose swords."

"I knew you would." Ethan was a wily and quick fencer, but Nick suspected he lacked stamina after living a life of dissipation for so long. He waved his hand and three burly servants got up on the lackey stand at the back.

"You have two days to summon your seconds. We shall meet at dawn on the third day, in the meadow at the north edge of my property. If you do not choose to come of your own volition, my servants shall bring you there."

Ethan cringed as if he'd seen the devil dance in front of him and slammed the door shut in Nick's face. He pushed away from the window, and all Nick could hear as the equipage turned around was a barrage of brimstone curses.

Rafe clamped his hand onto Nick's shoulder as if to lend his support. "A mouse caught in a trap. He will try to fight dirty."

"He's not leaving the field alive," Nick said between clenched teeth and went inside to polish his rapiers and hone his fighting skills.

The women heard of the duel through the servants, but even though Serena longed to beg Nick not to fight, she could not find the words. Delicia begged and pleaded, for naught. On the night before the duel, she flitted around the house unable to apply herself to anything. Callie said nothing, only watched Delicia's anguish with frightened eyes.

Delicia suffered the most, brother fighting brother, but Serena felt helpless in her efforts to soothe Delicia's agitation. Delicia finally crumpled in a heap on one of the sofas, her arms shielding her face and her shoulders heaving with muted sobs. The whippet dogs whined and tried to climb into her lap. Nobody could sleep. Serena and Callie sat beside her trying to soothe her, and right before dawn, they heard the commotion of the men leaving the house.

Serena thought she was going to faint with fear for Nick. She couldn't live if he lost his life in the meadow. Every one of her breaths was labored as if her anguish were too heavy for her body to bear. She counted the minutes, wondering if each brought a new wound to her beloved's body.

Just as the first rays of sun crept into the salon where they were waiting, she heard a horse galloping up the drive. She glanced outside, seeing a rider dressed in a thick wool cloak, a black cocked hat pulled low over the eyes. The horse drew to a halt in front of the entrance, and two minutes later, hard steps pounded the floor and the door was wrenched open.

"Adam!" Callie cried, and took two faltering steps toward her brother.

The man, his jaw darkened with black whiskers, gave an anguished growl and gathered Callie into his arms. He towered over his sister. Serena noted his strength and powerful physique. His face wore a stricken look, but Serena was aware that here stood a man used to command. The set of his chin and the hardness of his eyes said that he was a gentleman who brooked no nonsense. Someone had finally come to support Callie, someone from her past, her family.

A great weight lifted from Serena's shoulders as she watched, and despite her fear for Nick, she could feel happiness for her friend.

Wearing a shocked expression, the butler hovered in the doorway, and Serena asked him to bring some coffee.

"I want to know everything that happened, and then I shall set everything to rights," Adam Vine said, his fierce gaze sweeping the room.

"Thank God, you've come," Callie cried. "They are about to kill each other."

Nick and Rafe arrived early to the meadow, right before the daylight had truly ousted the night. A silver fog hung among the trees, and a glittering web of dew covered the grass. Nick surveyed the peaceful spot grimly. Dew would make the footwork slippery, and the sun might blind the duelists' eyes. He walked over the area, searching the ground for hidden potholes and stumps. He found none.

He inhaled deeply, thinking how beautiful the pink glow of sunrise was and how seldom he noticed such glory. This might be the last time he saw the sun spread its light upon the world. He shook off the disturbing thought. No, he would not let Ethan triumph in this last of their battles.

The rumble of a carriage sounded on the lane; he had arrived. Nick turned to Charles and Rafe, his seconds. Charles had tried to reason with him, to draw the rules up that the fight would end at the sign of first blood, but Nick was adamant. Ethan would have to pay with his life for his atrocities.

Rafe was polishing the rapier blade with a flannel cloth, and Nick flexed his arms and hands.

Ethan stepped down from the carriage, this morning dressed in black except for the white shirt and plain cravat. His seconds were no one Nick recognized, but one wore a guard's uniform. They consulted with Ethan, then stepped over to greet Charles and Rafe.

Ethan sent a cold, calculating glance at Nick, who felt a shiver down his spine. Ethan gave an exaggerated bow, sweeping off his hat. Nick nodded stiffly in return. Dueling etiquette demanded that you salute your opponent graciously before the combat.

The seconds compared the weapons, which had to be of equal length.

Charles, his expression set and grim, went to choose the best fighting spot with one of Ethan's seconds. The two others followed, carrying the long case with the rapiers. The gilded basket hilts glinted, reflecting the rising sun.

Nick took a deep breath to steady his racing heartbeat. A cold resolution settled in him, and his nerves steadied.

Ethan sported a pale face and hollow eyes, as if he'd had

difficulty sleeping the last few nights; but he also displayed a grim determination.

This is the day which might bring the culmination of Ethan's hopes, as well as mine, Nick thought. He felt a fleeting sense of sorrow as he remembered Sir James. *Father would have begged them to make peace.* It had always been his wish that Ethan would seek out his stepbrother in friendship, but even in the cradle, Ethan had turned away from Nick. Come to think of it, it was strange, as if they were destined to be adversaries from the start.

Nick marshaled his thoughts, tried to shut away the vivid images of his father. He wrenched off his brown velvet coat and simple waistcoat to reveal that he wore no protection against his skin. His white shirt fluttered in the cold breeze, and he shivered.

Ethan followed suit, his body slim, almost emaciated under the voluminous shirt. He detached his lace cuffs and placed them on top of the coat in the carriage. Then he wound a handkerchief around his hand and wrist to protect them.

"Listen here," Charles said out loud for all to hear. "You are not allowed to deflect thrusts with your left hand, and as soon as blood is drawn, the duel will stop. A decision whether to continue will be made at that point. Breaking of the rules of either party will end the duel."

Nick stepped up to the spot indicated by Rafe and received his sword. Ethan followed, rotating his arm and wrist. His blade glittered a threat as he slashed it through the air as if to measure its weight.

Charles and the others stepped back, and Rafe stood between the combatants, his arm up.

Ice filled Nick's veins as he looked into Ethan's feral eyes, but his hand did not tremble. They took up the guard position, knee bent, left arm up.

Rafe let his hand drop. "Commence!" he said and stepped back.

The blades clashed together, leaving a faint whining echo.

Ethan lunged, and Nick parried and riposted lightning quick, driving Ethan back in a series of rapid thrusts.

Ethan snarled and rallied, pushing Nick back with feints and thrusts. He sought to get under Nick's guard, but Nick expected his sly maneuvers and managed to deflect and sidestep the vicious attack. In guard, he circled his foe, trying to figure out the next strategy.

He made a lunge, but Ethan parried, the blades twirling around each other like stiff tongues kissing.

Even though the morning was cold, rivulets of sweat dripped down Nick's backbone and crawled along his hairline. He wiped his forehead with his sleeve, and at that moment, Ethan struck, the point of his sword streaking along Nick's arm, leaving a burning trail of blood.

Nick vaulted aside, knowing that the hit was only a scratch, if a painful one.

Charles stepped up, lowering a sword between them to halt the fight. "First blood." He turned to Nick. "Do you want to continue?"

Nick nodded, breathing hard. He watched Ethan as he exercised his stiffening sword hand.

Ethan spat on the ground. "To the end!" he snarled. "That cur shall not darken my doorstep again," he added, giving Nick a contemptuous glance.

Charles grimaced and withdrew after shouting "Commence!"

Nick went to the attack, pain and cold fury egging him on. The next minute he had pierced Ethan's shoulder, and Ethan staggered back, his face deathly pale. Sweat beaded on his brow, and deep lines of fatigue bracketed his mouth.

Yes, Nick thought, dear brother has no endurance.

He waited through the polite procedure of the seconds, but knew that Ethan would not give up. He had impaled Ethan's flesh, perhaps reopening the old wound but leaving the function of his sword arm still fully intact.

Confidence filled Nick. He knew he would win if he did not let Ethan fool him with his tricks . . .

The fight continued, Nick dancing in an ever quickening pace as he thrust and parried. One of Ethan's jabs, aimed at his heart, almost passed his guard, but he deflected it.

Ethan tilted his hand down in the blink of an eye, and the tip of his rapier would have pierced Nick's abdomen if he hadn't twisted away at the same time as he parried. *One deadly trick.* Nick thought, and there were others.

Ethan was stumbling back, slowly losing his coordination. Nick slashed the top of his brother's left arm, and Ethan shouted in pain, crumbling to his knees. The fight halted, and Nick fought for breath. Sweat covered the palms of his hands, and he wiped them on his thighs. His mouth was dry. God, he was thirsty.

The sounds of a trotting horse came up the lane. The surgeon waiting in Ethan's carriage stuck his head through the open window and gave a startled glance at the rider appearing out of the mist.

The stranger jumped out of the saddle and ran into the meadow, stopping only as he saw the group of men.

"What the devil?" Nick shouted.

"I'm Adam Vine," the stranger said. "Which one of you is Sir Ethan Leverton?"

Everyone stared at the newcomer. Ethan hissed a curse.

"Adam Vine, Callie's brother?" Nick asked. He stepped up to shake the stranger's hand.

"The same," Adam said angrily. "I've come to demand satisfaction of the man who ruined my sister. Are you Sir Ethan?"

"No, I'm Nick Thurston. You shall have satisfaction, but you'll have to wait until I've had mine."

Adam's lips pinched together, and his whole body trembled with impatience. "I have the right to avenge my sister's disgrace. She has suffered brutally and has to live with the pain for the rest of her life." He looked hard at Nick. "I *need* to avenge her misfortune."

Nick's chest tightened, and he looked at Ethan, who had ponderously risen to his feet.

Adam Vine did not wait for Nick's answer, but stepped through the trampled grass and slapped Ethan's cheek with his glove. "If you survive, we shall meet afterwards," he said curtly.

Ethan's expression grew ugly, and he slapped Adam across the face in return. "It shall be my pleasure. Your sister is a mealymouth and dimwit. She would never satisfy a man properly, and I am delighted I ruined her," he snarled. "To save someone else the bother."

Adam's hands clenched into fists, and the seconds had to step between the men and force them apart.

"Let the duel go on," Charles demanded.

"I need a drink of water," Ethan moaned.

"That is not permitted," Rafe said stiffly. "Not part of the rules."

Nick watched as Adam strode to his horse and delved into his saddlebag. The situation was getting out of hand rapidly.

"Let him drink," he said, wanting to get a grip on the strange feeling that had come over him. He sensed something was about to happen, and he watched Ethan stagger toward the carriage as if in a dream. Fog rolled over his boots, making him appear a ghost in a nightmare.

"I shall drink as well," he said. Nick could not take his eyes off his stepbrother as he walked toward his horse. The narrow back leaned forward into the coach. Ethan tilted a bottle to his lips. He set it down, then whirled around, a pistol in his hand.

Nick had known somehow. In a reflex, he crumpled to the ground just as two shots rang out. The bullet whistled past him, and as if still stuck in a sluggish dream, he saw Ethan fall to the ground, part of his head blown off.

Dead. It was over. A life—a *miserable* life—was over. Feeling weak and experiencing an inexplicable sense of loss, he got to his feet. Charles's arm came around his shoulders and Rafe loosened his convulsive grip on the sword's hilt.

Now that Ethan no longer stood before him, a visible obstacle to happiness, he should have cheered and shouted, but he felt only a bitter emptiness. He had lost part of his past, someone who had shared his years, however much it had been a relationship filled with acrimony.

"You shot him!" Ethan's seconds shouted belligerently at Adam Vine.

Adam blew at the smoking barrel of his pistol. "He would have shot Thurston with another pistol if I hadn't fired faster."

"Leverton has played his last underhanded trick," Charles said angrily. "This is the end of it. No more fighting!"

The seconds and the surgeon bent beside Ethan's body, shaking their heads.

The world would be a better place, Nick said to himself, but what would he tell Delicia? At one time, she had been close to her abominable brother—before the veil of trust and innocence had been ripped from her eyes.

"The death will be reported to the authorities, of course," Charles said grimly, "but have no fear of retribution, Nick. Ethan tried to shoot you—murder you—not following the code of honor."

Nick nodded, feeling suddenly very weary. "It is over."

He went up to Adam Vine and thanked him for his astute observation and subsequent action. "We'd better return home to tell the ladies the news."

"The *good* news," Adam said tersely and climbed into the saddle.

Nick wanted to agree, but could not.

Chapter 29

Serena watched the men alight from their horses, and she could have cried out in relief to see Nick step up to the door alive and almost whole. A blood stain on his sleeve spoke that he'd suffered an injury. But he was alive, which meant that Ethan would not come back. Not ever.

She glanced at Delicia, noting the haunted eyes and the pale cheeks. The door sprang open and Nick, Charles, Rafe, and Adam Vine strode into the salon where they waited. The surgeon followed, fluttering around Nick.

Nick sought Serena's eyes, relief and happiness springing up between them. Serena thought that Nick would come to embrace her, but Delicia interrupted his progress and threw herself into his arms. Tears contorted her voice. She cried, "Thank God you are alive, Nick! I could not have borne to lose you."

Nick held her convulsively, burying his face against her head. Serena thought she detected tears in his eyes, and his shoulders were hunched as if burdened with sorrow. Serena swallowed hard, feeling his pain. The whippets danced around, wanting their share of the attention. Serena pressed one against her leg and rubbed its ears.

"Ethan is gone," Charles said somberly. "He tried to shoot Nick in an unguarded moment and might have succeeded if Mr. Vine hadn't foiled his scheme."

Adam sat next to Callie, taking her hand. A look of gratitude passed from sister to brother. The dogs jumped and whined, infected by the tension in the room.

Serena was happy for Callie, but Delicia, who had lost a brother, would not feel the same gratitude even if she understood that justice had been served. And Serena doubted that Nick would feel the great relief he'd hoped for.

"It is over," Rafe said. "I'd say we all need something to drink. Brandy, perhaps," he added, glancing at Delicia with concern.

After the surgeon had bandaged the shallow wound, Nick donned a long wool waistcoat and sat down on the sofa beside Callie, holding Delicia close. Serena fought the threatening tears as she watched his haunted face. "I shall ask for a tray of food," she said to no one in particular, and went in search of the butler.

When she returned, Nick stared straight at her. She read doom and hopelessness in his eyes, and her heart jolted. She longed to throw her arms around him, but that was now the prerogative of his fiancée. Not that Callie showed any inclination to comfort him.

Serena set about refilling the glasses of brandy as the butler brought in the tray of roast beef and bread. As she handed out the glasses, Callie tugged at the lace at Serena's elbow. "Serena, I would like to speak—about you and . . . and Nick." She threw a cautious glance at Nick beside her.

His gaze intensified, and Serena sensed his longing as he looked at her. It echoed within her, and she ached to hold him in her arms.

"I'd like to speak for everyone to hear," Callie said hesitantly. "This is important."

Serena looked at each face, knowing they were her friends,

even Adam Vine, whom she didn't know at all. She nodded, in unison with Nick.

"You have all been my friends, my staunch support in my days of need," Callie began, her eyes filling with tears. "I would like to repay that generosity in some small way. I have realized that my life will go on, not the same as it was, but I have gained hard-won experience and I am at peace." She took Nick's hand. "I would like to release you from our betrothal, and nothing would make me happier than to witness your and Serena's wedding day." She took Serena's hand and placed it in Nick's. "I think you belong together. Anyone can see that you love each other."

He got up slowly and pulled Serena into his arms, hugging her so tightly she could barely breathe. He trembled, whether from emotion or exhaustion or relief, Serena did not know. But it mattered not. He was back in her arms at last.

"I love you," she whispered.

"And I love you, more than anything in this world."

An embarrassed silence hung in the room, then someone chuckled, bringing release. Everyone laughed, and Delicia joined in Serena and Nick's embrace.

"I wish you great happiness," she said, her red-rimmed eyes showing honest delight.

"I suppose we might as well use the brandy as a toast," Charles said, and raised his glass.

Epilogue

The wedding ceremony, in the fashion of the Middle Ages, took place on the church steps in the village of Hollow Fields, one mile west of The Hollows. A weak autumn sun shone benignly on the simple church party. Serena looked deeply into Nick's eyes as she said her vows, her heart swelling with love and happiness. He was splendid, her groom, wearing his most wicked grin and pressing her fingers in such a way that promised of intimacy to come.

"Are you happy?" he asked after kissing her in front of their friends, who cheered.

"Speechless," she whispered against his mouth.

He laughed in delight. "I like you best that way."

After receiving congratulatory slaps on the back from Charles and Rafe, Nick received a warm kiss on the cheek from the incomparable Marguerite. A knowing smile played on her lips. "I knew you would find the lady of your dreams, Nick. It was only a matter of time."

"You were right, as always."

Nick carried Serena to the waiting coach, which was adorned with branches of autumn leaves and gold silk ribbons. He set her down on the seat, and she laughed. Turning on the coach step, he shouted. "See you at the wedding feast, but don't expect us to arrive on time."

The coach rolled down the lane as the villagers waved their handkerchiefs. "Why did you say that?" Serena asked.

"You will understand in a minute," Nick said, busily setting to work unlacing her bodice. "I'm crazy with longing for you, so why wait until tonight when we can seal our vows now? I'll tell Noah to drive us to a secluded spot where we can end what we started this morning."

"With Noah as a witness?" Serena asked dreamily, pushing her fingers through Nick's hair.

"No, I'll send him away. I left a horse for him in the sylvan spot of my choice."

"Such meticulous planning," she chided gently, tracing his jaw with the tip of her tongue.

"A lifetime of happiness has to have a memorable start," he said, untying her quilted petticoat at the waist. The cream silk gown billowed around her on the seat, but no layers of material could stop Nick's exploration of her leg.

"You have not put aside the opportunist part of the Midnight Bandit," she said.

Nick shook his head, and his hair tickled her nose. "No." he said.

"You ceased your criminal activities even though you didn't pay off the orphanage mortgage. You did it for me?"

He gazed deeply into her eyes. "I learned a lesson. The Midnight Bandit lived a charmed life, but luck sometimes runs out. It did, and I was fortunate not to hang. I'll find the money somehow."

"Take mine. All that I have is yours from now on, and I insist you finish your mission. Sir James would be very happy to know how much you care, how generous you are."

He brushed the side of her face with his hand. "You are the generous one, my darling." His gaze slid hotly over her bosom. "Yes, thank you, the mortgage shall be paid in full once we return from our honeymoon, and Pegasus shall move north with

Rafe, his short glory on the roads soon forgotten. But first I have another mission to accomplish.''

''Oh yes? I'm burning to discover what it is.''

And he went on to show her just how efficiently he could arouse her passion, and slake it. An earnest application of his skills was all it took, and he didn't have to wear a face mask or a pair of white gloves to accomplish this kind of mission.

If you liked A LOVER'S KISS, be sure to look for Maria Greene's next release in the Midnight Mask series, A MASTER'S KISS, available wherever books are sold in October 2001.

Betrayed by the woman he loves, Rafe Howard purchases a commission in the army—and returns to England after an injury with no idea who he is. With the help of the Midnight Bandit, Rafe is seeking answers—but Andria Saxon cannot give them, and she cannot deny that her heart still aches for the man who claimed it long ago . . .